# Where Treetops Glisten

Praise for
*Where Treetops Glisten*

"What a treat—three of my favorite novelists have joined together to write a compilation of compelling World War II stories. The Turner family in *Where Treetops Glisten* captured my heart, and if you enjoy reading inspirational romance, I know these stories will capture your heart as well!"

> —MELANIE DOBSON, award-winning author of *Chateau of Secrets* and *The Courier of Caswell Hall*

"These are three wonderful Christmas stories filled with period details that 1940s fans are sure to love and with characters whom readers will remember long after they close the cover. I laughed and cried with each new story. All three were wonderfully woven together to make a cohesive whole. Sarah Sundin, Cara Putman, and Tricia Goyer are sure to make your Christmas a little brighter."

> —LIZ TOLSMA, author of *A Log Cabin Christmas* Collection

"The fragility of life, the certainty of loss, the daring of love… *Where Treetops Glisten* skillfully weaves a family's poignant loss with enduring faith and the sweet surprise of Christmas love reborn."

> —CATHY GOHLKE, award-winning author of *Saving Amelie* and *Promise Me This*

"Rich with faith and deep love, *Where Treetops Glisten* is a must-read for your Christmas season."

> —CINDY WOODSMALL, *New York Times* best-selling author of the Amish Vines and Orchards series

"Any book by Cara Putman is an automatic read. *Where Treetops Glisten* is a hometown World War II book that captures your heart with its charm. It made me wish I could experience Christmas in that era. Highly recommended!"

> —COLLEEN COBLE, author of *Seagrass Pier* and the Hope Beach series

# Where Treetops Glisten

Three Stories of Heartwarming Courage
and Christmas Romance During World War II

## Tricia Goyer
## Cara Putman  Sarah Sundin

WATERBROOK
PRESS

WHERE TREETOPS GLISTEN
PUBLISHED BY WATERBROOK PRESS
12265 Oracle Boulevard, Suite 200
Colorado Springs, Colorado 80921

John 8:32, quoted in chapter 10 of *White Christmas,* and Matthew 19:26, quoted in chapter 6 of *Have Yourself a Merry Little Christmas,* are taken from the Holy Bible, New International Version®, NIV®. Copyright © 1973, 1978, 1984 by Biblica Inc.™ Used by permission of Zondervan. All rights reserved worldwide. www.zondervan.com. Colossians 2:10, 13–14, quoted in chapter 9 of *I'll Be Home for Christmas,* and John 15:13, quoted in chapter 19 of *Have Yourself a Merry Little Christmas,* are taken from the King James Version.

Trade Paperback ISBN 978-1-60142-648-2
eBook ISBN 978-1-60142-649-9

Published in the United States by WaterBrook Multnomah, an imprint of the Crown Publishing Group, a division of Random House LLC, New York, a Penguin Random House Company.

WATERBROOK and its deer colophon are registered trademarks of Random House LLC.

Library of Congress Cataloging-in-Publication Data
Where Treetops Glisten : Three Stories of Heartwarming Courage and Christmas Romance During World War II / Tricia Goyer, Cara Putman, Sarah Sundin.
        pages cm
    ISBN 978-1-60142-648-2 (paperback)—ISBN 978-1-60142-649-9 (electronic) 1. Christmas stories, American. 2. Love stories, American. 3. Christian fiction, American. 4. World War, 1939–1945—United States—Fiction. I. Goyer, Tricia. II. Putman, Cara C. III. Sundin, Sarah.
    PS648.C45W49 2014
    813'.0108334—dc23

                                                    2014015556

Printed in the United States of America
2014—First Edition

10 9 8 7 6 5 4 3 2 1

*In many ways this is a story of siblings surviving and finding love during World War II. I've been blessed to share my life with three siblings. To Janna, Joshua, and Joel: I'm grateful we shared our childhoods, but even more that I can count you as friends today. And I'm delighted that each of you have found the love stories God wrote for you.*

—Cara Putman

❧

*In loving memory of my grandmother, Grace Potter Powell, 1915–2014, with deep gratitude for sharing her love of words and story and history.*

—Sarah Sundin

❧

*To Maaike van Beek, my sweet Dutch friend who shared her Uncle Arie's story and allowed his final letter to be used within the novella* Have Yourself a Merry Little Christmas. *And to all the dedicated women and men in World War II—from Army nurses to those in the Dutch Underground— who sacrificed their lives, and their immediate happiness, to serve and care for others.*

—Tricia Goyer

# Winter Wonderland

## by Sarah Sundin

*December 24, 1941*
*Lafayette, Indiana*

Even her morning rheumatism couldn't stop Louise Turner from decorating for Christmas.

Louise rubbed her sore hip. She'd been born the day the Civil War ended. Her husband, Henry, had fought in the Spanish-American War. Her son, Robert, had served in the Great War. And now her grandchildren faced another world war.

"War or no war, we simply must celebrate Christ's birth. Isn't that right, Ferdinand?"

Her black-and-white cat didn't even blink in response. He sat on yesterday's *Journal & Courier*, his front paws tucked in neatly, covering the horrid headlines that screamed death and destruction and panic.

After the cruel attack on Pearl Harbor, the Japanese had been barreling through Thailand, Malaya, and the Philippines and across the Pacific, taking another island every day, it seemed. The Germans loomed at the gates of Moscow, and in Libya the British and Australians battled the Germans and Italians.

The world was a horrible place.

Louise set her jaw. Gloom and despair led to defeat. Victory could only be achieved with faith, hope, and resilience. She'd learned that lesson well in her seventy-six years, and now she'd pass it on to her family.

She inspected the Christmas tree in the bay window. Thank goodness Robert and his wife, Rose, had set it up before Pearl Harbor, because after the declaration of war, all holiday preparations had screeched to a halt. Louise had been paralyzed like the others, but that would end. Today.

Humming "Winter Wonderland," she crossed into the dining room, opened the door that led to the side porch, and dragged in the box of greenery she'd paid the little neighbor boy to collect.

The song, a huge hit from a few years back, had been perky and festive during the ravages of the Great Depression. Now her family could use some cheer to get through the recent tragedies and coming trials.

Louise shut the door against the predawn iciness and pulled a chair to the transom separating the dining room from the living room. Robert would tan her hide if he saw her climbing onto the chair. That was why she'd gotten up early.

Louise peered through her thick glasses. Yes, the nails were still in place to hang the greenery. She stuck several lengths of string in her mouth, gathered an armload of pine boughs, and worked her way up onto the chair, gripping the doorjamb for balance. If she fell and died, at least she'd go out having fun.

"Grandma!"

Louise met the brown eyes of her grown-up grandson Pete, who burst into laughter.

He'd probably never seen his grandmother with string hanging from her mouth like the tongue of an anteater. Louise smiled around the string and wiggled her eyebrows.

Pete strode over to her in his bathrobe, his wavy dark hair mussed from sleep. He looked so much like her Henry fifty years ago. "Get down from there," he said. "I'll take your place. I'll even let you boss me around."

Sometimes good sense had to prevail. Louise took Pete's hand and eased her way off the chair.

Pete plucked the string from her mouth. "What are you doing?"

"Decorating. It's Christmas Eve, and the house looks forlorn."

"It's four o'clock in the morning."

"When else can I work in privacy?"

"You mean, when else can you work without getting caught."

She patted the young man's rough cheek. "Ah, to be twenty-nine again and know everything."

Her oldest grandchild leveled his lawyer gaze at her. "I know you're sneaking around."

"And you know why." Louise motioned Pete up onto the chair. "The family is in mourning—the whole country is. No one feels like decorating, but if I do it, no one will rip it down. They'll know it's the right thing to do. Turners don't let anything get them down, not even another war."

Instead of climbing onto the chair, Pete nosed around in the box of greenery. He pulled out a sprig of mistletoe. "Maybe so, but we need to set aside one Turner tradition this year. For my sisters' sakes."

"Oh dear." Louise rummaged in the box. "I told the boy no mistletoe. Poor Abigail. Poor Meredith."

Abigail's high school sweetheart had been killed at Pearl Harbor, and the girl was in the depths of grief. Then Meredith had come home from nursing school in Miami Beach, devastated. Instead of receiving an engagement ring for Christmas, she'd received a broken heart.

Pete grabbed a pine bough and climbed the chair. "Well, the British get through all that bombing with cheer and a stiff upper lip. If it works for London, it'll work for Lafayette, Indiana."

"That's the spirit."

He angled a smile down at her. "I'm just glad I can get in the fight."

Her heart lurched. Instead of aiming those fine dark eyes at judge and jury, Pete would be scanning for enemy aircraft. He'd done the right thing by enlisting, but as a pilot? It was so dangerous. At least when Robert did his duty in the Great War, he served as a lawyer in the army.

But the Lord would see the Turners through. He always did. He had seen Robert and Rose through miscarriages, a stillbirth, and the deaths of two precious children. Even if the worst happened, the Lord would hold them up by His mighty hand.

"Next?" Pete opened and closed his hand in front of Louise's face.

She blinked and passed him another bough and piece of string.

"Grandma! It's wet."

Louise chuckled. "Serves you right for interrupting me."

"Interrupting what?" a new voice asked. Abigail ambled in with Merry, both wrapped in red bathrobes and blue sorrow.

"Your parents' surprise." Louise gave the pretty brunettes a soft smile. The surprise was also for her granddaughters, to show them life went on even when your heart was torn to shreds.

"Oh." Merry's dull, dark gaze skimmed the boughs, and she joined her older sister on the couch.

Going back to school and keeping busy would be best for both girls. Abigail's studies in education across town at Purdue University would occupy her focused mind, and over time she would heal.

Merry had a year and a half left of nursing school in Miami Beach. She hadn't said a word about joining the Army Nurse Corps, but the need for nurses would be as great as in the last war, if not more so. How could a girl with Merry's adventurous spirit resist the call of her country?

Would she end up overseas with her big brother? Both of them in danger? Witnessing death and destruction?

Louise hefted up a smile to heft up her spirits. "One more bough should do it, Pete."

"This time, give me the dry end of the string first. Please."

Oh, but the damp end was so tempting. But she'd better be good. It was Christmas Eve after all.

"Well, well, well . . ." Robert shuffled in with his arm over Rose's bathrobe-covered shoulders. "Memories of Christmas past. Our children making a racket before dawn."

Rose tapped her chin. "Except as I remember, it was always Christmas morning—not Christmas *Eve* morning."

As one, the three grandchildren pointed accusing fingers at Louise.

She batted innocent eyelashes. After all, someone had to bring color into this household.

Last year, when she'd moved into her son's home—into a first-floor bedroom, nonetheless—she thought she'd taken one step closer to the grave. She couldn't have been more wrong. She had so much to give her family, and she relished doing so. Now she knew every day meant one step further into abundant life.

The next few years would bring turbulence to her family. They needed her faith. They needed her wisdom. And they needed her joy.

# White Christmas

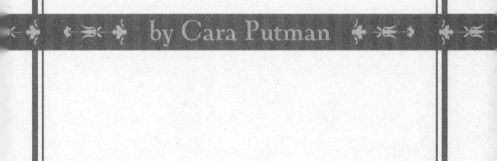

by Cara Putman

## One

*Thursday, October 29, 1942*
*Lafayette, Indiana*

*ackle your greatest fear?*

Professor Plante had smiled as he issued his challenge, as if the assignment was easy to achieve. Even a privilege. Yet five minutes after class ended, Abigail Turner remained frozen at her desk. A school project worth twenty-five percent of her grade tied to her greatest fear? And one that had to be developed and completed before the holidays? The professor called it a simple way to overcome the past by focusing on the future. A way to explore the principles they'd discussed and apply them to their own lives before trying the ideas on future clients. Didn't he see how tied the two were? How there was nothing simple about confronting dark moments in the past that were best avoided?

Abigail pushed back from the desk and joined the last students streaming through the door to the hall. She didn't notice anyone else who had broken into a cold sweat at the professor's instructions. In fact, most joked and bantered like another week of school was almost over, leading to another weekend of studying, Purdue football, and any odd jobs they worked. Maybe her fellow students didn't carry the fears and weight of the past as tightly as she did.

She tried to shake it off as she'd done over the years. She still had weeks to create the right experience for the project—at least until the end of the semester. Professor Plante had even made it sound like the students could have longer if they didn't mind an incomplete on their transcript.

As Abigail entered the hallway of Purdue's University Hall, she froze. The October wind gusted through the door and toyed with her hat, but that didn't account for her inability to move. No, she could only blame that on the reality that if she was truly to do this assignment, she had to find a way to open her heart to someone else. How could she make Professor Plante or anyone else understand that she couldn't do that? Not when it risked someone else leaving her.

"I have to get to work." She whispered the words as she tightened her grip on her bag, which was loaded down with textbooks, then forced her legs to move.

What would her life be like if Sam Troy, her high school love, hadn't enlisted and then died that terrible day the Japanese attacked Pearl Harbor? With his death, her carefully constructed dreams for the future crashed into an abyss, one she couldn't seem to climb from.

She glanced at her watch and frowned. If she dawdled any more, she'd miss the bus that would carry her down the hill, across the Wabash River, and to downtown Lafayette in time for her shift at Glatz Candies. With the weekend approaching, she looked forward to a couple of days to concentrate on the confections that made the restaurant and candy shop known around town. Soon she'd learn the secret to making the popular candy canes. Maybe she could coax the owner into teaching her the tricks to the twisted sweet that night.

"Slow down, Abigail."

Abigail grinned as her classmate Laurie Bertsche hurried up, her polo coat buttoned to her throat. Abigail nudged her friend in the shoulder. "It's not cold enough for that coat yet."

"I'm from Florida. We don't do cold."

"Then why pick Purdue?"

"It picked me, since it was as far away from home as I could afford." Laurie shuddered and gripped the coat around her throat. "What do you think of that assignment?" She rushed on before Abigail could interrupt. "It should be fun to think of something. There are so many people who need help." Laurie paused, frowned for a moment, then shrugged. "I'm not sure what I'll do yet. Do you have ideas?"

"Not yet."

"You're so intense; I know you'll come up with something brilliant." Merriment danced in Laurie's green eyes. "I need a favor tomorrow night. One of the guys I know from town asked me to a movie and dance. I said yes, but the problem is he has a buddy. Say you'll join us."

"You know my stance on boys."

Laurie singsonged as they waltzed through the doors. "No dating until this war business is over." She paused and a serious glint entered her expression. "This isn't a boy like you'd see here. He's not a student, but a man supporting his family."

"I can't, Laurie. If he's not in the military yet, he will be any day. Life is too uncertain to risk even friendship." Abigail had certainly learned that lesson between Sam, her brother Alfie, and her sister Annie. Professor Plante wanted her to confront her fears by acting in opposition to those very fears that life had branded into her. How could she do something and then write an essay explaining how the action had changed her? What if she did something and found she was still afraid of losing someone she loved? Should she help the military boys in some way? Or should she focus on children? Would either satisfy her professor?

"You mean you *won't*." Laurie's words jarred Abigail from her thoughts. "I intend to have a great time with Joey, but I wish you'd come. Joey's friend seems nice, and you don't need to worry that it will be for more than one night. Now if something develops with Joey, that's just icing for me."

"Try ice on the Wabash," Abigail mumbled. "The kind you fall through." The kind that broke your heart into shattered pieces, like the fragile ice coating the wide river, and left you frozen inside when you fell into the cold current.

Laurie shook her head. "Too early for that kind of ice. I'll have enough fun for the two of us. Call if you change your mind. If not, I'll see you in class Monday."

The rumble of the bus on State Street warned Abigail she'd better hurry.

*Don't leave! I can't be late for work.*

She waved frantically as the driver shifted the bus into gear. She rushed into State Street, waving. Brakes screeched and someone tugged her back to the curb right before a car whizzed by, horn blaring. Her heart stuttered in her chest. She'd come too close to landing under the wheels of that car.

"You all right, miss?"

"Thanks to you." She turned to her rescuer, and his gaze captured her, a mix of sadness and concern swirling in his eyes.

"You coming? Or standing out there all day?"

Heat flooded Abigail's cheeks at the bus driver's barked words. After checking for traffic, she hurried across the street, then tripped up the stairs, thrust a token into the box, and stepped down the aisle, barely noticing the young man who had rescued her following with a slight limp. The grinding gears and the bus's accompanying lurch pushed her down the aisle, and she collapsed onto an empty seat. The young man took the one opposite her.

She glanced at him under her lashes, noting the broad shoulders that indicated a life of work. There was something about him, as if his dog had just died, that made her want to reach out.

He slouched in his seat, hands clasped in his lap, shoulders slumped forward. A hat was crammed on top of dark hair that curled at the nape of his neck, longer than the regulation cuts worn by enlisted men. There was something familiar about him, yet she was certain they'd never been introduced. Abigail shrugged off the feeling. Even in the United States' heightened war machine during 1942, Purdue's campus flowed with men. The difference was many wore a uniform. This one didn't. Why? Could it be whatever had caused his limp?

His glance rose, colliding with hers. Caught. He'd discovered her staring.

Still she couldn't look away, not when such uncertainty resided in the pools of his hazel eyes. Something inside her froze, caught between wanting to help and distancing herself from the pain she saw reflected in the depths of his gaze. Maybe the pain was what she recognized.

She swallowed around a sudden tightness in her throat. "Thank you for what you did out there."

"You're welcome." His deep voice made it sound like it was nothing. He simply took heroic actions every day.

"I'm Abigail. Abigail Turner."

"Jackson Lucas." He looked back down at his hands.

Abigail felt the chill of the disconnection. She yanked a psychology text from the bag at her feet and opened it to the next chapter. The short ride would be better used preparing for Monday's class than wondering about the man seated across the aisle from her.

Her vow to avoid romantic relationships, no matter how casual, had not been some fly-by-night decision. She had carefully considered her course after Sam's death.

The war that had torn the world apart had arrived in the United States. Sure, it hadn't physically touched the nation since Pearl Harbor, but to see the war's effect, all one had to do was look at the men in uniform walking the streets or notice the blue and gold star flags hanging in homes across town. The war had touched so many lives, even in this sheltered city. She would never forget the pain that stabbed through her each time she drove by the Troys' home and saw the gold star flag hanging in the front window. Such a simple symbol that communicated so much senseless loss.

Abigail forced her gaze to remain firmly on the page even as her thoughts wandered. She'd made the right choice. She was certain. Nothing was worth risking the pain of losing more people she loved. Not when her big brother Pete was finishing requirements to be a fighter pilot while her sister Merry was training to be an army nurse. She couldn't bear the thought of losing them, and she

wouldn't risk opening her heart to anyone who could be taken by the vagran-
cies of war.

Jackson Lucas felt the weight of the envelope shoved inside his jacket as if each
page were a solid plank of the heaviest walnut rather than smashed wood pulp.
When had he started comparing weight to wood? His heritage belonged to a
farm, not a plant, yet he'd moved to Lafayette to work in a factory rather than
sell the farm and force his mother and sisters to move. He'd worked hard and
saved every extra penny, all in an effort to fix what the lean years, the thirties,
had stolen from them.

Now it was clear he shouldn't have moved away, even if it had meant earning the money his family needed to keep the farm.

The papers inside his jacket proved he'd failed in that effort. Somehow
even after all his work and focus, his family would still lose the only home his
sisters had known. What would Mother do now? How could he provide for
them without the farm?

What a mess.

He studied his hands. The calluses had shifted—similar but not the
same—as his work had changed. He raised a hand and twisted his wrist, examining every line, smudge of oil, and mark.

If only he could trace his thoughts as easily.

Without the sun shining on him, he felt different. Like one of the cardboard cutouts his employer transformed into toys that thrilled children. He
had nobody to thrill, not when he was as lifeless and bland as the cardboard
before the adhesive and pictures were applied.

The bus rumbled to another stop, and a young woman hurried on board.
This one wasn't as clumsy as the previous gal, Abigail. Jackson glanced her way
again. What had she seen when she studied him?

Did she find him wanting too?

He shook his head. He had to clear his thoughts, or he might as well not go on the date his buddy had set up. Why had he agreed to it? The words of the letter threatened to derail any chance he had of salvaging the evening, but Joey had refused to listen when Jackson argued he wasn't interested. He guessed he'd complained one too many times that Lafayette would never feel like home. His friend had lost patience and ordered him to appear at the Glatz Candies shop downtown on Friday night to meet a local girl.

*"Nobody likes being alone."* Joey's words couldn't have been truer.

"Excuse me?"

Jackson jolted as the gal across from him leaned into the aisle, the thick textbook in her lap threatening to tumble to the floor.

"Did you say something?" Her eyes danced as a curl slipped free of her headband.

"I don't think so." Surely he hadn't repeated Joey's words out loud.

Her smile widened. "Oh."

"Oh?"

"You're one of those." She tapped a page of the textbook as the bus lurched through another gear, chugging across the bridge that separated Purdue's campus and Lafayette.

"I don't understand."

"One of those men who likes to deny he might have a feeling." She eyed him a moment, then turned back to her textbook. "That's what my professor likes to claim, anyway. All men deny their emotions. I find his statements rather overbroad and all-inclusive. Don't you?"

Jackson felt his collar tighten as if someone had yanked back on it. How had he landed in the middle of this conversation? "I don't know."

"I'll admit my father and brother don't walk around spouting emotion." She paused as if caught in a thought, and her face twisted in a way that indicated it wasn't pleasant. "Still, they don't exactly hide what they're thinking. How about you?"

"I have sisters. Three of them."

"Oh."

After an uncomfortable moment, Jackson felt the bus grind to another stop. "Looks like this is me. Nice to talk to you, miss."

"Miss Abigail Turner," she said again. The smile that accompanied her name warmed him. "This is my stop too. Thanks again for your help."

Jackson nodded and waited for her to move ahead of him. She slipped past and then off the bus. He looked at her seat and saw a black book lying near the window. Picking it up, he noticed her name on the cover. By the time he stepped off the bus, book in hand, she'd disappeared.

How could he find her to return it? He cracked the cover and noted it was a calendar that included an appointment today at Glatz Candies. Since it wasn't out of his way, he could take the book there and try to catch her. He tucked it into his deep jacket pocket, and his fingers brushed the envelope.

Jackson's thoughts moved faster than his feet as he trudged toward the corner, weighed down by the words that filled the envelope. He pushed its message to the side, and his thoughts turned to the events on campus. Could a young woman like that ever give him a second glance? He doubted he compared favorably to the men she saw on Purdue's campus every day. At one time he'd dreamed of studying a subject like agriculture or engineering, using an education to get off the farm or improve it. After Dad died, he thought studying might give him techniques to improve the farm. Now he knew just what a pipe dream he'd fostered. He shoved his hands deep in his trouser pockets as he waited for the bus to move on and traffic to clear.

He crossed the street and headed up Main to the shop. It hadn't taken many days in Lafayette to realize Glatz's was a popular lunchroom and candy store, a favorite of locals and college students. Maybe on the way he'd find a convincing reason for why he'd agreed to this foolish date or a way to talk Joey out of including him. The bus ride served as exhibit A for why he shouldn't pretend to be suave and talk to young women he didn't know.

Who did he think he was? Cary Grant?

## Two

*A*bigail pushed through the heavy front door at Glatz Candies, enjoying the *ting-a-ling* of the bell. The solid counters stood separated by an aisle. One was lined with candy displays, the other with the soda fountain and a food preparation area. Large metal cash registers sat on each counter near the door. Business was slow as usual during this late-afternoon slot. The after-school rush had ended, and people's stomachs hadn't reminded them it was time to eat again.

"Good afternoon, Hannah," Abigail said to the girl behind the soda fountain counter.

"Like a Coke before you head upstairs?"

Abigail considered the idea for half a second before nodding. Once she started making whatever candy the store needed, she'd get hot quickly. "Add an extra squirt of cherry?"

"Of course." Hannah Morris blew blond hair out of her eyes and then pumped squirts of Coke chased by cherry into a glass before adding ice and the fizzy water. After a few quick stirs with a long-handled spoon, she slid the drink across the counter. "Here you go."

Abigail took a sip, savoring the sweetness. "Perfect. What do we need today?"

"Not sure. The boss said he'd leave a list for you."

"All right." She guessed she wouldn't make candy canes today. "See you later."

The book bag pulled at her shoulder as Abigail hiked up two flights of wooden stairs. Behind a closed door, away from prying eyes, stood the room where the magic of candy making occurred. Her parents had told her the store hadn't changed much since their visits during the early years of their marriage. Now she was part of its story.

Some would think it a nuisance to spend hours away from others while repetitively creating candy. Abigail used it as a chance to review whatever lectures she'd heard. Other times she'd memorize a list of terms while stirring the sugary or chocolate confections. She maintained top grades in her classes while earning the extra money to not be dependent on her parents. She might not have left home like Merry, but she liked gaining a measure of independence while she figured out her future, a future that would allow her to help struggling children. Her time at the Purdue Nursery School had only added to her commitment to learning more about how children coped with the strains of life.

Still, she couldn't study all the time, despite Merry's teasing, so she'd brought a small radio to break the silence. She flipped the machine on, found the list of candies, and started compiling the ingredients she'd need to make the candied fruit slices. Some girls might prefer the chocolates or caramels, but she'd take the lightly fruited sweets any day.

Time passed as she measured ingredients, stirred the concoction, and poured out the candy. After an hour, she wiped sweat from her brow. Time for a break while the latest batch cooled and set.

She slipped down the stairs, the empty Coke glass in her hand. Tables had begun to fill with a small supper clientele. Hannah took an order while one of the new cooks hustled about, filling other orders. Abigail slipped past him and refilled her glass with water. The coolness of the restaurant felt so good, she decided to sit for a few minutes and enjoy it before heading back to the superheated kitchen.

As she scanned the tables, her gaze landed on the young man who had saved her from being hit by a car. He looked as perplexed and lost as he had on the bus. His shoulders slumped over an empty plate from a weight she couldn't see, but she imagined it had something to do with the papers he studied. The way he looked at them that hard for so long, it was a good thing he didn't have Superman's x-ray vision, or the words might have burned off the pages.

There was only one thing to do—see if she could help.

No, she didn't know him. And yes, he might not be comfortable opening up to a stranger. But he bore the burdened look of someone who needed a friend. If her mama had taught her anything, it was to reach out to those who were alone. He certainly looked alone as he stared at the papers in his hands.

Abigail edged toward the empty seat at the small table next to his. In the tight space, she jostled his table before sitting down. "Sorry." She turned her brightest grin toward him. "I've been upstairs making candy and needed a drink desperately." She took a sip through the straw in her water glass. "Do you need a refill?"

"What?" The skin across the bridge of his nose and around his eyes wrinkled as he turned toward her. "Say, I've been looking for you."

"Really?"

He reached into his coat pocket and pulled out a small black book. "Is this yours? It was on your seat after you left the bus."

"My school calendar." She took it. How had it escaped her bag? "I didn't realize I'd left it behind." She exhaled heavily. Her life was cataloged in the diary's list of dates and assignments. "Thank you. I've got everything I need to get through the semester in there." She smiled. "Your glass is empty. Can I get you more? It's the least I can do. Please tell me you haven't waited for me for an hour."

"Has it been an hour?" He glanced at his watch. "I lost track of time after I ate. I don't need a refill."

"Are you sure?"

"I'm fine."

"You don't look it." She covered her mouth. That wasn't what her mama had in mind when she encouraged her children to befriend the friendless. "Sorry. My mouth can rush ahead of my brain sometimes. It's a real problem."

Silence settled over them, and she peeked at the papers. It looked like they bore a legal header. Bad news more than likely. He shoved the papers, words down, on the table. Heat climbed her neck. Had he caught her looking?

"I'm sorry. I shouldn't have tried to read your papers."

He expelled a heavy sigh. "I wish I didn't have to."

"Do you have anyone to help?" She raised her hand as he stared at her. "I don't mean me. My father's an attorney, one of the best in town. I'm sure he can help you. Well, unless you murdered someone. But I know you haven't or you'd be in jail. And even then, he's the only attorney in town I'd really recommend."

*Take a breath!* All this babbling made her look nervous. Surely she wasn't, not around a near stranger. Men simply didn't affect her that way. Not since her pact to maintain her distance for the duration of the war.

He chuckled, low and pleasant. "Are you always this talkative?"

"Not usually." She grinned. "If your problem is legal, you need to talk to an attorney before you decide what to do. I've heard my dad tell more than one person that he could have helped if they'd only given him time." A thought popped into her mind, and she blurted before common sense could stall the words. "Why don't you come to dinner tomorrow night? My mama enjoys cooking for company, and you can show Father the papers. It's perfect."

"I don't know."

"Really, I insist. After all, you did bring my book to me."

His intense eyes studied her a moment. What did he see when he looked through her like that?

"All right. I can reschedule an appointment." He shrugged as if shifting the weight that balanced between his shoulder blades.

"You're sure? You'll come?"

"I said yes, didn't I?" His lips tipped into the beginning of a smile.

"Wonderful. Our house isn't far from here." She gave him directions, then stood. "I need to get back to the candy. See you tomorrow night, Mr. Lucas."

"Until then."

The way he looked at her, sadness burdening him, almost broke her heart. What had she gotten herself into?

⋈

The next evening, Abigail scurried around the table adjusting the napkins and silverware until they were precisely placed at each setting. She'd already changed her dress twice since getting home from school and couldn't stand still.

Grandma came up behind her and reset the forks, a twinkle in her chocolate eyes.

"Grandma, please."

"Why are you so intent on the table?" A knowing smile settled over her face, as if she could sense tonight was more than a normal dinner for Abigail.

"I've invited someone to dinner."

"Really?" Grandma settled against the solid buffet that lined the wall, her gray curls shifting. "I knew something was up. You don't act like this normally. Is it a young man?"

Heat rushed into Abigail's cheeks.

"So it is."

"Grandma, I simply invited him so Father could give him advice. I want him to feel welcome while he's here."

Grandma tilted her head like a bird who'd identified her next meal. "Of course straight napkins will ease his loneliness."

Abigail picked up a navy-blue napkin, then set it down as Grandma chuckled.

Grandma turned as Mama entered the dining room. "Did you know about this, Rose?"

"I did." A soft smile curved Mama's mouth. "Abigail, what has gotten into you? You know we'll do all we can to make him comfortable and welcome."

Abigail huffed a curl out of her eye. She knew they meant well, but their attention could be intense without her siblings around to help deflect their focus. Still, why did she care? She barely knew Jackson Lucas. She shook her head. Maybe that would dislodge the interest she'd taken in him.

The doorbell rang and she hurried toward the door. Grandma followed, but Abigail stopped by the fireplace.

"Well, aren't you going to let him in?" The twinkle in Grandma's eye indicated she knew Abigail didn't want her grandmother to open the door. Who knew what the woman would say?

Abigail took a breath. Jackson had really come. She hadn't been sure he'd clear whatever appointment he'd had to dislodge. As soon as she'd heard he had an appointment, she should have offered an alternative, but she hadn't. Abigail caught her breath and prayed the evening would go well. Could Father ease the tension from the young man's face?

"Open it already."

Abigail scrunched her nose as she turned her back on Grandma. When she opened the door, Jackson stood there looking a bit like he was ready to bolt.

"You made it." Abigail shivered as a breeze swirled in the house, the bite in the air proclaiming it was nearly November. She took his arm and gently tugged him inside. "I'm so glad you found our house. Perrin Avenue is tucked at such a funny angle, it can be tricky to locate."

"Thanks again for inviting me." He held out a small box of chocolates. She smiled as she saw the Glatz label. "I wasn't sure what you'd like. Flowers are hard to find this time of year."

"Thank you. These are my favorites. In fact, I made some last night."

Mama cleared her throat.

"Jackson, may I introduce my mother, Rose Turner, and my Grandma Louise? Mama, this is the young man I told you about. Jackson Lucas."

"Ma'am. Thank you for allowing me to join you." He bowed slightly, his wool Mackinaw jacket tightening across his shoulders.

"So glad you could." Mama smiled as she gestured toward the matching wing chairs set near the fireplace. "We'll be ready to eat as soon as Mr. Turner arrives." She glanced at her slim watch. "That should be any minute, unless he got caught at court."

Abigail looked at their living room, which flowed into the dining room. A davenport covered in brocade tapestry sat in front of the window box, forming a comfortable conversation area with the navy wing chairs. An oriental rug covered the hardwood floor, and a marble-topped coffee table rested between the furniture. The roses carved into the couch and table brought the room together. To the side, by the wall between the living room and dining room, stood the piano that Merry hadn't played very well when she was home. Abigail had always thought it a welcoming room, but how would a man perceive it?

She jiggled the box. "Let me put the candy in the kitchen."

When she returned to the living room a moment later, Jackson stood in front of the fireplace, his coat now on the coat tree, staring at the family photo perched on the mantel. Abigail shoved down the bitter anxiety that chased the sorrow. The photo always looked incomplete, sitting there without any acknowledgement of her brother who had died in a car accident and sister who had died of influenza. They might have died years ago, but it still seemed wrong to have a photo with only the five who remained.

Her eyes landed on Pete, handsome in his dress uniform, pilot's wings affixed over his left breast pocket, the US and Army Air Force prop insignia on his lapels.

"Your brother?" Jackson asked.

"Yes. He's training to fly fighters. We don't know where or when he'll deploy." *Please keep him safe.* She couldn't bear to lose another sibling.

Jackson studied her as if something in her words hinted at more than she'd offered.

The door banged open. "I'm home and famished."

Her father's boisterous voice caused Jackson to turn. He stiffened as he did, feet spread wide.

Father walked toward him, his topcoat open to reveal the charcoal three-piece suit he usually wore on court days. He'd loosened the knot of his red and navy striped tie, signaling the end of a long day doing battle in a courtroom. He flipped his hat onto the coat tree nestled into the alcove, then slipped his coat off. "Welcome to our home, young man. I understand you have legal needs."

"I . . ."

"Robert, give the poor man a chance." Mama pulled off her apron as she stepped out of the kitchen. "Jackson, I apologize for my husband. He's very focused on fixing problems."

"Makes me a good attorney."

"An excellent one. But please save the legal discussions for after dinner." She gestured toward the dining room. "If you'll all have a seat, we can have our meal."

As Jackson held out a chair for Abigail, he cleared his throat. "Is that a roast, ma'am?"

Mama smiled. "With all the fixings."

Grandma leaned toward Jackson as he sat. "Rose makes the best mashed potatoes." Abigail bit back a giggle as Jackson nodded. Grandma edged even closer and dropped her voice to a stage whisper. "Butter would make them better though."

Father cleared his throat and led the family in a quick blessing for the food. As soon as he finished, he said, "So tell us more about yourself, Mr. Lucas."

Jackson shifted in his seat, rubbing his right leg as if it hurt. "I work for the puzzle company. On one of their lines."

"I love working their puzzles." Grandma waved her hands as she talked about piecing together one of the five-hundred-piece puzzles that had a dozen birds tucked within its perimeter.

"Do you like what you do?" Mama's tone was interested as she passed a basket of bread.

"Yes. It's not the same as being on the farm, but I enjoy it. I'm still getting used to working inside all day, but I enjoy watching the process. Right now we're working on toy kits for Christmas presents." There was a slight hesitation in his tone that made Abigail wonder what the *but* he didn't speak was. "It's a good job, and I'm grateful for it."

"Honest work is always something to be grateful for." Father launched into an example from a current client's battles. As he listened, Jackson rubbed his leg a few more times. It seemed to be an unconscious gesture, and he always returned to the same spot.

"We talked about the importance of meaningful work in one of my classes today." As Abigail had sat in the classroom, she had wondered what hers would be. She thought she knew, but sometimes she wondered if she dreamed of doing something impossible.

"I always thought my work would be on the farm, but life changed that vision." Jackson shrugged. "I'm learning to adjust my plans."

Father launched into another story, and Grandma interjected her insight with a touch of humor.

Abigail picked up the bowl of green beans and held them toward Jackson. "We canned these this summer. Hottest day of the year too."

"You should have seen her. Wet curls all around her face." Grandma's smile coaxed an answering one from Abigail, and Jackson turned to her with a smile. It was the most relaxed she'd seen him.

"My sisters aren't fond of canning either," Jackson said.

"Oh, it wasn't so bad. My sister Merry usually helps, but she was gone, so it was my turn."

The meal passed in a blur of circulating bowls, clanking silverware, and conversation. At one point Abigail noticed Jackson patting his shirt pocket. Did he wonder if the legal papers were still there? Abigail glanced at her father and smiled as he regaled them with another story. Surely he could do something to ease the shadows from Jackson's eyes.

She hadn't learned much about Jackson the night before, but he had a story. Would he reveal it to her and let her share the burden? She felt drawn to him, and it made her pause. What was it about this man and his quiet ways that made her want to help him?

After a bit, Mama signaled it was time to clear the dinner plates. "Abigail, will you help while I cut the cake?"

Abigail nodded and took Jackson's plate. "You'll love Mama's angel food. She makes the best cake in the world. I'm just grateful Father finally got her an electric beater, so we don't have to take turns whipping the egg whites into submission."

Grandma pulled a silly face as she studied Jackson. "If I'd known we'd have company, I'd have made some of my famous cookies and saved Rose from beating those eggs for twenty minutes."

"I don't mind." Mama handed a plate to Jackson. "I enjoy baking for company. We'll have a bowl of canned strawberries out in a moment if you'd like to add some to your cake."

Abigail returned from the kitchen with a bowl of strawberries and another of whipped cream. She set them in front of Jackson, then sat down as the easy conversation continued. She loved the way her family could make anyone feel at home. It was a special gift they offered others. Conversation slowed while everyone dove into the cake. Abigail enjoyed every bite of the fluffy delicacy. With sugar rationing in place and Grandma hoarding what they did have, she'd better enjoy the sweetness while sugar remained available.

Father patted his stomach. "Thanks for another great meal, Rose."

"My pleasure."

While they said the same words almost every night, it didn't stop Mama's cheeks from coloring with a sweet rose.

"Mr. Lucas, when you're ready, Abigail can show you to my office." Father nodded to them all, then stood and strode toward his second office.

Jackson pushed his plate back and placed his fork across it. "Can I help with the dishes?"

"Certainly not." Mama softened her words with a smile. "You're our guest. Besides, I know you have a problem Mr. Turner can help with. Go on back."

"Here. I'll show you." Abigail prepared to stand, but before she could, Jackson was on his feet and poised to help with her chair. "Thank you."

"My mother raised me to be a gentleman." The faintest twinkle surfaced in his eyes. "In a house full of girls, I had plenty of opportunities to practice."

"So I see."

"Let me grab my papers."

While he retrieved them, the thought flitted through Abigail's mind that with manners like that, any girl would be blessed to have him as a partner through the days of her life.

She tucked her chin and led him to the back of the house.

What had just happened?

It seemed like the manners his mother had drilled into him had somehow bothered Abigail. Yet she hadn't seemed offended. On the contrary, she'd seemed grateful, until she tucked her chin and wouldn't meet his gaze.

She led him to a small room behind the kitchen, then paused to point to the room beside it, which had a closed door. "That's Grandma's room. She's lived with us several years and keeps the door closed so her beast of a cat can't escape."

"She keeps things lively around here, doesn't she?"

"She does. I can't imagine her not being here." Abigail opened the opposite door. "Here you go."

She gestured for Jackson to enter the room, then closed the door behind him. At some point it might have been a bedroom, but now the walls contained Mr. Turner's home office. A small yet sturdy desk stood in the center of the room. A typewriter sat on a small table next to it, with a bookshelf behind.

Mr. Turner tugged a chair from the corner and set it in front of the desk. "Have a seat, Jackson. Ready to let me look at your papers?"

"I'd be glad to, sir." Jackson swallowed. "The thing is, money's tight . . ."

Mr. Turner held out his hand. "Let me read the document. If more is needed, we can discuss price. You may not need my services, so there's no need to discuss cost until we know what we're facing. I'm glad to do this for a friend of Abigail's when she asks."

Silence settled over them as Jackson studied Mr. Turner. He seemed sincere, but how could Jackson make him understand the serious nature of his family's finances? He didn't want to accept charity, not when he'd worked so hard so they wouldn't need it. Ever since Dad had died, Jackson had struggled to pull the farm out of the depths created during the years of economic depression. Should he mention he'd only met Abigail yesterday? Would that change Mr. Turner's willingness to help?

Jackson had to face facts.

He didn't understand how the bank could foreclose on the farm when he'd sent money for the payments to his mother month after month. What options did he have? Mr. Turner stood ready to help.

Jackson tapped the envelope, then surrendered it. "Here you go."

Mr. Turner settled back in his chair after placing an empty pipe in his mouth. Time passed with only the rustle of a turning page scratching the moments.

This night had made him miss the cozy kitchen back home and his mother's good meals. This time of year, the produce would be gone, but Mother would have canned enough to keep the family eating like royalty through the cold months.

If only he could somehow travel the thirty miles to Attica and spend one evening with his kid sisters. They poked, prodded, and loved each other with a fierceness he missed. Even more than the easy camaraderie between Abigail and her family. The Turners loved each other, but it wasn't the same as being surrounded by his sisters. Being here made him miss them all the more.

What would they do when he told them they had to leave?

He belonged there with them, on the farm where he knew what to do in every situation because he'd grown up trailing his father and watching his hero's response to each problem. Nothing had fazed the man . . . but Jackson couldn't say the same about himself. The packet of legal documents weighed heavy on his heart. The bank couldn't foreclose.

Not when he'd economized, pinched, and scraped every last penny together to send home.

It hadn't been enough.

All his effort and work hadn't been enough.

hat could they be talking about in there?" Abigail groused as she took another plate from the drying rack and wiped a dishtowel across it.

This length of time usually meant a serious legal problem, and she didn't want to think that a man like Jackson would carry that kind of burden. She'd hoped he'd missed a detail that made the papers unimportant, but they must be as dire as his body language had suggested. At dinner he'd answered Mama's questions with short answers—never rude, but distracted. As if the papers he carried weighed down his soul. Jackson had relaxed a bit as the evening progressed, but the sad aura she'd noted the moment she met him never lifted.

Father had worked miracles for people before. Surely he could do it again.

"Do you want him to sit with you on the swing?" Grandma held her hands under her chin and winked. "It's a perfect night to stare into his dreamy eyes."

"Mama, make her stop. It's too cold and she knows it."

"Just ignore her." Mama shot Grandma a look, then shook her head. "How did you meet him?"

"On the bus. Then at work. I accidentally left my calendar on the bus, but he figured out I worked at Glatz and brought it to me. I could tell he was burdened, and . . . I didn't think you'd mind."

Grandma brought a round of plates to the sink. "Well, he seems very nice. I'm glad you invited him."

"I always have room for one more, especially with Pete and Merry away." Mama rinsed a plate and put it in the drying rack. "We'll see if your father can help him."

"If I know Robert, he'll do all he can." Grandma headed back to the table.

Once the table was cleared and the dishes washed and dried, Abigail flopped onto the couch and pulled a textbook onto her lap. She read one page, then another, then stopped. So far, not a word had penetrated her memory. If asked, she wasn't even sure she'd know the subject. She flipped the book to the cover and sighed. Accounting was not where she wanted to focus her thoughts right now.

A door opened down the hall, and she shot to her feet.

"Relax, Abigail." Mama slanted a look her direction, before glancing back at her *Look* magazine. "I'm sure all is well."

"I appreciate your time and advice, Mr. Turner," Jackson said as the two men walked into the room.

Her father clapped him on the shoulder. "I'll do a bit of investigating and get back to you in a couple of days."

Jackson nodded, then turned toward Mama. "Thank you for welcoming me to your home and for the meal."

"Glad you could join us." Mama grabbed a paper-wrapped package from the counter. "I've put a few leftovers in here for you."

Color flushed his face. "My thanks." Jackson turned toward Abigail, and her breath caught as his hazel eyes found hers. Abigail waited, but he didn't say anything. She shifted her feet, and he blinked as if exiting a dream. "Well, I'd better head home. Thank you again."

He headed for the front door so quickly Abigail had to hustle to catch up. "Was Father able to help?"

He shrugged, a gesture burdened by more than his coat he reclaimed from the coatrack.

"Good luck to you." She bit down on her lower lip and took a step back.

"Thank you." He opened the door, then seemed to gather himself as he stood taller. "I appreciate the chance to meet your family. Good-bye."

"Good-bye." She watched as the young man slipped out the door and down the sidewalk.

"I can see why you need a no-boyfriend policy." Grandma leaned against the door, watching Abigail watch Jackson. "He'll be back."

"Only if Father needs something. And I bet that will be handled at the office. Good night, Grandma."

Abigail turned and hurried up the wide stairs to tackle her homework. As she wrestled with material for her psychology class, someone knocked at her door. She exhaled a breath. "Yes?"

"May I come in?" Father's voice was serious and insistent.

"Yes sir."

Abigail set her book to the side and watched as Father entered and glanced around her room. It was small, but the private space still felt strange after sharing it for so many years with Merry. True, she could now keep it as neat and organized as her studies and work schedule allowed, but she missed the late night talks and the way she could always count on Merry to brighten the dullest day. Even painting the walls a new color couldn't make the room feel like hers alone or remove the memories of years spent giggling together under the covers.

Now her younger sister would brighten the days of men in uniform as she nursed them back from injuries. As much as she sometimes envied Merry's purpose, Abigail knew she wasn't the right person for a nursing position—not when the sight of blood made her stomach turn and her head suddenly lighten. But with Merry finishing nursing school, this room and part of Abigail's life felt empty.

Father sat next to her on the bed. "Your friend is a nice young man."

"I don't know that I'd call him a friend. We only met yesterday."

"All the same, I'm glad you brought him home. He needs help, and you were right to invite him here."

"Can you help?"

"I'll try. There seems to be quite a mess to untangle, but I've done that before." He sighed and pulled his glasses off to pinch his nose. "It's hard to understand how some things happen, but God has a way of sorting it all out. If it doesn't, I'll just blame you. Say your enthusiasm got the best of you. Ignore the fact that you have one of the kindest hearts I know."

"Father!" He looked at her, and the twinkle in his eyes made her smile. "Is there any way I can help?"

Father's lips firmed into a straight line. "You know I can't discuss my clients' problems. Mr. Lucas is no exception, even if you did bring him to me."

Abigail knew that with those words, the conversation had ended. Father took his ethical obligations seriously and refrained from delving into specific details about clients' ongoing business at home. He might tell stories, but kept them general. That was one reason he kept his home file cabinet locked.

"Are you sure you can't make an exception this one time?" An urge to know what burdened her new friend burned through her. She wanted to help, and connecting him with Father wasn't enough. She wanted to do something herself, something that would ease his burdens.

Father shook his head as he leaned back and then stood. "Any information will have to come from him. I just wanted you to know I'll do my best to help. And I'm proud of you for offering him assistance and friendship. See you in the morning."

Abigail stared at the closed door for some time after Father left. He was proud of her. She would soak in that revelation for a moment. She knew he loved her deeply, but she often felt overlooked in between a fighter pilot and soon-to-be nursing sensation. Her life was quiet and small in comparison, yet she longed to make a difference.

Could that difference come through seeing the deep hurts and loneliness that others carried? No one should walk through life as burdened as Jackson Lucas. Yet could she risk her heart in accepting his pain and having a terrible result? Maybe it was easier—it certainly was safer—to walk through life sheltered from others' hurts. But she sensed an opening in her heart, and it felt good.

Given time, she'd learn his burdens, and if he'd let her, she'd gladly share them.

## Tuesday, November 10

Jackson slogged home after another day at the puzzle plant. The machines had been making cardboard play sets in addition to puzzles for months, in preparation for the rapidly approaching Christmas season. With so many raw materials reserved for war production, many young boys would find a cardboard Old West fort or Civil War play set under the tree this year. Jackson would take each of his sisters one of the dozens of puzzles the machines pressed, rolled, and cut. His ears rang from the level of noise that assaulted them during his shifts.

Days like this left him longing for the peace he'd find in the fields or the gentle sounds of the barn while he milked the cow. The mechanical whirs and bangs of the factory were a stark contrast. Should he look for a job at the Alcoa plant? Do something that was more geared to the war effort? When he'd first arrived in town, this had been the best job he could find, and he guessed if he had to stay inside, working on toys that would bring kids joy was a decent job to hold. It also wasn't as physically demanding as working at Alcoa, so it fit better with his afflicted body.

Some days he rode the bus home, but today he needed to clear his head. His leg didn't bother him, so he headed downtown on State Street. Traffic set a steady pace as he walked toward his boardinghouse, a clapboard home nestled in a small neighborhood near Columbian Park, halfway between the plant and downtown. Lafayette might not be the largest city in Indiana, but with industry ramped up at Alcoa and other companies to meet the military's needs, finding a room had been a challenge. Even if the boardinghouse's proximity to the Columbian Park Zoo meant the monkeys' calls and shrieks woke him in warmer weather, he appreciated the ability to walk to work or church on Sunday mornings when needed.

Today he'd use the walking time to pray about his family. He'd worked hard to provide for them, and even so, they stood to lose the farm. Then what? He stumbled at the thought. Should they join him in Lafayette? Should he return to Attica?

He shook the thought free. He'd left because he couldn't find a job in his small farming community. Not one that paid the cash his family needed. Until Mr. Turner contacted him, there was little he could do but pray.

Little he could do.

He suppressed a snort. His father would have told him prayer was the most important thing. Deep inside, he knew Dad was right. But God hadn't protected his father during the accident, and He didn't seem up to protecting the family home either. Jackson bit back the bitterness and tried to replace it with gratefulness. Bitterness wouldn't get him anywhere, and they still had the farm . . . at least for now.

His father had carried a tinge of anger over dreams unfulfilled. While Jackson had talked to Mr. Turner, he'd wondered if his dad had dreamed of doing something significant like the attorney. Mother had constantly reminded Dad that farming was good, honest work and necessary. Then the struggles of the thirties had taken the fight right out of Dad.

Jackson refused to let the same thing happen to him.

He hiked up the steps of the boardinghouse to the porch and then in the front door. The Craftsman-style woodwork was oak and gave the home a warm feel. His small room in the attic had the same wood floors and floral wallpaper he ignored. The narrow twin bed had a passable mattress and decent blanket. With the way heat rose in the house, he doubted he'd need a quilt even in the middle of winter. The small dresser served its purpose, since he didn't have much extra in the way of clothes. Three sets of work clothes, a pair of nice jeans, and a couple of shirts. One pair of suit pants for events like church. He'd sacrificed to send money south each month. It rankled that it hadn't been enough.

It wasn't the first time he'd failed, but the consequences were more severe this time. If only he knew where the money had gone. The best way to find out was a trip home. He'd have to find the time and funds to make the trip and talk to Mother, since catching her on the phone was difficult. Maybe then he could figure out what had happened and their situation would start to make sense.

Tonight he'd try to forget everything. Tomorrow he was headed to Purdue on an errand for his supervisor. Would he run into Abigail?

He snorted. On a campus that size, he thought he'd find one coed? No matter how beautiful she was, how bright her personality, it would take a small miracle to find her.

Could he have a future with someone like Abigail? No, he'd better get his expectations squarely where they belonged. Right now he needed to unravel the problems with the farm. He couldn't begin to think about a family of his own until his mother and sisters were taken care of. He needed to be realistic and responsible and pray for a solution to the problem perplexing him.

Beautiful women like Abigail Turner could play no role in his life right now.

## Four

*Wednesday, November 11*

A harsh wind blew across campus as Abigail hurried to the bus stop. She pushed against the wind, praying she'd timed it right and wouldn't need to wait a moment longer than necessary. She might freeze as brittle and unyielding as a Glatz candy cane if she stayed out in this cold much longer.

In the days since Jackson had dined with her family, Abigail had watched for him. He'd been elusive . . . or maybe he just worked and lived in a different part of Lafayette. She didn't want to consider why he mattered to her.

She had a firm commitment not to spend any effort or time on men. She could better protect her heart during the war if she simply focused on her classes and her work at the nursery school. So many of those little children didn't understand why their mothers were at work, and she enjoyed loving them. Add that to her school work and job at Glatz Candies, and she didn't have time to be swayed and distracted. Maybe if Father would simply say he'd resolved Jackson's matter, she could stop wondering if he was okay.

Instead, Jackson kept invading her thoughts. She'd barely heard today's lecture on toddler development because she wondered how he was.

Laurie had grabbed her arm as the lecture ended. "Have you picked your project?"

Abigail had sighed as she collected her books and stood. "No idea. You'd think this would be simple . . ."

"Maybe you can do something with the nursery kids." They walked out of the classroom, and Laurie leaned closer until the feather on the side of her box hat almost touched Abigail's cheek. "It's a good thing you didn't join us last week when I asked you to be part of our group. Joey's friend backed out. It worked out fine, but I was so relieved you weren't planning to join us."

"I knew it would work out for the best."

Laurie giggled as color slowly stained her cheeks. "I'd still like you to come sometime. You are all work and school. You need a little fun in your life." She glanced at her watch, then returned her attention to Abigail. "I've gotta run to my next class, but you know I'm right. Think about it, okay?" Laurie waved and then hurried off.

Abigail walked to the bus stop, considering the truth in Laurie's words. She did like to be busy. It kept her focused on the important things. What did it matter if she went out with a man for a night or two? Maybe it didn't, but she couldn't help thinking of the men and boys who were preparing for the fight. She didn't want to lead a frivolous life, even for a season. She sighed. It was easy to feel that way, but not so easy to explain to people like Laurie.

"That's a mighty big sigh."

Abigail startled at the sound so much that she dropped her books. "Jackson?"

The young man looked at her with a steady gaze. She straightened her shoulders and met his hazel eyes. Today they leaned toward green flecked with brown. A slow smile broke across his face. Oh, she could get used to watching that and then coaxing another smile to dawn.

"I wasn't sure it was you." Jackson grinned as his gaze swept over her. "Campus seems too big to bump into you again."

She pointed at the sign for the bus stop. "This is where we met. Well, we actually met on the bus, but only after you saved me over there."

"You're right." He shrugged. "I don't come to campus often, so seeing you twice seems like more than chance."

"It does." The bus arrived with a clash of brakes before she could respond further, and they stood in silence as a stream of passengers descended. Then Jackson waited for her to board before following. She nabbed a vacant bench in the front, and Jackson fell into the seat next to her as the bus lurched into gear. A faint tinge of color traveled up his neck.

The ride downtown was short ... too short now that she'd found him again. As the blocks passed, Jackson seemed content to sit beside her. Abigail fought the urge to wiggle as his stillness pressed against her. Would he find her normal chatter entertaining or annoying? He'd mentioned a houseful of sisters, so maybe silence was the ticket. She tried to stay quiet, but by the time they reached the bridge between Lafayette and West Lafayette, she burst. "What brought you back to campus?"

He smiled, that little crease to his mouth that made her want to know what would happen if she ever teased a real smile from him. He was mysterious, like there was much more to him but he couldn't quite release his control.

The moment stretched as the bus slowed through shifting gears. When she was about ready to ask the question again or turn away in frustration, he shrugged.

"My boss commissioned new art for a series of puzzles. He needed someone to collect the first piece, and I got tapped." He patted the bag he carried. "I've got it right here."

"Well, I'm glad he sent you. It's good to run into you." She collected her bag and shoved her textbook inside. "I get out at the next stop."

"I know." The quiet words let her know he hadn't forgotten. He turned to her, his attention pinning her in place, almost like the insects Pete had collected one year. "Join me for a movie?"

"I have to work tonight."

"Then tomorrow?"

There was something earnest and pleading in his eyes, something that made her move beyond the rule she'd erected to protect her heart. After all, they could go to the movie as friends.

She nodded. "Tomorrow it is."

"Great." He relaxed against the seat as the bus shifted to a stop, and Abigail stood. He hurried to his feet and into the aisle. "Where should I collect you?"

"Glatz's at seven? I work until then."

He nodded, then slid back onto the seat. "I'll see you then. Do you mind if I invite a friend?"

"Not at all." In fact, it felt less like a date that way.

Abigail felt a tinge of color blush her cheeks and fought it back. Jackson was lonely, and she could be a friend. She would get to spend more time with this intriguing young man.

She hurried across the street and down Sixth Street toward the store. Whether or not seeing one movie together was a good thing, tomorrow she'd learn more about the elusive, mysterious Jackson Lucas.


What had he been thinking, inviting Abigail Turner to a movie?

She was so far out of his league he couldn't believe she'd said yes. The moment he offered the invitation, he'd braced himself, waiting for her to laugh. Instead, she'd looked delighted.

What would her father think? He hadn't asked for permission first and desperately needed the attorney's help. At least by possibly adding Joey and his girl to the mix, the night would feel less intimidating. They could enjoy a flick and a Coke, then return to their normal lives.

Jackson brooded as the bus continued down State Street, now called South Street since the road had crossed the Wabash. When it reached Columbian Park he disembarked and headed to a park bench instead of his boardinghouse. A few trees held on to the last vestiges of fall's colorful leaves. Most had fallen into drying piles at the foot of the trees, waiting for someone to build them into a pile and then fling themselves into it. How many times had he done that at the farm? When he was in the park, he could close his eyes and almost pretend he was back home. Then a car horn blared, jerking him back to reality. A duck waddled by, possibly lost or confused since the pond was at the other end of the park and, according to the calendar, the bird should have migrated south.

He watched the duck amble by without a care in the world so long as the snow held off awhile longer. Yet as it waddled off in a circuitous path, Jackson wondered how similar he was. He'd thought his life was on a straightforward path. He'd put one foot in front of the other as he'd followed in his father's footsteps, intending to farm the homestead until another generation took his place. He'd applied to Purdue's College of Agriculture to learn the new techniques he believed it would take to farm in the future. Then Dad had died without a miracle to provide a new path.

Now the farm might disappear altogether. Then what?

Even during the long shifts at the puzzle factory and the even longer nights, he'd never considered what he would do other than return to the farm as soon as he could.

He propped his elbows on his knees and cupped his chin with his hands. *Do you have something else for me, Lord?*

The question echoed in the stillness inside him. God had a plan and future for him. He believed that. But at the moment, what that future held he couldn't begin to guess. His future seemed to collide with the uncertainty of his present, leaving him in such a fog he didn't know how to put one foot in front of the other anymore.

Maybe he should call Mr. Turner. Ask if he knew anything more. Or maybe he should return to the farm now. His thoughts clamored, knocking around in his mind.

*Wait.*

The word cut through the clutter, but it made no sense.

Wait to return when the farm could be taken by the bank?

Wait to see what his future held?

Wait to see what happened to his mother and sisters?

The questions pushed him from the bench and chased him to the board-inghouse, up the stairs, and into his room. Waiting didn't make sense, didn't seem possible, when action was required. Yet the word wouldn't leave him.

He sagged on the edge of his bed, ignoring the squeal of the springs. *All right, God. But You'll have to show me how, because everything in me wants to do something. Show me how to wait on You.*

The next evening, he hurried home after his shift and took a quick shower. Joey and his girl would meet them at the movie theater, but first Jackson would collect Abigail. It helped that the theater was across the street from Glatz Candies.

He caught a bus toward downtown. One benefit of living on such a main thoroughfare was the proximity of a bus stop. He could always catch an Alcoa bus if he missed the city's, and if he missed everything, it was a relatively quick walk to the heart of Lafayette. In short order, the bus veered off State Street onto Main at five corners, and then he was in front of Glatz Candies.

He checked his watch as the bus stopped. Six forty-five. Perfect. He'd arrive a few minutes early without looking overeager. He strode to the shop, its stoop set on an angle at the corner of the building, and held the door for an older lady. The bell *ting-a-linged* as he entered. A small crowd filled the tables beyond the soda fountain and candy displays.

His mouth watered as he passed the chocolates lined up next to other sweets. Which were Abigail's favorites? Or did she even like candy anymore after hours spent creating it? She'd seemed to appreciate the chocolate he'd brought to her home, but maybe working here made her tired of the treats.

He looked up the stairs and saw her bright expression as she hurried toward him.

She took his breath, with her plaid jacket thrown over an arm, her navy dress swishing around her knees. A few brunette strands had slipped from her ponytail, giving her a fresh, appealing air. His fingers tensed to touch her hair. The impulse shook him, and he squished out a smile as she approached. She almost missed a step as she watched him.

"Everything all right, Jackson?"

"Sure." Other than the fact that she captivated him more than he'd ever thought a young woman would. He was in trouble if he couldn't rein his thoughts into line. "Ready to catch the show?"

"Yes! I've so wanted to see *Holiday Inn*. Ever since *Look* talked about it months ago." She stopped in front of him, a hand resting lightly on his arm. "I just love Fred Astaire's dancing and Bing Crosby's voice. Can anyone croon like him?"

"I guess we'll find out tonight."

Abigail laughed as she let him take her coat. "While Fred can dance, he'll never sing as well as Bing. But that's all right. Bing will never dance as well as Fred." She slipped her arms into the jacket, then pulled the end of her ponytail from the collar. "Ready?"

"Would you like a Coke or some candy first?"

"Not tonight." She wrinkled her nose. "I've been surrounded by chocolate and nuts. A bag of popcorn might be nice."

They walked across the street to the Lafayette Theater and found Joey and his girl, Laurie, waiting at the ticket counter.

Laurie squealed as she playfully swatted Joey. "Abigail! Joey wouldn't tell me who we were meeting, just that we were going to the pictures."

"Jackson didn't tell me." Joey gripped his arm as if she'd wounded him, a teasing gleam in his eyes. "I've got your tickets."

"I'll get the popcorn," Jackson offered.

"Deal."

The marquee lights blazed in the twilight, letting the town know there was a show to see. Jackson held the door as the foursome entered the foyer. A small crowd milled about, waiting for the theater doors to open. Once they did, Jackson led Abigail toward the balcony stairs, while the crowd chose the main floor. Joey and Laurie followed a step behind.

Abigail let him lead her, then slipped into the first row. "I've always loved the balcony. Nothing to separate me from the movie."

Joey sat next to Laurie, then settled his arm around her shoulders. She snuggled in as if it were the most natural thing. Abigail leaned toward Jackson until their arms almost touched on the armrest. "I didn't know you knew Laurie."

"She's Joey's girl, and he's one of my friends at work. How do you know Laurie?"

"We take a couple of classes together." Abigail grinned at him. "You wouldn't happen to be the person they wanted to set me up with?"

"Maybe." He matched her smile.

The lights went down, and Laurie looked at them with a playful "shush."

A series of newsreels preceded the show, reminding them Pearl Harbor Day was almost upon them. Abigail stiffened next to him during the images of the burning ships. As soon as the newsreels ended and the movie began, she relaxed. The humor in the movie stood in contrast to the solemn reminder of that devastating event. They settled back while Astaire and Crosby sang and danced through a series of holidays. Abigail was so animated as she laughed and sighed through the flick that Jackson found himself watching her more than the actual film.

When the house lights came up, she remained against the seat back, her fingers brushing the soft velvet. "What do you think it would be like?"

"What?"

She looked at him. "To have a life that required working only a few days a year?"

"Very boring. Without work, days would lose their meaning."

"I don't know. It might be nice to try." She shook her head. "I'd probably go crazy if it really happened though."

He studied her, then shrugged. "All I've known is work. I can't imagine not having a mission or purpose."

"Well, I suppose we should get back, so we can have another day at the grind tomorrow." She stood, her jacket hanging around her shoulders like a colorful cape.

"You two want to join us for a Coke?" Joey threw out the question casually, but Jackson got the sense he wanted some time with Laurie.

Abigail gave a small shake of her head. "I've got homework to finish."

Jackson shook off a pinch of disappointment. "Maybe another time, Joey."

Joey nodded, then led Laurie down the block toward a restaurant.

"Walk me home?" Abigail studied him in the pool of light from the streetlight.

"Absolutely."

The blocks passed in companionable silence followed by pockets of conversation. Abigail didn't seem bothered by the quiet, and he was glad so long as she didn't find him boring.

He stumbled stepping into the street and caught her concerned look. "It's nothing. I had polio as a kid. Fortunately, it was a mild case. Not everyone is so lucky."

"Does it bother you?"

"Not much anymore. I do a few exercises, but for the most part I can forget about it." It wasn't the whole truth, but it was enough for her to know right now. He turned the attention to her with questions about her classes and what she hoped to do when she received her degree.

She allowed the conversation switch with a shrug, a movement he caught only dimly in the diffused glow from a streetlight. "I've thought of going to law school someday. I like listening to my father talk about his cases and clients. I've even helped at his office from time to time." She slanted a look his direction as if gauging his reaction. When he schooled himself not to respond, she looked back toward the front. "But it seems silly. Have you ever met a woman attorney?"

"No."

"That's why it's ridiculous to dream about it. I should do something practical, like be a teacher until I settle down and marry. That's why I'm getting my early childhood education degree."

"That's noble."

"But I'm not overly fond of other people's children." His eyes widened, and she hurried on before he could say anything. "I'm sure I'll like my own. But nine months of other people's children to be replaced the following fall with a fresh set?" She shuddered. "Sounds like torture to me."

"But didn't you say you work at the nursery school?"

"I do, but it's only a few hours a week. I enjoy that. And the kids are too young to push back if they don't like what I ask them to do."

"I guess teaching isn't for you."

"I don't know."

"So why not law?" She was dedicated to her studies and showed a real heart for others. Why shouldn't she explore her dream?

She stopped and studied him, something warm yet hesitant in her expression. "It's not done."

He touched the strand of hair that had slipped out of her ponytail and tucked it behind her ear. Intensity surged through him, the kind that made him want to give her the moon or whatever else she desired. She should have her dream or at least the opportunity to decide for herself. "Why does it matter whether it's done?"

She licked her lips, and he found his attention arrested by them, so much so that he almost didn't catch her words. "I can't change the world."

"You're already changing mine." She looked down and placed her hand on his arm. His thoughts evaporated at the power of her touch.

"I haven't changed anything." She stepped back and started down the sidewalk.

"Abigail, don't walk away." He kept his hand light on her shoulder, but he longed to urge her to stop. "I see a woman who cares about others, who has the ability to see what others don't. You saw me on the bus. You refused to let me hide my burden at Glatz's."

"But it hasn't fixed anything. Seeing isn't enough."

"So go to school and get that degree."

She looked up at him then, and he was surprised to see a tinge of moisture in her eyes. Was she a crier? One of his sisters was, and it undid him every time she let loose a wail.

"I think I'm not the only one who sees others," she said.

Her smile melted something inside him, something he hadn't recognized was hard and lost until that moment. What would it be like to spend a lifetime with a woman who saw into him?

Abigail looked down at the sidewalk, then swung around and returned to her walk home. He caught up and placed his hand on her arm. "I believe you could do it if that's what you want."

"Thank you." Her words were so soft he almost missed them.

They walked on, pausing for a car at a street crossing. Abigail's steps slowed, as if she wanted to delay reaching her home as much as he did. There was a magic to being with Abigail. She lifted his vision from the mess surrounding him to the possibility of hope in the future. He wasn't sure yet how she did it . . . he just knew he wanted to discover her ways.

Just down the street, soft light shone through the picture window of the Turner home. A few steps more, and they stood in that light.

Abigail smiled up at him. "I enjoyed tonight."

"I did too." Jackson led Abigail up the short walk to the front door, where her father stood framed by the light behind him. "Mr. Turner."

"Jackson." Her father sounded tired. "Would you like to come in for a moment?"

"Thank you, sir, but my shift starts early. Abigail, I enjoyed tonight. Thanks for joining me."

"Me too, Jackson. Good night." She gave him one last searching glance, then turned and entered the house.

Mr. Turner remained in the doorway. "Jackson, I hope to have something for you in the next couple of days. Call and make an appointment with my secretary, all right?"

Jackson nodded and headed up the street. It would be a cold walk up to South Street and then to the park. Especially with Mr. Turner's words making his uncertain future collide with the memories of a perfect night with a wonderful girl.

bigail sank into one of the wing chairs that flanked the fireplace. Mama had placed a red poinsettia on the white mantel in a nod to Christmas, even though it was still weeks away.

Father sighed and eased onto the couch. He acted older than his years, as if the weight of problems Abigail couldn't know pressed him against the cushions. "Are you all right, Father?"

"I'll be fine. Just one of those days that seems to continue without end and without one successful resolution."

Abigail toyed with a question. "Father, what would you think if I decided to go to law school?"

He straightened on the couch and studied her. "What brought this on?"

"Nothing much."

He waited until the silence stretched between them. She looked at him and had to laugh as he quirked an eyebrow at her. It was the look that got recalcitrant witnesses to speak and seemed to work as effectively on grown children.

"I guess I spent too much time working with you at your office," she said. "I want to make a difference like you do. I'm not doing that now, not like Pete and Merry."

"You don't need to be like them." He settled his arms on his legs as he leaned toward her. "God made you with unique skills and talents. Ask Him how to use those for Him and His glory. If that's law school, we'll figure out how to make that happen."

"Really?"

His smile was slow to form but sincere. "Yes."

"Thank you." Something inside her loosened at his words and acceptance.

"I have something for you." He pulled an envelope out of his shirt pocket and handed it to her.

She squealed when she saw the handwriting. "Pete!" She stood up and kissed Father on the cheek. "See you in the morning."

After she slipped into her room, she held the envelope for a moment. Pete wasn't the world's greatest letter writer, so the letter was a treat to savor. Slowly she slit the envelope, then tugged the single sheet of paper free.

*Dear Abigail,*

*How are you doing? Are you enjoying your classes this semester? Enjoy your days as a Purdue Boilermaker, because they'll be over before you know it. Of course, my definition of "enjoyment" stops at the academic level. Keep those college boys at a distance. I can't protect you from overseas.*

*Yes, we'll leave shortly. The 56th Fighter Group has finished training, and we're ready to take on the Germans, the Italians, and the Japanese—all at once. We don't know when we're leaving or where we're heading, and I couldn't tell you anyway, but we're ready.*

*I'm ready. For the past year I've learned to fly the P-47 Thunderbolt while I've watched the Axis powers rampage across Europe and the Pacific. Finally, we're getting into the fight—Midway, Guadalcanal, and soon North Africa. But progress is too slow for my taste. I want to help. I want to fly.*

*Besides, this is your black sheep big brother's final chance to do something wild before settling back into the stately life of a respectable lawyer.*

*But only one Turner is allowed to be dangerous at a time. Take care of yourself, little sister. And feel free to send me broken candy canes. I won't mind.*

*Love, Pete*

Her smile was tempered by his comment about being the family black sheep. He still walked under the self-imposed load of guilt for what happened to their older brother, Alfie. She prayed again that he'd gain the freedom that came with leaving his burden at the foot of the cross. The thought pricked her soul, but she shoved the discomfort aside.

She was doing just fine. Some days she even believed that.

Then why couldn't she come up with a greatest fear project for her class? Each time she sat at her desk, she heard another classmate talking enthusiastically about his plan or her idea. Each time she wanted to shrink into her seat so no one could see her and ask what she'd decided to do. She loved to help people, so this should be an easy assignment. Yet it tormented her with a dearth of ideas. All she could see was her A slipping away.

Several days went by and she didn't come up with an idea, nor did she see Jackson. Finally, when she couldn't wait another minute to know if Father had fixed Jackson's problem, she asked Father at dinner if anything had been resolved.

"No, but we're making progress. I've asked him to come into the office. Lottie scheduled an appointment for tomorrow, late afternoon." He pointed a fork loaded with roast beef at her. "If you'd like to come by, you can see how he is for yourself."

"Robert, don't tease her." Her mother placed her chin on her hand and smiled across the table. "Surely you remember what it was like. Not so long ago, was it?"

"Mama, it's nothing like that," Abigail protested. "I just wonder about him."

"He'll be there around four." Father studied her with a glint in his eyes. "I'm glad to see you take an interest in Jackson. He strikes me as someone who is very private and doesn't make friends easily. And you've shut yourself off from others in so many ways."

"I haven't." She choked out the words.

"Oh, leave the girl alone, son." Grandma diffused the tension building in

Abigail. "She's doing just fine and you know it." She turned to Mama. "What did you think about the study at church this morning?"

Abigail made it through the rest of the meal and helped clean up before she used an abundance of homework as an excuse to disappear upstairs. As she headed to her room, she paused and put a hand on Pete's door as she passed. She thought of his letter and said a quick prayer for his safety and that of his squadron.

So many men and boys were locked in combat, situations their parents had experienced a generation before. Maybe she didn't want to marry and have kids because of the risks. If a war that encompassed the world could break out twenty years after the last ended, maybe it was better to stay alone. Part of her longed to replicate the love her family experienced in her own home, but even that wasn't safe. Her family had the missing pieces to make her shy away from experiencing that kind of pain again. The world was a dangerous, scary place.

She wanted to live fully. Experience all God had for her. Yet something held her back.

She moved into her room and settled on her bed. She could name that something. It was the fear of loss. Between Sam, Alfie, and Annie, she'd experienced too much death.

What made her think she should be exempt from hardship?

The question echoed in her mind like it had so many times.

*God, I want to be free from this, but I'm so scared.*

So scared.

The next afternoon Abigail walked into her father's storefront office on the Courthouse Square, a small plate of truffles she'd made in hand. Lottie, her father's secretary, loved a good chocolate, as her full figure attested.

"Is that what I think it is?" Lottie reached up from her small desk, the surface as clean as if she'd just organized it.

"I brought them for you. Father might like the one in the middle. It has a pecan hidden inside."

Lottie shuddered. "My tongue itches like crazy when I eat pecans. I'll gladly leave that for your father."

"Has Jackson Lucas arrived?" Abigail took off her gloves and slipped them into her handbag.

"Is he why you stopped by? I suppose so, he's such a handsome thing and quite kind." Lottie gave her a knowing look. "He's been back with your father for fifteen minutes. I don't know how much longer they'll be."

"That's all right. I'll wait."

Abigail sat on the edge of one of the waiting room chairs. They were moderately comfortable, but one had a spring that poked through the seat. She shifted, then relaxed when she realized she rested on a safe chair. A large photo that Alfie had taken at Lake Anna was framed behind Lottie's desk, and a small walnut table sat near the chairs, the local *Journal & Courier* and the *Indianapolis Star* fanned out next to a few magazines. Father's clientele leaned toward businessmen and farmers, if his magazine selection was any indication. It wouldn't hurt to review the news so long as she avoided the casualty lists.

Abigail flipped through both newspapers while Lottie took several phone calls with a professional air. She was the perfect foil to Father's intensity as she smoothly scheduled appointments in between answering clients' questions. How she kept each one straight was a mystery to Abigail. Maybe she had a photographic memory.

Lottie hung up the latest call as Abigail set the second newspaper aside. "Do you want me to check on them?" Lottie asked.

"No." Abigail stood. "It must be important if they're still in there."

Mr. Turner leaned across his large desk and studied Jackson. "The key question is where the money went. Have you ever noticed anything disappearing from your mailbox?"

Jackson shook his head. "Our nearest neighbor is half a mile down the road, so it takes a bit of effort to get to us." He met Mr. Turner's intelligent gaze. "I've thought and thought, but I don't have an answer. All I know is each pay period I send half the money home. It should have been enough to keep the mortgage current."

"And your mother's never said anything?"

"No sir. She mentioned once a few months ago that the money was late, but she hasn't mentioned it since. I guess I should have sent it straight to the bank, but I wanted to make sure she had enough too." All that money, gone. And he had no way to re-earn it in enough time. "I was able to reach her and ask what happened, but she thought I'd sent it directly to the bank." If he had, all of this would have been avoided.

"Well, it doesn't look good." Mr. Turner shuffled some papers on his desk before picking up a pen. "There are some steps we can take. I've sent a letter to the bank on your behalf, requesting more information about the outstanding amount on the mortgage and when the last payment was made. We normally have twenty days to answer the bank's complaint, but I've filed for an extension of time with the court to give us an opportunity to investigate."

"Will it be granted?"

"More than likely. Up here the first request is granted almost routinely by right. I can ask for another extension if we need it."

"Will that be enough?" Dare he hope they could unravel the mystery?

"If not, I have a few other ideas. We'll start with these since they don't take as much time. If needed, I'll drive to the farm and do some checking."

Dollar signs seemed to twirl in Jackson's mind at the thought of what that would cost. "I don't have the money—"

"We'll cross that bridge when we get there. It might not be necessary."

Jackson nodded, praying it could be avoided. "All right. Thank you for everything you're doing."

"My pleasure." A genuine smile stretched Mr. Turner's rugged face. "I like a good puzzle, and that's certainly what you have here."

That wasn't the most comforting thing he could have said. Jackson would have preferred a simple problem with a straightforward solution. Instead, it looked like this process would continue at least through Christmas. Well, that meant his family could stay on the farm through the New Year. "If none of this works, when will they need to move?"

"We're a long way from that. Foreclosures can take a while. Don't give up hope."

"Yes sir." Jackson stood and brushed his hands down his pants. "Thank you again."

"Get on out to the lobby. If I'm right, my daughter's been out there for a while waiting for you."

Jackson froze. "I've meant to call since the movie."

"Don't explain to me, son."

"No sir. I mean yes sir." Jackson blew out a breath.

Mr. Turner grinned. "Get out there." He reached for his phone and buzzed his secretary.

Jackson walked out but stopped when he reached the lobby. The plate-glass windows framed Abigail, her bright red dress with some kind of tiny white flower scattered across its folds a flash of color against the beige walls. A red hat with a small feather was fitted around her locks, adding another breath of color.

She looked up and her eyes widened. A soft smile painted her face, and warm color flowed into her cheeks. She was beautiful. So beautiful that it felt like his tongue was welded to the roof of his mouth. He wasn't sure he could get a word past the lump in his throat.

"Jackson. I'd begun to think Father would keep you in there all afternoon just to spite me. He would, you know. Tell me I should stop by and then make it meaningless by keeping you occupied." She stopped. "Well, are you going to say something?"

"Give the poor man an opportunity." The secretary looked between the two of them, a knowing glint in her expression as she winked at Jackson. "That girl doesn't stop talking when she's nervous."

Nervous? Around him?

"Lottie." Abigail crossed her arms as she stared at the secretary. "That's enough."

"There's never enough of the truth, girl."

Abigail stared open-mouthed at the secretary, then burst into laughter. "You've got me." She turned to Jackson. "Walk me to Glatz's? I'm in the mood for a cherry Coke."

A cleared throat caused him to look and find Mr. Turner leaning against the wall. "Be careful with her, son. She's a handful."

"Father!"

"I don't mind." Jackson grinned. "Remember, I've got three sisters."

He offered Abigail his arm, delighted that she wanted to spend time with him. This was a woman worth knowing. And he was ready to start with a cherry Coke for her and a vanilla one for him. Or maybe he'd make it two cherry Cokes. If it was good enough for her, he could learn to like it too.

Glatz Candies was calm when they entered. Abigail took a seat, and a couple of minutes later, Jackson brought her a cherry Coke. She took the first sip as he slipped in next to her in the booth and then sipped his own drink. She laughed as his eyes popped open and his mouth torqued. "What did you get?" she asked.

"A cherry. I thought if it's your favorite I should try it."

"I'm guessing it's not your favorite."

He shook his head.

Something inside her warmed at the thought that he was trying it because she liked it. What would it be like to spend forever with a man who did that? "Take it up to Catherine. She'll be glad to make you whatever you do like."

Instead he took another sip, this time his expression not quite so comical.

"What are your sisters like?"

A smile lit up his face as he tugged out his wallet. "Here's a photo of them."

The photograph must have been five years old, because Jackson looked like he was still in high school. Three girls clustered around him, the youngest about eight.

"They're amazing girls, really. Each very different, yet they look a lot alike. Poor Claudine has spent her life being compared to Martha." He shrugged as he studied the photo. "I guess that's a hazard of growing up in a small town where all the teachers remember your siblings."

"Did you ever wish for a brother?"

"Sure, from time to time, but I'm grateful for the girls. They keep things lively at home with lots of laughter and silliness." He launched into a couple of tales about their antics that soon had Abigail giggling. The middle one, Roselyn, seemed a lot like Merry, while Martha seemed studious with a winsome streak, and Claudine must have had a bit of tomboy in her just to be different from her sisters.

"I can tell you miss them."

He tucked the photo carefully into his wallet and replaced it in his pocket. "I do."

Talking about them made him come alive. That kind of love was precious and could provide a solid foundation when he had his own family someday.

She took another sip of her cherry Coke. "Can Father help you? I know you might not want to say, but I've been so worried for you."

"No need to do that. I've done enough worrying for ten people." Jackson stared across the room, then slowly turned toward her. "I don't know if your dad can help. He's trying."

"Trying how?"

"Those legal papers were from the bank. They plan to foreclose on the farm."

"That's awful!" She couldn't imagine losing her home.

"What makes it worse is I've sent money home, but Mother never got it. Without knowing where the money went, there isn't much your dad can do other than delay the foreclosure. His questions got the same answers mine did. The money has disappeared." He swirled his straw around the edge of the glass. "Mother hasn't seen it, and neither has anyone else. She only mentioned once that she hadn't received the money. I guess I assumed she got it. Now I know I shouldn't have been so laid back about it."

Abigail's heart dipped, and she frowned. "It can't just disappear." She tapped a thumb against the tabletop, considering. "Has anyone ever taken anything from you before?"

"Funny, your dad asked the same question. Not that I know of."

"Well, if anyone can help you, it's Father. He's a great attorney."

Jackson patted his hands in a placating motion. "I appreciate all he's doing. I just wish it weren't so much money. If the bank doesn't have it, then there's no way to stop them from foreclosing. Not that I can see, anyway. And your father was talking about slowing down the bank, not stopping the foreclosure altogether. I can't earn that much money again in time to save the farm." His shoulders hunched as he leaned over the table. "I should have made sure Mother received it. I don't know why I didn't."

"You were busy earning it. I understand not questioning if your mother didn't mention it. I'd probably assume everything was okay too." She studied him and noted that the heaviness that settled on him had eased a bit as they talked. There had to be something more she could do. "How much do you need?"

At the amount, she whistled, then clapped a hand over her mouth. Mama would be horrified. "That's a lot."

"Yep. And that's the dilemma."

"I guess we should pray for a miracle."

Jackson looked at her with surprise, then with a slow smile that reached through her. "That's what I've been doing, but I'd take some help."

"I'll do it." She was silent a minute, using her straw to play with the ice in her nearly empty glass. "Money doesn't just disappear. Who would take it?"

"I don't know. I'm not sure who would know I sent money home."

"It's possible everyone did. You're from Attica, right?" At his nod, she continued. "It's a small town. I bet everyone knows you moved to Lafayette to make money to support your family. It was only a matter of figuring out when it would arrive."

"But like I told your dad, I don't have any ideas."

"Then we need to go down there and investigate."

Jackson slumped against the seat, his thigh brushing hers, and she almost jumped from the shock of electricity that coursed through her.

"I don't have a car," he said, "and it's not easy to get down there. Otherwise I'd have already gone. Even if I did have a car, it costs money and ration cards for gas. I don't have extra money to spend on an errand of futility, especially when it looks like I'll need every penny I can save."

"Then I'll talk Father into going. You can ride along. That will take care of everything."

If only it were that easy. Father didn't drive often. Most days the family's Hudson Terraplane sat behind the house off the alley while everyone walked wherever they needed to go. Father called it practice for gas rationing, which started in a few days. Four gallons a week wouldn't get them too many places, especially when Father had to save up for out-of-town trials. But she wouldn't complain about walking if it would help get Jackson home to investigate.

Something was wrong in Attica, and she wanted to help him uncover the answer.


As she set her jaw, Jackson wanted to shake his head. Abigail had decided she was going to help him solve this, but he couldn't decide whether he was a project or a friend. The night they watched *Holiday Inn,* he'd sensed a growing friendship and admitted he wanted to get to know more about her. What were her dreams? Her fears? Her desires?

Now he wondered if she were a bulldog focused on a problem and he'd merely become a project. That was the last thing he wanted. Would friendship be enough, or would he want more if time allowed them to explore what could be.

She glanced at her watch and startled. "I have to get home and study. Test tomorrow." She wrinkled her nose in an adorable expression.

"Walk you home?"

"No, I'll be fine since it's still light. But if I don't hurry, it'll get dark and Mama will worry. Besides, I need the time to think. That's always easier when I'm walking."

She pecked him on the cheek, then slid out of the booth while he sat dumbfounded.

She'd kissed him as if it meant nothing. Something friends did all the time. But it meant something to him.

He gathered his thoughts, then walked out of the shop after her, but she was already a block down the street. She must have to walk fast to generate ideas. At that pace, his polio-affected leg wouldn't let him catch up, not when it was this muscle-weary.

He crossed Main Street and then headed east on State, concentrating on keeping a steady pace and not limping. Prayers for direction and wisdom filled his thoughts as he strode toward the boardinghouse. He needed all he could get, along with favor and revealed truth. He had to believe that with God's help, he could unravel what had happened to all the money.

The amount of money that had disappeared could have paid for a year of college. He had read interesting techniques and theories in various College of Agriculture extension pamphlets that triggered the desire to know and understand more. As he thought about Abigail and her studies, he recognized the weight of his missing education. He'd never really minded before, but now he knew her. Knew that she'd have a college degree, maybe a law degree, while he'd work hard for the rest of his life without hope of obtaining a degree in agriculture or anything else.

He strode across Columbian Park toward the empty monkey cages. He didn't know whether he needed to do more or sit back and leave the problem in someone else's hands. Normally, he wouldn't wait, but unless Mr. Turner agreed to drive him to Attica, he felt hopeless. There was so little he could do. But then he remembered the impression he'd had the other night. The thought that he should wait. After meeting with Mr. Turner that seemed all he could do.

Complete darkness settled across Lafayette and the park too early for his liking. It was time to get back to his room, since he'd miss dinner if he didn't. He might *have* to start missing meals to provide for his mother and sisters. If they had to leave the farm, it would take that kind of sacrifice and much more.

No, he wouldn't think like that yet. Until the court authorized the foreclosure, he still had hope. He would cling to it with all he had because there was little else he could do.

"How's your young man?" Father's words startled Abigail as she walked up to the house.

"I didn't expect to see you on the porch this chilly evening."

Her father patted the space on the swing next to him. "I wanted to talk."

"All right." She settled next to him, and he set the swing in motion. She snuggled against him, content for the moment to be with this man she respected and loved. "Can you help Jackson?"

She felt his sigh. "It's unclear."

"That must bother you."

"Yes. I think an injustice is being done. The question is proving it in a way that will cause the bank to reverse its stand. Everyone I talk to on the phone insists no money has arrived. Without it, there's not much we can do."

"So how will you prove there was money?"

Father paused as if formulating his strategy. This wouldn't be the first time they'd discussed how he'd proceed in a case, all the names and identifying information disguised. This was simply the first time it had mattered so much to her, a turn of affairs she'd evaluate later. For whatever reason, Mr. Jackson Lucas was becoming someone she cared about. His deep love for his family drew her. He wasn't ashamed to talk about his kid sisters with affection. Underneath it all, she sensed that he felt responsible for what had happened to the missing money.

As the swing slowly rocked and she curled into her father's side, she wondered what it would be like to spend her life with a man like Jackson. Someday it would be someone like Jackson rather than her father who protected and cherished her. The thought warmed her through.

"Well?" she asked again. "How will you solve Jackson's problem?"

Father kept rocking, the steady squeak of the swing matching the motion of the chains. "We'll need to make a trip to Attica. Talk to the men at the bank to see how the account was handled in the past and what kind of notice they provided that the account was falling into default. Eyeball the mail carrier. Check the grounds and house. Money does not simply disappear."

"Do you have enough gas?"

"I should, but it's fortunate Attica isn't farther."

"It's too distant for Jackson to get home easily."

"All the more reason to take him. He's burdened for his family and seeing them will do him good." He shifted on the bench. "It's hard when you feel responsible for misfortune."

Abigail stilled, hoping Father would keep talking.

"His mother mentioned he still carries a burden from his father's death."

"Was he responsible?" She couldn't imagine such a thing.

"No. But he believes he was. His mother painted it as one of those terrible accidents that occurs on farms. There was nothing he could have done, but he doesn't accept that. She believes it's why he does so much for them now. She appreciates the help but hates the burden."

That explained the shadows that seemed to chase across Jackson's face from time to time. The way he walked as though he bore a heavy load. "How can we help?"

"Save the farm," Father said, as if it would be the easiest task of all. Somehow she knew it wouldn't be.

"How will you do that?"

"We'll see. But I promise I will do all I can for that young man." There was a tone of steel underlying his words. The tone that he used when he was firmly committed.

As she heard it, Abigail smiled. They would help Jackson. And Father would work a miracle because he was determined. Once that happened, he was unstoppable.

## Six

*Tuesday, December 1*

A week later, Jackson hurried downtown as soon as his shift ended. His next paycheck lay inside his billfold, and he needed to get the money home.

Lottie smiled as he entered the lobby of Mr. Turner's law office. "Why, Mr. Lucas. How are you this fine afternoon?" Her eyes widened as she looked at him. "Are you covered in sawdust?"

Jackson brushed a hand through his hair and shrugged. He hadn't taken the time to stop and clean up. He could only imagine what bits of cardboard and glue had settled on his clothes and hair.

"Well, never mind. What can I do for you?"

"Is Mr. Turner available for a minute?"

She glanced at a large desktop calendar and ran her finger down a list. "He should be back from a late hearing across the street shortly. Would you like to wait?"

"Yes ma'am."

Jackson settled on one of the waiting room chairs. A spring poked him, so he shifted until he found a comfortable position. Should he have stopped at the bank first? Gotten cash to send down? Maybe Mr. Turner would want to do something different with the money.

The front door opened and Mr. Turner hurried in. "It's turning bitter out there, Lottie. I wouldn't be surprised if a storm's blowing in." He stopped when

Lottie pointed her chin in Jackson's direction. "Why, Jackson. I didn't expect to see you today. How can I help you?"

"Do you have a minute? I won't take much of your time." He couldn't afford any of the attorney's time.

"Come on back to my office." Mr. Turner slipped out of his long coat and hung it on a hook behind his door. Once they were both seated, he focused on Jackson. "What can I do for you, son?"

Jackson pulled his paycheck from his wallet. "I have my check and need to send the money home. I thought you might have an idea on how I should best do that."

"I'll drive you down there."

"Sir, I can't let you do that."

"It'll give us a chance to do some digging. Something is fishy with this situation, and we're going to find out what. Besides, we need to prepare our answer to the bank's foreclosure. It's a fairly straightforward legal document, but it'll be easier to draft after we conduct an investigation. The best way to find out what's really going on is to get down there and start poking. When can you go?"

"I'll need to clear a day off with my supervisor. He's not keen on giving them out."

"This is a good time to ask. Today's Tuesday. How about we drive down Thursday? My calendar is clear of court hearings, so we can leave at nine and be there by ten. Even driving thirty-five miles an hour, it'll give us plenty of time to dig around."

"The mail doesn't get delivered until eleven usually."

"Perfect. I'll pick you up Thursday morning at nine."

"Yes sir." Jackson couldn't force himself from the chair.

"Is there anything else?"

"I still can't pay you."

Mr. Turner smiled, and it seemed genuine. "It's taken care of."

Jackson stiffened. Mr. Turner must have noticed his distress, because he hurried on.

"Don't worry. I'll let you pay as soon as you're able, but we need to go learn what we can. I can't do my job without this trip. Since I wanted to time our trip for the next time you would have sent money, this is the week to go."

"That's true. I always sent money the day after I got paid. And then again in the middle of the month if I'd managed to be especially frugal."

"We'll get to Attica, see what's going on, and get this mess straightened out. Plan on Thursday."

Jackson nodded and stood. He held out his hand, and Mr. Turner stood to shake it. The older man held his gaze so that Jackson couldn't look away.

"Accept a little help," Mr. Turner urged. "We want to, and God has placed us in your path at this time to do just that. It's our obedience to Him."

"Thank you."

Jackson left the office, Mr. Turner's words running through his mind. Could God have connected him with this family? He hadn't stopped to consider it from that angle, but it sure seemed possible, as they had exactly what he needed at the absolute right moment. He whispered a prayer of thanks as he headed down Main Street toward Glatz Candies.

⌘

Sweat slipped down the side of Abigail's face as she stirred the vat of sugar, water, and flavoring. Eventually this would transform into a hundred candy canes, but at the moment she felt like an overworked stepdaughter stirring a cauldron for an evil witch. It might be cold outside, but inside the third floor candy-making facilities, the heat was rising and staying. Even opening the windows on either side of the stove hadn't helped.

Over the last couple of weeks, she'd made batch after batch of the candy canes. So popular with customers, the candy sticks took a lot of effort to make. She had to watch the process carefully to make sure nothing went wrong.

Finally, the sugary concoction reached the right temperature, and she poured the batch onto the marble-topped table. She took the paddle and flipped the edges of the sugar mix to help it cool down until she could take a large portion to the pulling hook. Hannah would mix red coloring into the remaining section, which would later be twisted in so that the candy canes had the perfect variegated stripes running through them.

Hannah looked at Abigail and must have seen something that made her take pity. "Would you like me to pull the candy this time?"

Abigail straightened her back and grabbed the gloves. "No, I'll do it." Her muscles might ache from the physical labor of stirring and pulling, but she still loved the results of the process.

She tested the ball of amber-colored goo with her gloved hands and carried it to the hook. With methodical movements she swung it around and pulled, around and pulled, around and pulled. Slowly, it stretched, and even more slowly it began to turn white as the air mixed with the goo.

When they finished combining the two colors, running them through the heater to thin the mixture to candy cane widths and then twisting them into shepherd's hooks, Abigail was desperate for a drink. "I'm heading downstairs for a minute. Want anything?"

Hannah cut some candy cane ends into bite-sized fragments. "No thanks. I'll get the next batch ready to go while you're down there."

The tin metal tiles on the ceiling shimmered above her as she hiked down the wooden stairs. The air felt cooler with each step, and she wiped at the sweat on her neck. She might love making candy, but it was hot work. At least candy canes were made only during the Christmas season. While they'd made peppermint candy canes with red stripes, they still had to make the spearmint ones with green stripes.

Abigail slipped behind the soda fountain and poured crushed ice into a glass. Then she added carbonated water and squirted Coke flavoring followed by cherry. Taking a long spoon, she stirred it together. Someone handed her a straw, and she took a sip. Divine sweet liquid.

Abigail opened her eyes and started. "Jackson?"

She wanted to slip back upstairs before he noticed how completely disheveled she must look.

"Abigail. You look beautiful." His eyes twinkled, letting her know he was teasing. Probably just as he did with his sisters back home.

She pushed a strand of hair out of her face and grinned. "What brings you in?"

"A Coke and a certain girl."

As if she wasn't already flustered enough that he saw her looking as she did, he had to go and say a thing like that. "I've been making candy canes. It's . . . hot work."

He looked at her as if he hadn't heard a word.

"Jackson?"

He blinked as if waking from a nap, then smiled a slow smile that warmed her clear to her toes. "Your dad is taking me to Attica. We'll figure out what's going on."

"That's great! Do you know when?"

"Thursday. Want to join us? Your dad and I have a plan, and I thought you might want to come." He leaned against the counter, closing the space between them.

"What kind of Coke would you like?" she asked to buy herself some time to think.

"How about an orange?"

"All right." Skipping classes one day should be okay. Maybe her professors wouldn't notice.

She grabbed a glass and poured in the right combination of orange and Coke syrup, then added the carbonated water, stirred it, and added ice. All the while her mind worked. She wanted to join him as he went to Attica, but she hated that he'd seen through her and anticipated her desire. She didn't want to simply be his travel buddy.

She slid the filled glass toward him. "Is the factory busy?"

He watched her a moment, then nodded slowly. "Lots of orders for puzzles and play sets. Some days it feels like every kid in America is going to get something we make under the Christmas tree or in a stocking. It does make the days pass quickly." He shifted and caught his balance on the edge of the counter, then took a sip of his drink. "This is good."

"Thanks." She waited, wanting to say something witty, but her mind was empty of pithy comments. The bell on the door tinkled, and she pushed away from the counter. "I'd better get back to the candy making. We've got lots more orders for candy canes."

"I'll enjoy my drink and then head home." He shifted his weight as he studied her. "So can you come?"

She bit her lower lip, then nodded. "I'll have to get out of classes, but I'll try."

He paused as if hearing something in her voice, but then shook his head and placed a couple of coins on the counter. "Thanks for this. I hope I see you Thursday."

He grabbed the glass and walked to a chair, only a slight hitch to his steps. Had he walked downtown, been unable to catch the bus? She rarely noticed his limp, but seeing it reminded her of all he had overcome. How he pushed past the pain and refused to allow the diagnosis and its impacts to limit him. He was able to provide not just for himself but for his family. He might not see it that way, but she knew it was true. Without him, his family would be homeless right now. He had the fortitude to reach the other side of this current crisis.

As she hurried back upstairs, she worked through her calendar in her mind. She could join Jackson on his trip to Attica if her father allowed.

When she finished twisting the last candy canes, Abigail headed downstairs to find her father sitting at the counter, his coat still on and an empty glass sitting in front of him next to his hat. She could count on one hand the number of times he'd stopped at Glatz Candies while she was working.

After slipping into her coat, she approached him. "Father?"

"Hello, Abigail. Ready to head home?" His smiled reached his eyes but was tinged with fatigue. His days were long, the hours intense, the fights for his clients real.

"Yes sir."

He stood and offered her his arm, then slapped on his hat.

Cold air raced into Abigail as they stepped onto the sidewalk, the intensity of it threatening to freeze her breath in her throat. "I hope it snows in time for Christmas."

"I know you love a white Christmas."

"Yes sir." There was something magical about a white covering on the ground, making everything fresh and clean. She hummed a couple of bars of "White Christmas" as they walked.

"Your young man came to the office today."

"He's not my young man."

Father's steps never slowed, yet when she glanced at him, she saw the knowing set of his jaw. "He could be if you wanted. If you were willing to risk the future."

A soft sigh escaped her. "Maybe, but I don't think it matters. What if he just sees me as a friend?" Even as she said the words she wondered if she believed them.

Father's chuckle startled her. "Any man who sees you wonders if he could have more than friendship with you. You are a beautiful young woman with a sweet, feisty spirit. Only a blind man would miss that."

"Some men don't like that."

"And they're fools."

Their steps continued in a steady pace as they headed east toward home. Abigail snuggled against her father's shoulder, and their breath mixed in curls of frozen air, visible only in a misty dance.

They paused to let a car pass before them, then crossed the street and turned onto Perrin Avenue and toward home.

"Why bring this up now?" Abigail asked.

"I know him now." Father paused. "Working in a puzzle factory might not fill a direct war need, but it provides for his family and reinforces his focused nature. I don't know that I've met another young man who cares as deeply for his family."

"Those are good things."

"Yes, he's a good man."

Abigail nodded. As they turned up the sidewalk to the house, she wondered what it would be like to be loved by a man the way her father loved Mama. Theirs was a lasting love, one built on a legacy of love she'd seen her grandparents share. Even now, she'd sometimes catch Grandma with a faraway look in her eyes. When Abigail could get Grandma to talk about Grandpa, it was clear theirs had been a unique and lifelong love. Abigail didn't want to settle for anything less.

Not when the rest of her life spread before her like an empty scroll waiting to be filled with memories and love.

## Seven

*Thursday, December 3*

*J*ackson waited on the steps of his boardinghouse, the cold penetrating his corduroys as the sun's faint rays failed to warm the world. Traffic chugged by on State Street, but nothing turned in front of Columbian Park to stop for him. He rubbed his gloved hands together and blew on them.

*God, I need some answers today. I know I can't order You around, but it would be helpful to know where that money's gone.*

His right leg ached, a dull pain deep in the muscles. If he wasn't careful, he'd limp with every step. Maybe the car's heater would reach the backseat and ease the throbbing. He'd need to work the muscles harder, push them past their weakness. His doctor had suggested trying Sister Kenny's exercise regimen for current polio sufferers to strengthen his leg. While the exercises pushed back the residual effects of the disease like weakened muscles, some days he still felt the weakness and atrophy, especially on cold days.

While he waited, he reviewed the ideas he'd had since he'd talked to Mr. Turner about where to start and who to talk to about the missing letters and the absent money. The postman might know something. The bank too. Bankers usually knew everything in a small town like Attica. If someone suddenly had extra money, a bank employee would know and might think it odd. Mother might not know much, but maybe she did. He'd try again and hope face-to-face conversation worked better than his attempt over the phone.

A dark Hudson Terraplane turned the corner and pulled alongside the curb. Jackson waited a moment for his leg to steady, then started down the steps. The car idled and Abigail waved from the backseat. He guessed that meant he'd sit up front. He pulled open the front passenger door and slid inside.

"Good morning, sir. Thanks for the ride."

Mr. Turner nodded, then pulled the car into the street. "We'll get this figured out."

Jackson swallowed hard as a knot formed in his throat. His father used to say that all the time. If only Jackson had been able to run when the accident happened and reach his father in time to pull him free of the machinery that had fallen on him . . .

"Good morning, Jackson." Abigail leaned forward, and the scent of violets tugged his thoughts from the dark days on the farm. He shifted to take her in, and she blew a lock of hair from her forehead. "What's your farm like?"

Was she really interested? He guessed she wouldn't have asked if she wasn't. "It's small. The thirties hit us hard, so Dad had to keep it small, something he could manage on his own when it got too expensive to hire help."

He thought of the barn and other outbuildings. The way his father had worked hard to keep them clean and organized. The ways he'd tried to help when Dad wasn't chasing him back inside to keep him from getting hurt. Mother had finally had to tell Dad to let him help. Even then, he had been assigned tasks in the garden or helping with the couple of head of cattle and few pigs they raised alongside a loaded chicken coop. Just enough to keep them and a few folks in town supplied with a steady flow of milk, meat, and eggs.

"Do you raise animals?" Abigail asked.

"A few. I suppose you'll be most interested in any barn cats we have."

Abigail wrinkled her nose, an adorable movement. "Maybe. Grandma brought a cat with her when she moved in. It took one look at me and promptly scratched me. I decided if cats don't like me, I don't like them."

Jackson chuckled. "Cats aren't particularly fond of anyone. They grace us with their presence."

"Sounds about right."

After Jackson talked Mr. Turner through a couple of turns on the drive to Attica, they passed through town and then traveled a mile farther to the fork for the farm. The dirt road sent up a cloud of dust that looked more like the heat of summer than the approaching deadness of winter.

"Turn up there, Mr. Turner."

Abigail's father did as directed and in a minute pulled up alongside the small two-story farmhouse. The wood structure had been built by Jackson's uncle at the turn of the century. Did Abigail see a home that had been filled with love for fifty years? Or did she see a building in need of repairs that Jackson couldn't do, not when he couldn't climb a ladder? It didn't match the perfection of her home, not with the paint peeling and the shutters hanging listlessly to one side of the front window.

Still, love seeped in through the cracks and crevices, filling the vacant spots. Looking at it now, with the closed-off appearance it got in winter when Mother hung heavy curtains at each window to keep the wind out, it felt as closed off to love as he had been until he met Abigail.

Even after Mr. Turner shifted the car into park, Jackson remained in the car, hands resting on his knees. He should hurry inside to see if his sisters had already caught the bus into town. Then he glanced at his watch and realized they'd all be at school.

Mr. Turner opened his door and slid out. He opened the back passenger door and grabbed his briefcase, then held out a hand to Abigail. "Coming, Jackson?"

The kitchen curtain fluttered. Mother must have heard them pull up and was spying on them. She wouldn't know the car, but she'd know him.

Jackson patted his hands on his knees a couple of times, then opened his door and climbed out. "Come on in. Mother probably has coffee percolating on the stove."

Abigail hurried to his side and slipped her arm through his. "I'm looking forward to meeting her."

"I hope you'll like her."

"I will."

The question was whether Mother would like Abigail, or would the sight of a man in a suit and hat, carrying a briefcase, remind her of all the visits after Dad died? And how with each one another piece of their precarious world eroded under their feet?

Abigail sensed the tension in Jackson, from the muscles under her hand to his tight gait. For someone who was coming home, he was as tense as a recruit lining up for his shots. She wanted to say something to ease his concerns, but she had failed miserably on the drive. At one point, she'd settled back against the seat and simply prayed. She hadn't necessarily noticed a change in Jackson, but she'd certainly felt more relaxed.

The paint on the outside of the home peeled in places, and a collection of metal milk jugs, buckets, and other paraphernalia lined the porch. A tabby cat had curled up on top of a jug to soak in the sun. A kitten scampered by, then slid behind a chair that had lost part of its seat weaving.

There was a general air to the place that suggested they didn't get many visitors, but it was a comfortable home. She couldn't imagine what it would do to Jackson's family if they had to leave. Father had to find a way to help them.

The door opened as they crossed the small porch.

"Jackson?" A thin woman about Abigail's height stood in the doorway, her jaw slack as she watched Jackson approach.

"Hi, Mother."

"What are you doing here, son? Don't you have to work?"

"Not today. Mr. Turner brought me here so we can try to figure out what happened to the money. Mr. Turner, this is my mother, Agnes Lucas. Mother, Mr. Robert Turner."

"Pleasure to meet you, Mrs. Lucas. This is my daughter Abigail."

They exchanged pleasantries, and Mrs. Lucas invited them in. "I don't have much to offer, but there's fresh coffee on the stove and kolaches in the pantry."

Jackson caught Abigail's gaze as if to say he'd told her so. Soon they'd settled around an oval kitchen table covered with a simple red-checked tablecloth, steaming mugs of coffee in front of them. The walls were bare, and heavy red curtains hung in front of the windows.

Mrs. Turner bustled around the kitchen for a moment, then placed a plate of apricot kolaches in front of them. "I baked these yesterday, so they're fresh. Are you here to untangle this foreclosure mess?"

Jackson played with the mug but didn't meet his mother's eyes. "If anyone can, it's Mr. Turner. He's helped me understand the foreclosure paperwork and what we can do to try to stop it."

"Your son wanted to make sure he was doing all he could to save your farm. We're here as part of that investigation."

"Do you think it's possible?" A flicker of hope flashed through Mrs. Lucas's eyes.

"I'll do my best."

Mrs. Lucas grabbed a towel and swiped at nonexistent crumbs. "We can't afford to pay."

"It's all right. It's a privilege to help you and Jackson."

Abigail felt a swell of pride at the way her father deftly handled Mrs. Lucas's concerns. "My father is the best attorney in Lafayette. If anyone can help with your concerns, he can."

"I see." Mrs. Lucas turned her tired eyes on Jackson. "Do you think we can stop this?"

"I need to figure out where the money went first. You're sure you never saw it?"

She reached across the table for Jackson's hand. "I'm certain. Your letters haven't arrived."

"Not any?"

"Not for three or four months." She rubbed her temples. "I guess I was naive. I wanted to believe the money would arrive the next day. For the first couple of months it arrived on time. Then the letters stopped and my hopes for the next day stretched into several months. I'm just glad the garden produced well and Mr. Johnson helped us with butchering. The girls and I will have enough to eat this winter."

That assurance didn't seem to lighten Jackson's burden. Father asked a couple of clarifying questions, but it soon became clear Mrs. Lucas didn't know anything. Either she didn't want to think the worst of her neighbors, or no one around Attica had played a role in the disappearing money.

"It must have gone missing in Lafayette. Things like that don't happen in a small town. I've known our neighbors my whole life. Why, the postman attended my wedding." Mrs. Lucas shook her head, and her bun swayed at the nape of her neck. "It's impossible that any of them were involved."

Jackson reached inside his jacket and pulled an envelope from the inside pocket. He slid it across the table toward his mother. "Mother, here's this month's paycheck."

She eyed the envelope but didn't reach for it. "Maybe you should take it to the bank and see if it can stop the foreclosure."

"Good idea, Mrs. Lucas. I can help Jackson with those negotiations, though he's the kind of man who could handle it on his own." Father clapped Jackson on the back. "I appreciate the coffee. Should we leave, unless you need more time with your mother?"

Jackson shook his head, just as Abigail knew he would. He might like to spend time with his family, but she knew he wouldn't inconvenience her father a moment more than necessary.

"Jackson, isn't this about the time a letter usually arrives from you?" Abigail asked.

"Yes. That's why we decided to come today, so I could hand deliver it."

"Then don't you think we should wait, Father?"

Her father stood and carried his mug to the sink, over Jackson's mother's protests. He turned back toward Abigail and settled against the counter. "You think we might see something?"

"I don't know. But if we leave now, we'll never know."

He studied her, then nodded before turning to Jackson's mom. "Would we be an inconvenience, Mrs. Lucas?"

She stood and smoothed her hands down her faded apron. "Why, no, though it seems like a lot of trouble for you."

"Not as much as will come if you lose your home." Father glanced around the small kitchen and into the living area. "Where's the best place for us to sit and watch the mailbox?"

Jackson stood and walked toward a picture window in the front room. "Here's where we'd watch growing up. I think we should talk to the mailman too. Find out if he's noticed letters from me. Then we'd know if they made it this far."

"That's expecting a lot of George. Why, he delivers hundreds of pieces of mail a day." Mrs. Lucas twisted her hands in her apron, a ridge deepening the bridge of her nose.

"It's a good idea, Jackson." Father glanced out the window. "We'll see if we can chat with him. It should only take a minute."

A davenport rested in front of the window, parts of the red upholstery faded to salmon by the direct sunlight. Abigail settled on one end and patted the cushion next to her. "Keep me company, Father?"

He considered her a moment, then sat next to her. "Giving Jackson time with his mother?"

"I thought if we came all this way . . ." The kitchen table wasn't far away, but sitting on the couch gave Jackson and his mother the illusion of privacy.

"You have a kind heart, Abigail."

She took his words and sealed them in her heart as a wave of heat climbed her cheeks. That wasn't something that could always be said of her, but she hoped to become more like Christ in that area each day. "My supervisor at Glatz Candies asked if I wanted to help with a project at the hospital." She felt a boulder settle in her throat, one that she could barely breathe around. "I might be able to make it my class project too."

"Which one?"

"Home Hospital." She pulled the heavy navy velvet curtain to the side and then fingered the filmy lace curtain beneath it. After she brushed it aside, she had a better view of the postal box where it sat across the road. "He wants to do something for children who will be in the hospital over Christmas. If I made it a project, maybe more companies would participate."

"Do you think you can do it?" Father's words seemed simple on the surface, but she knew he was asking more. Would she confront her fear of the past repeating itself?

"I don't know, but it might be time to try."

Mrs. Lucas sucked in a breath and stiffened in the kitchen chair. "Christmas is a terrible time to stay in the hospital." She touched Jackson's shoulder as if to reassure herself he was next to her. "We spent more than one holiday in the hospital with Jackson."

"But now I'm okay."

She nodded but picked at a piece of lint on his sleeve without looking at him. What was she seeing? Did painful memories replay across her mind? Or did she imagine what someone else's mother had experienced this year?

"Maybe I'll talk to my boss." Jackson gave his mother a quick hug. "See if they'd like to donate anything."

"That's a wonderful idea." Abigail gave him a big smile, then turned back toward the window. Maybe she could make this her service project. If she could actually walk into the hospital without reliving the loss of her siblings. She swallowed hard, noting Jackson's concerned expression. "I'm sure puzzles and play sets would be a huge blessing to children trapped in hospital beds."

"Especially little boys. I remember how tired I got of constantly lying there, tied to the bed in awkward positions as the doctors did their best to help me. All those restrictive casts in an effort to keep my legs from failing after the polio passed." He firmed his stance. "I'll be sure to talk to him."

Abigail sat up straighter as a car chugged onto the road.

## Eight

*A* moment later the vehicle stopped in front of the postal box. Father launched to his feet, but before he got to the door, the vehicle moved down the road.

"I guess I should have been faster." Father turned to Mrs. Lucas. "Where does he go next?"

"Down the road a couple more miles, then back toward town. Everything around here is set in squares, so he works his way around the grid, in and out of town. He'll stop for lunch at the Hotel Attica lunch counter about eleven thirty."

"We'll be sure to find him there."

Mrs. Lucas looked at Father. "Should I go get the mail?"

"When would you normally collect it?"

"Not immediately. Sometimes it can sit there until the girls return from school. There's not much need to rush, since little good comes in the mail."

"Then let's wait a bit. See if anyone comes."

Jackson shook his head. "You can't wait all day."

"We won't. Let's give it half an hour. If someone wanted to take something from the mail, he'd make quick work of it rather than risk your mother getting there before he did."

Abigail felt tension coil through her muscles as she waited. She wanted so badly for someone to arrive, to prove that the money had been stolen. But with no envelope from Jackson in the mail this time, would the person take anything if they even showed up? Or maybe this was the one day the thief would be late.

"Jackson, do you have your envelope?"

"Yes, right here." He looked at her with curiosity in his gaze. "Do you need it?"

"Yes. No. I need you to fill it out like you'd mailed it to your mom."

"It won't be postmarked."

Drat. She hadn't thought of that. "Maybe whoever is taking the envelopes won't notice." He looked at her. "We need to hurry if we want to finish setting the trap. If he doesn't see an envelope from you, I bet he won't take anything. Then we can't prove anything other than he's nosy. He has to actually take something."

"Abigail's right." Father stood and handed Jackson a pen from his pocket. "Fill it out quickly just as you usually do, but be sure to remove the check. We don't want to give him anything more."

Jackson shrugged and did as Father asked. Then Father hurried the envelope out to the box before slipping back inside the house.

Not ten minutes later, a farm pickup turned onto the road. Rust edged the wheel wells and it wore plenty of dings, like it had been driven into a fence post or two. The tires spun as it skidded to a stop near the box, and then the door opened and a wiry man hopped out.

"Do you know who that is?" Abigail whispered, then bit down on her lip to stop a laugh because the man couldn't hear her.

Jackson stepped toward the window, stopping next to her. "Is that Saul Dunlop?"

His mother squinted. "It looks like him. Surely he isn't the one . . ."

Jackson shook his head. "I don't know, but I'm gonna find out." He hurried to the kitchen and out the back door.

Abigail watched as her father followed him. Could they be close to an answer?

～✺～

With as much stealth as possible, Jackson slipped around the corner of the house and in front of Dunlop's pickup. "Saul Dunlop, what are you doing?"

The sound of steps on gravel let Jackson know someone had followed him, but he didn't dare turn from Dunlop to see who. He prayed it was Mr. Turner and not his daughter. Unfortunately, he could imagine Abigail rushing into this with her can-do attitude.

Dunlop approached his truck, a smile slapped on his face as if someone had drawn it on with a sloppy hand, making him look even more like a skinny weasel than normal. "Why, Jackson. Didn't know you were back in town."

"That was the point." Jackson planted his hands on his hips and stared at Saul. "What are you doing in my mother's mailbox?"

"George put some of your mail in my box. Just being neighborly and bringing it by."

Dunlop had an answer prepared. Interesting.

Jackson squared his shoulders and stared at his neighbor. "Then take it to the door."

"Didn't want to bother your ma."

Jackson's jaw hurt as he clenched his teeth together. There were so many words he wanted to say, but none of them would please God or his mother.

Mr. Turner must have sensed the tension, because he chose that moment to step up next to Jackson. "Mr. Dunlop is it?"

Saul's brows puckered as he studied the attorney. "Do I know you?"

"Not unless you've been in trouble with the law around Lafayette. Which, considering what I think you're doing here, isn't outside the realm of the possible." He crossed his arms as he studied the rail of a man. "Do you mind showing me which letter you brought to put in the box?"

"Why, of course." Saul turned toward the box. "It's right in here." He started to pull out an envelope, but his hand trembled and he hesitated.

"I don't think so. I've watched you carefully, and you didn't have an envelope in your hand when you climbed out of your vehicle."

Saul's smile was as oily as his hair. "Then you noticed wrong."

"I'm pretty sure the local judge would agree with me." Mr. Lucas's face was calm, yet there was steel in his voice. "You see, we went to law school together. So you might tell me the truth. I've heard it sets a man free."

Saul's face hardened and he squared off with Mr. Turner. "You ain't got nothing on me."

"I disagree. But I'd be happy to let the police decide who's in the right. How about you, Jackson? This is your land after all."

Jackson forced his shoulders down as he kept a close eye on Dunlop. "Yes sir. That's all right with me."

"Then I think I'll have Mr. Dunlop come with me and you can follow in his truck. We'll get this squared away in no time."

"I ain't going nowhere with you." Dunlop crossed his arms and jutted out his jaw like a stubborn bull. Too bad he looked as intimidating as a calf.

"You can come with me, or we'll call the police and let them give you a ride to town."

Would the police take Dunlop in for them? Jackson wasn't as certain as Mr. Turner. The attorney might be used to the Lafayette police playing along with him, but he didn't think the Attica man would.

Fortunately, Dunlop didn't want to call his bluff. Grumbling the whole way, he followed Mr. Turner to his Hudson.

"Better not get the tiniest scratch on my truck," Dunlop warned Jackson. "I'll make you fix her if you do."

How Dunlop would notice a new scratch, Jackson wasn't sure, but he chose to ignore the man's grousing as he followed Mr. Turner into town. In just a couple of turns, he parked next to the Hudson in front of the small brick police station next to the post office on Main Street.

An officer Jackson didn't recognize sat behind a desk, filling out paperwork. He looked about as bored as a man could when he raised his head to take in the three men. "Can I help you?"

Jackson opened his mouth but closed it as Mr. Turner started filling in the officer on the situation. The police chief had dug pretty far back to find this man, who introduced himself as Officer Daubs. He had a paunch and enough gray hair to have served in the Great War. Whatever his age, his expression sharpened as he listened to Jackson's attorney explain the situation.

"What do you have to say, Saul?" The officer studied the man with familiarity.

Jackson winced at the officer's use of Dunlop's first name. Would the fact that they knew each other hurt or help him?

"I didn't do nothing wrong. I don't know why they thought they had to haul me in here when I'm just doing a neighborly thing, taking the mail to Mrs. Lucas."

"Then take it to her door. That's the reasonable thing to do. And where's this envelope you were delivering?"

"It's in my truck." Dunlop turned and pointed at Jackson. "At least it was until he drove it here. He probably let the envelope out the window on the drive."

The officer turned his attention to Jackson, and Jackson straightened. "I'd like to hear your story now, son. What's brought you to town?"

"It's like Mr. Turner said. I work at a factory in Lafayette and send money back to my mother every payday. Turns out she hasn't received a dime in months, and now the bank plans to foreclose. Someone's got the money, and right now Mr. Dunlop looks good for it."

"Yes. But why would he take it?"

Jackson shrugged. "I don't know, sir."

"I appreciate your honesty. Saul, you want to tell him about your gambling debts and how they've miraculously been paid? I do believe that's the word you used. 'Miraculous.' The chief and I have been eager to discover the secret to that miracle." The officer turned back to Jackson. "How'd you send the funds?"

"Cashier's check from my bank in Lafayette. I didn't want to send cash that would be easy to steal."

"You still bank at First Bank, Saul?"

"Yes." Dunlop stood defiant, but a muscle in his jaw twitched.

The officer considered Dunlop before turning to Jackson. "That where your mother has her account?"

"As far as I know, sir." Jackson replied.

"Then let's walk over and see what Stu can tell us. I have a feeling he can help us clear up the rest. If he's seen the cashier's checks, it'll put us a sight closer to wrapping this up. Don't you agree?"

Mr. Turner met Jackson's gaze and nodded. "I do believe it will. We appreciate your help, officer."

"Just doing my job. Ike'll be disappointed to have missed the fun. This is more interesting than paperwork or writing another ticket."

Jackson kept Saul in his view as Officer Daubs led the way down the block to the bank. The brick building had stood sentinel over the town since the turn of the century, lending permanence in the ups and downs of the economy.

Jackson worked his jaw back and forth as he kept pace with Saul. "Gambling?"

"Like you've never had trouble," Dunlop snapped back.

His words cut hard. Dunlop knew all too well the trouble that had befallen the Lucases and still chose to steal from them? His trouble must be dire or his nerve unwavering.

Officer Daubs opened the glass door to the bank and ushered the other three men ahead of him. Then he marched straight to the grate that separated the tellers from the lobby. "Is Stu in, Jane?"

"Sure is." The dark-haired teller smacked her gum and picked up the phone at her station. "Stu, Officer Daubs and a few gents here to see you." She nodded, then hung up. "He said to go on back."

Jackson followed the others behind the grate and toward a small office that sat next to a large safe. He'd often wondered who worked back here. Stu Newman stood behind his desk, a warm smile on his face, and gestured to the upholstered chairs in front of his desk. "Sorry I'm short a couple, but have a seat."

"I'll stand." Jackson leaned against the wall while Saul and Mr. Turner sat.

Officer Daubs closed the door and in short order updated Mr. Newman on what had transpired.

"That's interesting." Mr. Newman looked around the group, his expression more guarded. "What's it have to do with me and the bank?"

Officer Daubs nodded. "That's a fair question. Has Saul brought in cashier's checks made out to Mrs. Lucas?"

"Sure thing." Mr. Newman steepled his fingers in front of him. "Each was duly signed on the back. Nothing out of the ordinary."

Mr. Turner leaned forward. "Does she routinely use Saul for errands like that?"

"Only started a few months ago, but with Jackson gone, I figured it made sense for Saul to bring them in."

"Did you ever call Mrs. Lucas to confirm it was her intent?"

"Didn't see the need, since it was her signature on the back."

"You sure it was her signature?"

"No reason to think it wasn't."

Mr. Turner straightened in his chair, hands clasped in front of him. "Did you compare it to her signature card?"

"Why would we?" A look of confusion flashed across Mr. Newman's face. "He wouldn't have the check unless she gave it to him."

Officer Daubs nodded. "Did you deposit the money in her account?"

"No, though I wanted to, seeing as how the family was falling behind on the mortgage, but Saul insisted she wanted the cash. Had a typed note from her with instructions."

"We don't own a typewriter," Jackson mumbled, then caught himself. "And I called the bank to ask about the checks, but nobody saw them."

"What's that, son?" Mr. Turner turned to him, and the other three men followed suit.

Had the room somehow become stuffier? Jackson found it harder to breathe. "We don't own a typewriter. Mother couldn't have typed a note. And why didn't someone here tell me they'd seen the checks?"

Mr. Newman held his hands up in a placating manner. "Now wait a minute, son."

Dunlop jerked to his feet. "I've had it. Am I being accused of something? 'Cause if I am, I want a lawyer. If not, I'm done waiting around while you spin a story against me. I'm leaving to go find an attorney to sue you for hurting my reputation."

Officer Daubs ignored Dunlop as he studied Jackson. "You want to press charges, son?"

Jackson glanced at Mr. Turner, who gave a slight nod. "Yes sir."

"Good. I've heard enough to hold Saul while I talk to the prosecutor and judge." Mr. Turner's shoulders shook a bit as if he held back a laugh while Officer Daubs grabbed Saul's shoulder. "You coming with me quietly or do I need my handcuffs? I haven't had a good opportunity to use them yet. Might like the chance."

"I want a lawyer," Dunlop insisted.

"Sure thing, Saul. All in due time." Officer Daubs hustled Dunlop out of the bank.

After they left, Mr. Newman sat back down and looked between Mr. Turner and Jackson. "Anything else, gentlemen?"

Mr. Turner leaned forward. "Yes. Jackson has a good question about why no one on your staff admitted the cashier's checks had been received."

"Can't answer that. I'd guess that whoever he talked to wasn't involved in the transactions."

Jackson rolled his eyes at the thought the bank was so big anyone who worked there wouldn't remember the cashier's checks. Mr. Turner appeared ready to let it slide though.

Mr. Turner studied the man as if weighing his answer, then continued. "We can explore that matter later. However, we have the foreclosure to resolve.

As you can see, the lack of payments is due to theft. Based on the way you failed to exercise due diligence and check the signature, the bank contributed to the problem."

"If that's proven." Mr. Newman huffed out a breath, but then the bravado seemed to leak from him. He looked at Jackson. "Look, son, I really thought she had asked him to help."

Jackson nodded an acknowledgment, then cleared his throat. "It doesn't change the fact that you were part of the problem."

"A fact we'll prove in time, I have no doubt." Mr. Turner studied the shorter man as if daring him to disagree.

"All right." Mr. Newman sighed. "I'm really sorry for the mess. What do we do now?"

"I thought you'd never ask." Mr. Turner pulled his briefcase onto the chair next to him, popped the lid, and pulled out a sheet of paper. "Here is how I propose resolving this matter."

y the time the Hudson pulled into the farmhouse drive, Abigail wasn't certain who was more nervous. Mrs. Lucas had spent the first hour forcing idle chitchat. Then she'd dusted every surface in sight before turning to mixing cookie batter. A couple dozen sugar cookies cooled on the table by the time the door opened and Jackson and Father entered the house.

"Where have you been?" Abigail lurched from her chair and hurried toward Jackson. She stopped just before him, so close she could feel the cold he'd carried in on his coat.

"Watching your father work a miracle."

Warmth spread through her as she matched his grin. "Really?"

"Really. He was amazing."

"So you're glad I suggested you share your trouble with him?"

"Absolutely. I can't thank you enough, Abigail."

The way he said her name about stole her heart. Could she risk her heart again? With a man like this, she wanted to consider it. She leaned closer, eager to hear every detail of their time in town. "You look thirty pounds lighter."

"I feel it." And his posture showed it. No more slumping under the weight of a burden he couldn't solve. He looked ready to tackle his future with hope. This was the man she'd seen as if from a distance that first day and with a little more clarity each time since.

A throat cleared, and she stepped back with a start.

"We should head back to Lafayette," Father said. "I don't want to drive after dark if I can avoid it."

Mrs. Lucas stepped from the kitchen, wax paper packages in her hands.

"I've got ham sandwiches for each of you. Give me a moment, and I'll have cookies too."

"Thank you, ma'am. I appreciate your thoughtfulness."

She nodded, but looked at Jackson. "Is everything okay?"

"Yes ma'am." Jackson smiled. "It's better than okay. We get to keep the farm!"

Abigail grabbed her father's arm and tugged him toward the living area. "Give him time to fill his mother in. She's been frantic. I'm surprised there's any varnish left on some of this furniture."

"And you weren't?" Father asked.

"Of course not." At his look, she wrinkled her nose and shrugged. "Fine. I was worried too. Is everything okay?"

"There are still details to sort out, but the police are building a case against the probable thief. Maybe the bank too. We'll see what we can prove. As a result, the bank is willing to postpone the foreclosure. They'll drop the foreclosure once charges are filed and credit the Lucases' account with the payments."

"Really?"

"Yes. It seems the bank played an important role in the improper disbursal of funds."

Abigail reached up on her tiptoes to kiss her father's cheek. "You're the best!"

His chuckle rumbled as he pulled her into a hug. "It's been a good day."

An hour later the ride home was silent, but not because of tension. Unlike the drive to Attica, the car was now filled with a peaceful quiet, the stillness that comes from knowing it's been a good day, one in which much was accomplished.

Father broke the silence as they entered Lafayette. "Would you like to come for dinner, Jackson? I'm sure Rose has a tasty meal ready to go, and we can celebrate with you."

"I appreciate the offer, sir, but I've imposed enough for the day. Thank you for everything. I can't tell you how grateful I am."

Abigail started to comment but caught Father's glance in the rearview mirror and bit down on her lip.

"I'm glad I could do it, Jackson. It feels good to help right wrongs like this one. We had a helpful officer too. He had the missing piece."

"Sir?"

"Motive. Why your neighbor would steal." Father turned in front of the boardinghouse. "While your mother might have mentioned she expected the money to arrive, he had to choose to take it. The gambling debts were enough of a reason."

"Yes sir." The car stopped and Jackson opened the door. "Thanks again." He turned to look at her. "Thank you, Abigail."

Before she could say anything, he closed the door and walked up the sidewalk. She sighed and sank back against the upholstery. She should feel like all was right in the world. Instead, she felt deflated. Why couldn't he come back, take her in his arms, and thank her properly?

Why? Because this was real life and not some celluloid dream.

Jackson felt dazed as he walked into the house and then up to his room. A packet of Mother's sugar cookies waited in his pocket, but all he could do was sit on his bed and wonder what had happened. He felt like a different man than the one who had clumped down the stairs hours earlier. A weight had lifted, one that had burdened him for weeks.

*Thank You, God.*

The words had reverberated in his mind since they'd left the bank. It felt like a miracle had been worked on his family's behalf. A miracle that started when Abigail reached out to him with concern.

Today he'd imagined her in the farmhouse working alongside him. The image had pleased him, but how could he pursue a life with her when she wanted to do so much more than be a farm wife? Whether or not he went to college, his plan was to return to the farm. He couldn't really imagine anything else. How did Abigail fit with that vision?

He shook his head to clear the unanswerable questions.

Right now he'd focus on the fact that the foreclosure was essentially over. Thanks to Mr. Turner, he didn't have to worry about what would happen to his mother and sisters. He didn't have to wonder how to move them to Lafayette or if he should leave Lafayette and move all of them somewhere new. Instead, all would be right in the world.

But something still didn't feel quite as he'd imagined.

He didn't want to think about it. Surely he could have one night just to settle into the knowledge that his family was safe. That somehow God had led him to the man who could help rectify a terrible wrong. That was all good.

It was that man's daughter who had tied him in knots. When she looked at him, he felt like he could take on the world, at least the part he lived in. When she smiled at him with a hint of pride, he felt unstoppable, if a bit unnerved that she would grace him with the belief he could do anything. Didn't she know how hard his life had been? That he had no hope of the future being easier?

She knew pieces of his life but not the full story, because he hadn't let her. Should he?

Did he dare?

Would her impression of him change when she knew just how broken he was? That he couldn't save his father when it mattered most?

If he shared what he wanted to do, would she believe in him? Would she be willing to walk beside him through life? Could he dare to ask her?

He wanted to.

The next morning was too cold to walk, so Jackson blew on his hands and stomped his feet to try to stay warm and keep his leg from locking. Eventually the bus arrived, and in short order he was at the factory. The whirr of the machines became a backdrop to his thoughts. On his lunch break he asked his boss about participating in the hospital holiday event, which he learned the company had already committed to support. Then his shift ended, and he boarded a bus that carried him downtown to Glatz Candies.

Would Abigail be at work, or had he made the trip in vain?

When he pushed through the door, Hannah stood behind the counter. She grinned when she noticed him. "I wondered if you'd make it in tonight. Want me to get Abigail?"

Jackson sank on a stool. "Is she busy?"

"Sure, but if I know her, she'll take a break to see you. She's been up there long enough to take a short one."

"Thanks."

"Better yet, I'll send you up with a Coke."

Head up to the candy floor? "I'd be glad to do that."

"Sure you would."

A minute later she handed him two Cokes, and he climbed the stairs. When he reached the third floor, he pushed through a door into an expansive open space.

He walked past a small room where someone stirred chocolate and peanuts together. A sweet smell assaulted him from deeper in the main room. The large windows on two sides of the floor were open, even though it was December, and Abigail stood next to a long marble table, manipulating a mound of waxy goo. She hummed along with the radio, and he whistled to let her know he was there.

She startled and looked up. "Jackson? What are you doing here?"

He held up a glass of Coke. "Hannah thought you'd be thirsty."

"Great." She nodded toward a large wooden table against the far wall. "Can you put it over there? I have to keep working with this candy, or it'll be ruined."

"What's it going to be?"

"Our famous candy canes."

He set the Coke where she'd indicated, then leaned against the table. "Can I watch?"

"As long as you don't give the secret recipe away."

She never stopped moving as they talked. In a couple of days she'd start finals, and he mentioned how his company would include puzzles in the hospital event.

"Maybe we can deliver them together," he said.

Abigail hooked a glob of goo on a hook and started pulling it. "I'd like that. I've got a couple more companies to contact, but so far it's just Glatz and your puzzles." She tugged harder on the whitening candy. "I've never been a fan of hospitals. It seems silly to say that to you."

"I understand." He crossed his arms as he watched her yank and pull on the sweet mixture. "I don't much like going either, though I'm grateful for the care I received. And if I can help break the monotony for kids trapped there, then I'm happy to help."

"I'm sorry you understand their plight so well." She frowned as she yanked on the cooling glob again. A minute later she took the now white goo over to a marble table.

"I can see you're busy."

"I'm sorry. If I slow down at any point before this is done, I risk having to throw the batch away. I understand if you can't stay."

"Join me for dinner this week." The words erupted without forethought, but he was glad.

"Between finals and work, I'm not sure I can." She blew a piece of hair out of her face.

"We'll need to talk about the hospital delivery."

"I'm glad the professor is letting me carry his project over into the next semester. It seemed more meaningful to do this around Christmas." She rolled the concoction along the table. "Come to dinner tomorrow night. Mama and Grandma would love it."

It wasn't exactly what he'd had in mind, but it was more time with Abigail. He'd take it.

"All right. I'll see you tomorrow." He headed toward the door, pushing down the disappointment and frustration that she wouldn't be going out with just him, but at least she'd found a bit of time for him.

～∂∽

When she got home Abigail was hot, tired, and annoyed. She'd twisted candy canes until her fingers were scorched even though she wore gloves. Her back ached from standing for so long. She stomped into the entryway, knocking snow from her boots. After she slipped out of the boots and into house shoes, she looked up and noticed Grandma's concerned gaze.

"Everything all right, Abigail?"

"Just fine, Grandma."

Grandma arched a brow over her glasses.

"Sorry." Abigail slumped onto the couch next to her grandmother. "Can I just say it's been a long day?"

"Yes, but I still want to know why."

"Jackson came to work today." Abigail paused, but Grandma just waited. "He brought a Coke upstairs to me, and we chatted for a while. I'm not sure where we are now. Our reason for being together is over. His house is fine. He saved his family."

"Aren't you glad?"

"Yes. And no." Abigail scrubbed her face with her hands, smelling the sickening scent of peppermint. She used to love that scent and found it soothing and energizing. Now it made her think of work so hard her muscles ached. "Who am I to him now?"

"Someone special."

"Maybe. I hope so. He did ask me to dinner, so I invited him over here tomorrow."

"We'll love having him, but why not just go out with him?"

"I feel so pressured with school and work."

"That wouldn't have anything to do with going to the hospital, would it?"

Abigail winced, and Grandma scooted closer.

"You've got to let go of your fears. I wonder if you aren't pushing poor Jackson away because you're afraid of what could happen."

"I'm not pushing him away."

"Really? I'm sure he'd rather have you to himself." Grandma squeezed Abigail's hand. "Sam's death was tragic, but that doesn't mean you should wall off your heart and protect yourself from loving again. That's an empty life."

"Grandma, that was only a year ago. Can you believe it's been almost a year since Pearl Harbor? And it's not just losing Sam. We've lost Alfie and Annie too." A sigh shivered through Abigail as she tried to maintain control. "It still hurts, Grandma. Our family feels so empty, so small."

"Of course it hurts. But you have to choose whether to let fear and loss keep your world small or whether to let it expand to include others. Your heart is so soft, Abigail. But would you rather not have had those precious ones in your life to avoid risking the hurt when they left?"

"I know you're right."

"Of course I am. So why did you make poor Jackson agree to come here?"

"To chase him away? Oh, Grandma."

"He'll come back. It'll take much more than that. Especially when you don't want him to leave. He's special." Abigail started to protest, but Grandma raised a hand. "Trust me, child. I've seen a lot of young men and women fall in love. You both have all the marks of that ailment. If I'm right, you'll have to do more to chase him away. And if you're wise, you'll chase him back. Don't let Sam's death keep you from appreciating the young man God has placed in front of you."

## Ten

*Friday, December 11*

The days slipped ever closer to Christmas, but other than seeing Jackson at one family dinner, Abigail's life felt emptied of his presence. After he'd shared that meal with them, he'd offered to help her contact a few companies about the hospital project but hadn't found any more interest than she had. When he'd called to tell her his luck hadn't been any better than hers, she'd heard the disappointment in his voice. Then he'd asked her again if she'd have dinner, but her intense finals schedule consumed her time. Would he ask again, or had she disappointed him too many times?

In the quiet moments, she missed him. Desperately missed him. So much that she almost couldn't breathe when she walked down the stairs from the candy room and wondered if he'd be waiting at the fountain counter.

Or when she held her breath as she scanned the seats on the bus. A slump of disappointment would settle over her as she sat next to a stranger, longing to see her friend.

The letter she'd received from Merry that morning hadn't helped her frame of mind much. She slipped it from her pocket and read it again:

*Dear Abigail,*

*Greetings from sunny Florida. I'm just saying that because I know how those gray, rainy days can be so bothersome. The truth is I've been spending so much time in the books that I haven't gotten too many rays myself. New girls are showing up every week. Everyone's*

*here to "support the boys." Rumor has it that nurses will have to start*
*military training before they go overseas. Can you picture me trying to*
*hike with a pack or shoot a firearm? I bet Pete would like to see that!*

*Give all the family my love. And if they ask, I'm doing fine. I'm*
*telling myself that everything that's happened with David is for the*
*best. What does the Bible say? "The truth will set you free"? I'd hate*
*to think what could have happened if David had stuck around. Who*
*knows what I could have been pulled into? I tremble at the thought!*

*All I know is that true love is harder to find than anyone would*
*have thought. Don't you agree . . . or maybe you have something to*
*tell me?*

*Wish I could make it home for Christmas, but between the*
*travel restrictions and uncertainty about when army training will*
*begin, I've been told to stay in Miami. It won't feel the same without*
*you and some good Midwest snow.*

*With my love,*
*Meredith (what they call me here)*

Abigail tucked the letter back in the envelope, missing Merry even more.

"It's time to stop moping, young lady." Grandma settled next to her at the dining room table. "You've been pining after that young man for a week. What are you going to do about it?"

Abigail shrugged and slid the envelope into her psychology text. Could she pretend to be absorbed in her studies? Anything was better than listening to another lecture about how it was her fault for not encouraging Jackson more. When Grandma wasn't saying it, Abigail's mind picked up the refrain. It ran over and over as if it was the only song her mind could sing.

"Well then, help me decorate these Christmas cookies." Grandma handed her an apron.

"All right." Abigail set her book to the side and moved into the narrow kitchen, where Bing Crosby crooned "where the treetops glisten" from the radio.

"I've always said the best way to a man's heart is through his stomach. And if these Christmas white velvet cutouts don't do the trick, well, then you'll find a better man."

Abigail gave a startled laugh, then bumped shoulders with her grandmother. "Oh, Grandma. Life isn't so simple that a plate of cookies will fix the world's woes."

"Of course not. But it will fix yours." Grandma dusted the rolling pin with flour, then pushed it up and down in smooth motions along the dough. They worked in companionable silence, the pile of baked and decorated cookies growing steadily. "There. We'll let the frosting on these dry, then tomorrow when I take some to the neighbors for a Christmas treat, you can borrow your father's car and take a plate to Jackson." Grandma grabbed another blob of dough and sprinkled flour on it. Then she picked up the rolling pin. "That boy is probably pining for home. That boardinghouse keeper's cookies aren't worth the flour used to bake them."

"Grandma!"

"Did you eat one at the women's auxiliary meeting? I think not. I did. It is an experience I will never forget."

Abigail studied the pile of Christmas trees and stars. "I don't want to be afraid, Grandma."

"There's a simple solution to that. Turn it over to God." Grandma stopped her rolling and gave Abigail her full attention. "This life can be filled with pain. I'm not telling you to stop feeling." She touched her fingers to her chest. "I miss your brother and sister every day. There are times I ask God why He allowed their deaths. And I often ache with missing your grandfather. But I know God is here in the midst of pain. The Psalms even say He collects our tears. That's an image I have clung to at different times. No tears are wasted, unless you allow their cause to freeze you in place."

"Oh, Grandma." Abigail wiped a tear from her cheek. Grandma hugged her and whispered prayers in her ear. Abigail rested there another moment, then straightened with a wobbly smile. "We need to finish these cookies so I can make a delivery."

"Of course." Grandma's eyes twinkled as she nudged Abigail out of the way. "He'll be glad to see you."

"Only because of the cookies."

"And he'll need help selecting Christmas gifts for that passel of sisters."

The Worth Street minister's voice rolled over Jackson. He talked about how they were each to shine Christ's love just like the star over Bethlehem. Jackson tried to listen. Really he did. But instead the words flowed around him as he watched a particularly nice profile. Abigail was sandwiched between her mother and grandmother five rows in front of Jackson. Just enough to keep her in his line of sight but also out of reach.

He'd decided to try this church after Mr. Turner had mentioned it was the one their family attended. The sanctuary's ceiling rose to a point that made Jackson think of heaven, and the large stained glass windows lent a colorful dimension to the stories he knew. The large sanctuary was full, but it had taken Jackson only a moment to pick out Abigail and her family.

His days had lost some of their zest without her, but he'd decided he needed to be patient. She clearly felt pressured by work and school, and he didn't want to add to it. The time without her had reinforced his realization that he longed for something more than friendship between them.

People around him stood, and he lurched to his feet. Should he wait for her to see him or hurry through the sanctuary and out the doors before she caught him? He didn't want to imagine how awkward that conversation would be when he wanted to know her thoughts and heart.

The pastor stopped him at the door and reached for his hand. "Good to see you, young man."

"Nice sermon, Pastor."

"Anything to apply to your life?"

Jackson paused a minute. Something about stars? "Always good to want to be more like Christ. Shine His light."

The pastor chuckled and patted his shoulder. "Have a good week."

"Thanks, sir."

Jackson's steps slowed as he crossed the narrow hallway and exited the building. If Abigail had noticed him, she hadn't given any indication. He felt foolish as he vacillated between wanting to hurry to her side and wanting to give her the space she needed. If it were just because of finals, he'd be fine with it, but he had a sinking suspicion she wasn't sure about them. What would happen after her finals? Would she have another excuse? Or would she want to spend time with him?

One thing he knew for certain: he'd ask that question as soon as Purdue's finals ended.

He wouldn't let her disappear from his life without asking her for more than friendship.

"Isn't that your young man?" Grandma pointed behind Abigail.

"What?" Abigail glanced over her shoulder.

"Him."

"I don't know." She stood on tiptoe, but couldn't make out who spoke with the pastor. "I suppose we should hurry home and get dinner on the table."

As she pulled on her gloves, Grandma shook her head. "For someone who's in love, you sure aren't eager to chase him down."

"He's supposed to chase me." Abigail grimaced at her sharp tone. "Sorry, Grandma. At least I've got the cookies ready."

"Good thing."

Abigail nodded as she and Grandma joined the parishioners making their way down the aisle toward the pastor. Of all the Sundays for him to choose to greet each congregant. All she wanted to do was get home, eat, and then head to Jackson's boardinghouse. Would Jackson be home? She didn't really want to leave the treats with his landlady, though she should skedaddle home to study. Finals started in the morning, and she wasn't nearly as prepared as she'd like.

Lunch was quiet. The long week had taken a toll on Abigail without giving her enough weekend to compensate. She tried not to be tired thinking of all that was coming—a week of exams, then delivering presents to the children at the hospital and attending Christmas services. Thoughts of all she had to do kept her mind spinning.

With time short, Father suggested Abigail drive to Jackson's. She scooted out of the house with a box of cookies as she wrapped her scarf around her neck. She pushed the button to start the car and then backed into the alley. In a few moments she was at the park, the car idling as she studied the boarding-house. The only way to know if Jackson was home was to knock.

She'd barely climbed the steps when the door opened.

"Hello, Abigail." Jackson stood in the doorway, a sweater pulled over his collared shirt and corduroys. "Would you like to come in?"

She searched his eyes and smiled at the welcome on his face. "Thank you." A minute later she settled on a small davenport while he sat a respectable distance away on the other end. "Grandma and I baked some Christmas cookies. Here are a few for you. She . . . I . . . we thought you'd enjoy them."

She extended the box, and he looked at it for a moment before accepting it.

"Thanks." He lifted the lid and sniffed appreciatively. "These smell great."

"It's Grandma's secret recipe."

"I've missed being part of that back home. Thanks for bringing them. Can you stay?"

"I really can't." She bit her lip and met his gaze, willing him to understand. "I have to study for a final tomorrow."

"All right. I can't study for you, so I'll enjoy these instead." His intense gaze warmed her. "It's good to see you, Abigail. I'll plan to see you Friday night for our hospital delivery. If you get any time before then let me know, okay?"

"I will." She looked down at her empty hands, then back at him. "Enjoy the cookies."

"Every bite."

She nodded and stood. He followed her to the door, and she gave a little wave, then spun and headed down the steps. Her pace slowed on the slick sidewalk, and she glanced over her shoulder. Jackson still stood on the porch, watching her, one hand shoved deep in his pocket.

~oe~

The cookies didn't last as long as the questions. Why bring them over when she was so busy?

When only crumbs remained in the paper box, he still kept it. Seeing the box on his dresser reminded him of Abigail and her gesture. It also reminded him to pray for wisdom.

~oe~

## Friday, December 18

On Friday, his supervisor sent him to load the company pickup with puzzles and play sets. "Take at least twenty. I don't want any kid feeling left out. Not at Christmas."

"Yes sir."

"You'd better go if you're going to get to Glatz Candies in time." His boss pointed toward a pile of the company's most popular sets. "Those should do it. See you Monday."

Jackson loaded the boxes and wondered how he'd get them into the hospital. He might have to make a few trips, but he'd get it done. The thought of bringing joy and surprises to the kids made him work faster. He knew too well what it was like to lay in a hospital bored with nothing to do. Maybe the puzzles and activities would break the monotony for a while.

After a false start, he had the pickup chugging down State Street and then Main. He pulled into a spot down the block from Glatz Candies. When he walked inside, Hannah was helping the customer at the head of a long line. It looked like lots of people planned to take candy and treats home or to Christmas parties.

Maybe he should get something to take home to his sisters. They might like that more than anything else he could think to get them. They were too old for dolls or jacks. Too bad he didn't have a brother or two. They'd be a lot easier to buy gifts for.

During a break in business, Hannah hurried toward him. "I'm glad you're here. Abigail wondered if you'd been delayed and said she'd walk, but I told her she's crazy. The *Farmers' Almanac* predicts snow."

"Should I go up and get her?"

Hannah glanced at the line that reformed as quickly as she could serve people. "That would be great." She reached under the counter and held up a stack of papers. "Oh, and can you take these upstairs to her? The boss wanted these to be handed out with the candy canes."

"Sure. Merry Christmas, Hannah."

"To you too."

Before he'd stepped away, she was already smiling at the next person as she asked how she could assist them.

He climbed the stairs, turning ever closer to the third floor. He paused outside the door, then pushed through.

Inside Abigail ran back and forth, her scarf flying and beret threatening to pop off her hair. She grabbed a handful of candy canes and piled them into an overflowing basket. "It's just kids. I can handle an hour of this. It's the right thing to do."

What had gotten into her? She looked like a mother hen frantically searching for her chicks. After another minute watching her frantic activity, he stepped in her path. "Can I help?"

She startled and placed a hand over her heart. "Good night, Jackson! You should have said something."

"I just did."

She paused and then smiled. "Thank you for coming. Hannah said I'd be a fool to walk."

"She's right, especially when you knew I'd be here."

"I know. This has me so rattled." She glanced around the room without seeming to see a thing.

"Hannah asked me to give these to you. Something about giving them to the families."

"Okay." Abigail took the stack of papers without really looking at them. "I guess I'm ready." She picked up the basket, but he took it from her and offered his arm. She hesitated only a moment, then looked at him. Her pulse raced at her neck, but she took a deep breath. "I can do this because you're here."

He cocked his head and watched her. "They're just kids at the hospital."

"And you came out of the hospital fine."

"I think so."

"My sister didn't."

bigail could have bitten off her tongue. Why would she say such a thing? Jackson didn't need to know that hospitals frightened her.

What had seemed like the perfect way to serve some of the less fortunate at Christmastime and confront her fears as her professor had asked now struck her as a terrible idea. How could she walk into the children's ward and pretend to believe everything was fine? That the children would go home and back to their lives? Her family knew from hard experience the heavy hand of grief that often followed a child's stay at the hospital.

To this day she couldn't visit friends or loved ones in the hospital because the antiseptic scent would send her running for the door or she'd risk expelling the contents of her stomach. She'd been a young child when Annie died from influenza, but she'd been old enough to be scared and to associate the hospital with a place people didn't leave. Alfie had died before the ambulance reached the hospital, but she'd never forget seeing him in his casket.

Jackson stopped her at the landing. "Do you want me to do this alone?"

She bit her lip, the temptation to run inside the candy room and hide very strong. Yet she needed to do this for school. But even more, she *wanted* to do this, to be part of making a difference with these kids at this season. "I really don't want to go, but I will."

He stopped and waited until she looked at him. "I promise to stay with you."

"I believe you." She looked at the basket filled with a silly mix of sugar and flavoring. "I need you."

A slow smile broke on his face. "I'm glad. Come on, we'll do this and it won't be as bad as you expect."

He helped her to the pickup, and she examined the papers Hannah had sent with them. Half of each page was a coupon for a free meal at Glatz Candies. The other half was a short retelling of the meaning of the candy cane. As Abigail read it, she felt some of her tension leave. What had seemed like a silly thing to offer when she panicked at the store had meaning. The red to remind those looking at it of Jesus dying on the cross; the white to remind them that Jesus was sinless and pure. The candy canes would be a wonderful gift of hope.

Had anyone done something similar for her family?

The short drive to the hospital didn't take as long as she needed. Soon Jackson had stacked her arms with puzzles, then loaded himself up with play sets. Last, he stacked her basket on top of his load.

"Maybe we can leave the extras at the nurses' station while we deliver the first puzzles," he said.

She held back a giggle that threatened to erupt into panicked laughter. "That would be good. Otherwise, we'll leave a trail of boxes. At least they aren't heavy."

They crossed the reception area and took the elevator to the pediatric area. A nurse stopped them. "Can I help you?"

"We're with a class from Purdue," Abigail explained. "Our employers donated items for us to bring to the children. I set it up in advance."

"I'm so glad you could come. The Christmas season gets so long when you're cooped up in a ward." The nurse took in their towers of gifts. "Would you like to leave something at the desk?"

"If it's all right." Abigail lowered her stack to the desk, then took the basket from Jackson. "Is it okay to distribute the candy canes too?"

"Are those from Glatz Candies?" At Abigail's nod, the nurse lit up. "Wonderful. I don't suppose you have an extra?"

"A few." Abigail handed her one with a smile. "Thanks for all you do for the kids."

The nurse walked them from room to room, a candy cane hanging from her pocket. As long as Abigail focused on the kids and the way Jackson never left her side, she was fine. As soon as she thought about what the children faced or the fact she was in a hospital, her stomach roiled.

"You're doing great." Jackson's words were meant only for her, but they were exactly what she needed to hear. He approached a little boy lying in a bed that made him look even smaller. "Hey, Buster. What did you do?"

"Fell out of a tree."

"In December?"

The boy's blue eyes sparkled like sapphires. "My cat didn't know it was too cold and slippery to climb. Next time I'll leave him there."

"Ouch." Jackson tousled his hair. "How about a play set?"

"Really?" The boy sat up as much as the traction holding his leg in the air allowed.

"Sure. Cowboys and Indians or a store?"

From bed to bed, Jackson carried the conversation, talking to each child. Really seeing each child. His ease with the children was amazing, and it came from more than having spent time in their shoes. It was as genuine as Jackson and endeared him to Abigail. Through his example, she found it easier to approach the children and start a conversation. She stopped seeing the medical paraphernalia and saw them. Each precious in their own way.

An hour later Jackson was still talking with a couple of boys, helping them pop pieces out for a play set and explaining how to construct it. As she watched, Abigail felt the walls of the ward close in. The smell seemed to intensify, and she fought for breath.

A nurse looked at her, brows quirked. Abigail waved her away and then slipped out the door and down the hall to the chapel. As a child, this is where her parents had brought her and Pete to explain that Annie had died. The small space was meant to give peace and hope, but as she sat on a padded wooden pew, she felt despair coat her.

For years she had wanted a family, and the more time she spent with Jackson, the more she wanted that with him. But she'd experienced reality. Sickness happened, accidents occurred, and death resulted. Add the war, and it seemed the risk was too great. As she considered the pain her family had endured, the shadows that clouded her mother's eyes on certain days, she didn't want to risk opening herself to that kind of pain when she could avoid it by remaining aloof.

Now she knew Jackson, and remaining alone wouldn't satisfy. She wanted the love of a good man and a family of her own. In spite of everything she'd experienced, she wanted a family to love regardless of the risk.

She slipped to her knees in front of the pew.

Allowing the fear to rule over her wasn't right. Fear wasn't what God intended for her. No, God wanted her to be that light pointing to Him, but if she was too afraid to live boldly for Him, how could she point others to Him? The questions raced through her mind, one after another, in a confusing refrain.

*God?*

Did He hear and care?

She knew He did. On the darkest days, Mama sang hymns like "It Is Well with My Soul" and found acceptance. Maybe it was time for Abigail to do the same.

*Father, help me let go of the fear. I want to live a life that brings You joy.*

She knew that didn't include living a life constrained by the "safe" paths she tried to navigate. Slowly, peace crept up and through her. She held it to her, memorized the feeling. This was how she wanted to live from now on. Embracing the fullness of what God had for her and trusting Him to walk her through any valleys.

Hurried footsteps entered the chapel, and she launched back onto the pew. She wiped a couple of tears from her cheek and straightened her posture.

"Abigail? Thank goodness." Jackson rushed up the aisle toward her. "I was beginning to think you walked home."

She turned toward Jackson and smiled as she stood. "It's not that far."

"I know, but it's dark, and I'm your escort." He placed his hands on her arms and searched her face.

"I'm fine, Jackson."

He nodded as he stepped away. "Yes, I think you are. Want to tell me about it?"

She felt dazed as she shook her head. "Not yet. I'd like to, but I'm not exactly sure what happened. I just know I'm not afraid anymore."

He seemed to understand what she couldn't articulate. "Here's your basket. You left it at the nurses' desk."

"Thanks."

He led her from the hospital, and on the top step, Abigail paused. She took a deep breath and slowly expelled it, then another.

"Are you sure you're all right?" he asked.

She turned to Jackson, who stood next to her silhouetted by the lamplight. "Yes, I am. Thank you."

"I didn't do anything."

"Yes, you did. You reached out to those kids and gave them the gift of yourself. It was a wonderful thing to watch. You'd still be in there now if you hadn't run out of puzzles and play sets."

He ducked his chin and grinned up at her from under long eyelashes. "Maybe."

"You would." She swallowed around a sudden lump in her throat. "You are a good man, Jackson Lucas. I'm blessed to call you my friend."


Jackson offered Abigail his arm and helped her down the stairs. He wasn't sure what to make of her statement. He'd just been himself with the kids and tried to bring a little joy to the doldrums that existed in even the best hospital. He knew all too well that young bodies were not designed for enforced inactivity. The puzzles and play sets would help, but they weren't the perfect solution.

"Want to stop at my house?" Abigail asked after they'd both climbed into the truck. "If I know Mama, she'll have something hot waiting for us. And if she doesn't, Grandma will."

"You have a good family."

"Yes. Will you get to see yours?"

"I'll take the bus out on Christmas and stay for the weekend." He steered the pickup toward Perrin Avenue. In a few blocks he parked in front of her house. "Are you sure they won't mind if I stop in?"

"Certain." Abigail met his gaze. "Grandma would be devastated if you didn't."

"Devastated? That seems a bit strong."

"Not for my grandma. She believes things deeply."

"All right." Jackson hopped from the truck and walked around to open Abigail's door. As she took his offered hand, he felt the attraction between them ricochet. She was captivating and had found peace in the chapel. Whatever had chased her there, he sensed she was free. "I'll only stay a minute. I'm sure your day has been as full as mine."

"But now finals are over. All I have left is preparing for Christmas."

"Maybe you could help me shop for my sisters." He hurried on before she could tell him what a dumb idea that was. "All I've thought of for them is Glatz's candy. That won't last an hour."

She laughed, a rich sound that wrapped around him and included him in her joy. "I'd like that. And I won't suggest a doll."

"They'd appreciate that. What do you want for Christmas?"

"A white morning glistening with fresh snow." As her gaze met his, he noted the lightness in her expression. Something had definitely changed inside the hospital.

They stood on the sidewalk a minute longer, not quite ready to go inside. In the light spilling from the large picture window, Jackson tucked an escaped curl behind her ear. "I want to do a better job of caring for my family."

She cocked her head as if she didn't understand. "You already take good care of them."

"They almost lost the farm because I was careless. And Dad died because I couldn't help him." His words shuddered to a stop as she placed her hand on his arm.

"That's not what I heard from your mother." Her eyes were soft in the light from the window. "She said there was nothing you or anyone could have done to save him. His heart gave out first."

"There's no way she can know that for sure."

"Just like there's no way you can know you could have prevented it."

He squared his jaw and looked past her. "I want you to know I can care for them well so you'll know you can count on me too."

"I already do, Jackson." She leaned toward him, their breath mingling in the frosty air. "You are the reason they can stay on the farm. What a thief tried to steal, you discovered and brought back. They're blessed to have you, and I'm so glad I met you."

He felt her words and wanted to cling to them. His teeth clenched so hard he wondered if his jaw would crack as her words hit him deep inside.

She stepped even closer and tipped her face to his. "Jackson, hear me and understand me when I say this. You are the reason your family is safe. Without you, we wouldn't know who stole the money. You saved them when no one else could."

His blood thundered in his ears. He wanted to believe her. Freedom felt like it was right there, waiting to be claimed.

Then she reached up on her tiptoes, touched a gloved hand to his cheek, and leaned toward him. His heart threatened to stop as he felt the whisper of a kiss.

A rap on the window made her jerk back, a sheepish smile on her face. So he tugged her toward him and kissed her with all the emotion and promise he could.

## Twelve

*Sunday, December 20*

*S*unday morning Abigail looked for Jackson at church but couldn't see him. As a result, her thoughts strayed to him throughout lunch and the afternoon.

"You'd better send this girl to her room, Rose." Grandma shook her head as Abigail slouched on the couch with knitting needles and yarn resting in her lap. "She's no good to any of us. The only knitting she's done has more dropped stitches than we can use."

"I'm sorry, Grandma." Abigail touched her lips and felt the heat in her cheeks.

"We all saw that smooch, sweetie. I'd be distracted too. Where is your young man?"

Her young man was absent. Disturbingly so, especially when she wanted him next to her so she could learn more about him. The more she knew, the more she wanted to know. There were depths to Jackson she had not yet explored.

Her heart remained quiet in the face of what God had shown her at the hospital. Not only was Jackson not afraid to be back in a hospital after several long stays as a child, but he knew how to serve others. She longed to develop that ability. To not be held by the events of the past, but to push forward, relying on the knowledge that God was in control of all aspects of her life. She might not understand this side of heaven why her brother and sister had died, but she could cling to the One who controlled her destiny. The thought gave her a sense of security she hadn't realized she'd missed.

As Sunday turned to Monday, Abigail felt a bit at loose ends. Without classes, she didn't have anything to occupy her thoughts, and Christmas wasn't until Friday. She needed a distraction before she spent the entire day thinking about Jackson.

She went in search of her mother. "Mama, I'd like to walk downtown and do some shopping. Do you need anything?"

"I'm fine."

"Grandma?"

"Should I come with you?" Grandma asked.

Abigail looked outside at the crisp blue sky. There might not be many clouds, but it was bordering on bitter. Not enough to keep her inside, but probably enough that Grandma should remain at home.

"It looks pretty cold."

"I can bundle up." Grandma sniffed, then opened the side door in the kitchen. Almost immediately, she jumped back inside and pushed the door shut. "On second thought, I'll let you venture out into the tundra alone. Better yet, stay here and read to me while I knit."

"Oh, Grandma." She'd go crazy if she had to stay inside. "It's not any colder than when I'm darting around campus." She grabbed her heavy wool coat, mittens, hat, and scarf. "I promise I'll stop somewhere to warm up."

The cold bit at Abigail's face as she walked downtown. The trip didn't take any longer than usual; it just felt like it did as the blocks seemed to lengthen in the cold. After ten minutes she crossed Columbia Street and entered the main door of Loeb's.

The department store sat across from the courthouse. While all four floors were filled with shopping delights, today she'd focus on the discount area. She wasn't sure what Jackson could afford, so she'd start there, scavenging for gifts for his sisters. If she couldn't find anything in that area, she'd expand her search.

After sifting through the inventory, she found a darling hat for his middle sister, Roselyn. The more she looked, the clearer it became that she'd need his help to determine what his sisters liked. He hadn't said enough about them for her to guess.

"Can I help you, miss?" A man approached her in a dapper suit.

Abigail smiled at the clerk but shook her head. "I'll be back later. Thank you."

She slipped outside and walked across the courthouse lawn to her father's office. She opened the door and smiled at her father's receptionist.

"Merry Christmas, Lottie."

"Why, Abigail, I didn't expect to see you out on this cold day."

"It's not so bad if I keep ducking into buildings." Abigail loosened her scarf. "Is Father in?"

"Wrapping up with a client. Then I think he'll want to walk you home."

"Probably." Lottie was a better person to ask than her father. "Any word on Jackson's matter?"

Lottie turned reproachful eyes on her. "You know I can't talk about your dad's cases. You'll have to take it up with him."

Abigail smiled. "You can't blame a girl for trying."

"Sure I can." Lottie stood and took her coat from the rack. "Now that you're here, I'll head home. You shouldn't have to wait long, and we don't have anyone else coming."

"All right. Stay warm." Abigail grinned at the older woman as she exchanged her pumps for practical boots and then wrapped yards of scarf around her neck and head. "Are you sure you can breathe?"

"Positive. Toodles."

A few minutes later, her father ushered someone from his office and then collected his things. The walk home was quiet, but in the comfortable way. The kind of silence that communicated she was with someone she loved dearly.

When they reached the house, her mother was practically waiting at the door. "Where have you been, Abigail?"

"I told you I walked downtown. It took long enough that I stopped at the office so I could walk back with Father." She slipped out of her coat and hung it on the coat tree. "I'm sorry if you worried."

"I didn't until a certain young man kept calling." Her mother pecked Father on the cheek. "He reminds me of a certain young man I once knew."

"Once?" Father gave her a devilish grin, one that sent Mama scooting for the kitchen.

"Supper will be ready in a minute." Mama's voice trailed back to the living room, and Abigail couldn't help laughing at her parents' antics.

She wanted to still feel that way thirty years after she married the love of her life. To be able to give one look and have her husband move toward her, longing for her.

"That's quite a sigh, young lady." Grandma looked over her glasses at Abigail, a knowing gleam in her expression.

"Yes, it is. I'm going upstairs for a bit." Upstairs to be alone with her thoughts and prayers. Praying that God would show her what He had in mind for her future.

⟿⟾

Jackson slogged up the stairs. The impromptu trip home that weekend followed by a long day at the puzzle factory had left him weary into his muscles. He was glad he'd made it home, but his usual day of rest had turned into a time to serve his mother and sisters. Couple that with his regular work, and he was tired.

He was tempted to crawl into bed, but first he'd try Abigail again, to see if she was agreeable to his offer.

He stopped at the hall phone and gave Abigail's number to the operator. After a couple of clicks, the call went through.

"Turner residence." Her voice sounded rushed, as if she'd hurried to the phone. Had she hoped it would be him?

"Hi, Abigail."

"Jackson! Mom said you called earlier. I'm so sorry I missed you. Do you still need me to go shopping with you? I stopped at Loeb's today but didn't see much. I realized I need to know your sisters better first."

"That's not why I called."

"Oh." He could almost see her settling back and the puzzled line across her eyebrows.

"Would you go to the Christmas Eve service with me Thursday night?" He wanted to tell her that she was the only person he wanted to spend that special time with, but his tongue refused to cooperate. Instead, it stuck to the roof of his mouth like someone had cemented it there.

Her hesitation seemed to stretch into minutes, longer and longer like the candy she pulled.

"If you already have plans, I understand," he said. "I'm sure your family will want to spend that time with you."

"No." A smile seemed to fill the line. "I'd like to go very much. Could you plan to come here afterward? We always have a late spread of treats. Mama says if one has to stay up so late, there should be something to look forward to on the other side."

"I'd like that. I'll come by at ten?"

"Perfect. I'll see you then. Good night, Jackson."

"Good night."

Even after she hung up, he stood there with the phone in his hand. In three short nights he'd see her. Now to find the perfect Christmas present for her.

He had an idea, but it seemed hasty. Too much too fast.

But he didn't want to turn away from it. Not when he could envision a life with this caring woman. Could she imagine the same with him? That was a question he wasn't sure how to answer, yet it held the key to everything. If she did, he'd do all he could to make her happy for a lifetime. If she didn't, then he'd completely misread her heart and the kiss they'd shared. It had seemed to him that their hearts had connected and spoken words of promise.

Did he dare risk believing a future was possible? That she would stake her future on a farmer who couldn't farm? On a man who'd always limp? A man who'd almost lost his family farm?

But a man who would lay down his life to protect hers.

## Thirteen

*Thursday, December 24*

Abigail swept a gaily colored red scarf from where she'd hidden it behind the Christmas tree and plopped it around her grandmother's shoulders. "My, don't you look lovely, Grandma."

"Just trying to keep up with you, dear. I didn't know you had a green dress."

Abigail grinned because Grandma knew she hadn't owned one until Jackson had asked to go to the Christmas Eve service with her. That had been a great reason to go back to Loeb's and purchase the dress that had whispered to her when she'd shopped there early that week. Now she twirled in front of the mirror, missing the full sweep of fabric but liking the effect all the same.

"I'm sure he'll love it," Grandma said.

"I didn't buy it for him."

Grandma patted her hand. "Feel free to tell yourself that. I know the truth. Do you think we'll get snow tonight?"

"I hope so, but the clouds don't look right."

"Oh, so you've taken up cloud reading?"

Abigail laughed along with Grandma. A knock at the door had her checking her hair one last time and then hurrying to get the door before Grandma. Who knew what she would say next?

When Abigail opened the door, Jackson stood there with ruddy cheeks.

She closed the door the moment he stepped inside. "Did you walk all this way?"

"Sure. Nothing to it. Just one foot in front of the other." His teeth chattered just a bit, and she tugged him inside.

"Silly man. We would have come for you if you'd asked."

He stood taller and looked down at her. "That's not the way it's done, and I said I'd come by."

"And what if you catch pneumonia from such craziness? Come stand by the fire, and I'll get you something warm to drink."

With a swish of her skirt, Abigail left him in front of the fire. She was right. It had been foolish to insist on walking this late at night. The cold had threatened to send him back inside, except he wanted to spend the evening with her. Celebrate the arrival of the King and sing carols together.

His fingers had tingled back to life about the time she brought him a mug of steaming coffee.

"Black like you like it." She wrinkled her nose.

"Simpler that way with rationing."

"I think I'd rather stop drinking it . . . though that might be reality eventually. I wonder what else they'll ration before the war ends." She shrugged and handed him the mug. "Why don't you sit down? We don't have to leave for a while."

He eased onto one of the wing chairs and relaxed as she sank onto the floor next to him. "You look beautiful, Abigail."

Her eyes sparkled as she looked at him from her place on the floor. "Thank you." She braced her elbows on the coffee table and leaned her chin on her hands. "Are you ready to go home tomorrow?"

They talked about his coming trip. The conversation was easy as he filled her in on his trip home the weekend before. It had been so good to see his mother and sisters. Abigail never pushed but coaxed him to tell her more and more about his sisters.

"I feel like I know your sisters better." Abigail shifted on the couch. "I'd know what to get them now."

The door blew open, and her father walked in, rubbing frost from his gloves. "The car's warming up. Time to bundle up and head to church."

A few minutes later, Jackson found himself squished in the backseat next to Abigail and her grandmother. After the short drive, Mr. Turner idled the car at the curb and Jackson opened his door.

He looked back at Abigail after he slid out. "I'm going to help your grandmother first. Wait for me."

Grandma preened as she waited for Jackson to open the door. As he helped her out, she tapped his arm. "He's a good man, Abigail." She turned to him. "And Abigail's a woman who will delight any man."

Yes, she was.

There was nowhere else he'd rather be on Christmas Eve than with her at the church service. As he caught her smiling at him, his hopes soared. Maybe she felt the same.


As Abigail walked into the church on Jackson's arm, her breath slowed and she matched her gait to Jackson's long pace. Everything felt right in that moment. She was surrounded by her parents, Grandma, and Jackson. People she loved and adored. The only people missing were Pete and Merry, each doing their part for the war.

Sliding into a pew, she tried to ignore how empty it felt without Pete and Merry and instead focus on the man who stood next to her. She wanted to remember every detail of the candlelit sanctuary so she could describe it to her siblings in letters. Muted Christmas greetings were shared as people saw friends. Pine boughs had been placed along the stained-glass window ledges and filled the air with the scent of Christmas. Glass balls hung from red bows in the middle of the branches. The candlelight sent a rainbow of reflections off the glass. The wood pews and women's jewelry shimmered in the light.

Pastor Hughes led them through the reading of Luke 2 interspersed with the singing of Christmas hymns. Abigail leaned against Jackson, and he slipped his arm around her shoulder. She felt nestled and protected against his side. Could she feel this way forever?

Before the closing song, small tapers were passed out to the adults. Then the lights were dimmed and the candles lit, one at a time. In the soft candlelight, the congregation sang "Silent Night" a cappella. Their voices swelled in harmony, Jackson's tenor mixing with Grandma's quavering soprano, until Abigail wanted to close her eyes and weep.

After the last note, silence reigned as if the congregation wanted to hold its collective breath and sweep the peace deep inside. Then a child cried, and the moment was lost.

It took a while to work their way down the aisle, where volunteers handed out bags with an apple, an orange, and a few peanuts to the children. A fitting gift for enduring the late service. Then Father urged them to wait while he started the car and brought it around.

When they reached the house, Abigail headed to the kitchen to help get the buffet items ready, but Mama shooed her out.

"You invited him to stay, so entertain your young man. He'll wonder why he's here if you don't."

"All right." Mama had a point. Abigail returned to the living room and grabbed a cribbage board and a deck of cards from the bookshelf. "Would you like to play?"

Jackson looked up from the *LIFE* magazine he'd selected. "Sure, but first will you come sit by me?"

She sank onto the couch next to him, and he put his arm around her shoulder. She nestled closer and sighed. "Thanks for going to church with us tonight."

His side vibrated as he chuckled. "Your dad told me I should stay on the couch tonight rather than walk home."

"He's right. You could even have Pete's room."

"I'll be fine. What I want to know, Miss Abigail, is whether you'll take a walk around the block with me."

"At this hour? In this cold?" He must have already developed a fever to think a walk in the early morning hours of Christmas morn was a wise idea.

"The snow's started to fall." He brushed the curtain back and she saw light flakes dancing from the sky. "It seems your request for snow has been fulfilled. Let's go play in it. Not for long, but long enough."

She nodded and, without taking her eyes from his, called to Mama, "We'll be back in fifteen minutes, all right?"

"At this hour?"

"Yes ma'am."

Jackson helped Abigail to her feet, then held her coat while she slipped her arms into it. He tugged Grandma's scarf around her neck. "You look like a Christmas tree now. All green in that dress and wrapped in a red garland."

She pirouetted. "Thank you, kind sir."

When they stepped outside, the night had transformed into a winter delight.

"It's a white Christmas," she said. Her breath hung in the air as snowflakes meandered down from the sky.

Jackson guided her to the porch swing. "Will you join me?" His voice cracked, and she smiled as she sat next to him.

"Anywhere."

"Do you mean that, Abigail? That you'd follow me anywhere?"

"Yes, I do." And she knew she would. If he asked, she'd go anywhere.

He slid to a knee in front of her. "Will you walk with me through life? The ups and downs? The moments we celebrate and the times we'll cry?"

"Yes, Jackson." Abigail nodded as he clutched her hands. A tear slid down her face and froze on her cheek as she realized what he was asking. "I want to live my life with you."

"I love you, Abigail Turner. Will you do me the honor of marrying me?"

Her heart thrilled at his words. He loved her. He wanted to marry her. The words sunk into her soul, where she wanted to hold them close. She shivered and he tightened his hold on her hands.

Could she promise him forever? As the snow filtered down, creating a winter wonderland, she could imagine the path their lives would take. And she knew she wanted to walk that journey with him. Always with him.

She tugged him up onto the swing next to her and nodded. "Yes, Jackson, forever and more I love you."

He launched to his feet with a holler. "Abigail Turner is going to marry me!"

As she tried to shush him, the front door opened, and Father leaned outside. "Get in here, you crazy kids, before you wake the neighbors."

A light flicked on across the street, indicating it was too late.

"Come on." Abigail led Jackson back into the house, where Grandma, Mama, and Father waited, each with knowing smiles.

As Jackson shared their news with her family, Abigail realized she had all she ever wanted. On a Christmas as white as the song, she'd found his heart, and her dreams seemed destined to come true.

# I'll Be Home
## for Christmas

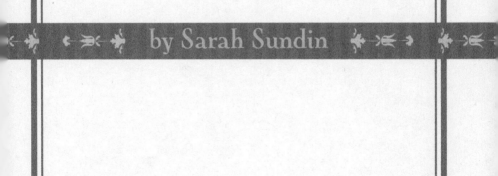

by Sarah Sundin

## One

Friday, December 3, 1943
Lafayette, Indiana

Grace Kessler poked harder at the typewriter keys, trying to drown out the song. Her fingers betrayed her and tapped to the rhythm.

Why did Ruby Schmidt insist on singing in the secretarial pool? Why did she have to choose Christmas songs? And couldn't she at least pick a song with a faster beat?

Grace deciphered her shorthand notes on the spiral-bound tablet to her right and finished a business letter from Mr. Dubois in Alcoa's procurement department to Mr. Parkhurst with the War Production Board. She zipped the letter out of the typewriter, removed the carbon paper, and laid the original in her outgoing basket and the copy in the file basket.

Alcoa was America's top producer of aluminum, crucial for the production of airplanes and other defense materials. A secretary's work might not be as glamorous as a nurse or a WAVE or a Rosie the Riveter, but it allowed Grace to support both her daughter and the war effort.

Grace's gaze slid to the silver picture frame on her desk, which held the last photo taken of George and Linnie together, over two years earlier. Linnie had just turned four. She sat on George's lap, and father and daughter grinned at each other with total adoration. No little girl could have loved her daddy more.

Pain rose in Grace's heart, and she ripped her attention back to the typewriter. The faster she typed, the faster Alcoa could produce aluminum, the faster planes could come off the assembly line, and the sooner this war would be over and no more men would be shot down by Japanese bullets over Filipino jungles.

They never even found George's body.

*"I'll be home for Christmas . . ."* Ruby's song drifted closer.

Grace winced. No, he wouldn't.

Something scratched the top of Grace's head, and Ruby giggled.

"Ouch." Grace extracted a little leafy branch from her hairdo—and a couple strands of her own dark brown hair.

"Mistletoe, sweetie." Ruby puckered lips as red as holly berries. "You need some Christmas spirit."

Grace replaced a bobby pin and forced herself to smile and wink at Ruby. "I need to get back to work, and so do you."

Ruby fluffed her platinum hair. "You need a date in the worst possible way. Bobby knows the nicest young man—"

"No." Grace pinned her strongest look on the girl. "No blind dates. Besides, who in this town would agree to baby-sit Linnie?"

"She's a handful, isn't she?"

"Yes, she is." Grace rolled new paper into her typewriter, flipped the release lever, and aligned the sheet. "You'd best get back to work before Norton sees you."

Sure enough, the door to the supervisor's office swung open.

Grace swept the mistletoe into her lap and handed a blank piece of paper to Ruby. "Thank you for taking care of this, Miss Schmidt."

"You're welcome, Mrs. Kessler." Ruby skedaddled back to her desk.

"Mrs. Kessler." Mrs. Norton glared at Grace. "Phone call. Your baby-sitter."

Sympathetic murmurs rose from the other secretaries, but Grace's lips and fingertips went numb. Not again.

Somehow she stood. She hid the mistletoe in the hip pocket of her bottle-green suit jacket and walked on wobbly ankles down the aisle between all the clattering typewriters.

"Thank you, Mrs. Norton." She edged past her matronly supervisor and through the doorway to the office.

Mrs. Norton crossed her plump arms. "You're the only one, Mrs. Kessler. The only one who takes so many personal calls. You need to get a handle on that child of yours."

"Yes ma'am." Grace turned her back on her supervisor to hide her anguish, and she picked up the receiver. "Mrs. Harrison?"

"I've had it. I've had it up to here." The baby-sitter's voice climbed and shivered. "When she's here . . . oh, my nerves! And when she goes wandering, well, just how much can a woman take?"

Grace clenched the cold black receiver. "Is Linnie there?"

"Of course not. She's trying to kill me, I'm sure of it."

Inside Grace, frustration with Mrs. Harrison wrestled with worry for Linnie. The clock read 4:05. Linnie should have arrived half an hour earlier. Teaching her daughter how to ride the bus had been necessary when Linnie started school in September, but it only encouraged her wandering. Her searching.

Mrs. Harrison jabbered about her nerves, and guilt filled Grace. What kind of mother allowed her six-year-old daughter to roam the city alone?

"Excuse me, Mrs. Harrison. I need to call the police." Again.

"This is it. This is the last time. I simply cannot take it any longer. I quit."

Outside the tiny office window, Alcoa's red brick smokestack jutted into the gray sky. Grace laid down the receiver, missed, and finally settled it in place.

Mrs. Norton sniffed. "Don't even think about asking to get off early."

"I know, ma'am." Grace's voice came out choked. "May I make another call, please?"

"I ought to charge you."

Grace dialed 4045 for the Lafayette Police Department, a number she knew by heart. While the phone rang, she rubbed the aching knot at the base of her skull. *Lord, please keep my baby safe.*

So many horrible things could happen to her little girl. And her job. She'd worn out every available baby-sitter. How could she stay employed without a baby-sitter? And without a job, how could she pay the bills?

Worst of all, Grace's love wasn't enough for her daughter.

That knowledge hollowed into her soul.

~∽⊙⊂~

Lieutenant Pete Turner trudged down Sixth Street, hands deep in the pockets of his olive drab trousers, his pilot's crush cap shoved low on his forehead.

He passed Glatz Candies on the far side of the street, angling his head away from the cheery red-and-white awning. A year ago, he would have bugged his little sister Abigail behind the counter and savored an ice cream soda.

Not now. Nothing sounded good. Not ice cream, not teasing, not even family.

A two-hundred-hour combat tour flying a P-47 Thunderbolt fighter plane over Nazi-occupied Europe had drained him of all grief, all anger, and all joy. So many deaths. So many good young men gone down in flames.

The marquee of the Lafayette Theater advertised *For Whom the Bell Tolls*. Pete had read Hemingway's book. He'd memorized John Donne's poem at Jefferson High.

"Never send to know for whom the bell tolls," Pete muttered, "it tolls for thee."

Today even Pastor Hughes hadn't helped. All Pete wanted was a few words of wisdom and comfort to make him feel again. Feel anything.

The pastor had gotten him through his big brother Alfred's death back in '27, when Pete was fifteen. Pete owed Pastor Hughes for his salvation, for his very life.

But today? Pastor Hughes had leaned back in his leather chair, holding his reading glasses and rubbing them with a handkerchief while Pete talked. Didn't he understand how hard it was for Pete to spill his guts? And the pastor just rubbed his glasses.

When Pete was done talking, Pastor Hughes leaned forward and said, "Give."

Give?

"When you're empty inside," Pastor Hughes said, "the best thing you can do is give. Find a need, step outside of yourself, and give."

Pete turned right onto Columbia Street. Maybe the pastor was going senile. Pete was an empty pitcher. How could he pour anything out from nothing?

He'd have to find his own way to fill up again. And soon. On January 1, he had to report for transition training with the Air Transport Command Ferrying Division. He had to fly again.

Maybe that was why he was roaming downtown. To fill up on all the sights he'd grown up with. The memories of a lifetime called out from each brick.

He squinted at the buildings, at the trees in their square holes in the sidewalk, at the overcast sky. He trained his senses to the chill in the air, the sounds of traffic—light as it was—and the conversations of passersby. But he didn't feel anything.

Ahead of him rose the high pointy dome of the Tippecanoe County Courthouse in all its Victorian glory. Pete and his best friend, Scooter, had loved running around the grounds, playing cops and robbers. How many times had they decorated the statue of the Marquis de Lafayette or added soap to the fountain at his feet? How many times had they been caught?

The thought should have summoned up either guilt or a smile. Nope. Nothing.

He headed down the left side of the street, across from the courthouse. A few blocks more and he'd reach the Wabash River. Maybe the sound of running water would awaken something.

The door of Loeb's department store opened, and Pete held the door for two ladies burdened with packages. When they thanked him, he said, "You're welcome" but couldn't smile. How could he with that infernal song billowing through the open door? "I'll Be Home for Christmas" made false promises, as if home could make you whole again. Baloney.

He let the door swing shut. Ahead of him, a little girl in a red coat pressed her face to the window. Pete stopped behind her to see the display.

A Christmas tree. A fake Santa Claus, and fake elves playing in fake snow. A wooden airplane that almost looked like a B-17 Flying Fortress, but not quite—too fat. A baby doll. A teddy bear. Lots of Built-Rite paper dollhouses and paper towns and picture puzzles, made right here in Lafayette.

Years ago, Pete and his brother, Alfie, filled with wonder, had pressed their noses to this same window. Golden-haired, golden boy Alfie. Black-haired, black sheep Pete. Was the display this cheesy back then? Granted, they had toys made with metal and rubber back when he was a boy.

*Back when he was a boy?* When had he turned into an old man?

The little girl in front of him hadn't moved. She belonged on the cover of a Christmas toy catalog with her red coat, her red mittens flat on the glass, and two little brown braids sticking out from under her red hat. Twenty-five years earlier, Pete would have tugged one of those braids just to hear her squeal.

"Please," she said, her voice no more than a whisper. "Please, Lord. Please."

For the first time in months, Pete felt something. A twinge in his chest. He remembered that longing for the perfect gift, the hope of seeing it under the tree, the joy of ripping off paper to discover his dreams fulfilled.

Her breath fogged the window. "Please, God. I promise I'll be good. I promise."

His lips twitched with the same emotion. How many times had he made that promise in vain?

"Do you see something you'd like for Christmas?" he asked.

The girl pushed back from the glass and met Pete's gaze in the window reflection. For her sake he had to smile, so he located dead muscles and coaxed them to do their job.

Slowly she faced him. She had wide greenish-blue eyes and a button nose.

A cute little thing. She reminded him of his old friend Scooter at that age, except Scooter never wore braids or a red bonnet with a bow under his chin.

A grin revealed two missing teeth—one of her front teeth and one farther back. The asymmetry made her even cuter.

Pete's smile felt more natural now. "Well, do you? Do you see something you'd like for Christmas?"

She studied him with a satisfied smile as if he were one of the toys on display. "Yes. Yes, I do."

race twisted the telephone cord around her finger. "Yes, Officer. I promise I'll stay home."

"You know it's best, Mrs. Kessler. Then we can call you if we need to. And when she comes home, you'll be there."

"You'll look for her?"

A sigh flowed down the line. "We'll keep an eye out, and if she comes to the station again, we'll bring her home. We always do."

She thanked him, hung up, and pressed her forehead to the wall above the telephone. How could she sit still and wait while her daughter roamed the streets? It was cold. Soon it would be dark. Cars and buses might not see a small child in the falling light. And Linnie trusted strangers far too much.

Grace had to keep busy until her daughter came home. "Linnie always comes home. Always."

The officer was right. Someone had to be there when Linnie returned—or when the police escorted her home—and that someone had to be Grace.

First Grace needed to find a new baby-sitter, or she wouldn't be able to go to work on Monday and she'd lose her job. She reached for the phone, then stopped. What if the police called while she was on the line?

Grace groaned and headed for the kitchen. After she tied on an apron, she opened the icebox and transferred the roasting pan to the oven. Last night she'd prepared chicken, potatoes, carrots, onions, and seasonings so she and Linnie could eat dinner at a decent hour.

If Linnie came home. Pain wrenched through Grace.

She closed her eyes and drew a deep breath. Worry, panic, and despair wouldn't help. *Lord, bring my little girl home.*

Grace grabbed the Bon Ami cleanser and scoured the kitchen sink to distract herself. She never had enough time to clean anyway.

Why had George bought such an enormous house? A house as big as his dreams and just as impossible to maintain.

She'd loved him, loved him so much, but he'd lied to her. Then he'd died and left her with this mess.

Water splashed her forehead, and Grace wiped it off with the back of her wrist.

The phone rang.

Grace dropped her rag in the sink, dashed through the dining room while drying her hands on her apron, turned into the living room, and lunged for the receiver. "Kessler residence."

"Hello, Gracie."

At the sound of her mother's voice, Grace closed her eyes and leaned back against the wall. "Hi, Mom."

"Are you all right, dear? Is it Linnie? Did she—"

"Yes. She's out searching again. And yes, I called the police."

"Oh my. I do wish—"

"So tomorrow you're leaving for San Diego." Grace brightened her voice to divert her mother's attention from a lecture about Linnie needing a good spanking. "I wish I could go and see Peggy and her baby too."

Her mother chattered about what a good mother Grace's older sister was and how well the children behaved, especially with their father off to sea with the navy. Grace gritted her teeth against the implied comparison to her own wayward child.

"Listen, Mom. I don't want to be rude, but I need to keep the line open."

Her mother clucked her tongue. "I tell you, sweetheart, for the sake of that child, you need a husband."

Grace massaged the space between her eyebrows. "All the men are at war or married. And how could I go on dates without a sitter?"

Mom stayed silent. She might want Grace to find a husband, but she wouldn't volunteer to watch her granddaughter. "Well, I'll pray the Lord sends you the right man."

The Lord would have to plop that man right on Grace's doorstep. "Thanks, Mom. Have a wonderful trip. Give Peggy and the children my love."

After Grace hung up, she opened the front door. Chilly air wound around her legs and her face. Up and down the darkening street, golden lights shone from homes with good mothers and living fathers and children who never wandered.

Grace shivered and shut the door.

⌘

Pete squatted in front of the girl and tilted his head toward the department store window. "What toy do you have your eye on?"

"My name's Linda Marie Kessler, but I go by Linnie. What's yours?"

She hadn't answered his question. "Lieutenant Turner."

The child shook his gloved hand. "What's your first name?"

"Pete, but you can call me Lieutenant Turner."

"I know." Her little round face nodded. "That's what Mommy says."

Her mommy. Pete frowned and glanced around. The sun was setting, and the stores would close at six. "Where's your mommy?"

"At home." Linnie hopped on one foot.

"Nearby?"

Linnie switched feet and hopped some more. "On Cason Street."

Cason? That was close to his parents' house—and about a mile away from Loeb's. "Shouldn't you be home for dinner?"

"Uh-huh."

"Does your mommy know where you are?"

Linnie stood still and laughed. "Of course not. She never does."

Pete's hands clenched. What kind of mother didn't know or care that her little girl was far from home, alone, with night falling? Most likely the father was off at war and the mother at work, but how could she leave a child without a sitter?

"How are you getting home?" he asked.

Linnie raised her eyebrows as if he'd asked the stupidest question in the world. "You're taking me, of course. Do you have bus fare? I do. I found a nickel on the sidewalk."

Scrounging for bus fare on the street? Poor kid.

"There's the bus." Linnie jumped and pointed. "Come on, Loo— Loo—"

"Why don't you call me Mr. Turner?"

"Okay."

The bus pulled to a stop in front of them. Linnie climbed the bus steps and paid her fare.

Pete followed and sat next to the girl. Pastor Hughes had told him to give. He could do one good deed, see this child safely home, and get the pastor off his back. Then maybe he'd get some real answers.

Linnie bounced in her seat. "I like this bus. I take it all the time when I explore. I like to explore, but Mrs. Harrison says it's naughty, and Mrs. Cole says I need to obey, and they all say I'm a handful. Mommy says I'm a handful too, but she hugs me and kisses me when she says it. Mrs. Harrison and Mrs. Cole frown."

A smile tugged at Pete's lips for the second time in only a few minutes. "You know, I was a handful too when I was a boy."

Linnie tugged one mitten off partway and flapped it back and forth. "Are you eunuch?"

Pete coughed. "Pardon?"

"That's why I'm a handful. I'm eunuch. Do you know what that means?"

"I . . . I do. And you're not a eunuch. Neither am I."

Her blue-green eyes widened. "Oh yes, I am. I looked it up, and it's me. I read it in a book. I'm a very good reader. Mrs. Cole won't never tell me what a word means. She says, 'Look it up and stop asking questions.' So I do. I know how to use a dictionary. Do you?"

"Yes, I do." He rubbed his palms up and down his trousers. He could see why this girl was called a handful.

"Good. I looked up *eunuch,* and it said, 'the only one, one of a kind, nothing else like it,' and I said, 'That's me!'"

Pete rearranged the syllables in his head and smiled. "U*nique.* It's pronounced u*nique.*"

Linnie pressed her lips together and batted her eyelashes in a long-suffering look she probably learned from her mother—if her mother ever came home. "No, it has an *i* not an *e,* and *i* says, 'ih' like in *pin.* You-nick."

Even though he hadn't laughed in months, Pete had to work to restrain himself. "Why don't you ask your daddy and mommy?"

"Daddy died. His plane crashed and he died. And my mommy . . ." She shook her head. "I don't think she can read a dictionary, because she doesn't say it right. And Mrs. Harrison just says, 'Stop talking. My head hurts.' Mrs. Cole too. I think they're sisters, 'cause they both smell like oatmeal, and not even oatmeal with brown sugar."

Pete puffed his cheeks full of air. So her father was dead, her mother neglectful, and Mrs. Harrison and Mrs. Cole—whoever they were—didn't have hands or hearts big enough for Miss Linda Marie Kessler.

Linnie swung her legs, bumping the seat in front of her.

The lady in front of them turned and scowled at Pete. "Do you mind?"

He didn't care to explain that Linnie wasn't his child. "Sorry, ma'am. It won't happen again."

Linnie kept swinging her legs.

"Watch out!" Pete said in mock horror. "The seat's on fire!"

"It is?" Linnie lifted her asymmetrical smile.

"It's a game my mama and I used to play. Remember, I was a handful too. And my legs never wanted to lie still."

"Mine too!"

"So." He lifted his foot. "You pretend the seat's on fire. Swing as close as you can, but if you hit it, you get burned and you lose."

Her eyes lit up, and her legs reached for the seat, then stopped short. She giggled.

He glanced out the window. "Say, what's your stop?"

"Right here." Linnie scrambled up to stand on the seat and yanked the pull cord. "I like ringing the bell."

"I bet you do." He led her off the bus and up Tinkler Street.

Linnie ran ahead. "Hurry! We're almost there."

Pete jogged to keep up. The homes in this neighborhood were nice, not what he'd expected for Linnie's neglectful family.

Linnie turned on Cason Street and climbed the steps of a large, well-kept Victorian house with plenty of gingerbread and a light in the window. The mother was home? Not even searching? Hadn't she noticed Linnie was missing? Or was she sleeping off a hangover?

As Linnie reached for the doorknob, the door flew open.

"Linnie!" A dark-haired woman dropped to her knees and pulled the child into a fierce embrace. "You mustn't run off like that! I was so worried, and the police insisted I stay home and wait for you. Don't you know how that makes me worry, sweetheart?"

Pete shoved his hands in the pockets of his flight jacket. So she did care. A lot. She had wanted to search for her daughter and even called the police. This widowed mother had waited at home, desperate for her child to come home. Not drunk. Not neglectful.

His insides squirmed. How ironic that he'd judged without evidence, when he'd suffered judgment himself. Well-earned judgment.

Pete acquitted Linnie's mother immediately, and not because she painted a pretty picture in her green suit hugging her red-clad daughter. Although she did. A very pretty picture.

If only she'd look up at him.

## Three

*G*race held Linnie tight until she realized she'd completely ignored the police officer.

"Thank you, Officer." Instead of dark blue trousers, this man wore olive drab. And a leather flight jacket and a service cap. An army pilot. "Lieutenant . . ."

She gazed up into a face too rugged to be truly handsome, dark eyes, and a mouth curved in appreciation.

A face she knew too well, a mean and taunting face.

Her stomach hardened. She released Linnie and stood. "Lieutenant Pete Turner."

His dark eyebrows sprang up, and he peered at her.

She crossed her arms and kept her voice as chilly as the air. "You don't remember me, do you? Grace Kessler, but you knew me as Grace Schuster."

His face fell. "Scooter's little sister."

What else did he remember? How he called her Greasy? How he pelted her with snowballs and put her toys out of reach and tossed her coat up into a tree? How he led Scooter astray into drinking and vandalism? How he and his gang stole liquor from a speakeasy and hid it in the storeroom at Schuster's Stationery? How her own father had been arrested until Scooter confessed? At least Scooter wised up after that horrid incident.

Grace patted her daughter's shoulder. "Linnie, go take off your coat and things."

"Okay, Mommy. Be right back, Mr. Turner." Linnie dashed away.

Bully Pete stared at his toes, his mouth scrunched to one side. "You probably don't remember me fondly."

"Not at all." She moved toward the door.

"I was mean to you, and I wronged your family."

The frank admission stilled her hand on the doorknob. "Yes, you did."

"Some of my many sins. I apologize."

She couldn't throw an apology back in his face. Besides, he had reformed enough to become a lawyer and an officer. "Thank you."

He edged backward. "Listen, I didn't mean to torment you by showing up on your doorstep. I just wanted to make sure Linnie got home safe. Great girl you've raised."

Grace blinked. "You . . . she didn't annoy you?"

"Not at all. She's bright and funny and imaginative. Great kid."

Grace glanced over her shoulder to make sure her bright, funny, imaginative daughter wasn't in earshot. "Most people don't share your opinion."

"Because she's a handful?"

"Yes."

"As a former handful, I understand."

His smile almost made her forget who he was. Before she could stop herself, she smiled back.

Linnie raced back onto the porch and tugged on Pete's hand. "You want to see my doll? My books? My treasures?"

He hung back and gestured over his shoulder with his thumb. "I need to get home for dinner. But thank you, Linnie. It was a pleasure meeting you."

Linnie's shoulders drooped, and she tugged his hand again. "You're staying for dinner, aren't you?"

*Heavens, no!* Grace grasped for words.

"Um, no. Definitely not." Pete took another step backward. At least he had the good sense to know when he wasn't welcome.

"Please, Mommy." Linnie turned up her sweetest face. "You have to invite him. I like him so much. He let me talk and talk and never once told me to be quiet, and he taught me a game."

Grace's heart twisted. How often did an adult treat Linnie kindly? But why did it have to be Pete Turner? "I . . . I do need to thank you for bringing Linnie home," she said to him.

"Seeing her safe at home is all the thanks I need."

Linnie hugged his arm. "Please stay. Please, please, please? Mommy made chicken and potatoes. I helped her last night, so I know. There's plenty of food. You can have my carrots. I don't like carrots."

For heaven's sake. How could Grace teach her daughter manners if she retracted an invitation? She swallowed hard and found her hostess smile. "Yes, do stay. For Linnie's sake."

Pete gave Grace a stunned, questioning look.

She nodded, an act of supreme effort, of courtesy over common sense.

"All right, little lady." Pete squatted down to Linnie's level. "Looks like you'll have to share your carrots."

"Hooray!" She pulled on Pete's hand.

He struggled to his feet, followed Linnie over the threshold, and shot Grace an apologetic look as he passed her. "Sorry."

She puffed out a breath and closed the door behind them. Of all the men to plop onto her doorstep. *Very funny, Lord.*

Now she had to figure out how to entertain a man she didn't even like. "Dinner's almost ready. Lieutenant, the *Journal & Courier* is on the coffee table in the living room. Linnie, you need to change out of your school clothes."

"But—"

"Rules are rules. Straighten your room while you're up there." Grace motioned her daughter toward the ornate twisting wooden staircase. Linnie obeyed with much thumping and grumbling.

"May I borrow your phone?" Pete took off his service cap and ran his hand through his wavy black hair. "My parents will think I'm lost and call the police."

She rewarded his joke with the slightest smile and pointed to the desk in the living room. "Let me make a quick call, and then you can have it."

After Grace notified the police that Linnie was home, she headed to the kitchen. Why on earth had she invited her childhood bully to dinner?

She opened the oven and tested one potato with a fork. Thank goodness, it was done. The sooner she could end this charade, the better.

"That's quite some girl you have."

Grace startled.

Pete leaned against the Hoosier cabinet and crossed his ankles. He'd taken off his flight jacket to reveal his olive drab shirt, as if he knew Grace disliked anything to do with planes and pilots. Why wasn't he reading the paper?

She wrapped towels over her hands and pulled the roasting pan from the oven. "Where did you find Linnie?"

"Outside Loeb's. Putting together her Christmas list, I guess. She said she likes to explore. Does she do this often?"

It really wasn't any of his business. Except he'd been kind to Linnie and brought her home.

Grace set the roasting pan on the counter, freed her hands, and pulled her platter from the cupboard. "She wanders as often as she can. Whenever she finds enough coins for bus fare and can sneak away after school."

"An adventurous soul. I like that."

"She's not looking for adventure. She's looking for her father."

"Her father? But she said he died in a plane crash. I'm sorry . . . I shouldn't be so blunt."

"He did die." With her serving fork and spoon, she got a firm hold on the chicken.

Pete grabbed the discarded towels and steadied the pan. "Then . . . ?"

She didn't know whether to be pleased that he was helping or annoyed that he stood so close, that he was probing into her life.

Grace sighed and settled the chicken onto the platter. "Linnie was four when George died. He was a fighter pilot based in the Philippines."

"I'm sorry."

He'd said that a lot today. Grace scooped the vegetables out of the pan and added them to the platter. "Linnie was heartbroken. After the memorial service, her great-grandma Kessler held Linnie on her lap and tried to comfort her. She told Linnie her daddy would never be far away. Wherever she went in town, she'd see him—in the windows of the stores where they shopped, among the trees in the park where they played, in the pews of the church where they worshiped."

Pete set the empty pan in the sink and turned on the faucet. Water sizzled in the hot pan. "Uh-oh. Let me guess. Linnie took it literally."

"Yes, she did." Grace stared at his broad back in amazement. No one else understood. "You have to be very careful what you say to Linnie."

"I can see that." Pete shook soap into the pan. "At her age how could she understand her great-grandma meant the familiar sights would bring back memories?"

"Yes." Grace frowned and reminded herself she was talking to Pete Turner. "So she . . . she wanders. She's convinced one day she'll look in a store window and see her father."

"Poor kid."

That poor kid came skipping into the kitchen, right up to Pete. "Come see my treasures."

"I think dinner's ready," he said.

"It is." Grace motioned to the dining room. "Linnie, set a place for Lieutenant Turner, please."

Over dinner, Pete was a strangely well-behaved guest, complimenting the food and asking Grace about her job and Linnie about school.

Perhaps she should reciprocate. Grace sliced the chunk of potato on her plate. "So, Lieutenant, you're a pilot?"

"Just finished a tour with the Eighth Air Force in England, flying a P-47 Thunderbolt."

"A fighter pilot." She put a piece of potato into her mouth, but it tasted dry and mealy.

"Not anymore." He cut up his chicken. "I am done with combat, thank goodness."

"You're still in the army, aren't you?"

"Duration plus six months." His face and his voice went flat. "I have a month furlough, then I report to Nashville January 1. But no more combat for me."

Grace had read something in the *Journal & Courier* about pilots being relieved from flying after they finished their tours. George hadn't lived long enough to earn a safe desk job.

As Pete concentrated on his chicken, she concentrated on him. In her experience, fighter pilots loved to brag about their exploits, but Pete remained silent.

Grace poured another cup of coffee, thankful that coffee rationing had been lifted in the summer. "I heard a rumor that you're a lawyer, like your father."

"That rumor's true." The flatness washed from his eyes. "I was practicing with a firm in Indianapolis before the war."

"I was surprised when I heard." Grace sipped her coffee. "I thought you were more familiar with the other side of the law."

"I was. Before I turned my life around."

Linnie let out a gigantic sigh. "Why do grownups always talk about boring stuff?"

"Linnie, your manners."

But Pete laughed. "We do, don't we? Someday you'll be a boring old grownup too."

"Are you done eating?" Linnie pushed away her plate. "I want to show you my treasures."

"Not yet." Pete lifted his coffee cup. "May I—"

"Of course." She topped off his cup, although she preferred not to prolong the meal. "Besides, young lady, you're going to bed early for wandering again. You'd already be in bed if the lieutenant wasn't here."

Linnie tapped her fork on her plate. "I won't wander ever again."

Grace's mouth drifted open.

Pete chuckled. "You've heard that before, haven't you?"

"No. No, I haven't." Grace scrutinized her daughter's face. "What made you change your mind, honey?"

Linnie beamed, exposing her missing teeth and a bit of chicken trapped in one of the holes. "It finally happened. It came true just like Great-Grandma said."

Grace's thoughts slowed. "What . . . what happened?"

Linnie bounced in her chair. "I saw my daddy."

Oh no. And in front of a stranger. She flicked her gaze to Pete but saw compassion instead of condemnation.

Grace leaned toward her daughter, her heart aching. "Honey, Daddy's in heaven."

"I know that."

Pete gave Grace a relieved look, which she returned. Then they both took sips of coffee.

"I didn't see my old daddy. I saw my new daddy." Linnie pointed at Pete.

Tandem spurts of coffee flew from their mouths.

Linnie giggled. "That was funny. Do it again."

Grace gasped and blotted her face with her napkin. "You shouldn't say such things."

"But you always say, 'Tell the truth,' so I'm telling the truth."

If only Grace could blame this fiasco on Pete Turner, but he looked baffled and embarrassed, and he dabbed at coffee dribbles on his shirt.

"Linnie," she said in a low voice. "We'll talk about this later."

"Uh-huh." Linnie stood the fork up on her plate, tines down, and walked it across the plate. "I was praying. I promised God I'd be good and stop wandering if only He showed me my daddy just once. Then I heard Mr. Turner's voice and I opened my eyes. There he was. Right in the window. And he has such a nice face, don't you think, Mommy?"

Pete dampened his napkin in his water glass. "As a lawyer, I recommend you plead the Fifth."

"It's not funny," Grace said.

"I know." He stopped cleaning his shirt and fixed a serious gaze on her. "You have to be very careful what you tell Linnie."

"Yes."

He pushed his chair back, came round the table, and squatted beside Linnie's chair. "I'm glad I met you, but I'm not your new daddy. I'll only be in Lafayette for a month, and then I go back to the Army Air Forces. Your mother's a lovely woman, and someday she'll meet a wonderful man to be your daddy, but it won't be me. Do you understand?"

One corner of Linnie's mouth dimpled. "You'll see."

Grace groaned. Her daughter had exchanged one delusion for another.

"I tried." Pete shrugged. "Maybe I should get going."

"That would be wise." Grace folded her napkin. "Linnie, get ready for bed. I'll come up in a few minutes to tuck you in."

Linnie's face reddened, and her foot banged the chair leg, the thunder before the storm. But then she looked at Pete, her foot stilled, and she hopped off her chair and skipped away.

Grace released her death grip on her napkin. If her daughter had to have a delusion, at least this one promoted good behavior.

Pete headed for the door, picking up his hat and jacket from the coatrack. As a good hostess, Grace went to see him out. She smoothed down her suit jacket and found a lump in the right hip pocket. She worked her fingers inside. Ruby's mistletoe.

Heat rose to her cheeks. Of all things, of all days, in front of Pete Turner, of all people.

Pete stopped at the door. "Thanks for a great dinner. I know it was hard for you, so I appreciate it."

"Thank you."

"And I know you'll get Linnie straightened out on this matter." He extended his hand. "Good night."

"Good night." The least she could do was shake his hand, but when she pulled her fingers from her pocket, the mistletoe tumbled to the ground. "Oh, goodness."

"I'll get it." Pete picked it up before she could. He studied it and turned it in his broad fingers.

"It's from work," she said. That didn't even make sense, and her face flamed.

His brown eyes glinted with mischief but none of the old malice. "Only a bully would use mistletoe to get a kiss from a lady." He held the mistletoe out to her. "I'm not a bully anymore."

She plucked the leaves from his hand. "I'm glad to hear it."

But she didn't quite believe it.

## Four

*Sunday, December 5*

astor Hughes's *amen* sounded through Worth Street Church, as rich as the polished dark wood and as bright as the stained glass.

Pete stood with the rest of the congregation and pulled on his olive drab overcoat. Across the aisle and two rows ahead, Grace Kessler sat alone. She'd distracted him the entire service. Her shiny brown hair curling on her slim shoulders. The curve of her cheek. The intent way she watched Pastor Hughes.

If only he hadn't been such a brat as a boy.

Growing up, he'd only noticed Grace as Scooter's kid sister, at least five years younger than he. While he'd been away at college, away in Indianapolis, away in the Army Air Forces, that skinny kid had become a lovely young woman. Who hated him.

With his family, he inched his way out into the aisle. When Grace's eyes met his, he smiled. Her gaze hardened, she flicked him a brief smile, and then she looked away.

"She's pretty, isn't she?" Grandma batted her eyelashes at Pete.

How could a woman half-blind see so much? Pete shrugged. "Yes, but she remembers me too well."

"She needs to get to know you as the wonderful man you are now. I know just what to do." Grandma tapped Mama on the shoulder and whispered in her ear.

Pete groaned. Why couldn't they leave well enough alone?

"Mrs. Kessler!" Ahead of Pete, Myrtle Rawlins barreled up the aisle toward

Grace. "I've been calling your house all week, and no answer. We desperately need volunteers for the Red Cross blood drive, and you'd be perfect."

Grace eased back from the older woman. "I'm sorry. As you know, I have a job. I'd love to help but—"

"But it's your duty." Mrs. Rawlins lifted her thin nose. "As an American, as a Christian, and as a woman."

If he wasn't trapped between pews, Pete would have revived his bullying skills for a good purpose.

Mama got there first. She set one hand on Mrs. Rawlins's shoulder and the other on Grace's. "Isn't it lovely that Mrs. Kessler is already doing her bit? You work at Alcoa, don't you, dear?"

Grace nodded, her cheeks red.

Mama heaved a dramatic sigh. "All that aluminum is vital to the war effort. You *are* fulfilling your duty as an American Christian woman, and as a mother with a child to support. Isn't that right, Mrs. Rawlins?"

Mrs. Rawlins stammered her reluctant agreement and moved on.

Pete nudged Grandma. "I guess Mama learned something from her lawyer husband."

"And from me. Watch this." Grandma inserted herself into the ladies' conversation. "Mrs. Kessler, your parents are out of town this week, aren't they? Would you like to have dinner after church with us?"

Grace's gaze darted over Grandma's shoulder and cemented on Pete, full of suspicion.

He put on his not-guilty face and stepped out into the aisle.

"Mr. Turner!" Little arms latched around Pete's legs. Sunday school must have dismissed.

"Well, hi there." Pete smiled down into Linnie's green-blue eyes, which mirrored her mother's.

Grandma leaned over to Linnie's level. "Do you like kitty cats? I have a cat named Ferdinand."

"You do? I love kitty cats."

"And he loves little girls. How would you like to meet him today? You could come have Sunday dinner at our house."

"With Mr. Turner?" Linnie jumped up and down, just missing Pete's toes. "Oh yes, please."

"Very well then." Grace's polite smile hinted at resignation. "We'd love to join you."

Pete stifled a chuckle. Poor Grace. Bullied by a little girl and a sweet grandmother into dining with a bully. Again.

On the walk home, Pete held Linnie's hand, which was encased in a red mitten. "What did you learn in Sunday school today?" he asked.

"Oh!" Linnie kicked at a tuft of grass by the sidewalk. "Mrs. Thomas told us the story of Elijah and the widow. I said my mommy's a widow, and Mrs. Thomas remembered me to raise my hand."

"A good idea. Makes the teacher happy."

He sneaked a glance behind him, where Grace walked with his sister Abigail and her fiancé, Jackson Lucas. He still couldn't believe his little sister was old enough to have graduated from Purdue, hold two jobs, and be engaged.

"Do you want to hear the story?" Linnie asked.

"Yes, I do." He knew it, but Linnie was sure to make it entertaining.

"The widow and her little boy were starving. All they had was a little meal—that's flour, Mrs. Thomas said—and some oil. The poor widow was going to make one last dinner for them, and then they'd die. Isn't that horrible?"

"It is."

She hopped along like a rabbit. "But you know what? Elijah told her to make a cake for him. Not a birthday cake with frosting but just flour and oil. I know, 'cause I asked."

"Mm-hmm." Pete pictured poor Mrs. Thomas trying to give the Sunday school lesson with countless Linnie-interruptions.

"Can you believe it? The widow was starving, and Elijah told her to give him a cake."

"She had nothing." Pete's thoughts swirled and sorted themselves, slowing his steps. "And she gave."

Linnie tugged his hand. "You know what? She didn't run out. God did a miracle. The more she gave, the more she had. And she and her little boy didn't die. Isn't that amazing?"

"Yes, it is." Pete's words sounded sluggish, mired in this new truth, this old, old truth. Even his one good deed the other night had made a difference. He'd smiled again. He wasn't himself, not by far, but he was closer than before.

Pastor Hughes, as always, knew what he was talking about. If Pete gave in faith out of his nothingness, God would replenish.

∽✢∾

Over dinner, Abigail chatted about her Christmas Eve wedding plans and how happy she was that their younger sister, Merry, was coming home from Miami for the wedding. After she graduated from nursing school, Merry had joined the Army Nurse Corps. She'd ship overseas soon and had a one-week furlough beforehand.

His kid sister was about to see the ravages of war. Could she handle it? *Lord, don't let her be drained like I was.*

Grace's eyes rarely met Pete's, even when he spoke, which wasn't often with the Turner family in high spirits.

"Guess what?" Linnie wiggled on her chair. "I don't have to go to Mrs. Harrison's anymore. I'm so happy."

"Mrs. Harrison?" Mama passed the bowl of rolls one more time. "Is she Linnie's baby-sitter?"

Grace's forehead furrowed. "Not anymore. I need to find someone new by tomorrow."

"By tomorrow?" Abigail leaned forward. "Isn't there a day-care program at the grade school?"

"There is." Grace's lips thinned. "Linnie isn't welcome."

"Uh-uh," Linnie said. "Susie Bishop told me to shut up, which isn't nice, so I pulled her hair. Then Bobby Carroll called me a know-it-all, and I hit him."

Pete almost choked on his creamed peas. That would get her kicked out, all right. Behavior like that had earned him many appointments with the principal's paddle.

Suggestions bounced around the table, but Grace shook her head to each one, her face reddening, her eyes moistening.

Pete pulled some fluff from his roll and balled it up in his fingers. "What happens to your job if you don't find a sitter?"

Grace fingered the rim of her plate and blinked too much. "I won't keep it if I miss another day. I've taken off too much time."

"Oh dear," Abigail said. "If I wasn't so busy working at Glatz's and the nursery school . . . and Linnie's too old for the nursery school."

Mama folded her napkin, smoothing out wrinkles even as new wrinkles creased her brow. "And if only I wasn't helping out in the law office this month. Lottie is still recovering from her gallbladder surgery. I would love to watch Linnie. It's only for a few hours after school, isn't it? And I'm used to active children." She winked at Pete.

He worked up a smile for his mother as an idea formed. A crazy idea. He was a man. And Grace hated him.

"Thank you, all of you." Grace raised a wobbly smile. "I appreciate the kind thoughts. I do. But it's all right. I'll find someone."

No, she wouldn't. Not by tomorrow morning anyway. Then she'd be out of a job.

Unless Pete gave.

Grace buttoned her gray tweed overcoat with shaky fingers. She needed to get home quickly to make phone calls . . . but whom could she call?

"Thank you so much for dinner," she said to Mrs. Turner. "It was lovely."

"Anytime, dear," Mrs. Turner said.

Pete stepped close, far too close. "May I speak to you in private? I'd like to ask you something."

Since his parents were occupied saying good-bye to Linnie, Grace could tell the truth. "I assure you, whatever you have to ask, the answer is no."

He glanced away. "I'm not asking you out," he said in a low, grumbling voice. "And I'm not asking you to like me or to trust me. I ask only that you listen to what I have to say."

Grace's stomach twisted around Mrs. Turner's fried chicken. "I need to—"

Pete's grandmother clapped her hands and leaned closer to Linnie. "Oh dear. I never showed you all my pretty yarn as I promised. We can't have that. May I borrow your darling daughter for a few more minutes, Grace?"

"Of course." Why did Grace have the feeling that sweet little old lady was in cahoots with her grandson?

Pete opened the front door for Grace. "Why don't we go to the side porch? There's a swing for you to sit on."

For heaven's sake. Grace marched outside and around to the long narrow porch along the side of the house. She plopped into the swing, smack in the middle, so Pete wouldn't get any ideas about joining her. "All right. I'm listening."

Pete gripped the porch railing and gazed out over the side yard. "You won't like what I have to say, I know. Please hear me through all the way to the end and think about it, all right?"

"All right." Grace set the swing in motion. The side chains creaked.

"My mother was serious about watching Linnie, but she can't help you until January. In the meantime, I'm home on furlough, doing nothing."

Grace planted her feet on the porch in case the swing's motion had scrambled her thinking. He couldn't possibly be offering . . .

Pete leaned back against the railing and stuffed his hands in his trouser pockets. "I'd like to watch Linnie."

"You must be joking."

"No ma'am." His dark eyes carried no mischief at all. "I like her. She likes me. I could pick her up at school, let her run off her wiggles, then make her do her homework and chores, whatever you want."

If almost any other person in town had offered, she'd have accepted. But Pete Turner? Heat filled her chest and puffed out her nostrils. "Why would I trust my daughter to the man who was mean to me when I was the exact same age? The man who almost ruined my family?"

Pete winced and stared at his shoes. "You'd rather lose your job than—"

"My daughter comes first." Grace's voice wavered, half in anger, half from the fear of losing her job.

He expelled a long breath, which curled white in the crisp air. "No matter how much a man changes, he still faces the consequences of his sins."

"That's true." Grace scooted forward to stand. "I appreciate the offer, but—"

"Wait." He held up one hand with the forcefulness of a prosecutor. "Perhaps if you knew the full story."

"The full story?"

He crossed the porch, leaned against the wall, and gazed through the window into the dining room. "If you knew how and why I changed, you might believe that I did change."

Something made Grace sit back in the swing. Whether it was the pained look on his face, her promise to hear him out, the juicy lure of a story—she wasn't sure. Perhaps the combination of all three. "Did you get *your* father arrested too?"

He ducked his chin. "No. And I tried to warn Scooter. It was in '25, at the height of Prohibition. We were thirteen, the youngest kids in the gang, and we wanted to impress the older boys. So Scooter volunteered your dad's store to hide the stolen liquor—it was only a few doors down from the speakeasy. I told him it was a bad idea, but the gang latched on to it."

Grace rubbed her gloved hands to keep warm. That did sound like Scooter, always trying to please.

"The fellows from the speakeasy couldn't report the robberies since they were running an illegal business. They had a thug follow us one night, then called in an anonymous tip about your father. They must have figured that would stop the robberies. It did."

Her father had never forgotten the indignity of being arrested. "Thank goodness the police released my father."

"Making that confession was the hardest thing Scooter and I ever did."

"You . . . you confessed too?" She was only seven years old at the time. Perhaps she'd forgotten some details—or had never been told.

"Of course." His dark brows pinched together. "That was all Scooter needed to turn his life around. I wish it had been enough for me."

Grace rocked the swing. He still hadn't told her why he'd changed. "What happened?"

"You know my brother, Alfie, died in a car crash in 1927, right?" His voice barely reached her ears.

"Right."

"What you don't know—what nobody knows other than my parents, grandma, and Pastor Hughes—is that I'm responsible for his death."

Grace pulled her coat tighter around herself and tried to keep the shock from her face. Why did he think this story would persuade her to put Linnie's life in his hands?

Pete crossed his arms over his service jacket and stared through the window. "I was fifteen, and I was drunk. I was down by the river with the gang, long past midnight, almost passed out. My parents sent Alfie with the car to search for me. He shoveled me into the car and headed home. I was in big trouble, and I begged Alfie to let me out, let me sober up and come home in the morning. He refused."

Grace nodded. She was only about nine when Alfie died, but she remembered him as a nice young man, steady and kind and dependable. Everyone loved him.

"So I . . ." Pete's face scrunched up, and he moved one fist up and down like a piston. "I grabbed the steering wheel, yanked it, tried to make him pull over. He veered off the road, into a tree. The steering wheel—it crushed his chest. And he looked at me as he died—right at me—with complete forgiveness in his eyes."

Grace sucked in her breath. She couldn't imagine living with such guilt.

"How could I forgive myself?" He crossed his arms again, bare hands jammed into his armpits. "My family—everyone was grieving. They couldn't see—how could they?—that I was falling to pieces. But Pastor Hughes noticed. He noticed."

"He's a wonderful pastor." Pastor Hughes was the reason Grace had stayed at Worth Street, George's church, and hadn't returned to her parents' congregation.

"He saved my life." Gratitude broke through the pain in Pete's eyes. "He called me into his office and coaxed the whole story out of me. I broke down, told him the wrong Turner boy died in that accident. Alfie was good, and I'd never be good like Alfie."

Grace chewed on her lips. How many times had she heard her parents say the wrong boy died that day? How many times had she thought it herself?

"Pastor Hughes said I was right. I could never be good like Alfie. God made Alfie compliant and thoughtful and eager to please, while God made me bold and energetic and full of life. God didn't want me to be good like Alfie, but to be good like Pete. Pastor Hughes told me to grab hold of all the great gifts the Lord had given me and to throw out the trash I'd added, and then I could be good like Pete."

Compassion squeezed at Grace's heart and chipped at her resolve.

Pete strode back to the railing. "That day I turned my life over to the Lord. I gave up the old gang and all my stupid ways and threw myself into my studies. I was—*am*—determined to be the best Pete I can be."

She found her voice. "I'm glad to hear that."

"But I bear the consequences. People in town—some of them still don't trust me. That's why I practiced law in Indianapolis rather than here with my dad."

Grace squirmed. She certainly understood about people not trusting him.

"How about you?" He fixed a sharp gaze on her. "Do you believe God can change people?"

When did the porch swing transform into a witness stand? "I . . . I . . . of course."

"So will you let me watch Linnie? It would only be for a month. Then I'll be out of your lives forever."

Grace pushed off with her feet. Back and forth the seat swung. Back and forth her thoughts swung. Pete and Linnie did like each other. But how could she trust this man? She held her grudge close, cocooned in painful memories.

Yet how could she say she believed God could change people and not demonstrate it? And if she didn't take Pete up on his offer, she'd lose her job.

She could keep her grudge or keep her job. Not both.

"Please, Grace." Regret swam in Pete's brown eyes. "Let me make it up to you. Let me give."

She stood up on stiff legs. "One day."

"One day?"

"Tomorrow. I'd appreciate it if you could watch her tomorrow. That'll give me time to make some more calls and ask—"

He grinned. The first true, joyful, face-altering grin she'd seen from him. It stopped her heart.

"Tomorrow," he said. "You won't be sorry."

## Five

*Monday, December 6*

A stream of first graders poured out of Ford School's Room 2 on their way home.

This was the same school Pete had attended, a Victorian castle of red brick and turrets and gables that had stood since 1869. He poked his head in the classroom door.

Linnie stood next to the teacher, Mrs. Cole, a middle-aged woman in a beige sweater and brown skirt.

"Mr. Turner!" Linnie said, eyes bright.

"Lieutenant Turner, Linda. One must address an officer by his proper rank." Mrs. Cole extended her hand. "Mrs. Kessler sent a note to expect you."

Pete shook her hand. "How do you do?"

"Very well, thank you." She straightened the girl's hat. "It's unusual for a gentleman to pick up a child. Are you taking her to the new sitter?"

Pete shifted his weight from one leg to the other. "I'm the new sitter."

"But you . . . you're a man."

"Yes ma'am." His smile felt stiff. "I'm home on furlough. Helping a family friend."

"What has become of this world?" Mrs. Cole fluttered one hand in the air. "The war's turned everything topsy-turvy. Women doing men's work, and now men doing women's work."

"If it helps us beat the Nazis, it's worth it."

"Well, it wouldn't be necessary if certain children learned to be good." She leaned closer to Pete. She really did smell like oatmeal, without a whiff of sugar about her. "Then Mrs. Kessler could keep a proper baby-sitter."

In his pocket, Pete's hand fisted. Only his legal training prevented him from speaking his mind. "Thank you for your advice. We'll take it into consideration. Come along, Linnie."

The girl took his hand and followed him out of the classroom, her feet shuffling, her head bowed. "She always says I need to be good. She says I'm naughty. I don't feel naughty inside. I just can't stop talking and moving."

Pete's jaw clenched, and he shoved open the front door of the school. That was how it started with him too. Everyone called him naughty when he didn't mean to be, and eventually he decided if he couldn't be good, he might as well be bad.

He squeezed Linnie's hand and headed down the long bank of steps to South Street. "Don't lis—" He stopped. How could he tell a child not to listen to her teacher? She had to be respectful. But she had to know the truth too.

"Tell you what, Miss Kessler. Why don't you decide where we go today? The park, Igloo Frozen Custard, the—"

Linnie jumped and yanked his hand. "Can we go to the river? I love the river."

"Absolutely." He led her to the city bus stop on the corner of South and Main. "What do you like best about the river?"

Linnie's whole face crumpled in a frown. "I got in trouble last time I said."

"I won't get you in trouble."

She picked up a stick and twirled it like a majorette-in-training. "Pastor Hughes talked to my Sunday school class and said we don't have to be in church to pray, 'cause God's everywhere. I asked if He was by the river, 'cause I like the river. Pastor Hughes laughed—I like his laugh—and said yes, God's even by the river."

Pete smiled. One more reason to like Pastor Hughes.

"So one time when I went wandering, I went to the river and talked to

God, and He talked back. I could hear His voice all watery and strong. But when I told Mrs. Harrison, she told Mommy I was a pagan 'cause I prayed to the river. I had to look up *pagan*. I don't like that word."

Neither did Pete. "You'd be a pagan if you prayed *to* the river, not if you prayed to God *by* the river."

"That's what Mommy said."

And yet another reason to like Grace Kessler. His own parents had always loved him as he was, and Grace loved Linnie as she was.

Pete hailed a bus, paid the fare, and selected a seat. "Remember our game. Seat's on fire."

"I know." But her legs hung limp.

"I told you I was a handful too, didn't I?"

"Uh-huh."

"And I had a big brother named Alfie, who was very well behaved. Everyone always said, 'Why can't you be good like Alfie?'"

Linnie made a face. "I'm glad I don't have a big brother."

"Well, I'm glad I did. He was a good brother. He was always nice to me even when I really did bad things."

One foot swung a bit. "I still don't want a big brother."

"You know what Pastor Hughes told me? He told me I couldn't be good like Alfie, because I wasn't Alfie. But I could be good like Pete. And you can be good like Linnie."

"Good like Linnie?" Her blue-green eyes narrowed.

"The Lord made you just the way you are—bright and curious and talkative and wiggly. He loves you. But He wants you to be the best Linnie you can be. That means absolutely no hitting or hair pulling, and it means learning to talk in class only when the teacher calls on you, and to sit as still as you can."

"It's so hard."

Pete chuckled. "I know. That's why we're going down to the river, so you can run and climb and de-wiggle yourself."

At the far end of the Main Street Bridge in West Lafayette, Pete led Linnie down to the Wabash River. The west bank was shallower than the east. The water flowed gray-green under the clear sky, with no sign of ice yet.

While Linnie ran and gathered treasures and climbed trees, Pete studied the river and listened to the quiet rush of the waters, savoring the calm and his sense of purpose.

Linnie skipped over, her hat hanging down her back by its ties. "See the rocks I found?"

Pete squatted down. "Very nice. Look how smooth they are from the water."

"Do you hear Him too?"

"God?" He looked into her intent little face. "I guess I do. But then I also heard Him up at thirty thousand feet."

"Thirty . . . ?"

"Flying." The word came out short and curt. The last thing he wanted to talk about was flying.

"My daddy flew airplanes. He died."

"I know. I'm sorry."

"Did you shoot down any planes?"

His throat thickened. "Five." That made him an ace.

"Did the people die?"

Images flashed through his head—flaming Messerschmitts, billowing parachutes, exploding Focke-Wulfs. "Some got out. Some died."

"Did any of your friends die?"

More memories surfaced, faces gone forever, names he'd tried to forget, as if that would cancel their deaths. Jake Cohen. Bill Abernathy. Red McClanahan.

Pain gripped his chest. He'd wanted to feel again, but this was why he'd gone numb in the first place. Feeling hurt.

"I'm sorry." Linnie slipped a little round rock into his hand.

He swallowed hard around the pain in his throat and smiled his thanks. Why did one gesture by a child bring more healing than a hundred sermons?

Grace walked at a fast clip from the Alcoa factory toward Main Street. With the temperature in the high forties, she didn't have to slow down to put on her gloves or button her coat.

"Why such a hurry?" Ruby Schmidt's high heels clicked on the walkway behind Grace.

"I need to check on Linnie. I don't quite trust her sitter."

"You don't? Why'd you hire her?"

Grace blew out a breath. "Not her. Him. He's watching Linnie for one day only, so I can find someone else."

"A man." Delight ruffled Ruby's voice. "Is he single? Handsome? Who is he?"

Grace ignored the first two questions. "His family is wonderful, really nice people, but Pete? He was my brother's best friend, and he bullied me when we were children."

"A bully? You're letting him watch Linnie?"

Grace sighed. "He's changed. He has."

"So . . . you never said if he's single and handsome." Ruby nudged Grace with her elbow.

"Yes, he's single." Thank goodness the bus waited at the stop. "And I suppose some people would consider him handsome."

Ruby squealed and jogged up the bus steps. "What's he do?"

"He's a fighter pilot." Grace couldn't keep the contempt out of her voice. "But he's done flying now."

"Ooh! Don't tell Bobby. His job with the railroad is important war work, but oh, a man in uniform . . ."

Grace had already loved a man in uniform, and he was dead. She settled in her seat next to the window. "So—"

"So this handsome, single fighter pilot—was he a horrible bully?"

A long list of his deeds raced through Grace's mind, but forgiveness meant not dwelling on them. "I didn't like him at all."

"You could get him back for all the mean things he did." Ruby twirled a pale blond curl around her finger. "Do you think he's interested in you?"

On Sunday, every time Grace had looked his direction, Pete had been watching her. And it had taken everything in her power not to look his way more often. "He's smart enough not to ask me out."

Ruby smacked her lightly on the arm. "You need to change your strategy, toots. Make him fall in love with you, then cast him aside like an empty ration book. Best revenge ever."

Grace had to laugh. Ruby's plan did have a certain diabolical appeal. "I could never do that. Besides, he's been kind to Linnie—and to me."

"Anyone who's kind to Linnie is aces in my book. If I could talk Bobby into marrying me, I'd quit this job and watch the girl myself. She's a hoot."

"She is." Grace smiled, then pulled the cord for her stop. "See you tomorrow."

As she walked up Cason Street, the glowing light in her living room window filled her with relief. But what if Pete was teaching Linnie to set off firecrackers or something? She darted up the steps, gripping the cast-iron banister, and opened the front door.

Linnie sat curled up next to Pete on the sofa in the bay window, reading him a storybook.

"Mommy!" Linnie bolted toward Grace.

Grace stooped down to hug her daughter. "Hello, darling. How was your day?"

"Wonderful. Mr. Turner took me to the river, and I found lots of treasures, and I climbed trees. Then we came home, and I had an apple and some milk. Then I did my homework, and now I'm reading Mr. Turner *The Poky Little Puppy*. He's never read it before. Can you believe it?"

Pete fetched his service jacket from the coatrack in the entryway. "The airfield library was sorely lacking in children's books."

Grace glanced up at his smiling face—his rather handsome face—while her mind sorted through Linnie's words. She couldn't imagine a better afternoon for her daughter. "Thank you, Lieutenant."

"No. Thank you." He pulled on his jacket and gave her a significant look—he appreciated her trust in him. He turned to Linnie and bowed. "Goodbye, Miss Kessler. It was a pleasure."

"Why, thank you, Mr. Turner," Linnie said in a regal voice.

For some strange reason, Grace didn't want him to leave yet. "Linnie, why don't you set the table?"

"Okay." She dashed back to the kitchen.

Grace followed Pete to the door. "How was she?"

"Great. She just needs to talk and run. Apparently . . ." His voice lowered, and he peered over Grace's shoulder toward the kitchen. "Apparently Mrs. Harrison didn't let her play after school and made her sit still all afternoon."

"I know." Grace chewed on her lower lip. "I didn't like that at all, but I didn't have a choice."

"Well, don't worry." He tugged on his hat and opened the front door. "My mother will make sure Linnie plays before homework. She understands."

So did Pete.

"Good-bye, Grace. Thanks again." He trotted down the steps.

He hadn't even asked for another day, much less the month he'd originally suggested. He accepted her one-day offer and didn't push for more. Like a gentleman.

She leaned against the doorjamb. "Um, Lieutenant?"

"Yes?" He turned and looked up at her from the sidewalk.

"Would you be willing to . . . to watch her for the rest of the month? Well, just till Christmas. I have the week off between Christmas and New Year's."

A slow smile rose on his face. "One condition. Call me Pete."

For the first time, she let herself give him a full, genuine smile. "I will."

## Six

*Thursday, December 9*

What was it about the scent of pine that brought with it that feeling of Christmas? Pete inhaled deeply as he and Linnie passed the Christmas trees in front of the Piggly Wiggly. The smell teased up memories of joy and the hope of joy's return.

Linnie stopped in front of the tallest specimen. "I wish we had a tree."

Pete tweaked one of her little braids. "I'm sure your mom will get one this weekend when she has a day off." The Turners had set up their tree the Saturday after Thanksgiving, but Mama and Grandma bled red and green.

"No, she won't." A sigh lifted Linnie's small shoulders. "Mommy says we can't 'ford one."

Pete hadn't seen any sign of financial difficulties other than Grace's desperation to keep her job. Linnie wouldn't meet his eyes, a reminder of how he used to act when telling a lie. Except why would she lie about that? If anything, she'd disguise family troubles, not make them up.

Another shoulder-heaving sigh. "We didn't have a tree last year either."

Oh, for heaven's sake. Pete could afford a tree. "Do you have ornaments?"

A bright-eyed gaze flipped up to him. "Yes. I saw them in the attic. I had to ask Mommy what *ornaments* meant, and she told me and said maybe next year."

Maybe this year. Pete hailed the saleswoman and paid $1.10 for a six-foot tree. Not tiny and cheap. Not big and pretentious. Just right.

Linnie skipped and sang "Jingle Bells" all the way home. After Pete sent her inside to do her homework, he poked around in the shed, found a saw, and evened up the trunk. Then he let Linnie take a quick break to show him the ornaments in the attic. She was right—more than one year's worth of dust covered the cardboard box.

While Linnie finished her homework, Pete rearranged the living room furniture and set up the tree in the bay window. Linnie insisted he draw the drapes so Grace would be surprised when she came home.

He couldn't wait to see the look on her pretty face.

Every evening, her greeting increased in friendliness. Every evening they talked longer at the door before he left. Every evening she looked more relaxed, more forgiving, more trusting.

Pastor Hughes was a genius. Giving made Pete feel great.

When the doorknob turned, Linnie startled and hid behind Pete. Why wasn't she rushing to her mother as usual? A nasty squirming feeling filled Pete's stomach.

Grace plucked off her gloves and smiled at Pete, her cheeks pink from the cold. "Good eve—"

Her gaze slid to the tree, and she froze. Her face puckered up, and she clapped a hand over her mouth. Her eyes glistened.

Oh no.

"Linnie," Pete said, "are those happy tears or sad tears?"

"Sad." The child's voice came out tiny and knowing.

Silvery trails ran down Grace's cheeks.

What on earth had he done? He never wanted to see tears in those eyes again, and now he'd put them there. Even when he had good motives, he managed to hurt her.


The tree blurred in Grace's vision. She'd told Linnie why she didn't want to decorate.

"Grace?" Pete sounded hesitant. "Are you all right?"

She moved wooden feet forward, pried her hand from her mouth, and fingered a bough of the tree. "George's plane went down on December 9, two . . . two years ago today. I received the telegram on December 22."

"For crying out loud." Pete leaned over and shouldered the tree, preparing to pick it up. "I didn't know. If I'd known—"

"I just wanted a tree," Linnie said, her voice wavering.

Grace touched Pete's arm. "Wait. Don't."

He looked her full in the eye. "Let me get rid of it. If I'd had any idea, any at all—"

"Linnie asked you to buy it."

"She said . . . she said you couldn't afford one."

Grace pulled a handkerchief from her jacket pocket and wiped her face. "She knows why we don't put up a tree."

Pete set down the tree and squatted in front of Linnie. "You have to be honest with me, young lady. You tricked me into doing something you knew your mother wouldn't like."

"I . . . I'm sorry." Linnie pressed a knuckle to one red eye.

"Apologize to your mother, not to me."

Grace dabbed at her own eyes, impressed with Pete's gentleness laced with authority, his stand for honesty, for respect, for . . . her.

"I'm so . . . sorry." Linnie looked up to Grace and broke down sobbing.

Grace knelt and pulled her daughter into her embrace.

"Well, look at that." Pete ran his hand through his hair. "I tell you I've given up bullying, and then I make two girls cry."

"It wasn't your fault." Grace used her damp hankie on Linnie's face. "We'll keep the tree."

"We will?" Tears darkened her daughter's eyelashes.

"Yes, but no dessert tonight because you lied to Mr. Turner."

Pete gestured with his thumb at the tree. "It's no trouble. I can get it out of here."

Grace shook her head. "It's been two years. It's time."

He gazed down at his shoes, then back at her, his look rich with meaning. "You never fully get over a loss like that."

She understood. Not only had he lost Alfie and his sister Annie, but he'd been in combat and had certainly lost friends. "No, but you can move on."

"Mommy?" Linnie tugged on Grace's coat sleeve. "May we decorate the tree now?"

"After dinner." Grace stood and took off her coat. "Let me get dinner started and—"

"I almost forgot." Pete headed toward the kitchen. "Come with me."

Grace unpinned her hat, tossed it onto the cabinet by the door, and followed him. What was he up to?

Pete pulled a casserole dish from the refrigerator. "I was bored this morning, so Grandma and I mixed up a double batch of her famous macaroni and cheese. Half for the Turners, half for the Kesslers. I brought it over before I picked up Linnie."

Grace stared, dumbfounded, as he lit the oven. "You . . . you didn't have to do that."

He slid the pan into the oven. "As I said, I was bored. Now you'll have more time to decorate. Good night, ladies." He gave them a mock salute and turned for the door.

"Pete, wait. Why don't you—please join us."

"Nonsense. My parents are expecting me, and there's just enough for the two of you."

"How much do you think we eat? That casserole is enormous. Besides, you bought us a tree. At least let me reward you with the food you prepared. Please stay."

Linnie grabbed his hand. "Please, Mr. Turner? Please? You can help with the tree. Oh! I forgot!" She ran away. Footsteps pattered up the stairs.

Pete glanced up as if he could see little feet upstairs. "Looks like I'm staying for dinner."

A strange thrill rolled through Grace's chest. "It's only fair. Do you need to call home?"

"I do." He stepped closer, dark eyes sparkling. "Honestly, I didn't plan it this way."

"I know." Feeling warm and relaxed, she indulged in a wink. "If you had, I wouldn't have invited you to stay."

He laughed and headed for the phone. "I don't doubt that for a second."

Grace set the egg timer, then returned to the entryway. She glanced in the mirror and smoothed a few errant strands of hair. If only she could reapply lipstick without looking like a teenage girl preparing for a date. She certainly didn't want Pete to think she wanted to look pretty for him.

Even if she did.

Oh brother. A handsome man showed kindness to her and Linnie, and she tossed common sense out the window.

Grace knelt by the box of ornaments and unwrapped glass balls and other trinkets she and George had purchased, laying them on the coffee table. Her chest felt tight.

Each ornament was wrapped in newspaper dated December of '41. The headlines screamed of panic, of attack, of a nation unprepared, of a divided people huddling together in grief, gearing up every aspect of society for war.

Grace smoothed a crackling sheet of newspaper. How much had changed in two years. Now the Allies had taken back North Africa, Sicily, and southern Italy. They'd turned the battle in the Pacific and were expelling the Japanese from the Solomons, the Gilberts, and New Guinea. The nation hummed with hope and purpose and productivity.

Pete hung up the phone and sat on the sofa. He leaned his elbows on his knees. "Are you going to be all right?"

Grace held an ornament up to the light, and her heart jolted. A plain, silvery glass ball, but George had painted a sprig of mistletoe on it for their first Christmas. What fun they'd had kissing and reveling in their love. She'd only been eighteen. So young, so naive.

"This is . . . this will be good for me." She hung the ornament on the tree.

"Maybe it will," Pete said. "Something I learned this week—boxing up memories doesn't make them go away."

"No, I suppose not." She fingered the paint strokes. Even if her memories had been boxed up, bitterness had leaked out. Maybe if she unwrapped the memories, good and bad, and exposed them to light, she could forgive her husband.

Linnie came thumping down the stairs. "Now I can put this on the tree."

"What do you have there?" Grace asked.

"Um . . ." Linnie hesitated, then held out a small clay heart painted with red polka dots and hanging from a piece of red yarn. "I made it in school. I told Mrs. Cole I made it for you, but I knew it'd make you sad, so I hid it in my room."

Oh, what had she done? Grace had let her grief and anger run this household, and now her sweet little girl was afraid to give her a present.

She sank to her knees, pulled Linnie onto her lap, and buried her face in her daughter's soft brown hair. "I'm sorry, sweetheart. I'm so sorry. You deserve to have a wonderful Christmas."

"But I'm already having a wonderful Christmas. I'm getting what I wished for."

Grace stiffened. Not this again. Linnie had kept her promise so far and hadn't said one more word about wishing for a new daddy.

"What did you wish for?" Pete asked.

Linnie looked at Grace in anguish. "You told me never to talk about it again, but he told me to be honest."

She winced at her daughter's moral conundrum.

Pete's face blanched, and comprehension flooded his features. "A toy. What toy do you want for Christmas?"

Linnie scrambled off Grace's lap and inspected the ornaments on the table. "I want a doll carriage, but there's a war on. Mommy says even dollies have to make do and do without."

"I never understood about girls and doll carriages." He plucked an orna-ment from the box. "Why do you want one?"

"Mommy says she and Aunt Peggy pushed their dolls around the neigh-borhood and met their friends and had tea parties. Doesn't that sound like fun?"

Pete shot Grace a mischievous look. "I'm a boy. So no, it doesn't."

She smiled back, but uneasiness twined around her stomach. She knew where this story was going. "Linnie, come hang that one—"

"Until that day." Linnie leaned over the coffee table, her eyes wide with foreboding.

Pete returned the look. "That day?"

"Not that story, sweetheart," Grace said.

Linnie picked up a tin star and hung it on the tree. "That day Mommy was giving her rag doll a ride, and a mean boy said she was going too slow. You know what that mean boy did? He tied Mommy's doll carriage to the back of his bike and rode away superfast, and the doll carriage broke to pieces."

Pete closed his eyes and tucked in his lips. He was that mean boy.

Grace's heart wrenched for him. "Pete . . ."

He opened eyes full of regret and pain. "I'm sorry for all the mean things I did."

"I know," Grace said. And in that moment, when his pain became her own, she knew she'd forgiven him.

## Seven

*Saturday, December 11*

In the shed, Pete squeezed past the lawnmower and garden tools.

"In the corner," Father said.

There it was. The go-cart he and Alfie had built one summer out of old crates. It was smaller than he remembered, and the whitewash was chipped and grayed. Pete traced the red circle on the side with "T2" painted in the middle, for the two Turner boys.

He moved his jaw around to loosen the thickness in his throat. "You sure you don't mind?"

"Alfie would have wanted it this way."

Yeah, he would have. His brother didn't have a selfish bone in his body.

Pete peered underneath the go-cart. Both axles and the steering mechanism remained, and best of all, the rubber-rimmed tires. "I can't believe these weren't sacrificed for metal and rubber scrap drives."

"You know how sentimental your mother is."

Pete glanced up in alarm. "Are you sure—"

"Yes." Father's brown eyes bore the strong determination he used with great effect on judge and jury. "As I said, she's sentimental. When she finds out you're making a buggy for that cute little pixie, she'll be tickled. She'll probably sew up all sorts of blankets and things."

"She will." Pete set down his legal pad, pulled off his gloves, and felt the tires. They were still in good shape considering the ravages of time and two boys. "I'll leave the frame intact. I only need the axles and wheels."

Father poked around beside the workbench. "I have some good-sized ply-wood scraps over here, an old broomstick, and cans of paint. Help yourself."

Pete hefted up a paint can. "Red. Linnie's favorite. Grace will be pleased."

"Sounds like you're falling hard."

Why try to hide it? He shook the can—half-full. "Maybe."

"Which girl?"

Pete laughed. "Both, I guess."

Father sorted through the plywood, and Pete sketched a doll carriage on his legal pad. How tall was Linnie? He held up a yardstick to estimate her height and then figured out how high the handlebar should be.

After Father set a pile of plywood on the workbench, he smoothed back his salt-and-pepper hair. "Grace has been through a lot. George's death was hard on her."

The muscles in Pete's back tensed, but he pretended to measure the wood. Was Father warning Pete to be gentle with Grace's heart? Didn't he trust his only remaining son?

Father wiped his nose with his handkerchief. "Your mother and I think you'd be good for her."

Pete's stomach jolted, and he gaped at his father. Why did he always assume people thought the worst of him? Perhaps he was the one who needed to trust others more. "Thanks."

"If you ever want to take her out, your mother and I would be happy to watch Linnie."

Pete let out a wry chuckle. "I doubt I could talk Grace into a date."

"Even so, those two young ladies have been good for you this past week. You haven't been the same since—"

"Since I came home. I know." Pete set aside a cracked piece of plywood. "That combat tour drained the life out of me."

"Actually, you haven't been yourself since Alfie died."

Pete's mouth fell open. "Aren't you glad?"

Father rested his hip against the workbench. "Not entirely. Yes, you were a scamp as a boy, and we were heartbroken and sick with worry when you turned to vandalism and drinking, but perhaps you went too far when you straightened out your life."

"Too far? I didn't think that was possible. My life was a disaster."

Father tilted his head and frowned. "Sometimes I think you're trying to live Alfie's life for him, even choosing law."

"I love law. I'm good at it."

"I know. You made the right choice. You're a better lawyer than Alfie would have been."

Pete rubbed the back of his neck. That might have been the first time in his life he'd been favorably compared to his brother—but he didn't like it.

"I hate this dust. I'd be a lousy carpenter." Father wiped his nose again. "You see, you used to be lighthearted and fun loving, always with a crowd of friends. When you cut all the evil from your life, you also cut out a lot of the good things too. We've missed that."

Pete turned to the workbench and scrunched his eyes shut. Since Alfie's death, he'd hidden himself in work and punished himself with solitude—a cage that didn't suit him.

Grace and Linnie were reawakening the lighthearted part of him, the social part of him. Maybe he could finally learn what it meant to be good like Pete.

## Sunday, December 12

Grace set the pile of dirty dishes next to the sink in the Turner kitchen.

Mrs. Turner carried in the platter holding a picked-apart roast chicken. "Two extra red ration points. Won't that be lovely?"

Pete's grandmother peered inside the coffee can by the stove, where they stored cooking grease. "This is almost full. So all we have to do is collect our waste fats, turn them in to the grocer, and we receive two points for each pound of fats?"

"Starting tomorrow," Grace said. "Then the grease is turned into lubricants for guns and glycerin to make explosives."

She traced the whimsical frost designs on the kitchen window from the weekend's cold snap. She could use the extra red ration points to purchase meat, cheese, and fats. If only she could earn extra blue ration points for canned goods. With her full-time job, she didn't have time to tend a victory garden and raise and can her own vegetables.

Outside the window, Linnie screeched and ran past, a streak of red. Pete ran behind her and wound up to pitch a snowball. Grace inhaled sharply. She remembered how hard Pete Turner could throw a snowball. She leaned over the kitchen sink to follow their path along the side of the house to the backyard.

Pete lobbed the snowball so slowly it barely whiffed the hem of Linnie's coat.

Grace smiled and leaned back. He was so kind and gentle with her daughter.

"Why don't you join them, Grace?" Mrs. Turner rolled up the sleeves of her dress. "I'd never dream of making a guest help with dishes, and Abigail is playing in the snow as well."

Grace hesitated, but only for a second. While she wouldn't play in the snow, she'd enjoy watching Linnie. And Pete. After she pulled on her outerwear, she headed outside.

In the backyard, Linnie tossed a snowball at Pete. Her throw was far too short, but he dashed forward and took it in the knee.

"I'm hit!" He dropped to the ground.

Linnie giggled and jumped up and down. Grace laughed too, warmed by his care and her daughter's joy.

"Hi, Grace!" Abigail waved at her from the other side of the yard, where she and her fiancé were building a snowman. "Come help. Jackson wants to build a two-ball snowman, but everyone knows a snowman needs three."

"All right." Grace crossed the lawn, which was covered in three inches of fresh snow, thankful for her boots.

"You want three? There you go." Jackson plopped a puny snowball on top of the snowman. Abigail squealed and pulled it off. He laughed, pulled her close, and kissed her. "All right. Three it is."

Perhaps Grace should give the sweethearts some privacy. She glanced away. Linnie lay on her back making a snow angel, and Pete approached Grace, tossing a snowball up and down with a mischievous smile.

Old fear clamped around her heart—she couldn't help it. "You wouldn't dare."

His face softened. "I pelted you with a lot of these, didn't I?"

"Yes, and smashed quite a few in my face." She didn't want him to feel guilty, but he did need to know his limits.

Pete held out the snowball in his open hand. "An eye for an eye, a snowball for a snowball."

"What do you mean?"

"Go ahead. Smash it in my face. Hard as you can."

She edged closer, but he made no move to throw the snowball or to grab her and wash her face with snow. "Do you mean it?"

"Absolutely."

Grace plucked the snowball from his hand.

"Linnie!" Abigail called. "Why don't you find something for the snowman's eyes and mouth?"

"Okay." Linnie scrambled to her feet and trotted away.

Pete clasped his hands behind his back, lifted his chin, and closed his eyes. "I'm ready to take my punishment like a man." All he needed was a cigarette and a blindfold to look like a prisoner facing a firing squad.

Grace studied his comical expression, and a laugh bubbled out of her. "It's awfully tempting."

He opened one eye, warm and brown. "I dare you."

How could she resist? She grabbed his shoulder and squished the snowball in his face. His shoulder muscles went taut under her hand, but he stood his ground as promised. Then he spat out snow. The ice crystals encrusting his eyebrows and lashes accentuated the sparkle in his eyes. The rascal had enjoyed it.

"Are we even?" he asked.

Something blossomed inside Grace, something forgotten and girlish. "Do you know how many snowballs you sent my way?"

"You counted?" His tie was loosened, his top button undone.

"No, but it was a lot more than one." She bent over and scooped up a handful of snow. "Not to mention how many ice cubes you dropped down my back on summer days."

"What are you up to?"

"Nothing."

A smile surfaced that she hadn't used in years, verging on flirtation. She grabbed his tie and stuffed snow down his shirt.

Pete gasped. His chest caved in as he flinched from the snow. He grimaced, yanked his shirt from his waistband, and shook the snow to the ground.

Grace's laughter was echoed by Linnie and Jackson behind her. Abigail whooped for joy.

Pete's face lit up, his gaze locked onto Grace, and he scooped up snow. "Why, you little brat. I ought to—"

She screeched and ran away, too slow in her boots and the snow. Pete's laughter followed her, big and merry, making her rethink her memories. In her childhood, how many of Pete's pranks were motivated by malice and how many by good-natured mischief? Had she exaggerated the cruelty of his motives in her mind?

A snowball hit the small of her back, but not hard. Now he was unarmed. She dashed for a tree, grabbed the trunk, and swung around it, placing the tree between them.

He gripped the trunk from the other side, his hands a few inches above hers. Laughter brightened his eyes and lifted a smile so engaging, so contagious, she wanted to—

"Let's go out to dinner," he said.

Grace sucked in her breath. "What?"

His grin didn't fade. "At Avalon."

One of the fanciest restaurants in town? Her breath froze in her lungs. She needed to divert him, so she forced a laugh. "Linnie isn't ready for Avalon."

"Of course not. Just you and me."

She eased back. "A date."

"Yes." His voice and face turned serious. "My parents offered to watch Linnie for the evening."

He'd thought this through. This wasn't a spontaneous, impulsive invitation. She rubbed her thumb over the rough tree bark. "I don't think so. Goodness, Pete. Only a week ago, you said I didn't have to like you or trust you, and now . . ."

"Now you trust me with your daughter." He rested his chest against the tree and gave her a crooked smile. "Don't you like me, even a little?"

She inclined her head and leaned back, letting the tree hold her weight. "Maybe a little."

"Good, because I like you more than a little. I thought it'd be nice to go out to dinner and get to know each other better. I know it's fast, but—no, I refuse to give you the line about my furlough only lasting a few weeks."

"You just did." She flicked one finger, tapping his overcoat.

He laughed and gave her a sheepish look. "I guess I did."

She smiled and nodded, waiting to see how the great lawyer would recover from that faux pas, waiting to see which way her heart would bend.

"Tell you what." He rested his cheek against the tree trunk. "Let's set a date for next Saturday evening. That gives you six days to reconsider. You can break the date anytime, no questions asked."

Her arms relaxed and drew her closer, and she brushed the snow from one of his eyebrows. "All right. It's a date."

From the way he looked at her right then and the way her heart responded, she knew she wouldn't reconsider.

## Eight

*Saturday, December 18*

$\mathcal{P}$ete opened the door of the '37 Hudson Terraplane, rescued from imprisonment under a tarp and filled with three precious gallons of gasoline. Grace stepped out and murmured her thanks, pale and quiet as she'd been since he picked her up.

He walked by her side along Ninth Street, refusing to interpret her silence as failure. After all, she hadn't cancelled the date, and she'd invited him to stay for dinner twice this week. They'd talked and laughed together until Linnie's bedtime, growing closer each day.

But tonight was different. Tonight was an official date.

Grace wore red lipstick and a whiff of perfume, and she'd curled and rolled her hair. But she held her shoulder bag across her stomach like a shield.

One tactic Pete took with his legal clients was to ask the big, hard questions straight out. He puffed a breath into the crisp evening air. "Is this your first date since . . . since George—"

"Yes." Her cheek twitched. "And he was my first boyfriend."

At least she gave the big, hard answers straight out. This evening had to be tough for her. Did she feel like she was betraying her husband's memory? "Then I appreciate you accepting my invitation even more."

She raised a twitchy smile. "How about you? Did the big handsome pilot leave a string of broken hearts across the British Isles?"

"Hardly. I haven't dated in . . ." When had he gone out with Betty Jean?

The senior partner at the Indianapolis law firm had begged him to date his pretty niece. That was 1939. "In four years. Wow."

"Oh." She slipped her hand into the crook of his elbow. "Then I appreciate your invitation even more."

All sorts of sensations zinged through him, unfamiliar and fantastic. Father and Pastor Hughes were right. It was time to give, time to come out of solitude.

"You know, since Alfie died, I've had this—" He tapped his nose. "I've had it buried in schoolbooks or pressed to the grindstone."

The corners of her mouth tipped up. "Better than poking it in other people's business."

"True." At Avalon's entrance, he held open the door and took a deep sniff. "But it's time to inhale fresh air and good food and . . . perfume."

She flushed, and once they were inside he helped her out of her coat. Her dress, a dark greenish blue, made her eyes stand out. Two jeweled pins were clipped to the corners of the square neckline, but she didn't need adornment. None at all.

Pete guided her to the table with one hand to the small of her back, relishing the silky material of her dress. When was the last time he'd touched fabric other than military cotton or wool or leather?

They passed tables filled with Lafayette's finest couples, some of whom he knew and some he didn't. Mr. and Mrs. Clyde Rawlins he knew. Officer Rawlins had dragged Pete's drunken, semi-conscious form home on many occasions. Now the policeman settled a hard gaze on Pete, while Myrtle Rawlins gasped, glancing back and forth between Pete and Grace.

Pete's gut constricted, and he dropped his hand from Grace's back. What had he been thinking, taking her out in public?

He settled into his chair and studied his menu. "I'm sorry. This was a mistake."

"A mistake?"

He cocked his head toward the Rawlinses. "Some people in town will never see me as anything but the black sheep. If they want to talk about me, fine. But now they'll talk about you too, and that's wrong."

Even in the dim light, her eyes shone. "Let them talk. If I want to have dinner with an upstanding lawyer and an officer in the service of our nation, then I will. Let them talk about that."

If he hadn't been falling in love with her before, he was now.

Grace returned her attention to the menu. "What looks good to you?"

His date. She looked good to him. But he played along. "I've heard great things about everything—steak, chicken, lobster, frog legs."

After the waiter took their orders, Grace traced the rim of her crystal water goblet with one slim finger tipped in red. "It's not often a humble secretary dines at Avalon."

Pete leaned one elbow on the table and rested his chin on his fist. "You don't talk about your job much. Do you like it?"

"No, but it pays the bills."

As long as he was asking hard questions, he might as well broach the subject that had nagged him for two weeks. "Then why work? I don't mean to be crass, and if it's none of my business, tell me, but didn't George have G.I. life insurance?"

Her mouth pursed. "Ten thousand dollars."

Five years' salary for the average man. "So why—"

Grace barely raised one hand, and she blinked over and over. He'd struck a nerve.

"I retract the question," he said. "The witness may leave the stand."

A smile flickered on her face, then extinguished. "I haven't even told my parents all the details."

"You don't have to tell me."

"Yes, I do. I think telling someone will help me forgive."

He nodded his encouragement.

Grace smoothed the white tablecloth. "George and I adored each other. We were very happy together."

"I can tell."

"But he had problems with money. His dreams were bigger than his wallet. He loved to fly and wanted to start an airline, so he bought one plane, then another, and another. But it was the Depression, and no one could afford to fly. Then one day he crashed. No passengers, thank goodness, and he wasn't hurt, but the plane still had to be paid for. Suddenly George dropped everything and joined the Air Corps. He didn't even discuss it with me. Then he was gone."

"I see. He had some debts?"

"Some?" She let out a short laugh. "I had no idea how many until his memorial service. His brothers, uncles, friends—I forget how many—they'd all loaned him money. A hundred dollars here, a thousand there, and they had paperwork to prove it. He'd bought our house outright, from a business windfall, he told me, but he'd actually borrowed from family."

Pete winced. "He owed a lot of money?"

"Every penny of the insurance. So I need the job to meet our daily expenses." Grace gazed at the chandelier above them, her eyes watery. "But what hurts most is that he lied to me. Over and over, he lied to me. We were in financial trouble, and he concealed it from me because he didn't think I could handle it."

"Or he couldn't bear to admit his failure to his wife."

She gave a sharp nod. "Either way it was wrong."

That explained a lot of her reactions. "Thank you for trusting me with your story."

She lifted one shoulder, and a jeweled pin twinkled in the light from the chandelier. "You trusted me with yours."

Pete's chest filled with admiration for her strength, for her maternal love, for her willingness to listen and forgive and change her opinions. He stretched his hand halfway across the table, palm up, a subtle invitation.

Grace stared at his hand, then up at him, but he didn't retract or waver.

Her hand inched across the table and across his palm, and he drew her slender fingers into his grip. She let out an audible breath and squeezed back.

"There." She raised her chin. "Now busybody Myrtle Rawlins has something to talk about."

Pete grinned, his heart full. "She certainly does."

⚯

"So on Tuesday I gave Linnie twenty pennies." Pete drew a straight line in the frosty night air. "She sets them on her desk. Mrs. Cole takes one penny every time Linnie comments or asks a question and two pennies if Linnie forgets to raise her hand. When she runs out of pennies, she can't speak one word."

"What a clever idea." Grace held Pete's hand as they strolled down Main Street. They'd driven downtown after dinner to take a walk. Gloves eliminated the stimulating warmth of his touch, but not the soft strength of his grip. "Did it work?"

"On Wednesday she ran out before lunch, but on Thursday she did fine. Then on Friday, Mrs. Cole couldn't figure out why twenty questions felt like forty. She counted the pennies she'd collected. Linnie had given her thirty-two, not twenty. The little rascal had slipped in some of her own coins."

"Oh no."

"Then Mrs. Cole asked Linnie to empty her pockets so she couldn't sneak in any more pennies."

"Her pockets?" Grace clapped her hand over her mouth. "Her treasures."

Pete laughed, a rich, rollicking sound. "Sticks and stones and acorns—all over the floor."

Grace broke out laughing and leaned her shoulder against Pete's. "You're so good with her."

"Well, she's good for me." He led her up onto the Main Street Bridge over the Wabash, abandoned by cars and pedestrians at that time of night. Then he slipped his arm around Grace's waist. "You're good for me too."

Although her heart spiraled in the most exhilarating way at his nearness, she reached her arm across her stomach, took his hand, and rolled out of his embrace as if dancing.

He laughed and beckoned her closer.

She gave her head a flirty little shake. "If I didn't know better, I'd say you were using Linnie to make me fall for you."

"I could say the same thing."

"What?"

Pete gripped the bridge railing and faced the river. "You could dangle that cute little thing like bait, reel me in, then cast me aside—pay me back for every mean prank I pulled on you."

"I could." She leaned against the railing. "In fact, my friend Ruby suggested that."

He chuckled, his expression warm in the light of the streetlamp. "Your plan's working."

Grace gazed down at the river, at the dark ripples, and let her shoulder rest against Pete's strong arm, their hands entwined. This was happening so fast, but it was too wonderful, pulling her along like the current below.

Their conversation over dinner had ranged from humorous to deep, and he'd shared how he felt empty after his combat tour and how Pastor Hughes had urged him to give. Gratitude wrapped around her heart in a neat bow. He'd chosen to give to her.

Pete rubbed her back. "It's well below freezing. Are you warm enough?"

Teasing playfulness flipped up her smile and sent her strolling away along the bridge. "First you try the furlough line, and now you try the warm-enough line."

Laughing, he trotted up behind her and spun her into his embrace.

She gazed up at him, breathless, both hands splayed on his solid chest.

"How about the simple truth?" His voice rumbled through her. "I want to hold you in my arms."

Despite the power of his words and of his grip, something gentle in his eyes told her that if she pushed away, he'd let her go. Yet that same power, that same gentleness drew her in.

"Truth—" The word came out hoarse, and she swallowed and moistened her lips. "Truth is refreshing."

Oh goodness, that captivating dark gaze. How had she ever thought him anything but handsome? He was more than handsome, his strong features sharpened by the hardness of life but tempered by the humility required to surrender, to change, to endure.

And he planned to kiss her. He was gathering her closer, the lawyer in him probing every corner of her face for hesitation. Something deep inside her screamed *no,* but something reckless and brave wanted him to kiss her, desperately wanted it.

He leaned in, his lips parting.

*No.* She ducked her head, pressing her brow to his shoulder, and her breath returned hard and fast.

He leaned his cheek against her hair, nudging her hat to the side. "Too soon?"

"Yes. No. Oh, I don't know." She gripped the lapels of his olive drab overcoat. "Two weeks ago I hated the sound of your name, and now . . ."

He caressed her back, firm and comforting. "It's more than that, isn't it? You trusted George, but he lied to you. And then he died, abandoned you and Linnie, and burdened you with debt. It's hard to trust again."

She nodded, inhaling his scent. Although he and George wore the same uniform, it didn't smell the same. They weren't the same.

"You're afraid if I kiss you, you'll fall in love with me, and I'll die and leave you too."

Grace cringed. "That does sound ridiculous." Especially since he wouldn't fly again.

"I guarantee no woman has ever fallen in love with me after one kiss. It takes at least twenty. I happen to be quite resistible."

His coat felt rough under her touch, and she snuggled closer. "You're trying to trick me into a kiss."

"I prefer the word *persuade.* I'm trying to persuade you to kiss me."

"Truth *is* refreshing."

"Mm-hmm. I have an idea." He brushed his lips over her ear.

Everything in her longed to turn to him, but she pulled back a safe twelve inches. "You can't talk with an ear in your mouth, and I want to hear your idea."

"Is that so?" Amusement danced in his eyes. "All right then, my idea. When you go to Glatz's and don't know which flavor of ice cream you want, they give you a sample on a little wooden spoon, right?"

"Right." As if her arms had a mind of their own, they slipped up around his neck.

"How about I give you the tiniest kiss," he said, "and you can see if you like it, see if you want the whole scoop?"

She raised one eyebrow. "A sample spoon?"

His shoulders convulsed, and he laughed good and hard.

Then she recognized the pun, remembered the old songs about lovers spooning in the moonlight, and laughter drew her closer until her cheek pressed to his. "A spoon . . . a sample spoon."

"You want one?" His voice came out low and husky. And irresistible.

She nodded, just the slightest movement, but enough to communicate.

He pulled back, read her expression, and leaned in. His lips barely touched hers, only for a second, and her mouth tingled, warm and alive.

A car drove past, the headlamps illuminating the longing and vulnerability in his face. "Well . . . ?" he murmured.

"May I please have a triple scoop with chocolate sauce, sprinkles, and—"

Pete silenced her with a kiss, full on the mouth, long and powerful and gentle.

Everything inside her melted, swirled, bloomed. Oh, he was wrong. One kiss—one spectacular kiss—and she was falling, tumbling, careening into love.

## Nine

*Monday, December 20*

Pete knocked on the door of Grandma's bedroom downstairs. "It's Pete."

"Come in, sweetheart."

Inside, Grandma's Singer electric sewing machine whirred. Pete peered over her shoulder at the flowered fabric flowing through the machine. "How's it coming?"

"The cushion and pillow are finished. I made them all one piece so Linnie's less likely to lose the pillow. I'm almost done with the coverlet."

Pete sat on Grandma's ancient green velveteen sofa. Beside him, Ferdinand curled up on the cushion for the doll carriage. The fabric looked like Linnie, with girlish flowers, but in bright reds and yellows and blues. "Linnie will love it."

"Grace too." A teasing tone rang in Grandma's voice.

"Yeah." He stroked the cat's soft black-and-white fur. Only seven hours until Grace came home from work and he could sneak a kiss as he had yesterday after Sunday dinner. The looks she'd given him since their date—wow. As sweet and spicy as Mama's gingerbread.

Grandma's time-gnarled hands pressed flat against the fabric and fed it through the sewing machine. "Things are moving quickly with you and Grace."

"Remember I'm only home for another week and a half." He still didn't want to think or talk about flying, but knowing Grace would write to him and wait for his next furlough would make it easier to step into the cockpits of the planes he'd be ferrying.

"She seems quite smitten with you. So does Linnie."

"Well, I'm smitten myself—with both of them." When the cat craned up his head, Pete obliged him with a scratch under the chin. "I feel alive again when I'm with them. I feel complete. I feel like . . . I'm home."

The sewing machine's whirring stopped, and Grandma's brown eyes narrowed at him in that way she had, seeing, knowing, analyzing, deciding.

He cocked half a smile to let her know he was fine. In fact, he hadn't felt better in years.

Grandma went to her nightstand and returned with her Bible. She rotated the chair to face Pete and opened the Bible in her lap. A mix of eagerness and apprehension rolled in Pete's stomach at the sight of those thin pages warped by age, use, and love. When Grandma pulled out her Bible, something good always happened, but sometimes it hurt.

"Okay, Grandma." He made a show of drawing in a deep breath as if bracing himself. "I'm ready. I can take it."

She smiled and shook her head at him. "It does my heart good to see you joking again."

"It's all because of you." He winked at her.

"You charmer. You inherited it from me, you know." She flipped through her Bible. "Here we are. Colossians 2, verses 13 and 14. 'And you, being dead in your sins and the uncircumcision of your flesh, hath he quickened together with him, having forgiven you all trespasses; blotting out the handwriting of ordinances that was against us, which was contrary to us, and took it out of the way, nailing it to his cross.'"

"All right." Nothing Pete didn't know. He'd experienced that forgiveness, the blotting out of countless sins.

Grandma leaned forward. "Don't you see? You are quickened together with Christ. You are alive in Him."

Pete inhaled slowly, feeling for the truth. Hadn't he told his grandmother he felt alive again when he was with Grace?

"A little higher, in verse 10," she continued. "'And ye are complete in him.' In Christ, sweetheart. You are complete in Christ."

He sagged back on the stiff sofa. He'd said he felt complete with Grace. And at home with her. "And my home's with Christ."

"Always and forever."

Pete raked his hand through his hair. Part of him wanted to get defensive, but the other part realized Grandma had a point. Was he searching for fulfillment with Grace and Linnie—fulfillment only Jesus could give?

Grandma rested her hand on his knee. "You came home from England with a hole in your heart. You haven't talked about it, but I know war can be unbearable."

He set his jaw and nodded. Thank goodness she didn't pry.

"Now, I'm happy for you and Grace. I think you're wonderful for each other, but be careful not to use those two little ladies to fill a hole only God can fill."

Pete stood and pressed a kiss to her forehead. "As always, you've given me a lot to think about and pray about."

But something didn't ring right to him. After all, maybe God sent Grace and Linnie to fill that hole in his heart. In fact, Pete was certain He had.

―⁂―

In the dwindling light, Grace paused on the sidewalk outside her parents' store. She could buy Pete's Christmas gift somewhere other than Schuster's Stationery, but she'd only delay the inevitable. Her parents had returned from San Diego last night, and she needed to tell them about Pete before the gossips did.

She steeled herself and entered the store, where Mom straightened the racks of Christmas cards and Dad stocked bottles of ink.

The familiar clean scent of paper and ink filled Grace's nose, and she waved. "Hi there. How was the trip? How are Peggy and the baby?"

Mom embraced her, kissed her cheek, and chattered about the adorable baby. Grace murmured and responded in all the right places while she scanned the display case. Asking about Peggy wasn't cowardly procrastination, she assured herself. No, it was only polite.

What should she give Pete? His pen bore scuff marks and scratches from years of hard use. An officer starting a desk job deserved a nice new pen. However, since civilian manufacturers had converted to military production, the selection was meager.

In a lull in the conversation, Grace pointed to a silver pen. "May I see that one, please?"

Mom slid open the drawer. "That's a man's pen, dear."

"I know." Grace held the box and stroked the metal pen. The burnished finish would stand up well to Pete's rough handling. "It's for the man I'm dating."

"Dating?" Mom's face lit up, and she clapped her hands. "Gerald, did you hear? Gracie is dating. Why didn't you say something, dear? But you weren't . . . when we left . . ."

Her father approached, and Grace gave him an acknowledging nod. "I know. We met—or were reacquainted—the night before you left. Remember when Linnie went wandering? He brought her home. Oh, he and Linnie are so good for each other. He's watching her right now. He picks her up after school—he's on furlough this month. And I . . . well, we started dating." With each word, her cheeks became warmer and warmer.

The light had dimmed in Mom's blue eyes, and Dad's graying brown eyebrows drew together.

"Goodness." Grace forced a laugh. "I thought you'd be happy. You're always telling me I need to date."

Mom frowned. "I heard a rumor today. Mrs. Rawlins, spreading gossip as always, and I told her there was no truth to it."

Grace's cheeks tingled. Mrs. Rawlins had seen her at Avalon.

"She said she saw you with Pete Turner, of all people." Dad straightened the sleeves of his gray suit. "I said she was mistaken, because no daughter of ours would be seen with a bad apple like that Turner boy."

Mom leaned over the glass display case, her eyes beseeching. "I guess she did see you after all. But who was the man?"

Grace kept her shoulders straight. "Pete Turner. We're dating."

"That can't be." Mom's hand fluttered to her mouth. "Darling, don't you remember what he was like? How he picked on you?"

"How about your brother?" Dad's eyes flashed. "Remember how he led Scooter astray and got him into trouble? How I spent the night in jail because of him?"

Why did they lay all the blame on Pete's shoulders? Why didn't they ever admit their son's role? "Scooter wasn't innocent in the matter, and Pete's changed." Her voice wavered.

"No one could change that much." Dad pressed a fist onto the display case. "You were too young to know, but after we laid down the law and Scooter straightened out his life, that Turner boy went from bad to worse. Everyone in town talked about it. He was a menace. If his father weren't so powerful and respected, that boy would be in jail where he belongs."

"Pete straightened out too." Grace's eyes stung. "His brother's death shook him up, and he gave his life to the Lord. He's a fine man. He's a lawyer and an officer in the Army Air Forces."

"He's Pete Turner." Dad's mouth warped. "How could you . . . how could you date him after what he did to your family?"

Grace clutched the little pen box. "He's a good man. I haven't been this happy in years. And Linnie adores him. She's stopped . . . she's stopped searching."

Mom pressed both hands to her cheeks. "You said he's watching her? How could you let him watch our precious granddaughter?"

"Because I trust him." Now Grace's eyes burned. "I've forgiven him because I believe God can change people, and I see it in Pete's life. Or don't you believe the Lord can change people? You certainly believe Scooter changed."

"But you were always such a sensible girl."

"Don't worry." Dad rubbed Mom's shoulders. "It won't last. Gracie is too smart for that."

She had always been the good daughter while Scooter and Peggy pushed the limits. Her hands shook, but she managed to open her purse and her wallet. "How much is the pen?"

"Gracie . . ." Her mother's voice warbled.

"How much?"

"Two ninety-eight."

Grace set down the money and put the pen in her purse. "Don't worry about wrapping it. I'm sure a smart and sensible girl can wrap a present."

"Your mother and I don't want to see you hurt," Dad said.

"Good." Grace settled a strong gaze on her parents, careful to filter out her anger. "Then I pray you give Pete a chance. If you don't, I'll be very hurt indeed."

## Ten

*Wednesday, December 22*

*P*ete led Grace and Linnie under the red-and-white striped awning of Glatz Candies and through the door in the corner. The sweet smell of ice cream and candy made his mouth water.

Linnie dashed to the candy counter on the right and pressed her mitten-covered hands to the glass. "Oh, look."

"One treat this evening," Grace said.

"And I'll buy you ladies a box of candy canes to take home." Pete sidled up to the soda counter on the left and addressed Abigail's friend Hannah. "What ice cream do you recommend?"

"We only have vanilla today," Hannah said. "Shortages, you know."

Grace rubbed her arms. "Isn't it rather chilly for ice cream?"

Pete winked at her but addressed Hannah. "May I please have a sample spoon?"

Grace colored nicely and dipped her head.

"Sure thing, sir." Hannah gave him a little wooden spoon with a taste of vanilla ice cream on it.

Pete licked it clean, never moving his gaze from Grace's pretty face. "I'd like the whole scoop, please," he told Hannah.

"Yes sir."

Pete stashed the spoon in his pocket. "So I don't forget."

"Peter Turner," Grace whispered in a scolding tone, but then she addressed Hannah. "I'd like a sample spoon too."

Linnie ran over. "May I have one?"

"Sorry," Pete said. "You're too young."

Grace laughed, her face as red as candy cane stripes. "Ice cream or candy. Pick one."

"Ice cream." Linnie hopped up and down, and her braids bounced.

Hannah handed them both sample spoons. Grace licked hers, tucked it in her pocket, and gave Pete a sly glance. "I'd rather have candy."

No doubt about it. He'd fallen in love.

He let Linnie pick a table in the back, and he and the little girl enjoyed their dishes of ice cream while Grace nibbled from a bag of chocolates.

Pete had known for certain he was in love on Monday evening when Grace came home from work, hauled him into her kitchen, shut the door behind them, took his face in her hands, and kissed him with tears in her eyes.

She'd told her parents. They didn't approve. But she was proud of him, proud to be with him, and she begged him to take her out in public as often as possible.

She was strong, this woman, and he loved her.

Pastor and Mrs. Hughes approached their table, bundled up in coats, hats, and scarves. "Pete, Grace, Linnie—how nice to see you."

Pete rose to shake the pastor's hand. "Nice to see you too."

"You're looking well." The corners of Pastor Hughes's eyes crinkled.

"Haven't felt this well in years."

The pastor leaned toward Linnie. "I understand you've been watching the lieutenant in the afternoons to keep him out of trouble."

Linnie giggled and wiped ice cream from her mouth. "That's silly. He's a grownup. He watches me."

Pastor Hughes patted her shoulder, then straightened and spread a smile around the table. "This is very good."

Pete's chest felt warm and full. Someone outside of his family was happy to see them together.

After Pastor and Mrs. Hughes sat across the room, Grace slipped her hand under the table and squeezed Pete's hand. "He's right. This is very good," she whispered, her eyes glowing.

If only he could claim that whole scoop right now—or even a sample— but he needed to keep things discreet for the sake of Miss Linnie. He squeezed her hand in return. "Very good."

"Only nine more days." Her glow dimmed. "And then . . . ?"

"Then I'll write every day, and whenever I get furlough, I'll come home."

"You'll be in Nashville?"

"I'll be where they send me. But let's not talk about that. Let's enjoy these nine days."

She flattened her empty candy bag. "I don't want it to end."

"It won't." He laced his fingers through hers. "It's only beginning."

Her watery eyes, her wobbly smile—they gripped his heart.

"None of that." He wiped an imaginary speck of chocolate from the corner of her mouth. "No more talk of January. December talk only. Understood?"

"Understood."

After Pete and Linnie polished off their ice cream, they all headed outside. Across the street, a crowd flowed out of the Lafayette Theater from a showing of *The Man from Down Under,* while farther down Sixth Street another crowd flowed into the Mars Theater to see *You're a Lucky Fellow, Mr. Smith.*

Everything looked bright and colorful. The twinkling marquees, the store windows decked out for Christmas, and the townspeople in a rainbow of scarves and hats and coats. He inhaled the crisp fresh air.

Linnie skipped ahead, singing "Silent Night," and turned right onto Columbia Street.

When the little girl was out of sight, Pete grabbed Grace around the waist and stole a quick, fervent, chocolate-flavored kiss. "It's rude to take a sample and not buy a scoop."

She smiled, returned his kiss, then extracted herself from his embrace. "Linnie!" she called. They had to jog to catch up with her.

A few blocks down, they arrived at Loeb's. This was where it had all started. The Christmas display with its cotton snow and whimsical Santa and appealing toys—and the same little girl in red. But everything else had changed.

Pete held open the door for the two girls he adored, and he grinned at the lights and displays and the song playing overhead: "I'll Be Home for Christmas."

He was. He was home and he was complete. Grandma was only partly right, for the Lord had sent Grace and Linnie to fill his life again.

---

*Friday, December 24*

Grace breathed in the scent of the pine boughs that adorned the walls of Worth Street Church for Abigail and Jackson's wedding. The piano played softly as the guests arrived.

Beside Grace, Linnie wore her new smocked red-and-green plaid dress, her hair in curls. Her legs swung close to the pew in front of them.

Grace set her hand on Linnie's knee. "Don't do that, sweetie."

"It's a game," she said in a hushed voice. "Mr. Turner taught me. I pretend the seat in front of me's on fire, and I see how far I can swing my legs without touching it. If I do, I lose, and I have to sit as still as a statue for the whole wedding. Isn't that awful?"

"That would be." Grace smiled and crossed her hands in the lap of her teal dress. She'd debated about wearing the same dress she'd worn on her first date with Pete, but she didn't have many nice winter dresses.

Pastor Hughes approached the altar, and then Jackson joined him, along with his friend Joey from work and Pete. Jackson looked handsome in a dark suit, but he twitched and pulled at the collar. Pete turned to Joey to answer a question.

While Pete was occupied, Grace admired his wavy black hair and his shoulders, so straight and strong, and the perfect fit of his olive drab dress uniform. Better yet, underneath that fine exterior lay a man of humility and courage and vitality, a man caring and wise enough to teach Linnie a game that allowed her to be herself while respecting those around her.

Grace loved him so much, an ache pressed against her breastbone. How could this have happened so quickly? How could she have passed from hatred to adoration in three short weeks?

As if he could hear her thoughts, Pete looked over and gave her a long and meaningful gaze. He hadn't spoken about love, but he was serious about her and cared for her deeply.

Next week, she and Pete planned to invite her parents to her house for dinner. Pete wanted to apologize. Maybe they'd give him a chance, but even if they didn't, it wouldn't change how she felt about him.

The music changed keys, the wedding march began, and everyone rose to their feet.

Abigail's friend Hannah glided down the aisle, and Merry followed, recently returned from Florida. They wore floor-length, robin's-egg-blue dresses and carried single red roses.

Then Abigail appeared in the doorway on the arm of her father. Her dress was lovely, with a sweetheart neckline, long sleeves, and a gently flared skirt that floated around her feet as she came down the aisle to her groom. Under a filmy veil, she wore her brown hair swept up.

She was so beautiful, and her love for her groom shone in her big brown eyes.

Grace's eyes moistened, and for a moment she allowed herself to dream the next wedding might be hers. To have Pete for a husband? To share the rest of her life with that fascinating man? It would be wonderful. And if she married Pete, she could quit her job at Alcoa, stay home and give Linnie the attention she needed, and even do volunteer work.

Grace closed her eyes. How could she think such things? They hadn't talked about love, much less marriage. It was far too soon.

As everyone turned to watch the bride and her father approach the altar, Pete alone faced the back of the church, faced Grace. Was it her imagination, or did she see love and marriage in his eyes?

Forgiving Pete Turner had led to a greater reward than she could ever have imagined.

## Eleven

Mistletoe dangled from every doorway of the Turner household, taunting Pete. He couldn't kiss Grace in front of Linnie, in front of his parents.

He and Grace spread jigsaw puzzle pieces on the dining room table, and Linnie knelt on the chair between them, bouncing on her knees. The newlyweds had departed for their hotel in Chicago, dinner had been swept from the table, and the last guests had said good-bye.

Jackson had a new design position at the puzzle factory, and he'd left his latest creation, a five-hundred-piece puzzle of a mountain scene, for the family to assemble over the holiday. Which might take longer than they'd expected, since Ferdinand the cat sat on the table and kept batting puzzle pieces to the floor.

By the bay window in the living room, Grandma, Mama, and Merry rearranged gifts under the tree, and Father sat in his armchair, smoking his pipe. At least half an hour of puzzle-solving time remained before Grandma would declare the house ready for festivities. Since Merry's birthday fell on Christmas Day, the family always opened gifts on Christmas Eve.

"Work on the edges first, Linnie." Grace pulled aside some edge pieces, then stood. "Pete, would you come with me? I'd like to talk to you about something in private for a minute."

He searched her face for any sign of trouble but found only a benign expression. She strolled into the kitchen and across the room to the door that led down to the basement. Then she leaned back against the doorjamb, her hands crossed behind her, and tossed a flirty smile upward.

Mistletoe hung in the doorway. She'd read his mind.

Pete closed the kitchen door behind him, ambled over, and leaned back against the opposite doorjamb, his toes touching hers. As much as he wanted to kiss her, he wanted a bit of fun first. "What's up?"

She batted her dark eyelashes at the mistletoe.

He put on his most serious face. "Only a bully uses mistletoe to get a kiss from a lady. I'm not a bully anymore, remember?"

"What if the lady wants a kiss?" She directed those gorgeous eyes at him, and those eyelashes did their magic.

"Sorry. Gave my word." He held up one hand as if under oath.

"Well, I didn't." She leaned into him, wound her arms around his neck, and kissed him.

He sank into the depths of her kiss, drew her close, and caressed her back. Thank goodness she'd worn that silky green dress again. He loved it. He loved her.

Pete nuzzled into the warmth of her neck, and her brown curls brushed his face. "Oh, Grace. I love you."

"You . . . you do?" Her voice sounded soft, strained.

He grimaced and pressed back against the doorframe, his eyes shut. "I shouldn't have said that yet."

"Oh, Peter. My Pete." She stroked his cheek. "I'm glad you did."

"You are?" He opened his eyes, and the glow in her face nearly undid him.

She kissed his chin. "I . . . I love you too. I don't know how I can love you so soon, but—"

He didn't need to hear the rest, and he cut off her words with the longest, sweetest kiss, running his hand into hair as silky soft as her dress. If only he could marry her, marry her right now. Then he'd never have to be apart from her again.

"Pete?" Mama's voice drifted from the living room.

Grace sprang out of his arms.

"I'm in the kitchen." He chuckled and beckoned Grace back into his embrace.

She shook her head, smoothed her hair, and patted her lips as if that could replace her long-gone lipstick.

"We're ready to open gifts," Mama called.

Pete took Grace's hand and murmured, "I've already had mine."

"There's nothing more for me."

"Hush," Grace whispered in Linnie's ear and held her tighter on her lap. "We talked about this earlier. We'll open our presents tomorrow at Grandpa and Grandma Schuster's. But wasn't it nice of the Turners to invite us to stay after dinner for cookies and apple cider and Christmas carols around the piano? And don't you love the matching Christmas aprons Mr. Turner's grandmother made for you and me?"

"I do. They're so pretty." Linnie flapped the red-and-white striped apron tied around her waist.

It was hard to believe her baby was almost too big for her lap. Grace glanced around the living room. Pete played Santa Claus, distributing presents. His parents sat in the navy wing chairs flanking the fireplace, Merry had pulled up the piano bench, and his grandmother sat beside Grace on the sofa, all of them occupied with boxes and tissue. Thank goodness they hadn't noticed Linnie's complaint.

"Excuse me a second." Pete passed behind the sofa, squeezed Grace's shoulder, and headed to the back hallway.

Pete's grandma folded a lavender sweater and placed it on the marble-topped coffee table. "Such a lovely color. You're so sweet, Merry. Knitting for me when you're busy with the Nurse Corps."

"Nonsense, Grandma." Merry smoothed a square of tissue paper. "Until we ship out, we just sit around and do nothing. Knitting keeps me busy."

Grace restrained Linnie as the child reached to finger the sweater. "So you'll head overseas soon?" Grace asked.

"Yes. I hope we go to the Pacific. It's warmer there. And I wouldn't—" Merry clamped her lips together, and her brown eyes glazed over. "I don't want to go to Europe."

"I understand why, dear." Grandma Turner shot Grace a look, an odd mixture of compassion and warning.

Grace responded with a slight nod. For some reason, Europe was a forbidden topic. "Are you looking forward to it?" she asked.

Determination broke through Merry's glaze. "I can't wait. I want to help. I want to make a difference. I want to make sure our boys come home again."

"Well, this is strange." Pete came down the hall, rolling a cart with a blanket over it. "I found this back there. The tag says it's for Linda. Do we have a Linda here?"

Linnie slithered off Grace's lap. "That's me!"

Pete set his hands on his hips. "Don't try to fool me, missy. I know your name's Linnie."

Linnie's brown curls bounced into a blur. "But my real name's Linda. Tell him, Mommy."

Grace shrugged and fought a smile. What had Pete given her daughter? "She never lets me call her Linda."

Pete turned the cart around. "Must be for someone else."

Linnie chased after him. "It's me. I'm Linda. I am."

Grace couldn't contain her laughter. "It's her given name."

"All right then. I'll let you have it." Pete pushed the mystery object to Linnie.

She whipped off the blanket and squealed. A boxy red buggy with a sunshield of colorful calico stood before her. "It's a doll carriage!"

"Oh my goodness." Grace stood and peered inside. A matching floral cushion, pillow, and blanket rested inside, ready for Linnie's doll. Her hand flew to her mouth. It was perfect.

Pete sank his hands into his trouser pockets. "The axles and wheels came off a go-cart Alfie and I made when we were boys. My father donated the wood and paint, and Grandma made all the frilly stuff."

Linnie kept squealing, running her hands over the red broomstick handle, stroking the linens, and raising and lowering the shield, but Grace could barely see through her tears.

"That's the most—" She gulped back a little sob. "The most beautiful thing I've ever seen."

Pete leaned over and inspected the lines of the buggy. "Not as nice as one you'd buy in a store, but I sanded it well. No rough edges."

"It . . . it's perfect." Grace pulled a hankie from her pocket and wiped her eyes. Not only had he given Linnie the only item on her Christmas list—and one unavailable in stores—but the color and fabric fit Linnie's personality.

Best of all, the gift sang of sacrifice and atonement, replacing what he'd taken as a boy and giving it back tenfold as a man.

"Thank you." She groped for his hand, thankful she'd already told him she loved him, because now—when she loved him even more—she couldn't say it.

"I have something for you too." He pried his fingers free and returned to the tree.

Grace sank to the couch. But the doll carriage *was* for her.

Merry crossed the room, opened a drawer in the Hoosier cabinet, and pulled out a rag doll. "Linnie, this is my doll. You can borrow her this evening if you want to give her a ride around the house. Walking, of course. Running might scare her."

"Oh yes." Linnie hugged the doll and tucked her into the carriage.

Pete sat on the couch between Grace and his grandmother and handed Grace a small square box wrapped in green paper.

Grace thanked him with her eyes. Inside the box rested a gold necklace with a delicate old-fashioned heart pendant. "Oh my goodness."

"It belonged to my other grandmother, Grandma Gerhardt."

"It's so beautiful. Would you put it on for me, please?" She twisted away from him and gathered her hair off her neck.

He fastened the chain around her neck. "Read the note in the box."

With her free hand she smoothed the slip of paper in her lap to read his strong slanted handwriting: *My heart is yours.*

She faced him, her chin quivering, and pressed her hand over the necklace, so warm and right, his heart over hers. "I wish I could thank you properly."

"You already have," he said in a husky whisper.

"Oh." She pointed to the tree. "I have a gift for you too."

"These last few weeks are the only gift I need." Pete waited for Linnie to pass by with the doll carriage and then retrieved the present from under the tree.

"It's not much," Grace said. After his deeply meaningful gifts, hers seemed rather flat.

He ripped off the paper and opened the box. He smiled. "So you've seen my old pen."

"I have." A sense of satisfaction straightened her posture. "I thought you should have a nice new pen when you start your desk job."

Pete chuckled and hefted the present in his hand. "Well, that won't be till the war's over, but a man can always use a good pen."

*Till the war's over?* Something squirmed in her belly.

"Speaking of that desk job." Pete grinned at his father. "Are you still willing to take on a partner?"

Mr. Turner leaned forward with his elbows on his knees, his eyes bright. "Always have been. Have you changed your mind?"

Pete's jaw pushed forward. "I want to come home."

Five minutes earlier, Grace would have thrilled at the implication—she was part of the reason he wanted to live in Lafayette. But now the unsettled feeling grew inside her.

"Pete?" she asked. "Your new position with the army . . . it's also a desk job, isn't it?"

He frowned at her, his eyebrows twisted in confusion. "Um, no. I'm a pilot. I was assigned to the Air Transport Command. I'll ferry aircraft—some stateside, some overseas."

"You'll fly?" She fought to keep her thoughts and her voice calm. "You said you were done flying."

"No, I said I was done with combat."

"Look, Mr. Turner." Linnie parked the carriage right in front of Pete. "I found a bottle for the dolly."

"Uh-oh." Pete pulled a little brown glass bottle out of the carriage. "Vanilla? Uh, Mama, are you missing something?"

Mrs. Turner came out of the kitchen with a plate of cookies. "No, dear. It was empty, and I gave it to her."

Pete's dad laughed. "Straight vanilla? Should we put it on the rocks?"

Everyone in the room laughed.

Everyone but Grace, who plastered on a fake smile despite the fear and betrayal clawing at her heart.

Pete would still fly? He'd go overseas? He could be killed just like George and leave her alone again.

All this time, he'd led her to believe he'd be safe. Just like George, Pete had lied to her. He'd told her he was done flying. What else had he concealed from her? Why, oh why, had she let him into her life, into Linnie's life, into their hearts?

For the sake of his family, for the sake of Linnie, the holiday, the wedding—for the sake of all these things, she clamped a lid on her roiling emotions.

The necklace burned like fire against her chest.

## Twelve

With every step toward the Kessler home, the temperature fell in the air and in Grace's demeanor. Linnie strolled ahead with the carriage, singing away, but Grace stayed several feet from Pete, her hands jammed in her coat pockets.

Despite the chill, heat built in Pete's head. He constructed each word of his defense and aligned his points of argument. He'd resolve this tonight. He wouldn't let her go to her parents' house tomorrow harboring false notions about him. After all, he had logic on his side.

Grace opened the front door. "Linnie, park your carriage under the tree and go straight upstairs to bed. It's past your bedtime."

A grumble, but the child obeyed, hugged her mother good night, then hugged Pete. "Thank you, Mr. Turner. This is the best Christmas ever."

He kissed the top of her head. "It sure was." Until Grace overreacted to his new job.

Linnie headed up the stairs. Time to resolve this situation.

"Grace, I know you're not happy—"

She held up one hand, gazing up the staircase. A door shut upstairs, and she wheeled around, fire in her eyes. "Not happy? You lied to me."

He clamped his lips together, determined not to let anger triumph over reason. "I didn't lie to you. Never once did I say anything about a desk job. In fact, if I had a transcript of our conversations, I guarantee the phrase 'desk job' would not be present."

Grace tossed her purse onto the hall table and crossed her arms over her gray coat. "Is that so, Counselor? How about the phrase, 'I'm done with flying'?"

This was where truth would win. "I never said that. I said I was done with *combat*."

"So you'll still fly?"

"Yes, I'll still fly. I'm a pilot, Grace."

She turned to the mirror and unpinned her hat. "You could crash and be killed."

Pete groaned. "It's a lot less likely than when I battled the Luftwaffe."

"But it could still happen."

"Sure, it could. Or I could step outside and get hit by a truck."

Grace turned a wounded gaze on him. "Don't you know what George's death did to me? To Linnie? I won't go through that again. I refuse to."

"I won't—" He stopped himself. How could he promise he wouldn't die? "Do you want a guarantee I'll live to the age of seventy? I can't give that to you. No one can. Life is full of risk."

"But some risks are greater than others, and pilots are the greatest risk of all. If I'd known you'd be flying again, I'd never have gotten involved with you."

Pete set his hand on his hip, looked up to the ceiling, and counted to three. "You knew I was a pilot when we met."

"I thought you were finished." Her voice climbed and quivered.

"Why would you think that? Why would the army stick an experienced pilot behind a desk?"

"Because you've done your bit. You're done. You led me to believe—"

"Hold on there." Pete raised both hands to calm her down. "I never led you to believe anything. The only thing I'm guilty of is *not* talking about my new position."

"Now I know why you didn't talk about it." Her eyes narrowed, intensifying the fire. "You wanted to conceal it from me. George lied to me because he thought I couldn't handle our financial troubles. And you lied to me because you thought I couldn't handle your flying."

"What?" His voice rose, and he wrestled it back down. Anger never won arguments. "Don't put words in my mouth. First you misinterpreted what I said, and now you're misinterpreting my intentions."

"Misinterpreting? Oh! Isn't that just like a lawyer? Twisting my words and using them against me. You haven't changed one bit, Pete Turner. You're still a bully."

Everything he'd kept under control boiled up inside, and he leveled a strong gaze at her. "Bully, huh? Are you going to throw that in my face every time I have the gall to get angry at you?"

"If it fits." She wiggled out of her overcoat and hung it on the rack. "You *are* still a bully. I can't believe I fell for you. I can't believe I fell for another liar."

"I didn't lie." His voice came out low and hard.

"A pilot. I knew better. I will *not* go through that again. I refuse to." She reached for the necklace clasp.

The night Alfie died, when the car hit the tree, when the last breath escaped Alfie's lungs, a sudden realization had slammed into Pete. Everything could change in a moment, and some things could never be undone.

This was one of those moments.

Grace fumbled with the necklace, red faced and muttering. She hadn't truly forgiven him for bullying her, and she never would. She hadn't truly forgiven George for lying to her, and now Pete bore the brunt of that fear and anger.

"Here." Grace held out the necklace, her eyes blue-green ice. "I don't want it."

Pete opened his hand. The pendant plopped into his gloved palm, and the chain collapsed around it in a tangled mess.

He stared at the little gold heart while his own heart emptied. Logic had failed him. Words had failed him. Nothing could be done.

Pete opened the door and stepped outside. A brisk wind blasted ice crystals into his cheek, but he didn't feel it.

He didn't feel anything.

The door closed with the thud of finality. He was gone. Thank goodness he was gone.

Grace breathed hard, the emotion she'd restrained churning up inside, and she wrapped her arms around her middle, staring at the shut door.

Despite his lawyerly words, she could still see the truth. He'd lied to her. And the nerve of him, turning her own words against her. Misinterpreting his intentions? Lawyers!

She marched up the stairs. "Just a dressed-up bully, that's what—"

Linnie sat at the top of the stairs, hugging her knees, her eyes wide.

"Linnie!" Grace gripped the banister. "Were you eavesdropping?"

"No, just listening. You were mad at Mr. Turner, and I wanted to hear."

She must have shut her door to fool Grace and then sneaked back. Grace pointed a shaking finger toward Linnie's bedroom. "That's eavesdropping, young lady, and it's rude."

"Why are you mad at him? Why did you make him go home early?"

"That's a grown-up conversation and none of your business." Grace pulled her daughter to her feet and guided her down the hall.

"You said he lied, and he said he didn't lie, and you said he was going to crash and die like Daddy."

"Linda Marie! That was a private conversation." Grace pushed open the bedroom door.

"He . . . he was mad when he left. What if he doesn't come back?"

Grace folded back the bedspread. "He won't. He won't ever come back."

Linnie's eyes flooded with tears. "But . . . but he has to. He's my new daddy."

"Oh no, he isn't." Grace untied the red ribbon in Linnie's curls. "He will never be your daddy. I won't let him hurt you."

"But Great-Grandma said—"

"That's not what she meant." Grace threw the ribbon onto the dresser, grabbed the hairbrush, and worked on the tangles in her daughter's hair. "I've told you, over and over. She meant you'd remember your daddy, you'd see him in your head. She didn't mean you'd see him with your eyes, and she certainly didn't mean you'd see a new daddy in a department store window."

Linnie cringed and clapped her hand to her head to protect her scalp. "But I prayed, and there he was. God answered my prayers."

"No, He didn't. It was a coincidence, nothing more." Grace set down the hairbrush and yanked Linnie's red flannel nightgown from the bottom drawer of her dresser.

"Did . . . did God lie to me?" Linnie asked. "Why would He do that?"

"He didn't lie. You just . . . you just . . ." Misinterpreted the Lord's intentions? Why would she use those words? That horrid Pete Turner, infecting her very thoughts.

Linnie wiped her eyes and scowled at Grace. "But I want him to be my daddy."

"Well, I don't." Grace flung the nightgown on the bed. "And I'm the one who'd have to marry him. Now put on your nightgown and go to bed."

Linnie's face contorted, and she stamped her foot. "You're mean. You can't send him away."

Grace left the room before she said anything worse. "Go to bed. I don't want to hear one more word about that man."

"I hate you!" Linnie slammed the door and then shouted through it. "And I hate God! You're both mean."

Grace clenched her jaw and marched away. Let the child throw a tantrum. It wouldn't change Grace's mind.

She yanked the bobby pins out of her hair. Pete Turner was the biggest bully of all time—sweeping in, flipping their lives inside out, making them hope and dream. All this time, he knew full well he'd return to the cockpit, and he never bothered to inform her. He knew she was a widow. He knew she had to protect her daughter. How dare he lie to her?

Grace changed into her nightgown, not bothering to wash her face.

She'd let herself like him, trust him . . . love him.

The devastated look in his eyes as she dropped the necklace into his hand.

Grace held it in, held it all in, until she fell into bed and pressed her face into the pillow.

Great sobs wrenched through her body and soul. She'd loved him, and he'd lied to her, and now she and Linnie were alone again.

## Thirteen

*Saturday, December 25*

Grace woke up groggy, her eyes crusty. Why?

Memories swamped her, curling her body into a ball under the covers, and she pressed her hands over her face.

Pete. She'd lost him. Lost his love.

"I don't want it anyway." But her voice sounded feeble.

She tossed off the bedclothes and forced her sore body to stand. In the dresser mirror, her pale face and red eyes startled her. Even her hair looked dull.

Only a day before, she'd overflowed with joy and hope. Only a day before, Pete had looked at her with love and marriage in his eyes. He'd kissed her fervently, tenderly. And the gift, the carriage for Linnie—so sweet, so thoughtful, so humble.

A dry sob convulsed her chest, and she leaned over the dresser and buried her face in her folded arms. How could he be the same man who lied to her? Oh, why had he come into her life? He was a bad apple, just as her father said.

Grace groaned. Her father. Today was Christmas, and she had to face her parents. To think she'd stood up to them and defended that scoundrel. Now she'd have to admit they were right.

Christmas. That also meant she had to pull herself together for Linnie's sake. Grace put on her red gabardine dress to look more festive than she felt, but even powder and lipstick couldn't conceal her misery.

Seven o'clock. For once she had to wake her daughter on Christmas morning. Poor little thing had probably cried herself to sleep.

Regret punched Grace in the belly. She longed to hold her little girl and apologize for being cross. After all, Linnie's dreams had been dashed too. And with her mother heartbroken and furious, the child had no one to comfort her.

Grace opened Linnie's door. She'd even been too upset to come back and kiss her daughter good night. "Lord, forgive me."

The bed lay as it had the night before, the covers folded back in a neat triangle, the nightgown draped over the edge, empty and lifeless.

"Linnie?" A sick feeling wormed through Grace. Where was her daughter? She trotted downstairs. "Linnie!"

No answer. No one in the living room, no presents disturbed. Except . . .

The doll carriage was missing. Linnie had parked it under the tree last night. Cold fingers dug into Grace's heart.

"Linnie! Where are you?"

The coatrack—Linnie's red coat was missing, along with her snowsuit, her hat, scarf, mittens.

"Oh, dear Lord." Grace ran her hands into her hair. "My baby. Where's my baby?"

Linnie had run away again. In the middle of the night. In freezing temperatures.

Grace ran to the telephone, dialed the police, and explained the situation to the officer in the longest, most frantic sentence ever.

Silence on the other end. A deep sigh. "Mrs. Kessler, it's Christmas. Do you expect me to call an officer away from his family to look for a child with Linnie's history? She always shows up. She's probably searching for Santa Claus. She'll come back when she wants her presents. You know she will."

"But this is different, Officer. It's different. She's never run away during the night before."

"Listen, Mrs. Kessler. We'll keep an eye open, and we'll call if she comes in. But don't you fuss. She'll come home. Now good-bye. And Merry Christmas."

The line went dead, and Grace stared at the receiver, mouth agape. He didn't believe her. He wouldn't search for her daughter.

Linnie had been out at night in frigid weather. A sob ripped its way from Grace's throat, and she pressed her fist to her lips. "Oh, Lord, my baby. Please let her be alive."

She grabbed her coat and hat and dashed outside into the frosty morning.

Where had Linnie gone? Grace scanned up and down the deserted street. Usually Linnie went downtown to look for her daddy, but this time was different. This time she had run away because she was angry with her mother.

Grace clutched her roiling stomach. Oh, why had she let her temper get away from her? Why had she taken her anger at Pete out on her child, her heartbroken child? The poor baby had her sweet heart set on having Pete as her daddy.

Grace sucked in an icy breath. Pete as her daddy.

That was where Linnie had gone.

Grace broke into a run.

❦

Pete poked at the scrambled eggs on his plate, which were nice and fluffy, just the way he liked them. But not this morning. His family's sympathy hung in the air, as suffocating as summer humidity. Last night as he struggled to sleep, Grace's words replayed in his mind, as clear as a legal transcript.

Grandma was right. He'd tried to use Grace and Linnie to fill the hole in his heart, and now they were gone. The hole remained, ragged and raw around the edges.

Pete divided his eggs into three equal piles. He'd started with noble aspirations. He'd done the right thing, giving to Grace. He'd solved her baby-sitting dilemma and allowed her to keep her job.

Then he'd used her to escape. He hadn't lied, but he also hadn't told her the hard stories from England or shared his concerns about returning to the cockpit.

That wasn't fair to Grace. He knew she feared loving and losing another pilot—she hadn't concealed it. But he'd dismissed her fears, all so he could dismiss his own pain. All so she would kiss him and fall in love with him.

Pete stabbed his fork at a chunk of egg, splitting it into pieces. *Congratulations, Turner. You succeeded.*

The doorbell rang. Pete lifted his heavy head.

"Who could it be so early on Christmas morning?" Mama frowned and headed for the entryway. The front door creaked open. "Well, hello—"

"Is she here?" That was Grace, and she sounded panicky.

Pete got to his feet.

Grace dashed through the living room, her coat unbuttoned, her hat askew. "She's here, isn't she? Please tell me she's here."

"Who? Linnie?" Pete balled up his napkin.

Grace's gaze darted around the room. "She ran away in the middle of the night to find you."

Everything froze inside him. "She didn't come here. I'd have brought her home."

Her eyelashes fluttered. "She's not here? Oh no. Oh no."

"She ran away in the night? Are you sure?"

Grace covered her mouth with her bare hand. "She . . . she heard us last night."

"Ah." His head sagged back, and he raked his hand through his hair.

Father came around the table. "Did you call the police?"

"Yes. They won't . . . they won't listen to me. They think it's nothing to worry about because she wanders all the time."

Pete's gut felt as scrambled as the eggs on his plate. "But she's never wandered at night, has she?"

Grace gulped and shook her head.

"Come on." Pete charged for the door. "Let's go look for her."

Grace strode up behind him. "I don't want your help."

He thrust his arms into his coat sleeves and returned her glare with his own. "Listen. You don't have to like me, you don't have to trust me, and after today you'll never have to see me again, but I'm helping you find her."

Father and Mama grabbed their coats too. "The more eyes searching, the better," Father said.

Grace blinked and nodded. "All right."

"Where does she usually go?" Merry wrapped a scarf around her neck.

"Downtown." Grace pressed her hand to her forehead. "But this time is different. She's angry with me, angry at God."

"Angry at God?" Pete jammed on his service cap.

She glanced away. "Because she thought He answered her prayers, and now . . ."

Pete yanked on his gloves. He was the answer to that prayer. "Knowing Linnie, she probably went somewhere to give the Lord a piece of her mind."

"The church?" Mama asked.

Light rose in Grace's eyes. "Yes, the church."

"No," Pete said.

The light in her eyes turned to fire. "You think you know my daughter better than I do?"

A vile feeling, slimy as algae, rose in his throat, and he swallowed hard. "The river."

"The river?" Her anger changed to comprehension and then to horror.

"The river?" Merry asked.

"She says she can hear the Lord there." Pete opened the door. "Father, Mama, Merry, head down Columbia, check out the riverfront down there. I'll take Grace in the car farther north. I think I know where she went. Grandma, stay here and man the phone."

In minutes, Pete drove the Hudson down Ferry Street, scrutinizing side streets for Linnie. Grace leaned her forehead on the window, silent. If anything happened to Linnie, how could he bear it?

"I'm not enough for her," Grace said in a choked voice.

Pete frowned at the back of her head. Just yesterday he would have pulled her close to comfort her. "You'll never be enough for her."

"That wasn't very nice."

He groaned. "No mother could be enough. No father could either. Only God can fill the hole in her heart."

Grace's posture softened.

Pete turned onto the road paralleling the river, slow enough to search the trees and slopes.

All three of them had holes in their hearts, and all three of them had tried to fill those holes with each other. And they'd failed. It wasn't enough. It couldn't be.

Pete gripped the steering wheel. *Lord, help us. Help us find Linnie. Fill the holes as only You can.*

Maybe that was the point of giving after all. He thought he'd given to fill others. He thought giving would allow others to fill him. But he'd had it wrong. Giving laid the holes bare and revealed his insufficiency to fill or be filled. To truly give, he had to lean wholly on God. The Lord alone could use him to help others, and the Lord alone could replenish his empty stores.

"There!" Grace pointed ahead. "Stop!"

Something red by the side of the road caught his eye and stabbed him in the gut. "Oh no."

He pulled closer. The red object wasn't Linnie, thank goodness, but the doll carriage, tipped over.

Grace scrambled out of the car. "Linnie!"

A tiny voice came from down the slope. "Mommy?"

"Thank God, she's alive." Pete dashed to the side of the road and skidded on ice by the carriage, barely catching himself. That was what had happened. Linnie had slipped on the ice and tumbled down the hill. A track in the snow ran down through the brush.

"Linnie! Are you all right?" Grace called, her voice high and frantic.

"My foot hurts, and I'm cold, and I'm stuck, and I'm scared."

"I'm coming, sweetie." Grace stepped off the road.

Pete clutched her arm. "No, let me. I'm stronger." He raised one finger to silence the protest forming on her lips. "And despite everything, you must know I'd never let anything happen to that little girl."

Her face crumpled, and she nodded.

He took off his hat and overcoat and handed them to Grace. "Toss these in the car. Linnie's carriage too."

Pete picked his way down the slope, grasping branches to steady himself. He wouldn't do Linnie any good if he went into the river. "I'm coming. What happened, honey?"

"It was . . . it was so dark, and I slid all the way down here. And my foot got stuck in the bush, and I could hear the water. But every time I move, the bush makes breaky noises, and my foot hurts. I'm scared, Mr. Turner."

"Stay put. I'm coming."

Pete made his way to the patch of red below, and his breath caught. Linnie lay sprawled over a bush, which had bent over, partially breaking the trunk. The branches—and most of Linnie's body—dangled over the river, about a six-foot drop.

"Don't move," Pete said. "Let me figure things out."

Linnie's boot was caught in the roots. If he freed her foot without securing her, the trunk could snap and send Linnie into the icy river. She turned her frightened face to him and extended her arm—just out of reach.

He rested his hand on Linnie's foot. *Lord, help me save this child.*

"Linnie?" Grace called.

"She's here. She's in a . . . precarious situation." Best to use a word Linnie wouldn't know.

"Be careful!" Desperation climbed into Grace's voice.

"What's precarious?" Linnie peered at him through a tangle of brown hair.

He forced a grin. "You'll have to look it up in the dictionary when you get home."

"I want to . . . I want to go home." Her voice shook.

"I know you do." He braced his knee against the root ball and grabbed a fistful of snowsuit fabric by her knee, as far as he could reach and still keep his balance if she fell. "Okay, Linnie, I need you to scoot toward me."

"The bush makes breaky noises."

"I've got you. I won't let you fall." And if she did, he'd jump into the water to save her.

"Okay." She edged toward him an inch or two, then yelped. "My foot!"

"This might hurt too. I need you to be brave." With his free hand, he tugged on her boot and popped it out of the clump of roots.

Linnie cried out, echoed by her mother above.

"Pete! What happened?"

"I had to free her foot." He took hold of Linnie's other leg. "Okay, Linnie, ease your way back to me. You can do it. One hand at a time, like climbing down a ladder."

Soft sobs rocked the girl's body, but she worked her way back from the edge. As soon as possible, Pete gripped her around the waist and pulled her to him. She clung to him, crying, shivering, her face chilly against his.

"I've got her!" he called up the hill.

Grace gave a gasping sob. "Thank goodness. Oh, Linnie."

Now to get Linnie up the slope. "Okay, sweetie, you get a piggyback ride." He knelt in front of her. "Hold on tight with your arms and legs."

"My foot hurts." She wrapped her arms around Pete's neck.

"I know. Do your best." He fought his way up the hill, grasping the sturdiest bushes, his knees slipping in the snow and mud.

Grace stood at the top of the hill, reaching toward them. "My baby."

Pete huffed his way to the roadside and transferred the child into her mother's arms.

Grace clutched Linnie. "Are you all right? You're so cold. Oh, baby."

"Mommy, I'm sorry." Linnie sniffled. "My foot hurts."

Pete opened the back door of the car. "Who's your doctor?"

"Dr. Canfield." Grace slid into the backseat with Linnie in her arms.

"He's our family doctor too. I know where he lives." Pete shut the door for them, climbed into the driver's seat, and drove away.

Only then did he realize how hard he was shaking.

race hovered over the cot in the doctor's examining room and stroked her daughter's cheek. "Feeling warmer, sweetie?"

"Uh-huh."

Dr. Canfield pulled the pile of blankets up to Linnie's chin. Thank goodness he'd been home. He'd arranged to meet them at his office downtown in the Lafayette Life Building, and his wife had called the Turners—and the police—to tell them Linnie was safe.

The doctor motioned Grace to the side of the room. "You found her just in time," he said in a low voice.

Grace swallowed hard and nodded. It could have been much worse.

He folded his reading glasses and tucked them into the pocket of his white coat. "I'll keep her here in the office today for observation. No need to admit her to St. Elizabeth's."

"But your family. It's Christmas."

A smile crinkled the corners of his eyes. "My four boys are off in the service, and my wife said she'll bring a tray of turkey and trimmings and keep us company. Sounds like a fine Christmas to me."

"Thank you." Grace gave him a jittery smile.

"Mommy?"

Grace rushed to her daughter's side. "Yes, sweetie?"

"Mr. Turner—is he still here? I want to talk to him."

Guilt jabbed Grace. She'd barely thanked him. "He's in the waiting room. I'll send him in." No matter how he'd treated Grace, he'd saved Linnie's life.

Pete sat near the door, his bare head in his hands, the sleeves and knees of his olive drab uniform coated in mud. He looked up, anxiety etched into his face. "How is she?"

"She'll be fine. Her ankle's badly sprained, and she has mild hypothermia. Dr. Canfield wants to keep her for observation, but she's fine."

Pete buried his face in his hands again. "Thank You, God. Thank You."

Her heart twisted. He'd never been anything but kind to Linnie. If only that were enough. "She's asking for you."

He sprang to his feet, then paused. "May I?"

"Of course." She took his chair, the seat still warm.

Pete entered the room and sat by the bed, his back to Grace. From where she sat, she could see and hear Pete, but he blocked her view of her daughter.

"Hi there, missy," Pete said. "How do you feel?"

"Warmer," Linnie said.

"Good. You really scared your mommy this morning. Don't ever do that again."

"I won't."

Grace let out a sigh. Linnie told the truth—this incident would scare the wandering out of her forever.

"No matter how angry you get at your mommy, you have to obey her," Pete said.

"I know." Linnie gave a small sob, and Grace scooted forward in her seat, ready to fly to her daughter's side. "I . . . I just wanted you to be my new daddy."

Pete's shoulders slumped. "I hoped I could be your daddy too, but that isn't the plan God has for us."

Eyes stinging, Grace sagged back in her seat. She'd entertained the same hope for a glittering moment. But Pete was right. It couldn't be part of God's plan for her to love and lose another pilot. Pete could die. She had to protect her daughter.

Yet she hadn't been able to protect her daughter last night. Linnie could have died. There were no guarantees in life. None. How could she ask for a guarantee Pete wouldn't die? No one—pilot or lawyer or shopkeeper—could make such a promise.

Grace groaned and hugged her stomach. The only way to avoid loss was to avoid love. Did she really want to sentence herself—and her daughter—to a life alone because of her fear?

Pete patted Linnie's blanket-covered legs. "When your daddy died, he left a hole in your heart, and you thought I could fill it, but I can't. Only God can. He's your perfect Father. He'll never leave you. He'll never die or go away to war. Even if you never have another daddy here on earth, you'll be fine. God's your true Father."

"That's 'xactly what He told me." Linnie's voice rose in excitement.

Grace leaned forward to hear better despite her guilt. Hadn't she chastened her daughter for eavesdropping?

Linnie's feet shifted under the blankets. "Last night on the river, God talked to me. Not in words, but He did, and that's what He told me. And I could feel Him holding me and keeping me safe and warm."

Pete chuckled. "Well, what do you know?"

Grace gripped her coat lapel. Was she willing to let the Lord fill the hole in her own heart? To trust Him alone to protect her and Linnie? To allow love into their lives despite the risks? She thought she could protect herself and her daughter, but she couldn't. Today proved it.

"I still believe God put us in each other's lives," Pete said. "You helped me, you know. And I think I helped you and your mommy. I'm very glad we met."

Grace squeezed her eyes shut. All month long, he'd given to both of them. And what had she given him? She'd made him labor for every crumb of trust, and then she'd thrown him out. And he still gave.

Oh, how could she love him? He . . . what had he done? She could barely remember.

He'd lied.

Grace pressed her hand hard over her eyes. Had he? She racked her brain, trying to remember their conversations. She'd heard him say he was done fly-ing, hadn't she? Or *had* he said he was done with combat, and she'd edited it in her head and inserted her wishes? What if she'd gotten it wrong? What if he hadn't lied to her at all?

Pete stepped out of the exam room, closed the door, and stood a few feet in front of Grace. "I talked to my mother last night. She'd still like to watch Linnie in January."

"Oh." After Grace had broken Pete's heart, Mrs. Turner was still willing to help her? Why did that feel like a punch to the chest? "Thank you."

"If you could send me word how Linnie's doing—through my mother—I'd appreciate it."

"Of . . . of course."

"Do you need a ride home?"

How could he be so kind to her? "I'm staying."

Pete lifted one hand in farewell, a mild smile failing to conceal the pain in his eyes, and headed for the door.

But he couldn't . . . he couldn't leave. She got to her feet so quickly she al-most lost her balance. "Are you . . . are you going to be okay?"

One hand on the doorknob, he turned to her. Irritation flitted around his eyes, but he blinked it away and raised half a smile. "I will. Pastor Hughes was right. I need to give. I'd retreated into numbness, into hard work, into solitude. Giving brought me out of that, and I won't go back. I'll be fine, and so will you, and so will Linnie."

He touched his forehead as if tipping his cap to her, and then he was gone.

All the breath gushed from her lungs. Why did he have to be so nice? It'd be easier if he were angry or if he pouted, but this quiet acceptance shredded her heart. For heaven's sake, she loved him even more now.

She drew the edges of her coat tightly around her. Nothing of the bully remained in him. Nothing.

What on earth had she done?

Grace pressed her open palm against her forehead and inhaled slow, even breaths. Although she longed to run after him, she couldn't. Right now her first and only priority was her daughter.

Back in the exam room, Linnie slept, her brown hair fanned out on the pillow, yesterday's curls long gone. If only Grace could brush her child's hair with soft, loving strokes, erasing last night's sins.

Dr. Canfield rose from his chair in the corner, set aside a clipboard, and tipped his head toward the waiting room. She followed him out of the exam room, and he closed the door behind him. "She's sleeping well. Poor thing must be exhausted."

Grace twisted her fingers together. "She probably didn't sleep a wink last night."

"How about you, Mrs. Kessler?" He patted her arm. "Why don't you go home? You could use some rest."

"I should stay here."

"No need. She's safe now, and she'll probably sleep till suppertime. Get some rest and come back this afternoon. Doctor's orders."

With the authority in his clear blue eyes, she had no choice but to agree.

As she walked home, only Grace's footsteps sounded on Main Street. In the darkened store windows, the holiday decorations seemed colorless and dull.

She balled up her bare hands in her coat pockets. Colorless. Dull. That was how she felt.

In trying to protect her daughter and herself, she'd broken the heart of a good man and ironically made things worse for both her daughter and herself— and almost gotten Linnie killed.

What aching pain. If only she could go numb. But wasn't numbness worse in the long run? Hadn't Pete experienced that very thing? Pastor Hughes had told him the cure—to give.

To give?

Grace stopped at the corner of Main and Sixth, under the red-and-white awning of Glatz Candies. Peering through the dark window, she could almost see Pete leaning against the ice cream counter, winking at her, asking for a sample spoon.

"Give."

Her fingers closed around the smooth wooden spoon in her pocket.

～✧～

For the second time that morning, Grace rang the Turners' doorbell, her cheeks hot with shame.

Mrs. Turner opened the door. "Oh, Grace. I'm glad you came by. Thank goodness Linnie's all right. We've been praying hard all morning."

"Thank you." Grace clutched a box wrapped in green. "Is Pete here? Do you think he'd see me?"

Mrs. Turner's cheek dimpled in sympathy. "He's in the study talking with his father. Make yourself comfortable." She motioned toward the couch and headed to the back hallway.

Grace hung up her hat and coat, set the box on the coffee table, and paced in front of the Christmas tree. The smell of roasting turkey filled the air, Bing Crosby crooned "White Christmas" on the radio, and pans banged in the kitchen—probably Pete's grandmother or sister.

Make herself comfortable? How could Grace be comfortable when she'd never felt more awkward?

Floorboards creaked across the room, and Grace looked over.

Pete stood on the far side of the dining room table, staring at her in silence, wearing a clean olive drab shirt and trousers.

Grace didn't speak either—she couldn't. She fussed with the sleeves of her red gabardine dress, glad she'd freshened her hair and makeup, but Pete Turner was too smart to be moved by curls and lipstick.

She sucked in a breath. "I gave you the wrong gift."

"The wrong gift?"

"Last night. I gave you the wrong gift."

"I do need a pen."

She couldn't face him, so she fingered a pine bough on the tree, the needles fragile and dry. "It was wrong. It was for the man I wanted you to be, not the man you are."

"Oh." His voice hit the basement of resignation.

Could she possibly make things any worse? Avoiding Pete's gaze, she gestured to the marble-topped coffee table and returned her attention to the tree. "That's the gift I should have given you."

Behind her, his footsteps thudded across the hardwood floor. "You don't have to—"

"Yes, I do. Please open it."

The rug muffled his footsteps. An armchair creaked. Paper rustled. "A . . . a woman's scarf?"

"It's the best I could find. The stores are closed, of course. But it's silk."

"Silk? Are you feeling all right?"

She spun around. Oh dear, the confusion on his face. "Fighter pilots wear silk scarves, don't they?"

"Yeah." The word stretched longer than any scarf.

"I should have given you a silk scarf. You're a pilot. I had no right to try to make you into something you aren't, just because I was scared. I'm sorry, Pete. So sorry. We're at war, and our country needs you. Yes, you could die, but so could Linnie, and so could I. I can't protect myself. I can't protect my daughter. I have to trust God."

"Thanks," he said in a throaty voice, frowning at the scarf, at the diamond pattern in shades of blue and green. A woman's scarf indeed.

What on earth was she thinking? "There's more."

"More?" His dark eyes swam with concern.

"In the box." She pointed, keeping her posture straight and her voice assured.

Pete pulled out white tissue, then the second package wrapped in green tissue paper.

When she stepped closer, her knees wobbled and exposed her lack of composure. "Last night you gave me a necklace—your heart—and I threw it back in your face. I'm so sorry."

"Grace . . ." The tissue crinkled in his grip. "You did what you thought was right."

"And I was wrong. I was a bully. I didn't listen to you, didn't trust you. Now I know you didn't lie to me, didn't lie at all. I . . . I heard what I wanted to hear, inserted my wishes into your words. Please . . . please open the gift."

He sighed and ripped open the paper. "The ornament Linnie made you."

"Yes, she gave it to me, so it's mine—my heart. And I'm giving it to you. It belongs to you. Do with it as you wish." Her shaking fingers clutched the side seams of her dress.

Pete stroked the uneven red polka dots. "It's clay. It's fragile."

"I know. I'd be shattered if anything happened to you, but God would see me through. And if you . . . if you don't want to take another chance on me, I'll understand. I'll be broken, yes, but no more than I am right now. God will see me through."

Pete stared at the gift. Then he riveted his gaze on her, more powerful and more gentle than ever. He held out the ornament in his open palm and closed his fingers around it. "I'll keep it safe. Forever."

Oh goodness, he was forgiving her. He . . . he . . . She gulped in a breath and clapped her hand over her mouth.

He moved to stand.

"Wait." She pointed to the box, her voice in tatters. "There's more."

He raised the ornament with a slight smile. "What more could I want?"

"Please?"

"All right." After he settled back in his seat, he opened the final package, wrapped in red tissue paper. He lifted a sprig of mistletoe and the wooden sample spoon, and his smile deepened. "Are you asking what I think you're asking?"

Her pulse hopped around more than Linnie did. "After the way I acted last night, I figured the only way to get a . . . a kiss from you would be to bully you into it."

"Or trick me." He waved the spoon and gazed at her from under his brows with a look half-tender, half-mischievous, and utterly captivating.

Warmth bloomed inside her, melting away her jitters, and she tilted up a smile. "I prefer the word *persuade*."

Pete set down both offerings and beckoned her with one finger. "You don't need to do either."

"Oh, Pete." She rushed to him, and he pulled her onto his lap.

But as she dove down for a kiss, he stopped her with one hand to her arm. "Now I need to ask your forgiveness."

"No, you don't. I was the childish one."

He rubbed her arm, warming her all the way through. "I should have told you everything that happened in England. I should have told you about my new position, about flying again."

"There's nothing to forgive. Nothing at all."

"This week. This week we'll talk." Something dark flickered in his eyes, and his forehead wrinkled.

Her heart squeezed. The stories would be painful for him. She kissed away the forehead wrinkles. "Thank you."

"My mouth is down here."

He cupped his hand around the back of her head, and her lips trailed down his nose to his waiting lips. He drew her in to his kiss, to his embrace, to his love, so passionate and strong and deep.

Somewhere on the edge of her consciousness music played, and the tiny part of her brain not tangled up in the kiss identified the song.

Yes, she was home for Christmas—with a man who loved her and Linnie too, who would give his life for them, who was humble enough and strong enough to change and to forgive.

Pete murmured under her kiss, "I'm home."

"I was thinking the same thing." Grace chuckled and ran her fingers into the dark waves of his hair.

He leaned away from her but examined her face lovingly. "This week we'll talk, and this week we'll have your parents over for dinner, and then, if you're still speaking to me, on New Year's Eve, I'll ask you to be my wife."

She gasped and sat up straighter. "So soon?"

"I know what I want."

Grace sighed and snuggled closer. She knew what she wanted too. "I'll have to say yes, you know. Linnie picked you out in the store window as her Christmas present. I have to keep you."

Pete laughed. "That's the strangest reason to get married I've ever heard."

"Not at all. You're the answer to her prayer—and mine." She turned his face to hers and kissed his fantastic lips. "I'm keeping you."

He traced the outline of her mouth. "For the record, I haven't asked yet."

"And for the record, Counselor, I haven't said yes."

But she would.

His eyes glowed, as wistful and warm as the song wrapping around them. "Home."

# Have Yourself a Merry Little Christmas

by Tricia Goyer

## One

*Thursday, December 21, 1944*
*Nieuwenhagen, the Netherlands*

*G*ray. The color of the sky outside the makeshift hospital.

Gray. The bare tree limbs that reached into the horizon, as if offering naked prayers for the Dutch countryside and its war-torn people.

Gray. The ashen faces of the soldiers as the stretcher bearers carried them in on litters. American soldiers, mostly, but Germans too, like the man who lay on the cot before her.

Meredith Turner tried to be gentle as she bandaged the shoulder of the unconscious German before he awoke confused and in pain. The bleeding from his ears meant he had a concussion—a serious one—but there wasn't much they could do for that except keep him still. She worked quickly. Her fingers did their job with skill and speed so that she could get back to the cleanup work in the operating room.

Not ten minutes ago, Dr. Anderson had shaken his head, telling her their patient hadn't made it. They'd tried their best to save the young American soldier, but his injuries had been too extensive.

She'd stood there, clamp in hand, unmoving. *Another life gone. Another family whose boy wouldn't be coming home.* Pain knotted her gut.

Dr. Anderson had looked at her with compassion. He was one of the few field doctors who understood the nurses' pain when seeing the limp bodies of the soldiers being carried away.

"Change the bandages on that German brought in earlier, and then you can come back and deal with the mess," he'd told her and then walked toward the front door, going outside for fresh air and to clear his head.

Meredith couldn't help thinking of her brother Pete as she bit her lip and finished winding a clean bandage around the arm of the injured German. Pete was home. He was safe. She thought of another man she'd loved once, wondering if he was in harm's way, but she quickly pushed the memory of David's handsome face from her mind. She wouldn't think of him now. To do so would only bring hurt, and she carried enough of that.

Meredith gazed down at the dark-haired man before her. His head was traumatized, and shrapnel had been dug from his arm, shoulder, and neck. His wounds weren't any worse than many others. In time he'd recover and return to his family, who probably waited and prayed. While it wasn't popular to say, German mothers loved their sons as much as American mothers, she supposed. German hearts loved too.

She'd known that kind of love. She'd seen it in David's eyes. The only thing that pushed his abandonment from her thoughts was caring for the soldiers who returned from the front lines in the ambulances' steady flow. Her mind stayed busy doing her part in making sure those men returned home.

*Home.*

Someday she'd return to Lafayette, Indiana. She wanted that more than anything. But since she wouldn't be returning anytime soon, did she dare hope that the Germans wouldn't get too close? That their American field hospital would stay out of harm's way? And maybe, well, was it too much to wish for a little music this Christmas, singing around the piano as they always had in the Turner house?

Looking back, she couldn't believe she'd run so far, leaving behind the family she loved. Meredith had thought she was too big for that town. She couldn't wait to see what the expansive, wide world had for her. To find sunshine and worth. But it hadn't worked.

Well, at least not the sunshine part. Winter in Nieuwenhagen in the Netherlands was the worst she'd ever faced.

Meredith shivered as a cold wind hit the window of the schoolhouse where their unit had set up. The school had four wings, and they put them to good use as a receiving room, a shock ward, surgery, and post-op. She liked working in the post-operation room the best. Even though it tugged on her emotions, she liked being there when the soldiers awoke from surgery. She liked encouraging them, talking of home, and praying with them. She wanted to be the first friendly face they saw when they realized that the war was over for them. Because their injuries were debilitating, for most of them it meant they'd be going home.

There was also a wood-burning stove in each room. There wasn't enough wood to keep the place much above freezing, but the walls offered some relief from the frigid chill outside.

At least it was more protection than the medical tents she'd worked in since July. The maps, posters, and children's pictures pinned to the walls of the schoolhouse brightened her spirits. They reminded her of why she was here— who the American soldiers were fighting for.

The nurses had landed on Utah Beach July 15, a month after D-Day. Meredith had expected to see signs of the struggle. Blood on the sand. Even though the beach was broken up, hit by war, there was no evidence of the thousands and thousands of lives lost there. What the soldiers hadn't cleaned up, the sea had washed away.

From France, they'd moved leapfrog-style, following the movement of troops to the front line. There were three field units in the 53rd Field Hospital. Meredith was in the 3rd Unit. Soldiers with stomach and chest wounds who needed immediate care were sent to them first.

And the sooner the better. Everyone called the first hour after an injury the "golden hour." Depending on his injuries, if the field hospital could get the wounded soldier within that time frame, stabilize him, and treat him for shock, then the chance for survival was good.

Another round of artillery boomed in the distance, causing a shudder to move through the small brick school.

Meredith willed the front lines to stay far away and the supply lines to stay open. She released the breath she'd been holding. Her fingers trembled as she worked, and she wondered if she'd ever be used to war.

Footsteps sounded outside, and two ambulance drivers rushed into the hospital with an injured man. The wounded soldier shivered. His face was as pale as the snow outside.

"He's in shock. We need plasma now!" Dr. Anderson called from across the room. He'd returned without Meredith seeing him.

Dina, one of the other nurses, rushed to assist him. They all took turns with the bad cases. Meredith was thankful it was Dina's turn. She had cleanup to attend to. Would she be able to wipe up the spilled blood without shedding a few tears for the lost soldier this time? She doubted it.

Meredith tried not to think about that as she listened to the shuffle of nurses' feet scurrying around the room. She finished her bandaging, said a quick prayer over the German soldier, and moved to the bucket in the corner to retrieve the mop. Thankfully someone had brought in clean water.

The last operating area waited—empty, silent. She moved toward it and with a swish of the mop started sopping up the blood.

As the mop swished in a swooping pattern, she looked out the window at the mother and three children who hurried by with bundles of wood in their hands. They'd been fighting for those kids. For their freedom. The Dutch people had been under Nazi occupation for years, but the Americans had freed them. The big booms of the distant artillery and the news from the front lines that trickled down to them proved the Nazis wanted to reclaim their lost hold, but the American boys were here to make sure that wasn't going to happen.

Meredith was witnessing history, and all the nurses were glad to be doing their part, though their part was far from easy. A few nurses had already lost their lives on the front lines. To the readers of *Stars and Stripes,* they were sad stories, but to Meredith they were Francis and Betty. Friends she'd laughed with and talked late into the night with, sharing secrets and stories.

Meredith returned the mop to the bucket. As she plunged it down, the water turned red. How much blood had been spilled on foreign soil? Too much. That was why it was so important to find a way to make Christmas special for the injured. Special Christmas music—it was the one thing that wouldn't leave her thoughts. Meredith knew how to sing a number of Christmas carols, and she was sure they'd find more talent among the other nurses and doctors. Maybe they could even practice a few new numbers to help the soldiers feel not so far from home.

In the classroom next door, Dr. Anderson's frantic voice interrupted her hopeful thoughts. The injured soldier who'd just been brought in had been placed on the operating table, and Meredith could hear Dr. Anderson's pleading. "C'mon, boy. Hold on. Your mama wants you home, son . . ."

She nibbled on her lower lip and silently prayed for the soldier. When the doctor's voice lowered into a whisper, she knew they'd lost him too. Another family's prayers going unanswered. Yet they wouldn't know—not for weeks—that he was gone.

So many losses during this war. How could her heart ever handle them all?

eredith pushed the mop bucket back into the corner, and movement by the door of the post-operation section caught her attention. She looked up to see Henk standing there. The Dutch villager, who had to be in his late thirties, was ruggedly handsome, with white-blond hair and clear blue eyes. His cheeks were red from the cold. A stocking cap was pulled down over his eyebrows.

Heat rose to Meredith's cheeks when she noticed Henk's blue-eyed gaze upon her. He tilted his head, and she quickly looked away. He'd done the same thing yesterday.

Under his gaze her emotions stirred—ones she hadn't felt for years. Heat rose up her neck, and her earlobes tingled. She lifted her shoulder to rub her ear. It felt good to be noticed, to be thought pretty even. But the last time she'd let a man worm his way into her heart, she'd opened herself up to heartbreak and shame. Meredith pressed her lips into a thin line, telling herself it could not happen again, especially with another foreigner.

Nancy, a fellow nurse, was perched on a small student's chair, picking pieces of metal shrapnel from the arm of an unconscious soldier. The soldier's left ear had been nearly shredded, but the doctor had hope for his hearing. Dr. Anderson always had hope. Meredith guessed that was what got them all through these long days filled with injured, too-young G.I.s—hope that they'd make a difference and send a boy home in the best shape possible.

Meredith scrubbed her hands in the wash basin, grabbed another roll of bandages from the supply shelf, and then hurried to Nancy's side to assist. As Nancy continued to work on the soldier's left arm, Meredith gingerly took the man's right hand into hers and bandaged a large gash that had been neatly stitched up.

As Meredith sat with her head bowed over her work, Nancy eyed Henk and then leaned close to Meredith. "I think you have an admirer. Mm-hmm."

Meredith finished the bandage, tucking the end of the white cotton fabric into one of the folds. She shrugged. "I probably remind him of a sister or friend or something." She gently placed the soldier's bandaged arm at his side, patting it softly.

From the cocky gaze in Nancy's eyes, she wasn't going to let it slide that easily. Not by a long shot. She jabbed Meredith in the ribs with her elbow. "I wish I could ask Henk if he wants to ask you out on a date or somethin'. I tried to thank him yesterday for all the food and treats he's been delivering from the villagers, but we got interrupted. His English seems pretty good. I wish I'd had time for a longer conversation." She clucked her tongue. "Such a pity. I'd love to know what that handsome stranger is thinking. Of course, we come from two different worlds."

Meredith sighed. "Sometimes where one's from isn't as important as understanding one's heart." The words were out before she could hold them back.

"Are you talking about Henk, the villagers, or . . . what was his name . . . David?"

Meredith shrugged. "The villagers and Henk, of course. I don't want to think about David again." Saying his name left a strange taste on her lips. She quickly licked them, tasting sunshine and salt, like their days at the beach together. She told herself not to go there. Not to let those memories carry her back to her happiest days.

Nancy nodded and rose. "Yes, that's what you say over and over. You tell me just enough to let me know this mystery man broke your heart. Someday maybe you'll tell me the whole story. In the meantime, I'm going to thank our handsome delivery boy with a warm smile."

Nancy approached, and Henk removed his wool hat. His blond hair stuck up in every direction. Nancy took a small basket of eggs from him. Fresh eggs!

Meredith knew what a sacrifice it was for the hungry, war-torn people to share, but their appreciation for the American presence was obvious.

Henk's eyes were still on Meredith, so she moved to the window, pretending to stretch. She'd been tending to soldiers for hours, but she didn't complain. How could she, when so many lives counted on her?

The small village outside the window looked like a hamlet out of a storybook that had been frozen in time. They were in the province of Limburg at the southernmost tip of the Netherlands, situated between Belgium and Germany. The people here spoke a blend of Dutch and German. Nieuwenhagen was a village ten minutes by automobile from Brunssum and an hour east of Brussels. She'd never thought much about this part of the world before, except for the jokes about brussels sprouts in sixth grade geography.

Church Nieuwenhagen looked like any other Catholic church in the states, brick with a five-story bell tower. A clock on the face of the tower still ticked away the time. Maybe the time until the war ended? The edges of the tower, the eaves, and the circular windows of the building were trimmed in lighter colored brick, reminding Meredith of the gingerbread houses that she used to make with her sister Abigail. Across the street from the church, a sweeping knoll appeared to be a park, but it was hard to tell under the snow. A dozen bare trees stretched up into the sky, their lower branches having been cut away, providing heat for the citizens.

The convent was attached to the church, and it was a special place of refuge. The place the nurses called home for a time.

Meredith felt a sense of peace when she entered the convent doors. Just as she was able to rest her body for a time on the cots that had been set up for them, seeing the warm smiles of the nuns provided rest for her spirit too.

The nuns went out of their way to care for the nurses, so thankful were they for the assistance given to the sick and injured villagers. Yet that was what being a nurse was all about, and Meredith wasn't going to let herself get caught up in foolish attraction just because some villager gave her extra attention.

Especially so far from home. Especially with someone who no doubt would choose his loyalty to his country over his loyalty to her. She'd made that mistake before.

Meredith pressed her fingers against the cold glass of the window, and a shiver traveled up her arm and down her spine. She had no hope of finding love again—she refused to risk her heart like that. Instead, she cradled hope that she could make a difference in the field hospital. Another pair of hands poised to assist in surgery, bandage a wound, or clean burns was always needed. As was a kind word and a whispered prayer, comforting a pained man for a moment. As Christmas neared, she'd also do her best to bring a bit of holiday cheer to those who longed for their families and celebrations back home.

*A piano.* She could talk to the nuns and see if they had a piano in the parish. A glimmer of hope pierced through her heart at the thought.

With a deep breath, Meredith took a step back from the window. *Lord, give me strength. Give all of us strength. Help us to be beacons of light and hope to all those who are missing home, even as we're missing home ourselves. And if You could somehow find us a piano for Christmas, I'd be forever grateful.*

Meredith turned her attention to the next patient. His arm had been stitched up well, but he lay there refusing to talk. Refusing to even look at her as she changed his bandages.

She hummed "White Christmas," imagining Bing Crosby's rich baritone. From the way the patient glared at her, she knew this soldier was also German, but one would never know by looking at him. With their bloody, torn uniforms cast aside, the men appeared the same. They bled the same. They needed the same care. Yet it was the deceit of the heart that made the difference. Where one placed his allegiance.

She'd had to reconcile caring for the enemy while also hating his cause when the Germans started arriving in the field hospitals. As a nurse, she couldn't turn away from a man in need.

Finally, the enemy soldier offered her a weary smile, but Meredith's mind returned to another man's face. *David.* David had smiled kindly too. He lived like an American until his deceit carried him back to his home country, taking her heart with him.

*Enough. Think of something else. Think of Christmas. Of music and singing.*

She rose, and the sound of shattering glass met her ears as a small vial of antiseptic slipped off her lap onto the ground, breaking into a dozen pieces.

"Keep your mind on your work, Meredith," she mumbled as she looked down at the shattered glass. Yet how could she stay focused when she searched the face of each German soldier carried in? Her mind chided her heart. *How can you love the enemy?* Or worse: *How could you ever forgive him?*

Of course she hadn't known the whole truth. Hadn't known during their courtship, adventures, and laughter that the man she'd given her heart to would not only betray her but also her country.

Meredith used a dirty cloth bandage to pick up the shards of glass and tossed them into the trash. The rumbling of a truck rattled the window. Her heartbeat quickened as she recognized the sound of the truck's engine. Everyone waited for the supply truck. Not only did it carry whatever fresh food supply the army could find, but it often carried letters and news of home.

She looked around again, noting Henk had slipped out. He'd made his delivery of food, offered from the local villagers, and left.

Breathing a sigh of relief, Meredith hurried to the door of the classroom and moved into the small foyer area. Another Dutch villager mopped away clumps of muddy snow from the white tile floors. She nodded a thank-you to him as she hurried past and opened the front door, glancing outside. A cold gust of wind bit her nose.

She blew out a frosty breath. A soldier with a slight limp moved toward headquarters. On his shoulder he carried a bag of mail. He no doubt would pass around news from the front too as he made his deliveries. Knowing she'd soon get word if any of those letters were for her, Meredith made her way back toward post-op, her army boots leaving a pattern on the freshly mopped floor.

She twisted her lips. "Sorry," she quickly said to the man mopping, then hurried back to her duties.

"I heard a truck pull up. Is it an ambulance?" Nancy called from four beds down.

Meredith closed the door behind her with a small click.

She blew out a heavy breath. "No, the supply truck, and I'm thankful since every cot and litter is full. But I did see a mailbag!"

The weary faces around her brightened. Everyone looked forward to letters from home. Maybe she'd have something from Mama and Dad or Abigail or Pete. An ache filled Meredith's chest at the thought of them.

She guessed the men here had the same aches deep down. She had to bring Christmas to them. But even if she did, would it ease the loneliness in her heart?

$\mathcal{M}$eredith urged herself to finish her task before her mind got all dreamy with thoughts of home. The next shift of nurses would be relieving her soon. *Keep your mind focused,* she told herself as she returned to the German soldier. News of home would come soon enough. Good news, she prayed.

A slow throb of weariness touched Meredith's right temple as she continued changing the bandages on the blond soldier's right arm. His skin was warm under her fingers, and he winced slightly as she touched him. She never could get warm enough in this place.

"Sorry for the cold fingers," she muttered, wondering if he could understand.

Around her, her fellow nurses chatted about their favorite Christmas songs.

"Have you heard the newest one? My mom wrote out the words and music. It came from Judy Garland's new film," Nancy said. "It's called 'Have Yourself a Merry Little Christmas.'"

One American soldier with a large gash on his neck gingerly leaned up on an elbow, eyeing Nancy. "Can you sing it?" A sparkle of merriment lit his face despite his wound.

"I'll try." Nancy cleared her throat and began to sing, "Have yourself a merry little Christmas . . ."

The clangs and clatters of doctors and nurses tending patients dulled as they strained to listen. The stillness—or was it the music?—seemed to agitate Meredith's patient, though. He pushed her hand away, fidgeting. Then his eyes grew round and took on the wild look of an injured dog who'd just been cornered.

With unexpected quickness, he jerked his arm away from Meredith's grasp, pushed off the woolen army blanket, and jumped to his feet. The German's chest was bare—smeared with blood from his wound. Tattered pants hung on his thin frame. He still wore his army boots, caked with mud. In their haste to save his arm, the nurses hadn't removed them.

The soldier took two steps, stumbled, and then righted himself.

Meredith gasped, reaching for him. "No! You're going to hurt yourself. You've lost too much blood."

He turned away, refusing to listen. With shaky steps, he moved toward the dark-haired German soldier lying a few cots down. The blond man shouted something in German, anger clear on his face. He motioned to his friend, who struggled to open his eyes. In a quick movement, the German bent down and pulled something from his boot. A revolver smaller than Meredith's palm.

Voices cried out around them. Nurses dropped to their knees. Some raised their hands, and Meredith's eyes moved to Dr. Anderson. He held his hands steady, putting pressure on the wound of the soldier on his operating table. No one moved. Hardly anyone breathed.

The German shouted words Meredith couldn't understand. He said something to the injured man on the cot and grabbed his arm, trying to jerk him to his feet. The dark-haired soldier cried out in pain, and color drained from his face. He tried to sit up, but he swayed and held his head. Meredith gasped. He had a serious concussion. He couldn't leave.

The German soldier waved his gun at the Dutch villager, who'd just been mopping a moment before, and demanded something. Without hesitation, the older man removed his coat and gave it to the German.

When the soldier reached for his injured friend again, pulling him up, Meredith rushed forward.

"No. *Nein!* Stop . . . you're going to kill him." Ignoring the gun pointed at her, she gently eased the injured man back onto the cot and then stretched her body over his.

Meredith closed her eyes, wondering if this would be it. No one spoke, and she heard movement behind her. Was this the end of her? *Dear God . . . help me now.*

Thoughts of Mama, Dad, Abigail, Pete, and Grandma rushed through her mind. Her heart pounded against the soldier's chest. He released a moan of pain but didn't move beneath her. If the Nazi wanted to shoot her, he'd injure his friend doing it. All she knew was that if her patient tried to escape, he'd never make it. Brain trauma could lead to this man's death. If only she could tell that to the German soldier behind her.

The chatter of nurses' voices carried from outside. The group of women loudly teased and cackled as they walked toward the field hospital. Meredith held her breath, willing them to look inside. To see the danger. To go for help instead of walking in.

The sound of the school door opening split the air, followed by voices. Then the footsteps of the German running toward the women. Meredith turned her head just in time to see the German push through them, knocking one nurse over. His arm dangled at his side as he ran, and he winced in pain. The women cried out, looking over their shoulders to see him racing away. Then they looked at those inside, waiting for an explanation.

"It was one of the German soldiers!" Nancy explained. "Meredith was try-ing to tend to him and . . . he escaped."

Meredith lifted herself off of the injured man. Looking down, she noticed he'd passed out. Would he try to escape when he came to? Her knees trembled as it hit her what had just happened.

"Someone alert the MPs!" Dr. Anderson bellowed. Then, without a mo-ment's hesitation, he returned to the surgery at hand.

Meredith let out a breath and sank to the floor. It wasn't until Nancy rushed to her side that she realized her hands were trembling.

Nancy brushed a strand of hair from Meredith's forehead. "I can't believe you did that."

After seeing the concern on Nancy's face, tears filled Meredith's eyes. Her body softened as if all her strength had been sucked from her limbs. She'd heard of German patients escaping, but never like this. Hadn't someone thought to check him for weapons? No, not when they'd been working so hard to save his arm, his life. He was alive now only because Dr. Anderson had stopped his bleeding and sewn up his arm. Didn't the soldier realize that?

Nancy reached under Meredith's arms and helped her to her feet. "You're still shaking. If you'd like, I can walk you back to our room."

Meredith wanted nothing more than to escape to her room, wrap the rough gray army blankets around her, and be carried away to dreamland. Last night she'd dreamed she was back home. Mama had a ham in the oven, and Abigail and Pete were playing a heated game of checkers. It was a memory of a time before she'd gone to nursing school. Maybe tonight she'd dream about being back in Miami Beach, lying in the sun, breathing in the ocean breeze.

There was only one problem—the memory of that German's wild-eyed gaze.

A shiver crept down Meredith's spine. "Do you think he's still out there?" She turned to Nancy, studying her face. "Do you think he'll come back?" She bit her lower lip.

"No." Nancy shook her head. Her voice was firm. "This is the last place he'll want to show his face." She patted Meredith's arm. "You don't need to worry about him. No Germans will come back around here, Meredith."

Yet even as Nancy said that, Meredith's mind moved to another man. Another German. David had escaped—not in the same manner, but he'd escaped just the same, taking her heart with him.

Her family back home didn't know even half of what happened between her and the man she'd loved. They'd assumed she'd broken things off. She was too ashamed to tell them the whole story.

Meredith reached down and brushed dirt from her olive drab slacks. They were men's pants just like the other nurses wore. She'd cared for a man she now knew was the enemy—as much of an enemy as the man who'd just pointed a gun at her.

Thankfully, David was long gone, back in Germany, she supposed. Yet what about the man who'd just escaped? Was Nancy right? Would he stay away?

He could be lurking somewhere outside their small village even now. Or worse, he might bring others—more of the enemy—to their doorstep.

## Four

*D*aaf sat down to the meal on the table before him. Mash of potatoes and a few beets. No meat. No fat. He hadn't been full in weeks. Months, maybe. Had anyone?

The rations had lessened by the week, and he wondered how much people would have to sacrifice. It was difficult enough to encourage ordinary men and women to continue caring for the strangers they'd hidden away in attic rooms now that the threat seemed to lessen. The Americans were here. This brought them hope. But the Americans' presence also stirred up questions from the villagers. What now? Were they truly free? Would the Nazis return? If Hitler's men had their way, they would.

Daaf's eyelids grew heavy and fluttered closed, partly because he was weary from his work and partly because the calendar reminded him that Christmas neared. Christmas always reminded him of the woman he loved. How could it not?

It was easier to think of his work. Of caring for the children, the US soldiers, and any other declared enemies that Hitler had attempted to take to slaughter. They'd rescued many, hiding them away or getting them safely across the border, through Belgium and occupied France. Some hid in southern France, where the Nazis' grasp was not clenched so tightly. Others trekked over the mountains to Spain, and still others made the dangerous journey across the English Channel on chartered vessels to freedom in England.

But he hadn't always been successful. The faces of those lost weighed heaviest on his heart. Yet even those losses were easier than considering the woman he'd left behind.

Daaf hadn't thought much about falling in love until he met the American, but her smile and joy had changed all that. The glimmer of the summer sun on her dark hair. Her brown eyes full of wonder and marvel over every new experience. She'd wanted to know everything about his world across the expansive sea.

She hadn't looked down on him for being a foreigner. She didn't suspect anything. He had no doubt the hurt over his leaving had gone deep. Not one letter had passed between them since he'd returned to his home country, but he didn't need to read about her heartbreak to know of it.

Daaf scraped his fork against his now-empty plate, as if doing so would make more food appear. His stomach rumbled in protest, exclaiming the small meal hadn't been close to enough. He pushed back his chair—wooden legs scraping against the worn floor—and ignored the rumbling.

He rose feeling slightly lightheaded, but he ignored that too. His body felt weary, as if he were eighty-eight years old instead of twenty-eight. It made sense, though. He'd lived three lives. First growing up in Germany. Then moving to Miami, starting his own business, and falling in love. And now he was back on family soil. He'd traveled home across the ocean, but that didn't mean his heart had returned with him.

Seeing the American liberators, doctors, and nurses around town and hearing their accent brought it all back, slamming into his heart like a German bomb.

Through the frosted window, Daaf saw Henk hurrying down the sidewalk toward their small cottage. Henk waved at Daaf, excitement filling his face, but as he neared, a neighbor girl named Elly approached, pulling a jar of plums from her coat pocket. Even though Daaf couldn't make out her words from this distance, he could imagine them as she handed over the jar.

"For the Americans . . . thank them for me."

The Americans had come, yes, pushing out the Germans, but most local villagers had no idea of the sacrifices made by the unknown army, the Dutch Resistance, which he'd been a part of for the last four years. Even before he returned, the brave few in the Dutch Underground had risked their lives—given their lives—to help others. He doubted their brave deeds would ever be public knowledge, but they hadn't done any of this for fame.

Since the Americans had arrived, liberating them from the Germans, some of those in the Underground had given up their cover and made their efforts known, but Daaf held back. He'd seen the war turn too many times. One wrong move on the Americans' part, and this area could once again be overtaken by the Nazis, and where would that leave him? Where would it leave those who'd been hunted down by the Nazis throughout the war?

Caring for so many had helped keep Daaf's mind off all the ways he'd hurt the woman he loved. But no matter how he tried to fill his day with other thoughts, she'd visit him in the quiet moments before he fell asleep. More than anything, he wished for this war to be over so that he could write one letter and explain everything. He had no hopes that she'd still be single—no woman that beautiful would be for long—or that she'd still care about him, but he had to let her know that she'd done nothing wrong to push him away. He wanted to explain that his lies were meant to keep her safe. But would she believe him?

Daaf turned from the window and tucked his chair back under the table. His nerves had balled up right below the skin. While the presence of the US Army in their town brought the smallest peace, they'd know no victory until Hitler surrendered, and the idea of that seemed impossible.

*With God only,* he told himself.

They'd grown used to the fear of Nazi reprisals, if that was possible. Harder still was sharing one's food and watching children cry in hunger because it was never enough. His memories of America seemed like a picture show he'd seen or a novel he'd read. The friends he cared about were out there, but it would hurt too much to think about them. It would hurt too much to think of her. Besides, those thoughts were foolish, considering his biggest concern was where he'd get the household's next meal.

*Radio Oranje*—the voice of the Free Dutch in London named after the

Dutch royal family, the House of Orange—had confirmed the rumors. The Dutch government-in-exile had asked for a national railway strike as a resistance measure. With no way for the Nazis to get supplies to the western Netherlands, the Dutch hoped that hunger would fuel the German retreat, but now they all suffered the lack of food.

Daaf picked up the two plates of potatoes and beets from the kitchen counter and then moved to the back bedroom. A door had been hidden behind the tall wardrobe for many years, but since the Americans had arrived, the wardrobe had mostly been pushed out of the way so their guests could move around more freely. Not that they did. They hadn't left their cramped attic home much.

Daaf balanced the plates as he climbed up the narrow stairs into the attic. Two young women sat upon cushions—frail but alive. Their cheeks were pink, and they offered him a small hint of a smile. At least it was warm up here from the heat of the wood stove. If he couldn't fill their bellies, at least he could keep them warm.

Artillery pounded in the distance, causing the floorboards to quiver and the glass of the windows to rattle. Smiles disappeared, and fear widened the eyes of the two young women and dulled the looks on their faces. The enemy who sought to kill them were no longer walking the streets, but their presence was still within arm's reach.

The younger of the two young women reached for a plate and began to eat as soon as it was in her hands.

Aleida had been only seven years old when he'd brought them into his protection. Years had passed but she still acted seven in so many ways. Her sister, sixteen-year-old Hedwig, was just the opposite. She'd matured far beyond her years.

Hedwig glanced at the other plate, but instead of reaching for it, a soft smile returned to her lips. "Daaf, I made something for you."

"Really? What?" He squatted before her where she sat on a cushion on the floor, offering her the plate. His heart doubled in his chest. He thought of these girls as his daughters. If he ever had a daughter someday, he'd want her to be as brave as Hedwig.

She took the plate with one hand but kept her second hand behind her back. "Your hands. I noticed they were red and raw." Lowering her gaze and peering up at him under her lashes, she pushed a small package into his hands. "This is for your hands."

"There is nothing I need," he said. *How can I take anything from her? And what does she even have to give?*

Daaf glanced around the attic room. It was no more than four feet by five feet. There was a small covered window that let in more cold air than light. Yet this young woman offered him a gift?

He opened the yellowed newsprint and pulled out a pair of knitted mittens. They were rough and made of various strands of colors.

"I am sorry they are not more beautiful," Hedwig said. "I found a rat's nest in the eaves. Who knows how long ago the rat died, but he'd been efficient in gathering scraps of wool yarn." She shrugged. "You might want to wash them if you get a chance. I'm thankful I thought to bring my knitting needles . . ." Her words trailed off. She'd had more—a full suitcase—but she had to abandon most of her things in Germany. The run for one's life couldn't be weighed down with too much baggage.

His heart filled with warmth, and the joy that comes only from giving was evident in her eyes, even in the dim light.

"They are *gut*." He slipped them on, thankful.

A smile brightened Hedwig's face. A larger smile than he'd ever seen from her. Give her some fresh air, some light, and some hope, and she'd be a pretty girl.

Daaf stood, but not all the way. If he tried, his head would hit the ceiling.

The sound of the front door opening caused both young women to jump in fear. Daaf heard a familiar whistle from downstairs.

He waved a calming hand to the girls. "It's only Henk. He has just come from the *American* hospital."

He stressed the word *American,* but the terror in their gazes eased only slightly. Would they ever find peace in their souls? Maybe only when they knew the Nazis were far away for good.

Henk's footsteps stomped toward the bedroom, and Daaf moved back to the stairs.

"Daaf, Daaf! Come quick. You have to hear this . . . I have amazing news!"

## Five

The nurses for the next shift slipped off their gray wool coats and mittens, then warmed their hands by the wood stove as Nancy and Dina helped Meredith clean up. Nancy was the big sister of the group. She'd been a labor and delivery nurse for five years before joining the military. Dina was from California and had been serving at Pearl Harbor when the Japanese attacked. Meredith had often overheard her telling stories of the destruction, the injuries, and the losses, but Meredith never asked any questions about that day. As selfish as it was, her own heart had been smashed by the enemy on December 7, 1941, shattering into a million pieces around her feet. Just the thought of that day brought heartache. She didn't need more pain on top of pain.

Meredith was the youngest of the nurses—always the youngest wherever she went, it seemed. All the nurses had been impressed when she'd explained how she boarded a Greyhound bus, waving through the window at Dad, Mama, Grandma, and her siblings as it carried her out of town.

Looking back, maybe if she'd been older than eighteen she would have had more sense. She wouldn't have fallen for the green-eyed musician so easily.

Then again, even her older self might have fallen for the gentle music teacher whose voice rose and fell with a German accent that he worked hard to hide. Some days she couldn't tell if David's lilt was trying to mimic a melody he carried in his head or mimic the gentle roar of the tide that filled every summer day.

But no matter what her heart said, David was as much of an enemy as the man who'd pointed a gun at her today. How did she end up here so close to the front? When she'd been home last, she'd promised Mama that the army would keep the nurses tucked away at safe distances. Obviously that wasn't the case.

Mama's worried face filled her thoughts. Was it only a year ago that Meredith returned home for Abigail and Jackson's wedding? It seemed as if a lifetime had passed since then.

The cold brought thoughts of home, and the fact that Christmas was only a few days away added to it. Mama always made the day special, especially for Meredith, or Merry, as her family called her. Mama wanted to make sure Meredith's birthday was celebrated with extra treats, and none of the kids minded having "Christmas and a bonus," as everyone called it.

Now a second wedding would be cause to celebrate, with Pete and Grace saying their vows in two days. Oh, how Meredith wished she could be there. Maybe in a few months Mama would send her a photo of the special day.

Pushing down the ache in her chest, Meredith straightened the bandages on the tray. *It's important to leave a place better than you found it,* Mama would always say. That was easy when one dealt with setting up metal medical trays, but more difficult when dealing with one's heart. How could a person find healing when answers were so few and far between?

Dina, whose blond hair looked perky as it curled around her face, handed her set of charts to the replacement nurses. Most days they worked much longer than their twelve-hour shifts, but things were a bit quieter today, meaning they could get some much-needed rest.

Dina held back a yawn, covering her mouth with her hand. "You comin', Meredith?"

"Is our shift over already?" Meredith asked, even though she knew it was. She hoped Dina didn't notice the tears forming in her eyes. She dabbed at the corners of her eyes with her thumbs. Her fingers still trembled from the German's escape.

Dina brushed a strand of hair back from her forehead. "Yes, and I'm surprised you aren't the first to make a beeline to your pillow."

"It should have been expected." Meredith shrugged. "I'm surprised one of the Germans didn't try to escape sooner."

"I'm not talking about that," Dina said. "I heard you tossing and turning last night." She sidled up to Meredith and wrapped an arm around her shoulders, offering a quick squeeze. "Thinking of home?"

Meredith crossed her arms over her chest. "Yes. How could you tell? My brother Pete is getting married tomorrow, and my sister Abigail is in the family way. Is it too much to dream that we'll be home before the baby arrives?"

Dina shrugged. Who could tell with this war? Who could tell what the madman Hitler would dish up next?

"And I've been thinking about my grandma too," Meredith continued, happy to get her mind off of David. "She's taken a turn for the worse, and she's had a difficult autumn. My mother's weary from caring for her. I wish I was closer to help. Of course, I know my brother and sister help as much as they can."

Dina smiled. "Sounds like you have a wonderful family. Maybe tonight you'll have sweet dreams about them."

Meredith nodded. "Of course." She thought of her bed at the convent. The nurses had stayed in this village longer than any other place since they'd landed in Europe. The nuns had transformed a large storeroom into a dormitory for them. Meredith understood the sacrifice. The nuns themselves and dozens of war orphans slept in the basement. It seemed a waste to have a cot she rarely slept in, but how could she sleep when one more man—ten more—needed a bit of care and a friendly face?

But today . . . today she'd welcome the sleep.

"I'll be over in a little while, Dina. I need to update a few of my charts first."

Dr. Murphy, a kind, older officer and their best surgeon, waved a hand toward Dina as she strode toward the door. "Nurse Martin, can you ask Mother Superior when the doctors and corpsmen will get a turn in a real bed with real sheets?" He chuckled. "I've heard some corpsmen conspiring to don a nurse's uniform and sneak in."

"I can ask, sir," Dina answered, "but she doesn't speak a word of English, and hand motions only go so far. Yesterday when I asked for a cup of hot water for tea, she heated me a hot bath." She patted her freshly washed hair. "How could I say no when I saw all the work she put into drawing the water, bringing in the wood, and keeping the fire going? It was delightful."

"The people here are kind." Meredith pulled rubbing alcohol and swabs from the supply trunk, adding them to the prep tray. "We've been here ten days, and I wouldn't mind another ten . . . or at least a few more to celebrate Christmas."

"And your birthday!" Nancy piped up. "It makes sense that someone as kind as you would share their birthday with our Lord. A special day."

"Christmas is your birthday, Meredith?" Dr. Murphy asked. "You must tell me what type of present you want."

She smoothed a hand down her army pants and sighed. "To stay here in Holland for a while and have a few more days of calmness on the front."

Dr. Murphy crossed his arms over his uniform and nodded. "Is that all? I'll ring up Patton and let him know. I heard we'll be crossing the border into Germany before the beginning of the New Year. Won't that throw Hitler for a loop?"

Meredith laughed, and she hoped it hid the pain in her eyes. David was in that country somewhere. A shiver trailed down her spine.

"Maybe we'll drink from Hitler's own wine cellar by Easter," one injured soldier piped up, and everyone called out their agreement.

Meredith, too, lifted her hand in a pretend toast, even though she never drank alcohol. She was thankful that no one was dwelling on what had happened with the escaping German earlier.

Lowering her pretend glass, she tucked a strand of dark hair behind her ear and continued the banter. "And wouldn't it be wonderful to have a piano to play Christmas carols?"

"It would be wonderful." The doctor clicked his tongue. "But I heard someone chopped up the parish's piano months ago to use for firewood. They never did catch the culprit."

Meredith's eyes widened. She turned to Nancy. "Would someone really go that far?"

"If you're cold and hungry, no saying what one will do." And without dwelling on that thought, Nancy looked down at the charts still in Meredith's hands. "Anything I should tell our replacements about your charts, in addition to the fact they should worry about another escapee?" Nancy chuckled, but Meredith didn't think it was funny.

Meredith scanned the room. "Tell them the men are doing well. Some are able to eat. A few were singing Christmas carols this afternoon," she said, holding an IV tube steady as Nancy changed the saline bottle.

"I wish all of them were doing well," Nancy said. "It's hard leaving some of them behind when our shift is over." Her eyes were full of concern.

Meredith followed her gaze toward a nearby soldier whose stomach wound caused her own stomach to turn. He moved his head and let out a moan. Bright red blood seeped through his bandages. Nancy's bloodshot eyes gave evidence of her weariness, but instead of complaining—instead of leaving with the changing shift—she hurried over to the man and set to work trying to stop the bleeding once again.

Meredith joined her. A few other soldiers nearby laughed and joked, but this man still fought for his life.

Meredith took his hand, pressing it between hers. It was cold and clammy to her touch. "We can move you back to a quieter area."

"Please no, miss. I'd like to stay here. I . . . I feel more secure around my buddies." A man a few cots down started humming "White Christmas" again, and a small smile lifted the lips of the soldier who lay before her, despite his obvious pain. Nancy finished rebandaging his wound, and within a minute he fell into a fitful sleep.

When Nancy had cleaned up the last of her supplies, she washed up and then slipped her hand inside of Meredith's, giving it a squeeze. There would always be more they could do, but today they'd offered all they could. They headed toward their coats, which were folded and sitting on top of boxes of medical supplies.

"It's amazing, don't you think, that the holiday spirit can be so strong even in the midst of war?" Nancy slid her arms into the sleeves of her coat.

Meredith nodded. "Maybe it's just human nature to want to be happy at Christmastime, even if it's a Christmas with the scent of sulfur from the bombs instead of cinnamon." She sniffed and then wrinkled her nose.

She was slipping on her coat when she saw a blur of color from the corner of her eye coming through the classroom door.

Nancy tugged on her coat sleeve. "Meredith."

She followed Nancy's gaze. The friendly Dutchman, Henk, had returned with a small basket of treats. His eyes fixed on Meredith. She quickly looked away, focusing instead on the six black buttons on her coat.

"He's taken a fancy to you for certain." Nancy snickered. "He must have spent the last hour visiting locals and gathering more small items for us just so he can get a chance to see you twice in one day."

The hairs on Meredith's arms stood on end. "Is that what you think?"

"Why else would his eyes be on you whenever you're in the same room?"

Meredith shrugged, then pulled her gray scarf from her pocket and wrapped it around her neck. "Perhaps I remind him of his sister," she said for the second time that day.

"I doubt it, but if that's what you think, maybe you should just ask him. He speaks quite good English. His mother is American." Nancy frowned. "Was American. I heard she died last year. Fever."

Meredith nodded, but she had no intention of talking to Henk. Why invite conversation? She led the way to the exit, hurrying past Henk and through the doorway before he had a chance to say a word. She could feel his eyes on her. Thankfully, Nancy followed without making a scene. With quickened steps, they left the schoolhouse and ventured into the cold night air.

What did Henk want? Why had he singled her out? She was almost afraid to know.

## Six

*D*aaf sat at the kitchen table and drummed his fingers on the tabletop. The red paint was chipped, and he paused to pick at a piece of peeling paint with his thumbnail. His eyes lifted and looked to the window again, watching for Henk.

He had made Henk go back. To look again. "You have to be certain," he'd said with a tremble in his voice. "You can't get my hopes up for nothing."

Henk had rushed inside Daaf's room earlier and called at the bottom of the stairs until Daaf had hurried down from the attic. "That photo—the one you carry with you. The photo that you think I don't know about."

Daaf's breath had escaped him. "What do you mean?"

"Don't pretend that you don't know." Henk had tilted up his chin, proud with knowledge. "You fell asleep with it lying on your chest once. I took it and studied it. From the smile in the woman's eyes, I could tell she was in love."

Daaf had patted his shirt pocket. How many times had he told himself that he needed to destroy all ties from the past? Yet he couldn't make himself destroy Merry's photo.

"Yes, that photo in your pocket." Henk had nodded. "That young woman, she wasn't a nurse, was she?"

Daaf's heart pounded so heavy that it echoed in his ears. "She . . . she was studying to be one."

"I think she's here. There are six American nurses. All of them are kind. Most of them are outgoing. Meredith is the quiet one. She doesn't joke around like the others. I often see her sitting on the cots, next to the soldiers. She does her part to heal their hearts as well as their bodies."

"Meredith?" Daaf had tried to remember what Merry had said her given name was. It could have been Meredith. That would make sense. But why was she going by that name?

More importantly, could it be true? Could she have ended up halfway around the world in the village of his ancestors?

He had to be certain, so he'd shown Henk the photo one more time and then sent him back. Now he waited, and the minutes seemed like hours.

*God, if it's not her, please don't get my hopes up.* He looked out the window, waiting for Henk and sending up the whispered prayer once again.

Daaf ran his fingers through his hair, feeling it stick up in every direction. How many times in recent months had he thought about his appearance? None. How many times had he even thought about music? He hadn't. That life was a different life. That person was a different person. He'd followed his own dreams, and where had it led him? It had led him to Miami. It had led him to her arms, but what good did that do? What good was acquiring everything your heart desired only to walk away from it?

He stood and moved to the kitchen sink, pumping cool water over the dirty dishes. He scrubbed them with a dishcloth and then set them on a towel on the counter to dry. His stomach growled, and his mind was already trying to think through the few items he had in the pantry. He'd have to figure out some way to make them last a little longer. Maybe tonight he'd visit Mother Superior. She usually gave him some bread, some cheese—enough for one person, for one meal. Yet he'd do his best to stretch it to feed four people.

Footsteps sounded outside, and Daaf hurried toward the door. Henk swung it open before Daaf could get to it.

"David, it is her!" Henk announced.

"Shh . . ." Daaf pulled him inside and shut the door hard. "Henk, my Dutch name, please."

Henk covered his mouth with his hand, and his eyes grew wide. His cousin hadn't made that mistake for a while, but it made sense. With the Americans here, everyone was thinking of how things used to be.

Daaf motioned to the rocking chair by the wood stove, which radiated warmth. He'd gone out this morning and stockpiled the wood.

Henk sat in the rocking chair and leaned forward, resting his elbows on his knees. He clasped his hands together, and his eyes were bright and full of excitement.

"I looked closely at the woman's face. It is the same face from the photo. I heard her talking with one of the doctors, and her birthday is on Christmas . . . just like your Merry."

Daaf's knees grew weak and he reached for the back of a second chair, sitting down hard. He looked up at Henk. He still couldn't believe it. "It's not her. It can't be her. She's back in the United States. Back where it's safe."

"It is her. Your Merry was studying to be a nurse. Now she is a nurse. She joined the military, and she has come."

"But I don't understand. This is . . . impossible." Even as he said the words, a Scripture verse ran through his mind—one his mother had taught him as a young child. *With God all things are possible.*

Daaf's heart doubled inside his chest. Joy filled him, quickly followed by worry. "The front lines are so close." He balled his hands into fists. If he were in charge, he would never let women this close to the front lines. He'd heard how the Nazis treated them, what they'd done. He'd heard of women who'd been raped and imprisoned. Many more—anyone considered an enemy— were killed.

*What if something happens to her?* His stomach flipped at the thought.

Henk rose and took two steps toward Daaf, placing a hand on his shoulder. "God is watching out for her, no doubt."

Daaf leaned against the chair back. "But how could this happen?"

"You've been faithful, David." Henk said his given name again, but this time it was only a whisper. "You gave up so much to return. Maybe God is rewarding you. God looked at your sacrifices, weighed them, and is returning a blessing. Maybe he's giving you back what broke your heart to give away."

"No." Daaf brushed off Henk's hand and then stood, forcing his cousin to take a step back. "I . . . I cannot let her know that I am here."

"But why . . . why not?" Henk shook his head. He waved a hand toward the door. "She's come all this way. God has brought her all this way. She has to know. I will tell—"

Daaf pointed toward Henk and then poked a finger into his chest. "No. You cannot tell her I am here."

Henk raised his hands and backed away. He neared the hot wood stove but didn't seem to notice. "But why not?"

"There is an enemy out there who wants to kill her . . . to kill any American." Daaf cleared his throat and pointed to himself. "But worse than that, I broke her heart. I need Merry to focus on her job and to forget me. Maybe after the war . . . after we are sure the Germans will not retake our village, I can go to her." Daaf raked his fingers through his hair and then nodded toward the window. "It'll be safer for her if she just keeps to her job," he repeated. "Because if the Germans do retake this village, I don't want her to have any worries for me. Not that I still expect her to care . . ."

He didn't finish the sentence. He couldn't finish it. If she cared for him, then she'd have a hard time retreating, knowing he was here. And if she didn't care . . . well, he didn't want to know that. He'd rather think of how things used to be.

Daaf released a heavy sigh. "You cannot tell her. She cannot know."

"God has brought her here for a reason." Henk's voice was low. "And she could be gone any day. I've heard that the Americans will be pushing into Germany soon. This . . . this might be your one chance. Why don't you pray about it? Ask God to give you wisdom."

Daaf didn't answer. What could he say to that? Didn't Henk know that he wanted nothing more than to sweep her up in his embrace?

He nodded once and then moved to his room. He shut the door firmly and settled on his creaky iron bed. How could he explain his mix of feelings? He was worried about her safety, yes, but there was something else he didn't want to admit to his cousin. Daaf swallowed hard trying to imagine the pain in Merry's gaze at seeing *him*. Would revealing himself bring her more pain?

He shifted again on the bed, considering all the friends he'd already lost. This war had claimed so many. The enemy had swallowed them up, one by one. He hadn't been able to save them, and he didn't want to consider losing Merry too . . . or seeing the anger and hatred in her eyes due to how he'd abandoned her with no explanation.

Daaf rose and moved to the tall bureau that blocked the attic door. He opened the top drawer and moved his hand to the back right corner, pulling out a pocket watch hanging from a silver chain. He ran his thumb over the cracked glass and then slid it back into his own pocket. He didn't look at it to tell the time. It had stopped working months ago. It was stuck at 3:47, the moment Raul's body had been tossed into one of the local canals. Later the Nazis had bragged about killing the old man for not saluting Hitler.

What Daaf had discovered later was that his friend's defiance—Raul's loud protests—had distracted the two guards long enough for a hay wagon to slip by. The wagon had carried two young Jewish children hidden under the hay.

Since the watch didn't tell time, Daaf looked at the cracked glass for courage. Courage not to go to Merry. Not to let his heart have more weight than his senses. It was also a reminder that there were causes worth fighting for. Causes worth leaving everything behind for, including true love.

And because of love he'd stay away. Merry was already in danger by being so close to the front. He didn't want to burden her mind with thoughts of him too.

## Seven

*Friday, December 22*

The room was a light shade of gray as Meredith's eyes fluttered open, and she was surprised morning had come so quickly. In less than an hour, she needed to be dressed and reporting for her shift in the field hospital.

Inside her, an uneasiness stirred. It wasn't due to her work—she enjoyed caring for the soldiers. Part of her was still bothered by the German soldier who'd escaped yesterday. She doubted he'd return, but just the memory of the way he'd waved his gun caused her heart to race. She was also bothered because there'd been no letters or packages from her family in the mail truck. Meredith had tried not to pout last night as Nancy read through a lengthy letter from her mother.

"Everyone's busy," she'd told herself. Her parents and siblings still cared. But it didn't take away the loneliness and the feeling of abandonment. Tomorrow was her brother's wedding, and she wouldn't be there to celebrate it.

She wrapped the gray army blanket around her shoulders and leaned against the cool brick wall. She was the one who'd left her family and joined the military. It had been her choice, but the emotions that came when David walked away had tainted every other relationship. Did anyone care for her? Did anyone miss her?

Nancy turned over on the cot next to Meredith, readjusting and pulling her blanket over her head. A minute later, Nancy's soft snores told Meredith that she was fast asleep again.

Meredith closed her eyes and tried to picture home. Was snow already covering the lawn and frosting the house's eaves? Was the fireplace bright with flames licking against the small logs that Dad always placed so neatly? Was Mama busy in the kitchen, making gingerbread like she always did the weeks prior to Christmas? And Grandma . . . her health was declining, Meredith had heard. Would Grandma hold on until Meredith could make it home—no matter when that was?

Meredith thought about Grandma and her wise advice. The older woman had faced a lot. Caring for a family, losing her husband and home, losing two grandchildren, and building and losing friendships over her eighty years. She always seemed to know what to say and do at the right moment, unlike Meredith, who often acted too impulsively and then later regretted it.

Meredith thought about when she was six and got into a fight with a friend at school. She couldn't remember what the argument was about, but she remembered the two days of silence between her and Janie that followed. She also remembered her grandmother's words.

Grandma had taken Meredith to the park down the street, and they'd walked to the small creek that ran through the park. Grandma shared about how conflict was like that creek, keeping one person on one side and the other person on the other.

"Forgiveness is a bridge that can join you again," Grandma had said, taking her to the small footbridge. "When you forgive you lay down the boards, but that's just the first act. Then you have to be willing to take the first step."

Meredith swallowed down her emotion, realizing that it wasn't a small creek but a wide ocean that separated her from the person who'd captured her heart—or at least that was what it felt like. She couldn't reach out to David. She didn't know where he was. More than that, how could she love and forgive someone who'd abandoned her to fight for an evil cause? She balled the blanket tighter in her fists and prayed for a way to release some of the pain, but the pain remained, echoing around the chilly room and filling the space.

She most likely never would find the answers to David's leaving or be able to extend the hand of forgiveness, but she could do better in building a bridge to her parents and siblings.

Morning light filtered through a high window, and Meredith rose and moved to her army bag. She shuffled through it, finding paper and a pen. She'd been negligent in writing letters. She'd blamed it on the fact that her work made her weary in both mind and spirit, but that was only an excuse. It was hard chatting about everyday things when she faced so much injury and pain in both her work and her heart.

She pulled out a single piece of paper and used her Bible as a small table on her lap. Then she began to write:

*Dear Family,*

*It's 0700, and I'm supposed to start work at 0800. I've been taking the day shift lately, although I enjoy the night shift more. Some nurses don't like that shift, but it's better for me than tossing and turning in the darkness, wondering just how close the enemy is. Thankfully, last night I slept.*

*It feels like I've been on European soil for years rather than months. It's cold outside, bone-chilling cold. Maybe it wasn't a smart idea to thin my blood in Miami Beach during nursing school.*

*Last Sunday one of the local families invited three of the nurses for a late dinner. It was clear they'd been wealthy before the war, but their fine clothes hung off their thin frames. Dark circles shadowed their smiles. They'd somehow managed to find enough food to make potato soup and biscuits for us, and on the wall was a fine painting of rolling hills and flowers. Their English was good, better than most villagers. And the mother of the home said that the image in the painting is how this area looked before the war.*

*The more time I spend here, I can't help thinking how similar to a human being this cold winter is. The soldiers come into the field hospital with barely a breath of life left. Their faces are gray and pale, but with care, color returns. Cheeks turn pink. Blue or brown eyes open in a handsome face. Just like spring comes after winter, life is renewed with care and tending.*

*I was telling this to my friend Nancy and she said, "And those who don't make it here can look forward to an eternal spring." That helped me. The next time I had to draw a blanket over the face of a soldier it helped to think of that painting and the beauty beyond.*

*Mother, how's the Christmas baking coming? Abigail, are you ready for that baby? I imagine you are. I cannot wait to hear about the arrival of a new niece or nephew. And who knows, maybe next year, 1945, will bring the end of the war.*

*Pete, tell your bride-to-be, Grace, hello. Actually after today she'll be your bride! Our family is changing so much—but all in good ways.*

*Grandma, Mama writes and tells me that things are ailing you. I hope that this note finds you feeling better. Overall, thank you for your prayers. I know they are being sent up, and I'm counting on them to keep me safe. And when I leave this foreign soil, know that I can't wait to come back to Lafayette for good.*

*Love,*

*Meredith (Merry)*

She sat for a minute deciding if she had time to write her grandmother her own letter too. Grandma had been as close as any friend. She always had time to listen, and Meredith always found herself pouring out what was deep inside. She pulled out another sheet of paper.

*Dear Grandma,*

*I'm sorry that I couldn't keep my promise about writing every week. My desire to care for Uncle Sam's boys often comes into conflict* with my desire to write home. You asked about my duties. We care for soldiers with stomach and chest wounds who need immediate care first. Others come in with wounded limbs. We also see many tanker crew men, called tankers. Some die en route here because of their burns. Mostly I work alongside the doctors and five other nurses—all friends—to apply splints, clean and bandage wounds, give injections, and check vitals. I also assist in surgery.

When we arrived in France in July, we had hopes the war would be over soon, but this horrible conflict in the woods has changed everything. We've seen France, Belgium, and now the Netherlands. Rumor has it we'll be in Germany soon.

When we first pulled into this village, we passed houses, stores, and a church. Our truck pulled into a schoolyard and stopped. The play equipment was empty and looked as if it had been that way for twenty years. War makes things feel that way.

An old priest met our truck. He wore a threadbare coat over his cassock. He spoke with our commander and pointed to the school. I knew what he was saying: we could set up in there. I breathed a sigh of relief. Real walls. They'd block out the whipping wind.

The people here are so thankful that the Americans have liberated their town. The nuns prepared a large storeroom as our dormitory. To sleep in a real bed, under a roof, seems so extravagant.

Whether we have much or little, pray that God will continue to use me here, and please pray that we'll have a good Christmas. My Christmas and birthday wish is for a piano to play carols on. The music will bring my heart home.

Love,

Merry

*D*aaf had dreamed of Merry. He'd dreamed that it was summer, and he was taking her home to meet his mother. When they arrived, Mother told him she'd been expecting them, and she'd sat at her sewing machine with a smile on her face and begun sewing a fine dress—a wedding dress.

Daaf could hardly remember a time when his mother wasn't at the sewing machine, rivers of fabric and lace pooling around her as she sewed drapes and curtains.

Mother always reminded him that he was just as much Dutch as he was German. She spoke to him in Dutch when there were no visitors in their home. At first Father protested, but after a while he just cast disapproving glares. It was the language that Daaf liked best. It was the one his mother used to read him Bible stories and whisper prayers.

He grew up in Dresden, Germany, where his mother had immigrated for a job. It was there they'd found a safe haven, even after his father became ill and could no longer work, leaving provision for his family to rest on his mother's shoulders. They'd planned on returning to the Netherlands to be closer to his mother's family, including his cousins, but it was 1929 and a severe depression had hit the Netherlands. He'd been thirteen years old. The depression hit the rest of Europe too, but not as badly. In Dresden his mother had a sewing job, and so they'd stayed.

Their cottage had been just a stone's throw from the theater. He spent all his time there and became friends with the musicians. Seeing his love for music, one music teacher gave him free lessons. His talent was clear.

In all his years Daaf had heard his parents quarrel only once. It was the day—when he was nearly an adult—that his father insisted he move to America to go to school, and his mother insisted that the Netherlands was a safer place. Safe from the draft in Germany. Safe from the war.

In the end, Daaf chose to follow his father's plan. He lived in the United States for three years, finishing college and then starting his own business. It wasn't the draft that called him back. It was his conscience.

It made no logical sense for him to return to Europe and move to an unfamiliar place—to the Netherlands. Yet that was where he felt led to go. To help an uncle he'd visited only during childhood summers and to risk his life for strangers.

His help was needed in the Netherlands. His cousins knew few people they could trust with their precious cargo. He'd sacrificed himself for others. Always put others first. Just as he did now with Merry. Yet as he prayed about releasing his love for her again and that God would keep him strong so he wouldn't approach Merry, the whisper to his heart said something different.

*Wait. Those who wait upon the Lord receive new strength.*

The directive wasn't just about not revealing his true identity, but also about not letting those still in hiding emerge from their safe corners. Someday, like butterflies escaping from chrysalises, the hidden would break free. But now was not the time.

Last night Henk had asked Daaf if they should urge those in hiding to come out. "Let them have a warm bath, sleep in a real bed," Henk had said.

"The war is not over—" Daaf had argued.

"The Americans are here," Henk interrupted. He waved a hand toward the town. "We cannot keep them caged forever!"

Daaf cleared his throat. "The Americans can be defeated. Lost ground can be regained."

He didn't want to think the worst. He hated the thought of the Germans returning, but he'd rather be safe than sorry. He longed to protect those still in his care. Maybe someday they would be truly free, but not today.

Today he'd just remember how things used to be. And maybe tonight he'd again dream of his mother meeting Merry, although that was not possible since both his parents had passed. Tonight he'd dream of a future with Merry that most likely would never take place.

~⁓∾⁓~

Meredith approached the brick schoolhouse-turned-hospital. Every time she entered these doors, she sent up a prayer of thanks. The desks and chairs had been removed the first day, replaced by cots. A place of learning had become a place of healing.

Meredith brushed her hair back from her face. When she had a moment's peace, she'd have to pin it up. She'd always been a tomboy, and her hair never seemed to stay in place. Abigail's hair had always stayed in the braids their mother had so meticulously woven.

The cry of an injured man echoed through the bustling recovery room as she entered. She followed the voice to a man lying on a cot in the back corner. Vie was trying to calm him. She looked weary and flustered. Vie much preferred the operating room, where she never had to relay the hard truth to damaged men or hear their moans and cries.

Meredith approached her friend, squatting beside her.

Tears rimmed the corners of Vie's eyes. "He's a tanker. I was just getting ready to bandage his wounds."

"I'll handle it." Meredith had seen this type of wound often, nearly two or three every day: tankers whose tank had been hit by flamethrowers. The heat inside seared any exposed area of skin—face, hands, arms.

She grabbed the Vaseline and bandages and prayed. Most of the time she had to ask for help—someone to calm her patients since they usually suffered several days of delirium. As busy as the hospital was today, she doubted anyone would be able to give her a hand. But God was with her, she knew. He helped her when she felt as if she'd come to the end of herself. Just as Jesus had calmed the storm for Peter, He also knew how to still the souls of hurting men.

*Dear Jesus,* she prayed as she sat next to the tanker's cot.

The man's dark hair, singed from the flames, caught her attention first. The right side of his face was untouched, and his features . . . Her stomach flipped as she realized how much he looked like David. Why was she thinking about him again? Maybe because they were nearing the German border. Maybe because it often crossed her mind that it was possible David could be brought into the hospital. Not in an American uniform, of course. Meredith shook her head, trying to shake off those thoughts.

The injured man fell into a fitful sleep, and Meredith was thankful. She'd set to work applying Vaseline bandages to the left side of his face, his arms, and his hands when she heard footsteps approaching behind her. They weren't the footsteps of one of the other nurses, but heavier. She turned around. Dr. Anderson approached.

"Nurse Turner . . . Meredith," he said. "There is a soldier, and well . . . the truth is, he's not doing so well. You spent time with him a few days ago, and he's asking for you."

As if on cue, a man's cries punctuated the air. She recognized the voice. It was Samuel, a young soldier from Shippensburg, Pennsylvania, and Meredith found her feet moving toward him even before she realized what she was doing.

Even though his eyes were bandaged, he must have sensed her presence.

"Tell me a story, Merry. Get my mind off all that I've seen."

"Merry." She offered a soft smile and took his hand into hers. "That's what my family calls me." *And David,* she added to herself. She pulled up a chair and sat beside Samuel. He let out a soft moan again. "I'm glad you called me that, Samuel. I miss hearing it. When I enlisted, I didn't think my nickname was suitable for an army nurse. Isn't that silly?"

Her throat was tight, and she remembered stepping out of that office feeling like a different person—as if that would help her broken heart.

She leaned closer to Samuel. "Do you want to hear a funny story?" She chuckled. "It was my older brother Pete who taught me to swim. Mother made him because the lifeguards at the city pool couldn't keep me out of the deep end. I suppose that's still me today, taking on more than I can handle."

"Do you have another story?" he asked, nearly gasping for breaths.

"Another story, let me see." She held his hand tighter and focused on him. "There is a small candy shop in Lafayette, Indiana, where I used to live. My sister works there, making candy . . . the most delicious candy anyone's ever tasted. I know. I find candy wherever I go to compare. My sister Abigail was working there and attending school when she met a man named Jackson who sparked her interest." Meredith told Samuel her sister's story as Abigail had written it in her letters.

"A . . . love . . . story." A smile touched Samuel's lips. "That helps to keep my mind off of things."

"Do you have a girlfriend back home?" she asked.

"No, but I'd like one."

Hope tinted his words. She knew from his injuries that hope was hard to come by. But at this moment that didn't matter. All that mattered was that she was here to tell him stories that would take his mind off his pain and fears. Maybe he'd go to sleep tonight dreaming of his someday girl. And as he dreamed of a future, it would give him a way to cling to life, if only for another day.

Meredith had just started to tell Samuel about how Pete met his new bride when his gentle snores told her that he'd fallen asleep. It was only then that she rose to take care of her duties. Caring for the soldiers was the hardest work she'd ever done, but the time went quickly. It was only after the end of her shift had come and gone that she returned to Samuel's side. No one told her she had to leave, and the other nurses were caring for the other men.

Meredith had first thought about being a nurse after reading a biography of Louisa May Alcott. While the rest of the class was enamored of *Little Women*, she couldn't read enough about Louisa as a Civil War nurse. She read *Hospital Sketches* so many times that Father had to tape the cover back on for her.

Like Louisa, Merry had grown up with a sense that she needed to do something. Something important.

In *Hospital Sketches,* when Louisa's young neighbor Tom said, "Go nurse the soldiers, the tented field," Louisa had answered with "I will!" And Meredith's heart had cried the same.

Her mother had believed in her dream. Her father had been encouraging but realistic. "Merry, aren't you the one who faints at the sight of blood?"

"I don't faint all the time, Daddy, but . . . well, what does it matter if I get weak in the knees? Every task is hard at first. Just because it's a difficult task doesn't mean my help isn't needed."

What she didn't tell him was that she'd do anything to keep other families from suffering like the Turners had after losing Alfie. Her memories of her older brother were few, but what she remembered most was laughter and joy in their home. She also lost her sister, Annie, yet she was too young to have any clear memories of her. After Alfie's death, things changed. Her family still cared for each other, but there was an emptiness that she couldn't put her finger on. Something was missing. Someone was missing. It had to do with the children her family had lost. If she could do anything to keep another family from going through the same trauma, she would. Becoming a nurse was a bold decision, but falling in love had come unexpectedly.

Meredith hadn't planned on falling in love not long after she'd arrived in Miami Beach. After spending the first couple of days at the beach, she'd set about unpacking her things—at her roommate's insistence—counting down the days until nursing classes would start.

Meredith had sorted through her things, deciding to give some of her warmer clothes to June Welch, her new neighbor a few houses down from the apartment where she stayed, who would head north to college. It had been nearly dinnertime, but Meredith figured she still had time to drop off the clothes and be back in time for the meal.

Meredith had knocked on the door to the Welches' house and without a moment's hesitation it had swung open. A man stood there. Tall, with striking features and green eyes. His hair was rumpled as if he'd run his hands through it.

"I was hoping you were the nurse."

*Gimme a few years, honey,* she'd wanted to say. Instead, she attempted to peer beyond him, into the Welches' living room.

"No, I'm not a nurse. Uh, is June here? Or Mrs. Welch?" She could hear voices and a wail from Mrs. Welch. She cocked her head and looked at the man standing in front of her. "Who are you?"

"David." He turned, hurrying back into the living room.

It was only then she saw Mr. Welch lying on the sofa. Blood dripped from a gash on his temple. She also noted blood on the sleeve of the strange man's shirt.

"Oh, Mr. Welch." She'd rushed forward, only to be pushed aside by Mrs. Welch.

"Give Howard air, Merry. He passed out climbing the ladder to clean the gutters. This dear man was driving by and saw him fall. June went for the nurse. Trudy lives just two doors down."

Meredith glanced outside, noticing for the first time the sedan hastily parked in front of the house. Mr. Welch seemed fine now, more embarrassed than anything, but it was the young man—David—she couldn't keep her eyes off of.

He sat at the older man's side, and his lips moved slightly. She couldn't hear his words, but she could tell it was a prayer. Her heart swelled to double its size within her, and she wondered where this stranger had come from. Had that been a German accent he'd spoken with? Maybe he was a teacher at the university.

After his prayer, David rose, went to the kitchen, and got a clean wet rag. After placing it on Mr. Welch's forehead, he took Mrs. Welch's hand and patted it, offering her comfort.

"I'm just thankful I could help, although I haven't done much," he said.

And as Meredith sat there, her fists tightened around the dresses she'd brought for June. She didn't know this man, but she knew immediately he was the type of man she wanted to marry. Someone who'd stop to help a stranger and who'd send up whispered prayers, not caring what anyone else in the room thought. Who'd give comfort to Mrs. Welch.

It wasn't until later that she realized David had put on a show.

"Daydreaming again?"

Meredith jumped. Nancy's voice interrupted her thoughts.

"Thinking about home, I suppose," Nancy said knowingly.

"Isn't that what we all think about these days?" Meredith replied.

"She was telling me a story." Samuel's voice was groggy.

"Oh, really?" Nancy placed a hand on her hip. "Anything good?"

"About her childhood. Her fam-family. Next . . ." He winced and tried to smile. "Next I was going to ask about where she was when she heard about Pearl Harbor. It's what everyone talks about."

"If you can get her to talk about that time in her life, then you deserve a medal, soldier," Nancy declared.

Meredith didn't let Nancy's words bother her. It was only natural that most people talked about December 1941. The day the Japanese attacked Pearl Harbor had changed everything.

Nancy left to care for another soldier, and soon Samuel fell into a fitful sleep, leaving her again with her thoughts.

There wasn't a person in the army who couldn't tell you where they were and what they were doing when news of Pearl Harbor hit the airwaves. Meredith had been at Miami Beach, and that day everything had changed.

Nineteen forty-one had to be the best year of Meredith's life. She met David and was busy in nursing school. After class a group of them would meet at Lummus Park. They'd run around on the grassy area and then jog over the white sand to the water. Weekends were spent doing much of the same. What was not to enjoy, with the sun and the sand?

That year they'd eaten Thanksgiving dinner at Pastor Garcia's house. The older couple didn't have any children of their own, but they had a long table that seated ten, and every holiday they filled it up with young people far from home.

As Meredith had gazed at David over the flickering candlelight of the Thanksgiving table, she had hoped this would be just the first of many holidays together. The love in his gaze was clear. And with the questions he'd been asking—about her hopes of the future, about where she saw herself settling down, about her taste in jewelry—Meredith had believed that a proposal would be coming soon. And she couldn't think of a more perfect month to accept a proposal than December.

"So where were you, you know, right before Pearl Harbor?" Samuel asked. His words escaped in a yawn as he tried to wake up fully.

Meredith gave him a brief summary of her time in Miami Beach and the friends she had there. She didn't tell him the rest. Couldn't tell him the rest. That she'd gone to David's small bungalow to see if he had heard the news about Pearl Harbor. And that she'd found his three roommates pacing in the driveway.

"I can't believe this happened. How could we not have known?" one roommate, she later learned was Josh, had asked when she arrived.

"I should have suspected something. We should have known," Tony said.

"Should have known what?" she asked.

Three heads swung around, eyes widening, as if they hadn't realized she was there.

"Merry, there you are. We . . ." Josh had shuffled uncomfortably from side to side. "We were just coming to get you. To find you."

"But I already know," she said.

"But how could you? We just found out ourselves."

"How could I not know? It's all over the radio. Everyone on campus is talking about it."

"But how is that possible? We just found the note."

"Oh!" Tony interrupted. "You're talking about Pearl Harbor?"

"Of course I'm talking about Pearl Harbor. We were bombed," she'd said. "Our country is now at war. What else could I be talking about?"

The three men looked at each other. Josh kicked at a rock on the ground, and for some reason they no longer made eye contact. A sinking feeling came over Meredith. Her knees softened, and she glanced around. The bright sun overhead seemed too bright, too glaring.

She shielded her eyes and looked up at Tony. "Where is David?" She choked the words out and studied their faces. There was a mix of confusion and anger in their gazes. No one answered.

She reached over and gripped Josh's white shirt sleeve, clenching it in her fingers. "Tell me what's going on. Where is he? Why are you looking at me like that?"

"There's a box of things in his room. Some of his stuff is gone, but what we found . . ."

She moved toward their bungalow, taking the front steps two at a time. She paused at the door. "Which one is his room?"

"Straight back." Tony nearly winced as he said the words. "The door right off the kitchen. His stuff is in there. Everywhere. Not like David at all."

"If that is his name . . ." Josh's words punctuated her steps.

Merry rushed into the back bedroom and noticed things strewn everywhere. The dress shirt David had worn on their dinner Friday night was tossed in the corner next to a pair of slacks. Music books filled a small bookshelf, but some had been pulled off and lay on the floor. A dresser drawer was open and empty. A photo booth picture of the two of them was ripped. Half of it lay on the floor.

Tears filled her eyes, and her mind tried to process it. Why had he ripped their photo? Did he leave? Had he gone somewhere? Where? And why in such a haste?

She glanced around, trying to take it in. The room smelled of him—of the sandalwood cologne that he favored. The window was open, and the sound of the ocean waves lapping against the shore met her ears. Was it just last night that he'd confessed his love and sworn his dedication to her?

Then she saw it. A shoe box. It had been opened and partly spilled onto the unmade bed. Pamphlets and fliers had been neatly packed inside. She couldn't read the words, but the images were clear. Nazi propaganda. Hitler's one-armed salute and glaring face mocked her in black and white.

"There's a letter for you." It was Tony's voice. All three of David's roommates crowded into the doorway.

She noticed it then. A simple white envelope lay on the pillow, which was missing its pillowcase. She grabbed it and saw the flap hadn't been sealed. Merry pressed the envelope to her chest. "Did you read it?"

From the look on their faces, it was clear they had.

"Why did you read my letter?" she demanded.

"Wouldn't you read it too if you just found out that you'd been living with a Nazi?"

She wanted to read it but not here. Not now.

She turned to leave, forcing herself to hold the emotions in. What had her dad always told her? *If something seems too good to be true, it probably is.*

David had seemed too good to be true.

"You're leaving?" Josh had asked.

"Well, I have no reason to stay. Unless . . . unless there's something you want to tell me."

Josh reached out and placed a hand on her upper arm, gripping her as if he was sure she'd collapse under whatever words he had to say.

"He was a spy, Mer. A German spy. I don't know why we didn't guess it before. Working so close to the military here. Tutoring officers' children. Befriending their families. He fooled us all."

Meredith had wanted to tell the three men that they were lying. She wanted to tell them that it was all a mistake, that David would soon appear and explain everything. Yet he never returned. It was as if he'd fallen off the face of the earth. She woke each day with tears—a mixture of anger and longing— and fell asleep each night with the same.

The tears came again now as she sat in the field hospital, although she tried to wipe them away before anyone saw.

Vie came to her, urging her to head back to the convent before it got too late.

Meredith looked at her watch. She'd been sitting there for twenty minutes at least, lost in her thoughts. The new rotation of nurses had come and busied themselves taking care of the patients.

Was it because of the sorrowful look she surely wore that they hadn't bothered her? Was it because Samuel wasn't doing well? His labored breaths told her that he was getting weaker. They probably all assumed that she cried over him. Maybe that was true. Maybe it was yet another loss that stirred the feelings of abandonment she couldn't keep away.

"Uncle Sam told me I had to be here, but what about you?"

Samuel's voice interrupted Meredith's thoughts.

She jumped slightly, but then reached for his hand. He was pale, and his breaths took great effort. There was nothing the doctor could do to help Samuel. Nothing anyone could do but hold his hand as his body grew weaker.

"He didn't force me, but I had to do my part," she answered. "This . . . men like you . . . are what brought me here."

"I heard just last month . . . that . . . a nurse was killed in Belgium. Are you afraid of dying, miss?" He squeezed her hand, as if wanting to reassure her, though she knew he was the one who wanted to be reassured.

"I'd be lying if I didn't admit that I tremble every time I hear those big guns booming. There's been more than one close call."

His grip weakened and for a moment she wondered if he was still conscious. Then he cleared his throat, as if holding back emotion.

"But," she continued, "since I was a child I've gone to church, and I've learned about the saving grace of the Lord Jesus. He died so that I could live. He came to earth so that I could someday be with Him in heaven."

"My mother taught me the same." Samuel's breaths were getting labored, heavy. "For so long I didn't believe."

"And now?"

"Well, as they were carrying me here on that stretcher, I . . . I prayed and told God if He was real, He'd let me be ushered into heaven by an angel." A pained smile crossed his lips. "Now I know He's real, because here you are. I feel the peace, miss, and I wonder what I've been fighting for so long. I'm His now."

A tear ran down her face. She clung to his hands, refused to release them to wipe it away.

"Can you tell my mother?" he asked. "Can you let her know her prayers for me will be answered and that she'll see me . . . on the other side?"

Meredith nodded and her tears came harder. Here she'd been moaning over her broken heart, and now some poor family was going to hear the news that they'd lost their son. That they'd never get a chance to spend Christmas with him again.

Samuel's chest rose and fell three times before stopping completely. Meredith clung to his still-warm hands, praying for his family. Then, before she alerted the doctor of his death, she squatted down and rummaged through his field coat. It was dirty from the foxholes and smelled of smoke and sulfur, but in the inside pocket she found what she was looking for. A Bible with Samuel's name and address inside the front flap. Without hesitating she tucked it into her trouser pocket and stood.

"Doctor," she called. "He's gone."

Dr. Anderson approached, weariness tugging down his eyelids. "It's sad to lose one so young just three days from Christmas."

"It's sad to lose any of them, but yes . . . you're right. I feel the same."

He reached up and placed a heavy hand on her shoulder. "You should go, Meredith. Get some rest. Your shift was over hours ago."

She nodded but still her feet didn't move. She looked down at the young soldier one more time, thinking about his words. Did God really use her—the fact that she was here—to point the young man back to Him? To answer a simple prayer here on earth to point him to his eternal home?

It had seemed that when she lost David she lost her purpose, but at this moment God was reminding her of it. He had plans for her now, here. And Samuel had showed her that.

eredith walked back to the convent with slow steps. The flat-faced brick buildings were the only things in the village that weren't sunken, gray, and lifeless. Meredith couldn't imagine the bare tree limbs full of green leaves, full of life. In broken English the groundskeeper had claimed it was one of the worst winters he'd known. Some worried that hunger would claim just as many victims as the Germans. And if it wasn't lack of food, flooding and the lack of heat were concerns.

Meredith lifted her face to the darkened sky. *Dear Lord, won't You give these dear people one spot of joy? One moment of unexpected happiness?*

She thought of the piano again and made a note to ask Dr. Anderson about it tomorrow.

The other nurses were sleeping when Meredith got back to their small quarters. Most of the time she was thankful for the quiet, but not today. She wanted to talk to someone. Needed to talk to someone. She sat on her cot and removed her boots, letting them fall to the floor.

Nancy's eyes opened. She glanced at Meredith, and her eyes widened. She rubbed the sleep from them. "Is everything all right?"

Meredith didn't know how to answer. "I'm fine . . ." Her lower lip trembled as she spoke.

"And the soldier?"

"His name was Samuel. He didn't make it." The tears came then and a soft, quivering sob emerged with them. "I . . . I don't know wh-why I'm crying. Other soldiers have died. But . . . but it's always so hard . . . this place. Maybe . . . oh, I don't know."

Even as she said those words, Meredith knew it wasn't only Samuel's death that bothered her. She was nervous about entering Germany.

She'd been shoving down her anger—and her shame—about David being a German spy, keeping her secret to herself. How could she tell anyone that she'd been in love with a Nazi? Yet the tension building inside her refused to be squelched any longer. She took a deep breath, telling herself that she'd been carrying this burden too long on her own. She needed to talk to someone about it. Nancy had proven herself trustworthy.

"Are you ready to tell me yet?" Nancy asked, obviously sensing that Meredith wanted to talk. "Are you ready to tell me about the man who broke your heart? Was he a soldier? A pilot? Those flyboys have a bad reputation."

Meredith pressed her lips together as she'd done every time Nancy had asked, but this time the words refused to be contained.

"Oh, he's not a soldier—at least not an American one."

Nancy lifted her eyebrows. "So he's . . ."

"German." Meredith blurted out the word and then covered her face with her hands. Shame washed over her. It draped over her back like a dark, heavy cloak. She couldn't believe she'd said it—admitted it. What would Nancy think of her now?

"You fell in love with a German soldier?"

"Yes. I mean no." Meredith lowered her hands and shook her head. "I'm not sure. He was German. His family, that is, but I met him in Miami Beach."

She went on to tell Nancy about how they'd met. About how they'd fallen in love. "To me he was just a gentle, caring music teacher. I didn't think of him as German—well, not until news of the war escalated. Not until he disappeared."

"So do you think he came back to serve?"

"Yes, yes I do. That's what he told me in a note he left for me. David said that he had to return to fulfill his duty. It was all he said."

Meredith angled her shoulders away from Nancy, wondering what her friend thought of her now. Knowing it wasn't good. She swallowed hard, trying to swallow her emotion.

"I'm sorry that you had your heart broken, Meredith, but maybe you should be more concerned by the other German soldier."

"The other German?"

"I'm not sure if you heard, but there are rumors that the German soldier who escaped is still around town. Houses have been broken into. Food is missing. Medicine was stolen from one of the supply trucks." Nancy's voice grew low. "I hate to think of him still around with that gun."

They were both quiet, listening to the night as if trying to distinguish the sound of footsteps from the sound of the wind in the tree limbs.

"Hopefully he's gone," Meredith said. "Maybe there's another explanation for the thefts."

"Yes." Nancy turned over on her cot. "And the truth is, I'd rather think of your broken heart than worry about an escaped Nazi. Please, tell me more of your woes before I die from a heart attack!"

Meredith offered a soft smile. Only Nancy could joke around at a time like this. "You must think I'm a fool, don't you? Getting so bent out of shape over someone from three years ago."

"The thing about love," Nancy said, more serious now, "is that it's slow to fade. It's not a bad thing. Love is meant to last."

Meredith nodded, wondering where that left her. Wondering if she had any hope of loving again. *Scrub David from my heart,* she prayed silently, but even as she thought those words, something inside fought against them.

*Hold on. Trust.* A gentle stirring moved within her. She didn't understand it. It made no sense, but by this time weariness had overwhelmed her. Finally.

Nancy closed her eyes and burrowed under her blankets. Meredith lay down and pulled her blankets around her. She could hardly keep her eyes open. Tomorrow was a new day, and it meant one day closer to the end of this war, whenever that was. And as she drifted off to sleep, she had a feeling she was also one day closer to a healing within.

With the slightest stirring, the pieces of her broken heart had begun to shift, giving her hope that one day she would once again find wholeness.

## Ten

*Saturday, December 23*

Meredith had a lightness to her step as she walked with Nancy away from the center of town the next morning. They'd come upon Mother Superior earlier. She'd been bundling up to head outside to gather wood, and the two nurses offered to go instead since they still had an hour until they had to report for work.

For the first time in many months, Meredith had awoken with a smile. Her problems hadn't been solved overnight, but it had helped to share her story and her tears with Nancy. Part of her burden had lifted when she'd told her friend the truth. It felt so good to get it off her chest. In fact, she hadn't realized what a burden her secret had been until she'd told someone.

She also felt lighter inside because Nancy hadn't judged her or chided her for dating a German. She hadn't been shocked that Meredith had dated a Nazi spy.

As they strolled away from the center of town, the day was no brighter and the sky was no bluer, but something inside Meredith told her that God would bring healing somehow, someday.

They didn't have to walk far. Mother Superior had told them that a local man named Daaf had gathered wood for the convent. They just needed to pick it up.

The two women chatted as they walked, and then Nancy's words stopped midsentence. In the distance they saw a small cottage. With its whitewashed walls, red tile roof, and large tree out front, it was just as Mother Superior had described. Henk stood on the front porch, talking to another man.

A smile burst onto Nancy's lips. "Henk!" she called and waved.

Henk looked at them, but instead of his face brightening and filling with his typical smile, his jaw dropped.

He grabbed the arm of the man next to him. The other man turned, and his face fell. He wore a beard, and his face was thin and gaunt. But his eyes . . .

Meredith would never forget those eyes. David's eyes had been large, full of life. His dark brows had perfectly framed them, and even from this distance, the man before her had the same eyes.

Meredith paused her steps. Her heartbeat quickened in her chest. "David." The name fell from her lips. She wanted to call to him. She wanted to run to him, but her feet stayed planted.

Before she could say another word, the man turned away and rushed into the house. His quick movements seemed unnatural, like an awkward colt trying to prance for the first time.

Nancy looked at Henk and then at Meredith, like she was trying to figure out what had happened. "No, that's Henk," Nancy said. She studied Meredith's face as if she was worried that her friend was losing her mind. Nancy lowered her voice. "David is someone you knew from Miami Beach, but do you remember Henk? Henk has been visiting our field hospital."

"I know who Henk is." There was a quiver to Meredith's voice. "I'm not talking about him. I'm talking about the other man who was with him. He looks just like David."

Nancy wrapped her arms around Meredith, pulling her into a hug. "Oh, honey, that wasn't David. You were just talking about him, that's all, and he's on your mind."

"I . . . I know what he looks like, Nancy. Believe me, I know." Yet even as she said those words, it sounded silly to her. "I . . . I mean, it did look like him. At least the eyes."

Henk waved them forward. A smile filled his face, but he seemed nervous. He glanced toward the house as they approached, then back to them.

"We came for the wood," Nancy explained. "We had time, so we told Mother Superior that we would come."

Henk jutted out his chin. "I told her I would bring it later."

"She was out of wood now. She needs wood to build a fire and cook breakfast for the orphans."

"I will fill my cart. You can help—"

"That man," Meredith interrupted. She pointed to the house. "He . . . he looks . . ." She paused, realizing how silly she'd sound if she said he looked like someone she knew. "That man," she started again, "is he all right? He rushed inside so quickly."

"Yes, he is good. He had work to do. Inside work. And he is not feeling well."

Meredith folded her arms over her chest. "I'm a nurse." She turned toward the house. "I can look at him if you'd like. He looks awfully thin."

Instead of answering her, Henk walked to the back of the house and then returned to where they stood by the woodpile, pulling a cart behind him. "Here, we can load it quickly, yes?" He seemed eager to get the wood loaded and get them on their way. "My friend, no, he is not that sick . . . he will be well soon."

Nancy began loading the wood, but Meredith hung back. She looked at the cottage, scanning the windows, trying to peer inside through the sheer curtains.

"So, are you supposed to be so far away from the field hospital?" Henk asked. "I thought you were supposed to stay close. I heard about the Nazi soldier who escaped—"

"That is worrisome," Meredith interrupted, not answering his question. They probably shouldn't have left the area, but it was only half a kilometer away. "But I'm also worried about your friend."

"My friend?" Henk rubbed his brow.

"That man. The one who was talking to you. The one now in the house."

"That's my cousin, Daaf," he said hurriedly. "He has been traumatized . . . by the war. He doesn't like new people. He does have work inside. And he is not that ill." Henk refused to meet Meredith's gaze.

"He reminds me of someone I once loved." The words were out before Meredith could stop them. Heat rose to her cheeks. She looked away and began loading wood into the cart.

Henk paused and turned to her. "Do you love him still, miss?"

Tearfully, Meredith nodded. She didn't know what had gotten into her. She didn't know why she was confessing it to this man now. "Yes, I suppose I do, but there are hundreds of reasons why I should not."

She couldn't look at Nancy as she said those words. She didn't want to see the concern in her friend's gaze. Instead of looking at Nancy or trying to explain any further to Henk, she grabbed a log with her gloved hands. And then another. Piece by piece, she added to the stack in the cart, telling herself that it wasn't him, it couldn't be him.

Still, she thought again of that man's eyes. Even though it wasn't David, just seeing those eyes had brought a bit of joy to her heart. And a lot of pain.

David slipped the photograph back into his jacket pocket right next to his heart. He leaned against the interior wall, telling himself to wake up. Surely this had to be a dream. Surely Merry wasn't in his town. And what had she confessed . . . that she still loved him?

Henk had come inside and told David what she'd said, and then he'd gone outside again to walk the women back to the convent. The idea that Merry still loved him was too much to comprehend.

He hadn't wanted to believe Henk. It was easier to think of Merry working back in the States, maybe inoculating draftees or caring for the wounded back at home. He always liked to picture her in Miami Beach, her sun-kissed cheeks, her dark hair pulling free from its pins and tossing in the ocean breeze. He'd planned on marrying her until the war got in the way. Leaving her was the hardest thing he'd ever done.

Yet thinking of all those children still locked in safe houses—thin but alive—and all those people their network had skirted across borders, he knew it was worth it. He hadn't been on the front lines, but he'd been fighting this whole war. Fighting to keep safe those who were hunted. Protecting the innocent from the hungry eyes of Nazi wolves.

Yet even though he'd walked away from Merry, expecting never to see her again, here she was.

*God, how could You let this happen? How could You bring her so close and remind me again of what I gave up?* It was easier to love the memory of her. Harder was seeing her in her olive-gray jumpsuit and heavy coat and realizing his love hadn't faded.

Henk had told him she had no beau, but how would he know? Merry wasn't the type to kiss and tell, especially to a stranger.

Footsteps approached again, and David turned. Henk had returned.

"So is it her?" his cousin asked. "The woman in your photograph? It is, isn't it?"

David placed his finger to his lips. "Shhh, you're too loud. Lower your voice before the young women upstairs hear you."

Henk paused before David and leaned close. "You have a strange look in your eyes, my friend. I told you it was her."

David sighed. "Not that it matters."

"What do you mean?"

"There is nothing I can do about it."

"Of course there is. You must go to her. You must tell her you are well. You must make plans for finding each other after the war."

"But to do so . . . it would blow my cover. Everyone knows me as Daaf, not David. No one knows that I used to live in the United States. They would wonder how I know Merry. Word would get out. Others would know I'm not a simple stone factory worker. Then I would have to reveal that we are part of the Underground. The young women in the attic would no longer be safe. There are still Nazi sympathizers in town, and if the Americans lose this ground, then all of us would be turned in."

"We do not know if that will happen. The Americans are here. They are strong. We are no longer under German control. The Americans are turning to Germany next. The Germans are running . . ."

"For this week, but what about next? To reveal myself is to put at risk all those who are still in hiding."

"And if you don't reveal yourself, don't you think you are turning against God? God brought her here. It is a miracle, don't you think? Out of all the nurses, *she* is stationed at your doorstep. It's a Christmas gift. For you. For her. For all of us. It's a reminder that God has not forsaken us. That even in the war there is hope of a future."

y the time the wood got unloaded and Meredith and Nancy made their way to the field hospital, an ambulance had pulled up and unloaded a half-dozen injured men. Their injuries were severe, and one of the young men didn't make it.

When things finally settled down and they had a chance to eat dinner, Meredith found her way over to a quiet corner. The other nurses and doctors must have noticed her need for peace because they let her be. She sat on a wooden box in a corner of the room and ate her food quietly. Her mind couldn't help but wander back to thoughts of David and their picnics at South Pointe Park.

Later, while she and Nancy worked side by side, cleaning pieces of shrapnel from the legs of an unconscious man, Meredith found herself sharing more of her life before the war. She didn't want to talk about it, but she couldn't help it. Perhaps she needed to get it all out to allow room to heal.

"Even though David had the maturity to start his own music school, he was only five years older than me," she told Nancy as they walked. "I started helping at the music school after I'd get out of my nursing classes. Mothers would arrive and drop off their children, and those first few days when I stopped by, I found the boys having sword fights with their violin bows and the girls in tears. I helped with the check-in system, and David taught. More than once I pictured our life being just like that. Him working with the students, and me supporting his work."

"And what about being a nurse?"

Meredith shook her head. "I was such a fool. My heart was so caught up with him that I was ready to give that up."

"That speaks of love to me."

"Or foolishness. When a class of nurses—my friends—graduated, we had a small party for all of them. David played the piano for the guests, and everyone in the room was mesmerized. Even though the music was beautiful, I could tell by the look on his face that something was bothering him. Foolish me, I thought he was just preparing to propose. My heart nearly burst out of my chest when he asked to say something in front of the group. I thought he was going to get down on one knee—or at least say something nice about our friends who were graduating. Instead, he talked about family and the beauty of gathering with those you love in a safe place. He didn't look at me during the whole speech . . . and there were tears."

"Tears?"

"Yes, when he mentioned that some things are worth fighting for."

"He was thinking about returning even then, wasn't he?"

Meredith's fists balled at her side and she nodded. "I had no idea he was talking about supporting the Germans. Nobody did." Her chin trembled, but she urged herself not to cry. She'd shed more than enough tears over the enemy.

"There were some in Miami Beach who were against him simply because he was German," Meredith continued. "Once a hate letter was slid under his door. Another time his windows were broken, but for the most part people supported him, trusted him."

She took the tweezers and resumed pulling small pieces of metal from the soldier's leg. Some pieces were embedded deep. She knew she couldn't get all the pieces out. It was impossible. The shrapnel would either work its way to the surface or work deeper into the skin, possibly causing infection.

*Is that what I've been doing?* Meredith wondered, digging deep. Have I let my wounds fester? It felt good to open up to Nancy. Meredith felt at peace, and what the soldiers saw in her face was what they often experienced. When she was at peace, they usually were too. How could she not remember that?

She hummed Christmas carols as she worked. The men around her perked up, and one young man who'd been lying down for over a week managed to sit up, watching her intensely. Could her choice to be joyful make that big a difference to all the men around her? From what she saw, it did.

"Where are you from?" the soldier asked, leaning up on one elbow. His opposite arm was in a sling and his leg was badly broken. She knew when he was better stabilized, he'd be sent home.

"Lafayette, Indiana."

"Really? I have an aunt from there!" The soldier smiled. "She'd come to St. Louis every Christmas and bring us Glatz Candies."

"You don't say." A smiled filled Meredith's face. "My sister Abigail used to work there."

She thought of the aromas of chocolate and peppermint candy canes from the store around Christmas, the *ting-a-ling* of the bell. Her stomach rumbled at the memory of candy displays and the soda fountain where she'd meet to hang out with friends. Her parents said that Glatz's hadn't changed much since their first years of marriage, and it gave Meredith a sense of peace that it was still the same today. Rationing of sugar and other ingredients might have slowed production, but everyone needed a place to go where time stood still and the simple pleasures of life could be enjoyed. Abigail would always bring them a small treat to "test" for her, and sometimes Grandma would ask her to bring home a special truffle. Meredith would do anything to have just one hour back there, to let the cares of the world be forgotten as she sipped on a malt.

"Oh my, you've brought back so many memories. Every Christmas . . ." she started, but then she noticed something in the soldier's face change.

He blinked back tears. "I'm not going to ever get back there again, am I?"

"Where?" she dared to ask.

"Back to the good ole US of A. Back to St. Louis. Back home. The doc says that there could be infection. That things can turn bad—"

"Or that everything will heal well," she insisted. "Actually, I think you will . . . and I'm not just saying that. You had one of the best doctors, and your vitals are looking good. You'll need time to rest and heal, and therapy, but you're going to make it."

It felt good saying those words, and she spoke them with confidence. A lot could go wrong, such as infection, but as she spoke, she noticed the man's face brighten, and she began to understand. Hope did even more good than the medicine and the doctoring. Hope changed things.

The mail truck arrived, and Meredith was pleasantly surprised a few minutes later to see the driver approaching. "Two letters for you today, Meredith."

"For me?"

Joy bubbled up inside, and she felt as if she could float up and touch the ceiling. She looked at the return addresses and noticed one letter was from Pete and the other from Abigail. She couldn't wait until her shift was over. Yet she had to. She had work to do, good work.

Meredith moved through the rest of the day's tasks with joy and a smile. The previous days, weeks, months had been hard, but she was learning to look at the positive. She couldn't wait to hear what her siblings had to say, and she again thought about after the war when they could meet more frequently. She was doing her part to make sure families had a chance for special reunions, and there was nowhere else she would rather be.

Was this change of attitude caused by simply opening up?

## Twelve

The shift had been long, and Meredith was glad it was over. She'd prayed with the soldier from St. Louis, and he'd drifted off to sleep with a look of peace on his face.

Now she was back at the convent, sitting by candlelight, thankful for the warmth in her room. Warmth provided by the wood they'd retrieved that morning. She didn't want to think of Daaf—the man who seemed to have David's eyes. Not when she had news from home.

Meredith glanced at the two letters on her lap. One from Abigail and the other from Pete. Growing up, she'd always been the baby, the caboose, the shadow. Pete had been the troublemaker and Abigail the peacemaker. She'd been the one they all liked to take care of.

She'd moved to Miami Beach partly for the reasons she'd claimed. She wanted warmer weather. She wanted adventure. But she also wanted to be her own person and not just the littlest of the Turner kids.

Wherever she went around Lafayette, folks had already written her script for her, and they tried to take care of her too. On the first day of every class she'd see the expectation in her teacher's eyes. "Merry, dear, let me know if you need any help."

But now . . . now she wondered. What was wrong with being a Turner kid? Maybe having older siblings to identify with wasn't so bad, and she couldn't wait until the day she returned to tell them so. She opened her first letter and began to read.

*November 1, 1944*

*Dear Merry,*

*I hope I'm getting this package in the mail in enough time for it to find you wherever you are before Christmas.*

*It's November 1st—you know how I like to cut things close. And I've got plenty to be thankful for. You're safe. Pete's off flying, and we enjoy having Grace and Linnie so close. He's been good for them, but they've been just as good for him.*

*Then in a few months, Jackson and I will welcome our own child into our family. Remember the nights we'd huddle under our covers and whisper about those far-off days when we'd get married and then have children? It seemed so distant, and now I'm married and talking baby names. I pray someday you'll find the man who makes your heart race and makes you want to spend every moment with him. I know he's out there for you. Whoever he is, he'll be God's best.*

*Grandma's the same feisty person. We wrote and told you that she had been feeling ill, but as of late, it looks like she's been bouncing back! I see her at least every Sunday, but she's certain I need help before the baby arrives. I wouldn't be surprised if she moves into the small room we'll use for a nursery—just to make sure everything is fine. You know how she is.*

*Much love. We miss you, and merry Christmas, wherever you are.*

*Abigail*

She opened up Pete's letter next, expecting the note to be brief, and just local gossip. Instead she was moved by Pete's words—so much so that she read it twice.

*Dear Merry,*

*By now I hope you received the Christmas package I sent in September. Rather, the package Grace sent. My lovely fiancée insisted on having the honors.*

*We both pray that you're well. I say this in every letter, but it bears repeating—we servicemen appreciate what you nurses do. Most of the men you treat were drafted. They didn't have a choice to serve, but you did. I know your living conditions are unpleasant—I chuckle to think of my snow-hating sister braving the coldest winter in recorded European history—so my appreciation runs even deeper.*

*The ATC Ferrying Division keeps me hopping around the country. I enjoy flying a variety of aircraft, shuttling them from the factory to the training fields and air bases. I often fly to Indianapolis, where I make my best lawyerly arguments for a Remain Overnight and catch a train home. My CO has a soft heart and a nostalgic wife, so I don't have to argue hard.*

*Our December 23 wedding approaches, but not quickly enough. Despite Grace's wish to keep it simple, she and Linnie are in a whirlwind. I should feel guilty that I only have to show up in dress uniform and repeat my vows after Pastor Hughes. But I don't.*

*Lately, you've been heavy on my heart. Three years seems like a long time, but it's only a blink of an eye when you've been hurt and betrayed. Even though you were the one who broke things off, I know David must have done something to bring you to that. A big brother knows these things. Forgiveness usually happens in a process rather than in a single moment, and I pray you'll let the Lord continue to patch the hole in your heart. Forgive me for being blunt, but what are big brothers for?*

*I love you, little sis, and I'm proud of you. Now tell a big burly medic to throw a snowball at you from me. Hard.*

*Love, Pete*

Laughter slipped from Meredith's lips, and she pictured Pete hurling a snowball at her as he'd done a thousand times.

She thought of Abigail—the caregiver and the friend. It had been Abigail who'd vowed not to date until this war business was over. Of course, that vow did her little good when Jackson Lucas came on the scene. Meredith, on the other hand, had always been open to following her heart. And where had it gotten her?

She read Pete's letter for the third time. He didn't know the complete situation with David—how could he know? Yet now he spoke of forgiveness. He no doubt struggled with forgiving the enemy he fought against on his missions as a bomber pilot, and that told her something. If he could work to forgive the real enemies he met in the sky, then maybe she needed to give it a try. The only question was how?

*Lord, I need You to do this. I give it to You—the pain, the rejection, the shame. I give it all to You.*

## Thirteen

*Sunday, December 24*

$\mathcal{M}$eredith hadn't planned on approaching Henk, but that is exactly what happened the next day when he arrived, bringing food to the field hospital. She'd approached with quickened steps, meeting him at the door.

"Henk, I need to talk to you about that man at your house."

"Daaf, yes, that is who you are talking about. I know you wish to thank him for his help with supplying wood for the convent." Henk peered down at her. His voice lowered as if he were going to tell her a secret. "But Daaf is not the only one bringing wood. There are many in our village who want to do their part to help."

"Yes, well, I'm very thankful about the wood, but . . . I'm more interested in the man. He looks familiar. Like I told you before, he looks like someone I once knew."

Henk's jaw dropped open, yet she couldn't help but note the twinkle in his gaze. "But how can that be? Have you visited our village before?"

"No, of course not. This sounds silly, doesn't it?" She studied his face closely, noting a feathering of wrinkles fanning out from his blue eyes. Henk had to be in his late thirties, and for the first time she wondered what he was doing here, rather than fighting on the front lines. Their commander had to trust him to allow him access to the hospital units, but was he trustworthy? How much did they really know about him?

Meredith rubbed her temple, wondering what she should do. *Don't trust him, Meredith,* she told herself. *Don't say anymore. Before you know it you'll be leaving this village—and leaving all the mysteries of this place behind.*

The clatter of an instrument tray hitting the floor just behind her caused her to jump. Henk let out a small chuckle and then shook his head. "I think you need to get more sleep. More rest."

"Yes, maybe that is it." She frowned up at him. "Maybe that's why I'm seeing things."

He strode away before Meredith could ask any more questions. She rubbed the back of her neck and then released a low breath. "Daaf . . . what kind of name is that?" she mumbled.

❦

Daaf sank down on his knees beside his bed. It was just a small cot. He didn't even have a blanket. He'd given it to someone along the way. The young mother with the nursing infant? The two twin boys whose eyes were bright and happy, as if hiding out in an attic room was a delightful game? He wasn't sure. It wasn't the only thing he'd given away. He'd shared all the clothes and food he could. He'd given away his plans, his future. He'd given away what he'd wanted most—*who* he'd wanted most—for the sake of a holy cause.

He'd first heard about Hitler's plans before he even left Europe. His uncle had attended some of Hitler's rallies, not because he believed, but because he knew how easily diseased ideas spread. The day Daaf had stood on the docks, preparing to board the ship to New York, his uncle had pressed Nazi fliers into his hands. "Remember that there are times when your life must take a backseat to the needs of many. Remember that you are Dutch as well as German. Remember that there are some things worth fighting for," he'd said.

His Uncle Arie had lived for his beliefs. He'd died for them too, just a few months after Daaf had left the United States and come to the Netherlands. Had it been almost three years already?

Daaf pulled out his uncle's last letter. He could almost picture him hurriedly writing it under the watching eye of the Nazi guards. The people in his uncle's life who meant the most to him were people Daaf had hardly known before the war. Now they were the ones he worked with to save the lives of the defenseless and helpless.

*Dear parents, sisters, and brothers,*

    *With this letter I give you notice that this is the last letter I can write. The reprieve has been refused and the sentence will be carried out.*

    *Mother, give the boys some of my things. It is up to you what to do with the vegetable business. The pastor has visited me in prison, and we prayed together.*

    *Mother, I know it is going to be difficult for you. For every one of you, but for you the most. But be not discouraged, Mother. One day we will see each other again.*

    *I do not know what to write. Greet all the people another time from me. Now finally I want to greet all of you one more time.*

    *Bye, Father, Mother, Marie, Jaantje, Nelly en Koosje, David, Henk. Mother, do not be afraid. I die as an honorable man.*

    *All my things are on the Haagsche Veer (the police station, MvB). When you receive this letter, I will be no more.*

    *Father, Mother, think of your other children and grandchildren. Do not think only of me.*

    *Love each other while you have the chance.*

    *Arie van Steensel*

Daaf set the letter on his lap. Pain radiated through his chest as he thought again of his uncle. An uncle who was close to his age and closer than a brother. Arie had been sentenced to death for favoring the enemy. Why? He'd attempted to help the crew of a British bomber escape, but the men were captured, and one wore Arie's cap. The civilian clothes of small-town citizens proved who'd been helping the enemy. Arie hadn't lived to see the day when the Germans had been pushed out of the Netherlands. If Arie had known of all the lives they'd saved, he would be proud.

Uncle Arie had written Daaf often while he was in the United States, asking him to return and help with the fight. He had sent Daaf more fliers, telling of Hitler's deeds. He'd written of the Jews being rounded up, sure it would lead to their destruction.

A battle had waged within Daaf upon hearing his uncle's words. There were many things he'd given up for the sake of strangers. Some things were harder to leave behind than others. Leaving the woman he loved was hardest of all. But Arie had given his life. Daaf felt guilty for wanting to gain back what he'd given up—Merry—especially when his uncle gave the ultimate sacrifice.

*Oh, God, what have You done?* Daaf pressed his forehead into the thin mattress. He'd been willing to walk away, and yet God had brought her—brought Merry—to his doorstep. *Why, God? To taunt me? To break my heart all over again? To bring on guilt for even considering pursuing happiness?*

Yet he had known God since he was a child, and Daaf had gotten to know Him even better over the last four years. First, during his time spent with Merry, understanding the goodness of God's gift to Him. Then the three years after as he was forced to walk away from that gift. Total need and dependence had a way of doing that. Maybe, as with Abraham's attempted sacrifice of his son, God's plan wasn't to strip away but to provide a better way.

But why now? Why here? The war wasn't over. The Nazis had made it clear that their fight was far from done. To reveal himself would be to put many lives at stake. At his insistence, those who'd hidden for the sake of their lives were still in hiding. After all, there were no guarantees that the Nazis wouldn't reclaim this ground. He'd heard rumors of a German superweapon—one that would turn the tide of war back to the advantage of that madman Hitler. He couldn't put those in his care at stake. He couldn't reveal his true identity. He couldn't bring any risk of connection to him, or to Merry either. More than one of his friends had suffered under torture and lost their lives to keep the secret of the resistance leaders. Yet a question remained: if he couldn't go to her, why had God brought Merry so close?

*A Christmas miracle. To bring hope to My children.* The words fell like a soft snow on his heart. His chest warmed, as if someone had placed a hand in the center of it, and Daaf blew out a breath, wondering how God could meet an ordinary man like him in such a way.

Could it be that easy . . . to just accept the gift?

The back door opened, and Daaf recognized Henk's footsteps. Henk walked as if he were stomping on ants with every step. He approached and sat on the handmade stool across the table from Daaf. His face was pale, making his freckles appear more prominent.

"What's wrong?" Daaf asked. "Is there bad news from the front?"

Henk swallowed hard. "No, but I have something to tell you. Do not be mad."

"Henk, how could I be upset with you? We've been through a lot. You've saved my life more than once. Do you think that I'd be unnerved so easily?"

"You don't understand. It started with good intentions. I truly believe that God brought Merry to our village to reunite with you. I never once thought any different."

"So what are you saying?"

"I couldn't keep it a secret any longer. I had to tell someone."

"You told her?" Daaf gasped and jumped to his feet. "You told Merry? You told her I'm here?"

"No, but I did tell her friend Nancy. I couldn't hold it in when she approached me today. Nancy was worried about your Merry. All Merry can talk about is the time spent with you and all her regrets. She said the man at this cottage looked like you. Nancy was so worried about her friend that she was about to go to the commander and ask him to take Merry off the front lines. Nancy is certain her friend was having some type of mental shock. But I told her not to tell . . . at least not yet."

Daaf rubbed his temples with his fingers, feeling a headache coming on.

Henk opened his mouth and then closed it again. He pulled his hat from his head and then combed his hair down with his fingers in quick strokes, acting as if that one simple act was the most important thing he could be doing at the moment.

Daaf didn't know what to say. He wanted to be angry, but he understood why Henk had done what he did. Henk thought God had brought this to be. And who could ever guess that Merry had been right. That it *was* him that she recognized?

His heart ached for Merry. He didn't want to think of the shock his leaving had caused. What did she think of him?

He expected her to be angry. She no doubt was. But Henk claimed she'd also declared her love. That wasn't something he'd expected. If she still loved him, could she also forgive him? And if he revealed himself, would it put those in his care at risk?

"If I reveal myself to Merry, then everyone will know," he said softly.

"Know that you're a hero?"

Daaf shook his head. "Know I've been lying to them."

"Yes, but it was for a good cause."

"True, but lies always hurt. If I could do things over, I would have told Merry more. I would have told her the truth. I didn't want her to wait for me. I didn't want her to think we'd ever have a chance to be together." He lowered his head and looked down at his lap and the letter from his uncle. He folded up the letter and put it back in the envelope.

"If you don't tell her, I will. I don't understand why you are so worried," Henk finally said. "You claim it's to keep the young women safe, but if it comes to that, we have places to send them. I think it's your heart that you're most worried about, my friend."

Daaf pressed the envelope between his fingers. What had Uncle Arie said? *Love each other while you have the chance.*

"If she finds out from Nancy and you don't come forth, then Merry will think you have abandoned her again."

Pain stabbed Daaf's heart. He didn't want that. He'd made that mistake before. "What do you suggest then?" he finally said. "How can I earn her trust . . . and remind her of my love?"

A smile brightened Henk's face, and he placed a hand on Daaf's shoulder. "Friend, I have an idea. You must start by letting Merry know that you've never stopped thinking about her . . . that every moment you had—and every memory that she shared—was important."

## Fourteen

*Monday, December 25*

Meredith awoke and sat up with a start. Something was wrong. She looked around and noticed the other nurses still asleep. Then she realized what the problem was. Silence. The ground fire had ceased —at least for a time. Did the fighting slow because it was Christmas?

Meredith snuggled back down, telling herself to go back to sleep, yet sleep evaded her. Instead, she thought of the man at the cottage. She replayed his features in her mind. Maybe Nancy had been right. She'd been thinking about David a lot—talking about him—and now her mind was playing tricks on her.

There were times over the years that she had tried to push David out of her mind. She wanted to forgive him, she did. Her Grandma had told her before that forgiving wasn't forgetting. There were some things you could never forget. Instead, it meant giving it over to God. Was God asking her to pray for David? She had no idea where he was or what he faced in this war, but while she knew him, David had seemed to be a man of faith. Was God asking her to pray that David's faith would be renewed?

She thought about the man at the cottage who looked so much like David, and she prayed. "Lord, that man reminded me of David. And I've been so worried about going into Germany and finding him . . . yet You know where he is. Will You be with him wherever he is? Will You remind him that You are in control of his life and that Your love for him is strong? Will You help David do the right thing and make the right choices? Amen."

It had taken awhile to get to this place—for her to be able to pray for the man who'd hurt her so. It had taken her being transported to the Netherlands during one of the coldest winters in history, helping broken soldiers, and being visited by a ghost from the past.

But it felt good to pray for him. And deep down, Meredith had a sense that her prayers mattered.

Nancy's snores eased, and she turned on her side. Her eyes fluttered open and a soft smile touched her lips. "It's good to hear you praying again . . . even if you're praying about him."

It wasn't until Nancy's comment that Meredith realized she hadn't been praying for herself. She'd been concerned about her patients, and she'd whispered prayers for them. But all her own cares? She'd stuffed them deep inside. Did she think that God couldn't handle them? Did she think that her broken heart was too big for God's grasp?

Nancy's soft snores filled the room again, and Meredith let out a gentle breath.

"I ask You to help *me* do the right thing—to make the right decisions too," she finally said in the softest of whispers. "I'm tired of trying to feel like I'm in control. I place myself in Your hands."

---

Not long after she'd arrived for her shift, Dr. Anderson approached, placing an arm around Meredith's shoulders. "Meredith, the nurses are talking about planning something. It's a Christmas celebration, but they really perked up, talking about your birthday."

"There's a war out there, doctor. We have very injured men here. I'm sure there are more important things for everyone to worry about than my birthday." Still, she couldn't help but smile.

"Don't you know that around here a little bit of joy is the best medicine? When word gets out that one's nickname is Merry because she was born on

Christmas, it's hard not to get excited about that." He pulled his hand from behind his back and emerged with a handmade Christmas card. "It's not from me . . . I wish I had thought of it, though."

*Merry, Merry, Merry!* the outside of the card read. She took it from him and opened it. *The most beautiful nurse in the Netherlands. Happy birthday!*

She took a step back. "You don't understand. I'm not Merry. When I enlisted I used the name Meredith. I *chose* to use the name Meredith, and my nickname stayed home with all my other childhood things." She crossed her arms over her chest, pulling them tight to her. "No one should know that name here."

She bit her lip, thinking of Samuel. He'd called her Merry. Had someone overheard?

Dr. Anderson winked. "Well, maybe we know you better than you think."

She opened the card again and looked at it closer. A gasp escaped her lips and she covered her mouth with her hand. Under the words *Happy birthday* someone had drawn a peony. A chill traveled up her arms. It was the Indiana state flower, but also her favorite. She glanced around the post-op room, looking to see who was playing this trick on her, but all the other nurses were busy at their tasks. *How did they know?*

"But . . . but . . ." she sputtered, looking up at Dr. Anderson. "Doctor, where did this come from?"

He shrugged. "I found it on a chair by the front door. I thought you'd know who it was from."

Meredith forced a smile. "Well, I can guess. Maybe Nancy? She knows me better than anyone else." Her voice sounded more sure than she felt.

Nancy was in the operating room, assisting one of the other doctors with a surgery, and Meredith planned on talking to her later. She tried to remember if she'd ever mentioned her nickname or her favorite flower. She didn't think so, but they'd spent a lot of time together. Who could remember all that they had discussed?

A few minutes later a soldier hobbled up to her. Charlie's arms, leg, and neck had been burned, but he was doing better. Meredith was surprised to see him up and around.

"Meredith, I found this hanging on the doorknob of the back door. It has your name on it," he said.

"My name?"

"Well, almost your name. It says 'Merry Turner.'"

Dr. Anderson happened to be walking by as she took the piece of paper into her hands. He let out a low whistle. "Nurse Turner, I do believe you have an admirer."

She tried to laugh, but when she opened the paper and read it, flutters filled her stomach, followed by a cold shiver. She wondered if she was going to be sick.

The soldier took her arm as if worried she would faint. "What is it? What's wrong, ma'am?"

"It . . . it's my favorite poem. I memorized it in the third grade." She held it up so the soldier could read it.

"A little bird I am, shut from the fields of air, and in my cage I sit and sing to Him who placed me there: Well pleased a prisoner to be, because, my God, it pleases Thee!

Naught have I else to do; I sing the whole day long; and He whom most I love to please doth listen to my song, He caught and bound my wandering wing, but still He bends to hear me sing," Charlie read.

"Louisa May Alcott is my favorite author," Meredith confessed. "And her work as a nurse inspired me."

She'd barely gotten the words out when Henk arrived with a small tree. He walked into the recovery room, and his eyes were fixed on her. "I cut this down. A Christmas tree."

"What a wonderful idea." She tried to act like she wasn't bothered by the way he'd just shown up with the tree. She smiled and sat on a nearby chair, certain she would faint if she didn't sit. Other than singing Christmas carols, her favorite thing about Christmas was the Christmas tree.

Abigail and Mother loved to bake. Pete loved the Christmas dinner. Grandma loved wrapping presents. But the one thing Meredith looked forward to most was Daddy setting up the tree. She was the one who organized everyone to add the candles and bulbs. But again . . . how did someone know? Was it just a coincidence?

"Hey, miss, do you have any K-ration cans?" another one of the injured soldiers asked.

Her eyebrows peaked. "You want cans?"

"Maybe we can cut them up to make decorations," he said.

Another soldier sat up, looking through a care package that he'd been given. "Look what arrived in our Red Cross packages. Life Savers! Do you have any bandages we can use to string these up and add them to the tree?"

"I don't see why not." Meredith rose and moved to the supply chest with a new lightness to her step. Someone was making sure she had Christmas—and a bonus—and Meredith decided to go along with it, to enjoy herself. The guns had stilled outside and a new peace settled within her. The joy on the patients' faces was clear. She supposed Dr. Anderson was right. Joy was wonderful medicine.

Meredith hurried to Henk, who was setting up the tree. She placed a hand on his arm. "Thank you so much for doing this. It means so much."

Henk turned to her and a smile filled his face. "Yes, but it is not me you should thank. Someone who cares for you very much made sure this came to be."

Meredith nodded, understanding. She looked over at the closed door to the surgery room. Nancy had taken her place in surgery today, giving her lighter duties. What had she done to deserve such a friend?

"Yes, I feel very loved," Meredith said, turning back to Henk. Nancy was a good friend, indeed.

## Fifteen

The tree was up and decorated, and Meredith hoped their hospital unit wouldn't be ordered to move before their Christmas celebration. She had overheard rumors that they'd be heading into Germany soon. Mentally, spiritually, she was more prepared for it. Yet for the sake of everyone here, she hoped they could enjoy a time of celebration together before they moved and the fight for lives started again.

"We have a pianist in town. He is a good friend and can be trusted," she overheard Henk telling Dr. Anderson. "Could he come and play for the men?"

"It would be fine if we had a piano." Meredith stilled the movement of her hands.

"Yes, well, I know a family . . . the Alberts family have a piano. I am sure they will not mind. They have asked me more than once what they can do for the Americans. Thankful they are, indeed."

"That's good news!" Dr. Anderson's voice rose with excitement. "I can send someone from operations with you to see if we could borrow it. If so, then we can move the piano into the recovery room. If it all works out, tell your musician friend that he can come tonight."

The doctor smiled. "If it's not too much work, the men would appreciate it."

Meredith hurried up to them. She clasped her hands together. "A piano? Really? That would be so swell. I've been meaning to ask if we could try to find one." A smile filled her face. "I'm sure I haven't told anyone, but one of my favorite parts of Christmas is singing Christmas carols."

Henk chuckled. "God has a way of letting us know, Merry."

She looked up at him and cocked her head. Had Henk meant to call her that? Had word gotten out about that being her nickname?

Henk nodded enthusiastically. "With a few of us, we could haul the piano in my wagon. It's not too large. I am sure the Alberts family will let us use it."

Meredith remembered the lovely family who'd invited the nurses to dinner when she first arrived. She clapped her hands together. "I think the soldiers would love that. Can I go with you, to thank the Albertses?"

"Yes, of course!" Henk motioned to Dr. Anderson. "If it is good with you."

"Yes, if it doesn't take too long. Our patients will be wondering where their favorite nurse went."

Meredith hurried to the coat rack, reached for her coat, and then paused. Her jaw dropped open in shock.

Taped to the wall by the window was a paper cutout of a Christmas stocking. JESUS was written in capital letters across the top. It was an exact replica of one she had at home, back in Indiana. Meredith must have been seven or eight years old when she'd made the stocking. It had been a school project, and each student was supposed to write his or her name.

When her mother asked her about it, Meredith had said, "Jesus and I share the same birthday, and I want to celebrate Him."

Her mother had tried to hold back a smile when Meredith had gone on to explain that she wanted to make sure He got gifts that day too. With tears in her eyes, Mama had explained that what Jesus wanted was their hearts. Meredith had heard that before, but that day she understood it completely, and she prayed with her mother, giving her life—a great gift—to Jesus.

Staring at that paper stocking on the wall, Meredith had never been so surprised. She'd also never felt more confused. She was sure she'd never shared that story with Nancy. And there was no way anyone could know about it. "Unless . . ." she said to herself, "unless Nancy has been reading my mail!" Meredith thought about the letters she'd received from Pete and Abigail. Both of them had mentioned her birthday in recent months. She had mentioned Louisa May Alcott and the Christmas stocking too.

The only one who knew where she kept her letters tucked away was Nancy. Had her friend—the woman she'd assumed was a friend—gotten into her mail?

Meredith turned on her heel and noticed Nancy across the room. She was just getting cleaned up from surgery. Meredith approached. She watched as Nancy finished washing her hands, chatting about the new song "Have Yourself a Merry Little Christmas" with Dina as she did. Meredith waited until Dina walked away, and then she placed a firm hand on Nancy's shoulder.

Nancy pulled back, surprised.

"If you want to give me a neck rub, you'll need both hands." She chuckled. Then her smile faded when she noticed the serious look on Meredith's face.

Meredith pointed to the corner of the room where an empty wooden bookshelf stood. "I need to talk to you. Over there. Please."

Nancy lifted her hands in surrender. "Yeah, sure, but whatever has gotten you all in a huff, I didn't do it."

Meredith marched toward the corner, and Nancy sheepishly followed. Meredith tried to pretend that a dozen eyes weren't on her. What did it matter? After a few days she would never see these men again. But Nancy—Nancy had been her closest friend since they met on the ship to England. They'd cried together over the first soldiers lost. They'd sat side by side during USO flicks. Meredith had dared to tell Nancy about David just a few days ago. She'd opened her heart up to her fellow nurse more than she had to anyone else in a very long time. The only person she'd opened up to more was David, and this was how Nancy treated her?

"What is my favorite flower?" Meredith jutted out her chin.

Nancy's gaze narrowed. "Is this a trick question?"

"No, I just want to hear your answer."

"You haven't mentioned it. I don't know. Rose? Carnation? Lily?" She scratched her head.

"Don't try to play it off, Nancy. Just tell me the truth. You read my letters from home. You read the one where my mother talked about planting my favorite flowers—peonies—and then you told Henk."

"Wait, wait." Nancy wagged her finger in Meredith's direction. "I did not read your letters. That would be as bad as reading someone's diary. You should know me well enough, Meredith, to know I'd never do that. Never ever. I had no idea about your favorite flower. Sheesh. Nice of you to blame a gal. How would you like it if I did that to you? If I—"

Meredith's mind began to spin. She searched for an answer. If it wasn't Nancy, then who? Who could know so much about her? Goose bumps rose on her arms.

Nancy also wore a look of shock. Then her face softened. She looked around the room, as if expecting to see someone. Her lips curled in a soft "oh."

Nancy tilted her head and looked at Meredith. "I know it seems as if you've been betrayed, honey, but just relax. Let yourself have fun with this. Open your heart. Maybe it's a Christmas miracle." Nancy offered her a gentle hug and then stepped back. "I have a feeling this could be your best Christmas ever . . . if you let it."

*A Christmas miracle?* It was a time of war. Pain, destruction, and death daily burdened her heart. Could there be such a thing as miracles in this war? And if so, why should she receive one? There were so many who needed them more. Surely there had to be a logical explanation.

"Something is happening . . . something strange." Meredith dropped her head so that her chin touched her chest. "It's as if someone who knows me better than anyone else is leaving me clues . . . but clues for what, I don't know. It's giving me the shivers. I mean, who could know all these things about me?"

Nancy curled up one side of her lips and shrugged. "Lucky guesses?"

Meredith let out a long sigh, trying to make sense of everything. Someone was trying hard . . . she had to give them that. And even if someone did read her letters—which she was no longer certain of—what did she have to hide? A loving family? A brother, a sister, a grandma, and parents who loved and cared for her? Why should one be so timid about sharing that?

"Listen." Nancy lowered her voice. "I didn't mean to confuse you. Maybe you should ask for a few hours to rest. It's your birthday. I'm sure Dr. Anderson will give you a pass. Then . . . I hear we will have someone here to play some special Christmas music later—"

"I can't rest. Not now." Then she remembered. "I'm going with Henk to pick up the piano for tonight."

Without hesitation she returned to the foyer area and put on her coat, scarf, and mittens. Outside, Henk was waiting with a tired-looking wagon and two even more tired-looking horses.

"Are you sure that can carry a piano?" she asked.

"It's a spinet. It will fit well, I promise." He offered her a hand as she climbed onto the front of the wagon. Meredith sat and then stood again and climbed down.

"Wait. Last time I was there, Mrs. Alberts had a nasty cut on her hand. I tended it, but I should take a first-aid kit just in case."

Henk clucked his tongue. "Once a nurse, always a nurse. You were made for this, Merry."

His words carried her as she moved inside, and deep down she knew Henk was right. God had brought her here for a reason. God had given her this Christmas for a reason. She wasn't here because of the whims of a schoolgirl. She wasn't here because she'd tried to run from a simple life. She was here because of God's design. It was the first time she'd ever really thought of it like that. Yes, she was serving others with her nursing skills, but tonight these soldiers would have a special Christmas. She'd do her part to see to that.

## Sixteen

The first sign that something was terribly wrong was that all the drapes at the Albertses' house were drawn even though it was a beautiful, sunny day. Meredith clasped her first-aid kit to her chest as she climbed down from the wagon with Henk's help and moved up the steps.

Henk knocked loudly and they could hear voices, then the shuffling of feet.

Meredith heard the strained voice of Mrs. Alberts say something in Dutch through the door. Henk answered, and she could tell that he was inquiring about the piano.

The woman spoke again, and Henk looked at Meredith. "Something does not seem right here. We need to leave," he said, and then a strange expression crossed his face. He grabbed her arm and took a step back.

"But the piano!" she protested.

"We need to leave—" he started again.

Henk's words were cut off by the door swinging open. Mrs. Alberts stumbled out, hands raised. A man stepped forward, following her. Mr. Alberts's clothes hung on him, but it was not Mr. Alberts. It was the escaped German soldier, his gun drawn and pointed at the back of Mrs. Alberts's head.

The German shouted something at Henk. Henk swallowed hard and answered. He raised his hands and stepped forward. "Merry, come inside."

"What is it? What's going on?" she asked.

"The German. It's his arm. They are asking for help. He has been keeping them hostage, but he needs help."

"The wound," she whispered, following them into the house. The door slammed shut behind them.

The German released Mrs. Alberts and then turned the gun on Meredith. Recognition lit his eyes. He remembered her from the field hospital, and she thought she saw relief in his gaze too.

Meredith ignored the gun and rushed forward. Henk followed.

"Tell him to lie down." Meredith pointed to the couch. "And open the drapes. We need light in here!"

Even though the German did what she said, with the help of Henk's translation, he still held the gun pointed at her. Meredith took a deep breath and knelt on the floor next to the couch. She quickly unwrapped the bandages on his arm. Someone had tried to cover her old bandaging job with pieces of a shirt, and as she unwrapped it, she understood why. Her bandages were soaked through and an awful stench rose from the wound.

She nodded and smiled at the German, and then she reached for her first-aid kit.

He jerked slightly at her movement and pointed the gun closer to her.

"Tell him I will fix him up," Meredith said to Henk. "And then tell him you'll give him a ride to the German front lines."

"What?" Henk's hands were still raised, and he shook his head.

"Just tell him," she said again through a smile and clenched teeth.

Henk said something in German, and the soldier seemed to relax. She continued to cut off the bandage, acting as if there was nothing wrong. She really wanted to gag from the smell of infected, decaying flesh. The members of the Alberts family stood to the side and watched in horror.

"We need to take this off," she said in a singsong voice.

"The bandage?" Henk asked.

"No. *All* of it—the arm." She motioned to the air. "We need to get him back to surgery. If Dr. Anderson works quickly, we can save his life. But tell him I said that we'll have him fixed up in no time."

Henk nodded, and she continued cutting off the bandage as if she didn't have a care in the world.

The German said something to Henk.

"He wants to know about his friend," Henk translated.

Meredith smiled for real this time. "Tell him he's doing well. He's up and walking."

Henk translated and the other man nodded.

"Okay, swell," she said. "I'm going to get some special medicine. I know what I'm doing, but as soon as you see my hand moving toward the man's face, I'd suggest that you hit the floor."

As carefully as she could, Meredith poured chloroform from her first-aid kit onto a rag without anyone being able to read the label. She knew the German wouldn't return to the hospital willingly, yet she also knew she couldn't do anything here to save his life.

*Dear Lord, be with me. Help this work.*

She dropped the man's arm to his chest. He cried out in pain at the same moment her hand reached for his nose and mouth, covering them with her cloth. She kept her hand against his face as she ducked away from the pistol.

A shot rang out, and the sound of a bullet whizzed through the air. Yet before the man could fire a second shot, the chloroform had done its work.

The German passed out, and the gun dropped to the floor. Henk lunged for it and picked it up gingerly. Meredith righted her body and released the breath she'd been holding. It wasn't until she dropped the rag to the floor that she realized how fast her heart was pounding.

"You moved so fast," Henk said. "Meredith, that . . . that was fast. I've never seen anyone move like that."

Meredith thought of the letter she'd read just a few days earlier. She smiled when she thought of her older brother. "My speed is what allowed me to get to adulthood." She placed a hand over her pounding heart and offered a comforting smile to the Alberts, who were still trying to figure out what was going on. "My brother Pete can throw a mean snowball. I guess you can say he's been training me every winter for just this moment. Now, let's get this man back to the field hospital as fast as we can. If we're going to save his life, we have to get him into surgery!"

## Seventeen

The field hospital was a flurry of activity when the piano was brought into the post-op room. Meredith and Henk had taken two trips, first to bring the injured German, and second to bring the piano.

Dr. Anderson indeed had to remove the man's arm, but he had saved his life. The German had not yet regained consciousness from surgery, but he'd been moved off site to be guarded, along with the other Germans. Dr. Anderson wanted to make sure that his nurses and patients would not be put in harm's way again.

"I can't control the big guns and hen tanks out there," Dr. Anderson had said, "but this I can do."

Meredith was in the process of rebandaging one of the soldier's wounds when the piano was finally carried in. Chairs had been brought from the other rooms and set up around the Christmas tree. The piano was situated just behind it.

Now, with the piano set up and the rest of the recovery room decorated with makeshift ornaments, Meredith looked around in amazement. This day had been such a wonder. She decided to do what Nancy had suggested, and instead of being bothered by the mysterious gifts, she just appreciated them. Someone here cared for her . . . very much.

Outside, snowed fluttered from the sky, and some random shelling could be heard in the far distance. But inside, the post-operation room was warm and filled with smiling faces.

"Meredith!" Dr. Anderson called. She looked up and he waved her forward. "When you finish that, we'll start. I'm saving a chair for you."

She nodded and forced a smile, still wondering who'd left the card and gifts.

She finished the bandage and approached the tree. The soldier Charlie was waiting by the back row and he ushered her up to the front. Piano music began, but she could not make out the musician. The Christmas tree was blocking the view.

Looking around, she noticed tears filling the eyes of the soldiers. They had faraway looks in their eyes and were no doubt thinking of home. And of buddies lost.

Footsteps sounded behind her, and she turned to see the priest making his way to the front. He spoke to the soldiers in Dutch, his voice filled with emotion. Henk rose to translate.

"Father says that for many years he has prayed for freedom, and it came in an unexpected way. But that's how God works. He uses the weak things of the world to defeat the strong." Henk cleared his throat and then turned to Meredith. "God also brings us unexpected gifts in unexpected ways."

The tears came then, and she realized how true it was. In her discomfort and uncertainty she'd found God again . . . and she'd turned over to Him the burden she'd carried for so long. She'd also started praying for David and hoped someday he'd find his way down the right path too. Now it was time to stop crying for—and stop longing for—David. Her good future was in God's hands.

When the priest joined them in the audience, the pianist began playing "Be Thou My Vision"—Meredith's favorite hymn. How could they have known? Warmth filled her, but then her stomach flipped when the pianist began to sing.

Be thou my vision O Lord of my heart
None other is aught but the King of the seven heavens.
Be thou my meditation by day and night.
May it be thou that I behold even in my sleep.

Be thou my speech, be thou my understanding.

Be thou with me, be I with thee

Be thou my father, be I thy son.

Mayst thou be mine, may I be thine.

It was David's voice! With trembling hands, Meredith rose. The doctors, nurses, patients, and a few villagers continued to sing around her, but she could not stay planted.

Meredith hurried around the tree to get a better view. Joy and confusion merged when she saw him.

It was the man from the cottage—thin and frail with threadbare clothes. He'd shaven, but she would have recognized his face anyway. He continued to sing as he looked at her, uncertainty and worry filling his gaze.

"David." The word slipped from her lips, and the emotions overwhelmed her. He'd left, and he'd abandoned her. But what was he doing here? Why wasn't he a German soldier? And Henk knew him and trusted him? Nothing made sense.

She needed some fresh air. She needed to think. Meredith turned and hurried to the door. Her heart pounded even faster than it had when that German gun had been pointed at her.

Henk stopped her near the classroom door. "I am sorry I lied. He is your David . . . but he is also our Daaf."

"You . . . you know about David? You know about us . . . and Miami Beach?"

Henk nodded. "I lived, too, in the States for two years. I thought it would be my forever home, but others needed me. Coming back, if we could save the life of even one child, it would be worth it. With Daaf's help—David's help—we've done more than that."

She turned, and seeing David was like a dream. He finished the song and then rose. He smiled.

"Three long years," she said to him. "It seems like it's been a lifetime since

I saw you. Then again . . ." Her voice trailed off. At the same time, it seemed like yesterday. After all, he often visited her in her dreams, but she would not tell him that.

David took three slow steps toward her. His eyes studied her face, as if having a hard time himself believing that it was really her. His hand lifted, as if to touch her face, and then he lowered it again. "You're all grown up."

Her nose wrinkled. She suppressed a grin.

"Is that your way of saying that I've gotten old?" She looked down at herself. "Baggy, drab jumpsuit. Combat boots, a thick jacket that's two sizes too large."

"You look beautiful. Even prettier than the last time I saw you."

She swallowed her emotion. She opened her mouth to say something, but no words emerged. What could she say? Over the years she'd come up with plenty of things she'd say to him if she ever saw him again. She'd chewed him out dozens of times. She'd cried that he'd left her to help the enemy. But now? Her mind was still trying to comprehend what she'd just heard. David hadn't left to hurt, but to help. Was that what Henk had said?

"I'm sorry for leaving as I did. I had to do something to fight the evil." He opened his mouth, and she could see from his eyes that he wanted to say more, but he didn't. Why not? David glanced around, and seeing that they had an audience, he pressed his lips tightly together.

"But why didn't you tell me that you were leaving for a good cause? If that's truly what it was about. You should have said something. Everything would have been different . . ."

"I did not want you to wonder about me and wait for me. I thought it would be better if you could forget about me. I thought you'd find someone else and fall in love. I knew that if you even had a glimmer of hope of us being reunited you would not give up, *ja*?"

He sighed. "The hardest thing I ever did was leave you, Merry. You are the joy of every memory."

She pressed her fingertips to her temples and closed her eyes. Was this the truth? What if David was lying? What if Henk was lying? *Loose lips sink ships.* If she'd heard or read the slogan ten times in the last three years, she'd heard it a thousand times.

She took a step back and narrowed her gaze, but before she could ask another question, David stretched out his hand and placed it gently on her arm.

"I can't explain everything, Merry, but can you trust me?"

Her brow furrowed, and fear pierced her heart. He was so handsome. The way he looked at her. The tenderness there made her want to believe him. And that was what worried her. The best spies, she knew, were those others found easy to trust.

"I'm not sure what you need from me." She crossed her arms over her chest.

"What I need . . ." He rubbed his forehead, unsure. "I just need you to know that I care, Merry. That I've always cared. But . . ." He sighed. "I . . . I suppose you don't have any reason to believe me. Do you?" He shifted his weight from side to side.

She thought about all those small gifts. The card. The stocking. The poem. Was that his way of letting her know that he hadn't forgotten one detail?

David softly started to hum "O Holy Night." She knew he always hummed when he was nervous. He looked out the classroom window behind her, and his brow was folded in concern.

"Why don't you tell me the truth?" she said. "What are you trying to hide?"

"I can tell you that I am here now. And I still have some people I need to protect. I need you to trust me. I can't tell you too much, Merry. The war is not over. Won't you just trust me?"

Meredith bit her lower lip. "You abandoned me. I can't . . . I can't allow myself to get hurt." She could tell that her words pierced his heart, but she considered how she'd been hurt. She couldn't trust him. No, she wouldn't do that to herself or to her hospital unit. The enemy had already tried to hurt her twice.

How could she trust him? And if she did, what would that mean? Meredith still needed time to think. To pray. She'd been praying that David would make the right choices. And now she needed to pray the same for herself too.

## Eighteen

Tuesday, December 26

*M*eredith woke up the day after Christmas with a feeling so strong she was sure a black hole of longing swirled in her gut. She imagined Mama bustling around the living room yesterday, with Grandma seated on the tapestry-covered davenport, watching and shaking her head. "You try to do too much, Rose," she would have said. "Let's do things a little simpler this year."

Of course, Mama never made things simple, especially with their Savior's birth to celebrate.

Meredith pictured her parents' living room: the oriental rug, the marble-topped coffee table, and the nativity scene perched on top. "Our Lord Jesus came for nights just like this," Grandma would say as she pointed to the sky. "And for troubles just like these." She'd point at her heart.

Meredith opened her eyes and turned her head. Nancy was already awake and dressed. She sat on her cot with paper and pen, but the paper was blank. It was as if she'd been waiting for Meredith to wake up.

"So . . . are you ready to talk now?" Nancy asked. "About last night?"

"What do you want me to say?"

"Well, I don't know." Nancy rubbed her chin. "But say something. I mean, you saw the man that you once loved yesterday. The man you still love, and instead of embracing him, you ran away."

Meredith shrugged. She didn't know where to start, so she decided to start with the last thoughts that had played through her mind as she'd drifted off to sleep.

"We'd been planning a trip home for Christmas. David and I were going to take the train. I was excited for him to meet my family. I was excited for them to meet him. I was sure they'd love him. He played the organ in church, for goodness' sake."

"But he was German." Nancy said. "Weren't you worried about that, especially with all that was happening in Europe?"

"You could hardly hear his accent. Besides, in Miami Beach, everyone was from someplace else. David had grown up in Germany, but he seemed like the rest of us. He seemed American to me. There were other things too. We'd talk about how we both missed our families. We'd sit on the beach and dig our toes into the sand and share memories of childhood. I'd never seen a guy open up like that. My brother Pete always put on a show that nothing bothered him. Often Daddy acted the same. Maybe that's why David was such a good spy. He knew how to make someone comfortable. Everyone considered him a friend. He'd gotten all of us to let our guard down."

Nancy listened, but Meredith didn't know how to explain the jumble of emotions that swirled inside her. Maybe she should have made the trip to Lafayette in late summer as her parents had asked. As an attorney, her father helped many people, and Mama always said he was a good judge of character. Maybe Daddy would have seen something in David that everyone else around her had missed.

*Daddy.* She thought about his tall frame, dark hair, and gentle eyes. He'd always looked so handsome in his three-piece suit and striped ties, and even though he was formal at work and with strangers, he'd always been a softy. She couldn't count the nights she'd snuck out of bed for one more hug, even after she'd been tucked in. She thought of the small yet sturdy desk in the center of her father's office. A typewriter sat on a small table next to it, a bookshelf behind.

Daddy never could deny his little girl. She'd curl up on him, wrap her arms around his neck, and breathe in the scents of his aftershave and his pipe. She'd taken him for granted for so long. Had taken for granted the way he provided for the family by caring for their physical and spiritual needs. And she'd realized as she'd drifted off to sleep the night before that she still struggled with trusting God like that. She'd been hurt, and she'd been mad at God for letting David break her heart.

"I don't know what else to say, Nancy. I'm still trying to figure all of it out." She entwined her fingers on her lap and peered into her friend's face. "I just want someone to protect me, I suppose. Someone to make sure I'm not going to get hurt again."

"Oh, sweetie." Nancy rose, approached her cot, and ruffled Meredith's hair. "All of us want that, but the world is a difficult place. It's filled with strife and war. The best thing we can do is just trust our hearts. Do you believe David was one of the good guys? If you do—deep down—you need to give him another chance."

"And if not?" Meredith asked.

Nancy sighed. "And if not, then you have to ask yourself why you haven't let go. Something—some type of hope—has kept you tethered to him. God knows the answer, sweetie, and He'll help you out. But it'll take stepping out of your safety zone. It'll take risking hurt. But it's then that we discover that God is who He says He is. He didn't bring you this far to abandon you, to hurt you, Meredith. You just have to trust that."

Meredith listened and took it in. She hurriedly got dressed, and together they walked to the field hospital. Dozens of eyes were on her as she entered the classroom. Everyone had witnessed the reunion yesterday, and no doubt they all had their own ideas of whether or not she'd made the right choice.

Acting as if it were any other day, Meredith pulled off her jacket, and it landed on the floor with a thump. It was only then that she remembered the Bible in the pocket. She thought of the handsome young soldier, Samuel. She thought of the family who loved him. Thought of the mother whose worst fears had come true, though she didn't know it yet.

Samuel's mother had given her son as a sacrifice. So many mothers did.

"She gave her son as a sac—" She tried to mutter the words as she pulled out supplies for the day's work, but the words wouldn't come. Face after face came to mind—those who'd survived and those who hadn't. She'd been happy to do her part. She thought that she was here to help them, but what if they were here to help her? To remind her of what really mattered. Of *who* really mattered.

"To love God and to love others as yourself," she whispered. It had always been the greatest commandment. "Lay down your life for a friend . . ." she whispered. These soldiers had done just that. Had David?

She thought about the song that David had been humming yesterday.

O holy night! The stars are brightly shining,
It is the night of our dear Saviour's birth.
Long lay the world in sin and error pining,
'Til He appear'd and the soul felt its worth.
A thrill of hope the weary world rejoices,
For yonder breaks a new and glorious morn.
Fall on your knees! O hear the angel voices!
O night divine, O night when Christ was born;
O night divine, O night, O night Divine.

She thought about David. His music had often expressed what he couldn't. He'd never been able to hide what was deep in his heart, not completely. He had looked forward to that new and glorious morn. He had dared to think that even after all the pain this war had brought, they might have another chance at love.

Thinking of that, Meredith suddenly knew the truth. She *had* received a Christmas miracle. She didn't deserve it, but God had led her here for this reason. Jesus, the Truth, had revealed the truth to her.

David hadn't left to serve the enemy. He'd returned to protect the innocent. He'd understood the sin and error of this world, and with God's help had chosen to make a difference to save lives.

And then he'd come to her. David had risked rejection to display his heart. And even though they couldn't be together today, he dared to hope for a future—their future.

Knowing that made her heart swell with love. David had stepped away from their love to serve mankind—to serve God. And now God had brought them back together again. Hope dared her to join in this miracle. Joy flooded over her, and she hoped it wasn't too late. Would he still be around? He hadn't left again, had he, nursing a broken heart?

She had to find him, and even though no injured men had been brought in this morning, she needed to ask Dr. Anderson for permission to leave. He was currently in the operating room performing surgery on a soldier's damaged leg.

The minutes ticked by, and Meredith tried to hide her impatience. She tapped her foot and looked at her watch. Finally, someone approached. She turned to see Dr. Anderson.

"You seem like you have somewhere to go. Someone to talk to," he said.

She glanced up at the doctor. "Actually, I do."

"I saw Henk walking by. If you hurry you can catch him."

She hadn't even had to ask. Dr. Anderson's eyes sparkled as if he'd known all along that she'd be wanting to find David.

"But my shift . . ." She furrowed her brow.

"I heard word that we'll probably be leaving today—heading into Germany. We'll start packing within the hour. The men are doing well. Ambulances will be arriving. I never thought we'd move out the day after Christmas, but the army has a mind of its own."

"Do you think I have time to find David?"

"Yes, if you hurry. Catch up with Henk. We have reason to trust him—trust them both. The villagers have been relaying many stories."

The joy that had taken root now blossomed fully in her chest. Meredith threw on her jacket and headed to the door without hesitation.

"Meredith, don't forget to thank him for the music yesterday!" It was Nancy's voice calling after her.

"Call me Merry!" she called back. "I have someone to wish a merry Christmas to. I'll be right back!"

enk was far down the road, and Meredith hurried to catch up. Her breath fogged on the chilly air, and as she approached he turned.

"Merry! You've come! I told Daaf . . . told David you would."

"Is he home?"

"Yes." Henk nodded. "We have a few small gifts to exchange, since David was in no mood to do it yesterday, but I had to take wood to Mother Superior first."

"We?" she asked, matching her stride with his.

"David, I, and two girls we've cared for during the war."

"So it's true?" she asked, peering up at him.

"Your David is a true hero. I know he won't tell you that himself."

They entered the cottage, and David sat at the table. Two young women sat next to him, eating what looked like mush. The young women looked scared and excited, but Henk quickly rattled off an explanation in Dutch.

Seeing her, David rose and hurried over. Meredith knew he wanted to hug her, to pull her close. She could see that from the look in his eyes. But there was something else too. Humor. David was hiding a smile.

"What's so funny?" she asked. Talking to him seemed so natural, as if this was how it had always been—him and her together.

"The girls were surprised by you. They didn't understand. They've never seen a woman in pants before, so Henk was explaining."

She reached out and took his hand. It was a simple gesture, but joy flooded his face. "Women don't wear pants around here?" she asked.

"No. In fact, the first night you were here, I overheard the nuns talking about you nurses. When you first rolled into town, they thought you were prostitutes."

"Prostitutes!"

"Yes, because you wore the same uniforms as the male officers, including the pants."

"And they still invited us to sleep in the convent?"

David shook his head. "Only after they discovered who you really were. They were quite happy to see you nursing the patients." His face changed, and Meredith had a feeling the conversation was going to change too. "Merry." He took her hand. "I—"

"Wait," she interrupted. She held up her hand, pausing his words. "Say that again."

"Say what?"

"My name. I haven't been Merry for a very long time. Everyone here knows me as Meredith."

"So I heard. Why?"

"Well, I enlisted under Meredith and left my old nickname behind, since this seemed like serious business."

"It is serious business."

She smiled. "Yes, but not so serious that I forgot what life . . . what love is all about."

He leaned forward and kissed the top of her head. His breath was warm, and tingles danced up and down her arms and through her chest. David tugged on her hand and led her to the living room area. They sat in two chairs so their knees touched. He didn't release her hand.

"Can you tell me the truth, David? Can you explain what you're doing here?"

He nodded, and she knew it would be hard for him. She knew he wanted to protect the young women, protect her, but still he continued. Maybe David had also learned to trust God?

"I was born in Germany, but my mother was from this village, Nieuwenhagen. She went to college in Germany. She settled down there, but at least twice a year we'd visit family in the Netherlands. I spent more time with my mother than my father—he was very ill. And even though we saw them less often, I had a closer connection with my Dutch relatives. My uncle especially. He was only three years older than me. We spent a lot of time together. Talking to Uncle Arie and writing letters back and forth gave me a whole new perspective of what was happening in my country.

"Of course, all I was interested in was music. I thought I could escape the whole mess by just moving to the United States. But my uncle continued to write. We'd figured out a secret code as boys, and he'd send me private notes. He sent me Nazi pamphlets, and . . ." David's voice trailed off. "I battled with myself about what I should do. I didn't want to involve myself. I had asked my mother to send me my grandmother's wedding ring just a few months after I met you. She did, and it arrived the same day as a letter from Henk. He told me they had rescued a dozen Jewish children, bringing them across the German border, but some had to be left behind. When he went back for them, they were gone. The Germans had rounded them up and put them into a camp."

Tears filled David's eyes. Then he pulled something from his pocket. A ring. "Someday I'm going to put this on your finger, Merry. Someday after the war."

"I would like that," she whispered.

He slipped it back in his pocket and then took her hand again. He'd no doubt hoped she would come. Maybe that was why he was carrying the ring in his pocket.

A strange feeling crept over Meredith as she sat there, looking into the face of the man she loved. She studied his face, noticing that the added worry lines only added to his character. David was even more handsome than before. His voice was different, though. When he first moved to the United States, he'd worked hard to blend in, and unless one was really paying attention, his German accent was hardly noticeable. He said that his mother had been the same way, speaking English with little accent. Yet when he'd talked with Henk, his guttural pronunciation came from deep in his throat. His English gave evidence of that now too.

"That night I lay on my bed with the letter in one hand and the ring in the other. I wept before God. I wept because of my love for you, and a verse filtered into my mind. *"Greater love hath no man than this, that a man lay down his life for his friends."* Even with those words filling my soul, I asked for a sign. It was the next day that I heard the news of Pearl Harbor. I knew the United States was going to be getting in the war. It would be not just a war against the Japanese but against the Germans too. My only chance to leave the country would be right away. I was going to be a part of the war whether I liked it or not. God showed me that. I returned by ship to the Netherlands, and my uncle helped me forge a new identity. Soon I was part of the Underground network. Uncle Arie died only a few months after I got back, but he'd set everything up for us to be successful. Many lives were saved because of him."

"Why didn't you tell me about this? About what was happening to the children? About your uncle? I would have understood."

"I knew if I was to return, it would be to work with the Underground. In order to keep you safe, my uncle safe, and the children safe, I needed to simply disappear from my old life and appear as a new person." He reached over and took her hand. "Leaving you, Merry, was the hardest thing I've ever done."

She let out a long, slow sigh. "A lot has happened in three years. I've experienced a lot. Seen a lot."

He released her hand and then placed a soft knuckle under her chin, tilting it up so that she looked him in the eye. "I've seen a lot too, but it's just made us stronger, more dependent on God—hasn't it? And look, He has brought you to me. My Merry." He winked. "I do see some merriment in your eyes still. I heard that bringing the piano in was your idea."

She brushed aside his praise, instead wanting to know more about his life over the last few years. Her small deed seemed so minor compared to that.

"Can you tell me what you've done? Your work to help."

"I can't give too many details, but we'd travel by foot or cart to villages on the German side of the border. I worked in a stone factory here. Let's just say that most German guards were too lazy to remove those big, heavy stones to search. We also carried messages between Resistance groups. I prided myself in never forgetting a word. No one could understand how I did it."

Meredith cocked an eyebrow. She rested her arms on her knees and leaned close. "You put it to music, of course."

His eyes widened and laughter spilled from his lips. He pulled his hand back and folded his hands on his lap. "Yes, that is correct, but how did you know?"

"You told me once that you memorized Scriptures that way."

"So I did." He was quiet for a moment. "Do you remember . . ."

"Everything." She finished his sentence for him.

He nodded. "Yeah, me too."

They sat there for some time, each in his or her own memories.

"I thought you were a spy." She tucked a strand of hair behind her ear. "I thought you'd taken what you learned from me and shared it with some high commander. Loose lips sink ships and all that."

"Believe me, Merry, what I learned from you . . . what I learned from your lips . . . had nothing to do with military tactics. I did have a friend, though, who I later discovered was a spy. In early '42, the Germans had worked their way into the Resistance groups. Some—like my friend—moved up to a place of leadership. He was eventually found out, and it cut me to the core. I'm sorry if that's what you thought, although I understand."

"So what are we going to do?" she asked. "What's going to happen?" She didn't finish the sentence "with us." But she could tell from the look in his eyes that he knew that was what she meant.

"The war has to end sometime . . . It can't last forever."

*Can't it?* she thought. "So is it hard, seeing all the pain your country has caused?"

"Germany is not my country. America is. I may not be official on paper"—he tapped his chest—"but it's official here, where it counts."

"So you're going to return?"

"As soon as I'm able."

"Where to? Back to Miami Beach?" Her lower lip stuck out slightly. In all the daydreams she had about the days after the war, she never thought of returning to Miami Beach. She liked the place fine enough, but every time she daydreamed, she thought of home. Of Daddy and Mama. Of Grandma and Pete and Abigail and all the new family members that she hadn't had the pleasure of meeting yet.

"Miami Beach maybe," David said, "or perhaps Lafayette."

"Lafayette?"

"The place isn't as important as being with a special person."

Meredith had worn the same heavy combat boots since they'd landed in France in July, but at this moment they felt as light as air, and she was certain she was going to float away. "With me?"

"Yes, with you . . . wherever you are, Merry. With you, I'll always be home."

Those were the words that she needed to hear. Those were the words that would carry her through the war. Today the hospital would be leaving, pulling out, but God had given her two good gifts. First He'd given her Himself, and then He gave her David. He'd also given her what she wanted most, a sense of home. There was no doubt she'd return to Lafayette, but between now and then, she'd have a Father's arms to rest in. He'd carry her. Merry did not question that.

"I love you, Merry." David's voice was gentle. "And I'll come. After this war I'll find you."

"I know, David." She leaned forward and placed the softest kiss on his lips. "If God brought us together here, He'll no doubt bring us together again. And maybe next Christmas we'll be together with all those we love. Wouldn't it be a wonderful God to see to that?"

"Yes," David said with a smile. "Yes, indeed, my dear Merry."

And with those words he gave her one more kiss.

# Let It Snow, Let It Snow

## by Cara Putman

*Tuesday, December 25, 1945*
*Lafayette, Indiana*

The chill of a damp winter morning seemed to soak through the walls into Louise Turner's bedroom. She pulled the quilt up to her chin as she snuggled into the warmth. Just one more minute.

It was Christmas morning. A day to celebrate for so many reasons. The long war was over on both fronts. Soldiers were returning home, and life had made progress toward normal. But things wouldn't feel right until everyone in her family was back home, around the dinner table, celebrating all that God had done for them.

The radiator hissed with heat. If Louise didn't climb from her bed now, she knew she'd be tempted to stay, and that wasn't how she wanted to spend Christmas. The winter mornings made her rheumatism tricky, but Rose would need her help. The house would be full even if a few were missing. Pete and

Grace would walk the couple of blocks from their home, Linnie dashing ahead in her red coat, hat, and mittens. That child could chatter like a robin, and Louise loved every moment. Then Abigail and Jackson would be here, Abigail's hands full with baby Stewart. Maybe Louise could steal him away and tickle a giggle from his rounded belly.

Louise's family was a living treasure that grew with each year. She thanked God for each of them as she dressed and brushed the rat's nest that was her hair. She glanced in the mirror while she slapped on some powder and lipstick. Her face had a few more wrinkles, but her life held so much joy she didn't care.

When she slipped from her room, she was surprised to see that no one was up yet. Well, that gave her the perfect opportunity to bless Robert and Rose with Christmas breakfast. Living with them had been such a good decision all those years ago. Soon the coffee percolated . . . genuine coffee, not the stuff they'd endured during rationing.

It was at the oddest times that she'd remember life had changed. The war had truly ended.

Thirty minutes later, Robert stumbled down the stairs. "What's that I smell?"

"Just some breakfast." She pulled a pan of oatmeal muffins from the oven. Someday, she'd add sugar, real sugar, for that added taste of sweetness. But for now, sugar was still rationed, one lingering effect of the war. "There's coffee on the stove."

"Thanks, Mother." He poured himself a mug, then gave her a quick hug. "Merry Christmas."

Her smile started from deep inside. "Merry Christmas, son."

Soon Rose joined them, and the activity increased. The noon meal would be at two to accommodate Pete and Grace having their family Christmas with Linnie. Louise couldn't contain her joy as she peeled potatoes and prepared stuffing for the turkey. God had been so good to them throughout the war. They'd never had to hang a gold star in the window, unlike so many of their friends. Her heart crimped as she thought of all the families who would forever miss a son frozen in time as the young man who left for the war.

Yet it was over. No more deaths. Now was the time to rebuild.

The morning flew by as she and Rose worked in companionable silence.

"I think we've got things ready, Mom. Let's rest for a bit." Rose filled mugs with fresh coffee and carried them into the living room, where Robert had a warm fire crackling in the fireplace. Snow danced in the air, visible through the large picture window. Louise eased onto one of the wing chairs and picked up the new issue of *LIFE*. The cover photo illustrated a gripping image of reconstruction. The credit showed it was one of Rachel Justice Lindstrom's and the one next to it had been taken by Lee Miller. Both women had taken amazing photos across Europe.

The front door flew open, banging against the wall. "I'm here."

Louise laughed as Linnie ran in, covered from head to toe in her red, white snowflakes dotting the fabric. That girl had more energy and zest for life than should be crammed into an eight-year-old body. "Granny, did you bake my favorite cookies?"

"The peanut butter?" Louise teased.

Linnie's pert nose wrinkled as she grimaced. "No. You know I don't like those."

"Ah, that's right, those are your daddy's favorite."

"What's my favorite?" Pete looked up, his arms loaded with brightly wrapped packages.

"Those icky peanut butter cookies." Linnie stuck out her tongue, as Grace stepped through the door.

"Linnie. Tell me you aren't being unruly already." She shrugged out of her coat, then turned toward Louise, an apology on her face. "I'm sorry for whatever she said."

Louise laughed at the contrition on Grace's face. "We were just teasing each other, weren't we, Linnie girl?" Linnie ran toward her and snuggled in for a hug. "If you ask your grandma, I think she can find a cookie for you."

"Only one, Linnie. I don't want you to spoil your dinner." Grace watched Linnie disappear toward the kitchen, then handed her coat to Pete, who juggled the packages to accept it. Her dress barely stretched over the new life she was carrying, another wonderful surprise for the family. Come May, the family would grow again.

"She's so excited to be here." Louise turned to watch Linnie's progress. "I don't think she's thought too much about presents."

"That's all she's chattered about this morning. She'd barely opened ours before she was thinking about what was waiting for her here." Grace stiffened but then relaxed as Pete slipped an arm around her shoulders.

"It's good, Grace. She should be excited." Pete tugged Grace closer.

Grace and Pete sat on the davenport under the picture window. Pete seemed so settled. Working with his dad at the law firm and having Grace and Linnie in his life satisfied him in a way he hadn't been in years. God was good.

Linnie raced into the room with a plate of cookies.

"Grandma sent enough for all of us." She thrust the plate at Pete. "Even one of those icky ones you like, Daddy."

Pete's smile grew, and Louise smiled. He delighted in that little girl, and it was good and right. He'd needed Grace, and Grace and Linnie had needed him.

Robert followed with mugs of coffee for the adults and a glass of milk for Linnie. They all chatted, until the door bounced open again. Jackson grabbed it right before it hit the wall. "Morning, everyone."

Louise glanced at the clock and grinned. Last time she'd checked, one o'clock in the afternoon wasn't morning, but she'd let it slide. Abigail slipped in behind, a large blanket-wrapped baby tucked against her coat. A fist pumped out as Stewart wriggled free of a layer. Louise pushed from her chair. Abigail would need it now that she was here.

"Sit down, Grandma. Stewart cooed the whole way here suggesting he needed some great-grandma time."

Louise settled back down and held out her arms for the bundle of delight.

Stewart pushed to a sitting position, then reached to grab her glasses. She chuckled and snuggled him close until he protested and pushed back. Such a strong little man. Then he grinned at her, and she knew he had to be the smartest baby boy since Pete was little so many years earlier.

A new round of cookies and coffee arrived as Rose puttered around in the kitchen attending to details.

Louise held Stewart and looked at her family, her heart so full she could almost burst. Her grandchildren were expanding the family, and with each addition, it felt right and good. She'd spent years praying for them and their future spouses. Seeing the fruit of those prayers made her heart sing. If only Merry had come home. Louise stifled a sigh. At least her youngest granddaughter would make her way home soon. She'd survived the war and that awful Battle of the Bulge. And if her letters were to be believed, she'd found the love of her life in the Netherlands—a hero who helped people escape through the Underground, someone she'd met in Miami Beach and who God had brought back to her during the war. God certainly worked in mysterious ways!

"If you aren't all filled up with cookies"—Rose grinned as she wiped her hands on her apron—"I think we're ready to eat."

Jackson helped Abigail out of her chair, as Pete pulled Grace to her feet. Both men pecked their ladies on the cheek, a gesture so like what her husband used to do that Louise's heart ached just a bit, though joy rushed in to squeeze out the pain. It took a few minutes to get everyone settled at the table.

Spruce branches lined the middle of the table, with bowls of mashed potatoes, canned green beans, yeast rolls, and fresh applesauce dotted around the decoration. Then Robert brought out the platter of turkey while Rose carried a bowl of stuffing. In short order the dishes were passed around as everyone took turns heaping the bounty onto their plates. Good-natured chatter filled the air, with ribbing thrown in to keep everyone laughing.

Time passed with the clank of silverware against china, the sound of laughter, teasing, and sharing mixing with the aroma of another wonderful meal. Bowls were passing from place to place for the second round when the door opened again. Louise turned in her chair, trying to spot who would be arriving. Everyone was here except . . .

Her breath caught and she pushed back from the table.

"I'm home!"

Louise barely made it around the table before the others stood.

"Is that my Merry?" Louise's voice quivered. Could it be? Had God given her the gift of her whole family?

Merry moved from the entryway, shaking snowflakes from her hair. "It's me. I'm home."

Louise pulled her into a tight hug, eyes squeezed closed as she held on tight to her baby granddaughter. Then she stepped back to take in the beautiful woman in front of her. "Why didn't you tell us you were coming home? A surprise like that could shock this old heart of mine. I'm not as young as I used to be, you know."

"I wasn't sure I'd make it. I didn't want to get everyone's hopes up and then get caught somewhere. There are a lot of people traveling right now."

A throat cleared, and Merry turned toward the man standing in the doorway, delight in her eyes. "Everyone, I'd like you to meet David. David, this is . . ." Laughter—merry laughter—tumbled from her mouth. "David, this is everyone!"

The home exploded into a celebration. Hugs and welcomes, claps on the back mixed with tears. Louise smiled until her cheeks hurt. They were all home. All of her babies were home with their families. Indeed, God had blessed them, everyone.

# Holiday Cookie Exchange

### GRANDMA TURNER'S WHITE VELVET CUTOUTS

2 cups butter, softened

1 8-ounce package cream cheese, softened

2 cups sugar

2 egg yolks

1 teaspoon vanilla extract (though Grandma likes to use peppermint
     to make them Christmasy)

4 ½ cups all-purpose flour

In a mixing bowl, cream butter and cream cheese until light and fluffy. Add sugar, egg yolks, and flavoring. Mix well. Gradually add flour, ½ cup at a time. Cover and chill 2 hours or until firm. Roll out on a floured surface to ¼-inch thickness. Cut into 3-inch shapes; place 1 inch apart on greased baking sheets. Bake at 350 degrees for 10 to 12 minutes or until set. (DO NOT BROWN.) Cool 5 minutes; remove to wire racks to cool.

### PETE'S FAVORITE PEANUT BUTTER COOKIES

½ cup butter, softened

½ cup creamy peanut butter

1 ¼ cups flour

½ cup sugar

½ cup brown sugar, packed

1 egg

½ teaspoon baking soda

½ teaspoon baking powder
½ teaspoon vanilla
Granulated sugar

Preheat oven to 375 degrees. Beat butter and peanut butter on high speed for 30 seconds. Add ½ cup flour, sugars, egg, baking soda, baking powder, and vanilla, and beat until combined. Beat in remaining flour.

Shape dough into 1-inch balls. Roll in sugar. Place on ungreased cookie sheet, and flatten with the tines of a fork.

Bake at 375 degrees for 7 to 9 minutes or until edges are lightly browned. Cool on rack. Makes about 36 cookies.

## GRACE'S MOLASSES COOKIES

### *(Sundin family recipe via Diane Sundin)*

¾ cup shortening
¼ cup molasses
1 egg
1 cup sugar
2 ¼ cups flour
1 teaspoon baking soda
½ teaspoon salt
1 teaspoon cinnamon
1 tablespoon ginger
Granulated sugar

Preheat oven 350 degrees. Mix shortening and sugar. Add egg and molasses, and beat well. Mix flour, baking soda, salt, and spices in a separate bowl. Add flour mixture to sugar mixture. Roll dough into 1-inch balls, then roll in sugar. Place on ungreased cookie sheet. Bake at 350 degrees for 6 to 8 minutes.

## LINNIE'S CANDY CANE COOKIES

1 egg
1 cup butter, softened
¾ cup sugar
1 teaspoon peppermint extract
1 teaspoon vanilla
2 ½ cups flour
1 teaspoon baking powder
¾ teaspoon red food coloring
Red sugar sprinkles
Egg white


Beat together first five ingredients until fluffy. Add flour and baking powder, and beat well.

Divide dough in two equal portions. Mix red food coloring into one portion. Refrigerate dough for 1 hour.

Preheat oven to 375 degrees. For each cookie, roll 1 teaspoon of each color dough into 4-inch ropes. Twist one red and one white rope together, bend into candy-cane shape, and place on ungreased cookie sheet. Brush with egg white and sprinkle with red sugar sprinkles.

Bake at 375 degrees for 8 to 10 minutes. Makes about 36 cookies.

# Readers Guide

1. The novellas in this collection were inspired by the great Christmas songs of the World War II era. How does each song fit each story? What's your favorite Christmas song and why?
2. How does Louise Turner help each of her grandchildren? Do you have a special person in your life like her? Can you be that special person to someone in your life?
3. The Turner family has experienced troubles and tragedies. Where do they find their strength? How do you see this in the stories? How can you and your family bear the troubles and tragedies you face?

## WHITE CHRISTMAS

1. Abigail Turner is dealing with the residual effects of grief. What tips would you offer Abigail to move forward in a healthy manner?
2. Jackson has done everything he can to help his mother and sister, yet life has intervened and now he is overcome with guilt. Have you ever experienced a situation like that? What advice would you give Jackson?
3. It is simpler to wall our hearts off rather than risk love. Is it worth the risk of future pain?
4. Grandma is a voice of wisdom in Abigail's life. Who has been that voice in your life?

## I'LL BE HOME FOR CHRISTMAS

1. Pete Turner feels empty after his combat tour. How does he try to get filled again? What works? What doesn't? What do you think about

Pastor Hughes's advice for Pete to give? In the long run, what does Pete learn through the process of giving?

2. Throughout the story, Pete, Grace, and Linnie give each other a variety of things—from baby-sitting to ornaments to wooden spoons. How do these gifts reveal the heart of the giver? What's the favorite gift you've ever received and why? What's the favorite gift you've ever given?

3. More than anything, Grace Kessler wants to protect her child—and herself. What good things result from this instinct? What mistakes does she make? What does she ultimately learn?

4. Linnie Kessler is a handful. Do you have any handfuls in your life? How can you encourage them to respect others without squashing their spirit? Were you a handful yourself? Any fun "handful stories" to share?

## Have Yourself a Merry Little Christmas

1. Merry Turner is a combat nurse and goes by the name Meredith. How does her name change reflect the changes within her? Why does she ask to be called Merry at the end of the story?

2. Daaf (David) is doing his best to care for those who the Nazis are trying to hunt down and hurt. Even when the Americans arrive he has a hard time believing that those in his care are safe. Do you ever let your worries overwhelm you? How do you deal with your worries?

3. Meredith's favorite part of nursing is talking to the injured soldiers. What drew her to nursing in the first place? How have the experiences in your life directed your life's path?

4. Everything changes in Meredith's heart when she realizes the real reason that David left. Do you think he made the right decision in leaving? Like Merry, when is a time that the truth set you free from past pain?

# A Chat with the Authors

*Readers often like to know the stories behind a collection. So we grabbed our favorite hot beverages and sat down for an interview with the authors of* **Where Treetops Glisten**. *How did the idea for this novella collection come to you?*

**Cara:** I'd written in a couple of novella collections and loved the collaborative aspects. Writing is often solitary, but when you're working on a collection with other writers, you have fun opportunities to work together. I asked Sarah and Tricia if they'd like to work together because I love their World War II stories, and I love their hearts. I also thought this was a sneaky way to get to know them better. It's so fun to now have a book that we've written together!

**Tricia:** The coolest thing about Cara approaching me is that I highly respect both Cara and Sarah for their writing abilities and their love of World War II. There aren't many people I know who enjoy both of these passions, just as I do, and it was easy to say YES!

**Sarah:** When Cara invited me to participate, I was thrilled. We all liked the idea of using one family's experience over the course of the war to tie the stories together. Since so many great Christmas songs debuted during World War II ("White Christmas" in 1942, "I'll Be Home for Christmas" in 1943, "Have Yourself a Merry Little Christmas" in 1944), I've often thought those songs would be a fun way to connect a novella collection, so I suggested it to Cara and Tricia, and they liked it too.

**Cara:** I loved the idea of using the Christmas carols to connect the stories. So many of those songs are a big part of Christmas even today! But we still had to figure out the rest. Christmas carols alone wouldn't be enough for three stories to come to life. Once we were all on board, we had a conference call to figure out the rest. Sarah and Tricia started throwing out elements that had to be in the stories to stay true to what our readers expect. Small town close to a major city. Industry that was involved in the war. Maybe a major university. I started laughing because that perfectly describes Lafayette, Indiana, where I live. While we were talking, Sarah hopped on the Internet and threw out ideas such as incorporating Glatz Candies (now McCord Candies), the puzzle factory, etc. It was perfect and became the setting for this collection.

*So that brings up another question. In this collection of stories, we could picture Lafayette as if we'd visited. Cara lives in Lafayette, but Sarah and Tricia don't. How did you make the town come to life?*

**Sarah:** Oh, my favorite part! I had the privilege of spending a couple of days in Lafayette, staying with the delightful Putman family. Cara—and her four children!—took me all around town. One of Cara's friends graciously loaned us her home to serve as the Turner home, and she let us traipse through, sketching floor plans and taking pictures. We visited the Alcoa plant, the bridge over the Wabash, and the charming downtown area. Driving around the area where I knew Grace would live, we saw the cutest Victorian—for sale! Since I figured they wanted people to look inside, I walked all around, peeked in the windows, and took dozens of photos. I also spent a few hours at the local library going through 1943 phone books and newspapers—a treasure trove. And of course, we had to sample the wares at McCord's!

**Tricia:** I was honored to travel to Lafayette to speak at a banquet, and Cara was a wonderful hostess while I was in town. We toured downtown, visited McCord Candies (and grabbed a soda there!), and we also visited some antique shops, which really gave me a feel for the area. Cara also drove me around to see the home of the characters in the book. It was a delight to see the town come to life!

**Cara:** One of my very good friends owns a historic home near downtown Lafayette, and I've known for years that it would be the perfect home for a heroine. So when we set the book in Lafayette, I asked Ann if we could use her home. Since I wasn't sure if anyone else would get to come to town to visit, I sketched out the floor plan and uploaded it to Pinterest so Sarah and Tricia could refer to it—reinforcing why I went to law school and not art school!

*Even with visits to Lafayette, was it a challenge to write three such interconnected stories?*

**Cara:** Sarah is the spreadsheet queen. Seriously! After our conference call, Sarah had character and timeline spreadsheets ready for us. We stayed in contact and used those spreadsheets to keep the details straight.

**Sarah:** I forget everything unless I write it down, and I have a genetic predisposition to loving tables and charts, so yes, I coordinated timelines and character charts. The interconnected stories were both challenging and inspiring. As each of us added to the Turner family history, the other authors' characters and stories were affected too. We often ran scenes by each other so we could stay true to the other characters, such as "What would Merry have been thinking at this time?" "What would Abigail's wedding be like?" "Would Pete say this?"

**Tricia:** There were also many e-mails that flew back and forth with questions like, "What year was Pete born again?" and "What was so-and-so doing in

1943?" It was fun figuring out this family and these characters together. And then once we figured out the information, Sarah put it in her spreadsheet!

*Fascinating! So now that you've written together, what was your favorite part of this collaboration?*

**Sarah:** I'd known Tricia and Cara for years from writers' conferences and online connections, but this project made us true friends. It was also great fun to see how other authors work. I'm a slow, methodical writer who takes a long time to find and develop ideas. Cara and Tricia are whirlwinds of energy and ideas—and they write like the wind! They definitely inspired me to be more creative.

**Tricia:** I loved spending time with Cara and Sarah and weaving stories together. As a writer I'm usually the one trying to figure everything out on my own. It was fun to do it as a team!

**Cara:** My favorite part was the collaboration and the excuse to spend time with my writing buddies. They probably wouldn't have come to Lafayette without this project, so that was an added bonus. The collaboration was so natural, I'd love to do it again.

*Thanks so much for joining us for this behind-the-scenes look, ladies.*

# About the Authors

Photo by Jessica McCollam

*Tricia Goyer*

*USA Today* best-selling author Tricia Goyer is the author of more than forty books, including the novelization for *Moms' Night Out*. She has written over five hundred articles for national publications and blogs for high traffic sites like TheBetterMom.com and MomLifeToday.com. Tricia and her husband, John, live in Little Rock, Arkansas, where Tricia coordinates a Teen MOPS (Mothers of Preschoolers) group. They have six children.

Website: www.TriciaGoyer.com

Facebook: www.facebook.com/AuthorTriciaGoyer

Twitter: www.twitter.com/TriciaGoyer

Pinterest: www.Pinterest.com/TriciaGoyer

Instagram: www.Instagram.com/TriciaGoyer

Photo by Linda Johnson

*Sarah Sundin*

Sarah Sundin lives with her husband and three children in northern California, where she works on-call as a hospital pharmacist and teaches Sunday school and women's Bible studies. She is the author of six World War II novels, including *With Every Letter, On Distant Shores,* and *In Perfect Time* in the Wings of the Nightingale series. In 2014, *On Distant Shores* was a finalist for the Golden Scroll Award from both the Christian Authors Network and the Advanced Writers and Speakers Association. In 2011, she received the Writer of the Year Award at the Mount Hermon Christian Writers Conference.

Website: www.sarahsundin.com

Facebook: www.facebook.com/SarahSundinAuthor

Twitter: www.twitter.com/SarahSundin

Pinterest: www.pinterest.com/SarahSundin

Photo by Emilie Hendrix

*Cara Putman*

Cara C. Putman, the award-winning author of nineteen books, graduated high school at sixteen, college at twenty, and completed her law degree at twenty-seven. *FIRST for Women* magazine called *Shadowed by Grace* "captivating" and a "novel with 'the works.'" Cara is active at her church and a lecturer on business and employment law to graduate students at Purdue University's Krannert School of Management. Cara also practices law and is a second-generation homeschooling mom. Cara is currently pursuing her Master's in Business Administration at Krannert. She serves on the executive board of American Christian Fiction Writers (ACFW), an organization she has served in various roles since 2007. She lives with her husband and four children in Indiana.

Facebook: www.facebook.com/caraputman

Twitter: www.twitter.com/cara_putman

Pinterest: www.pinterest.com/caraputman

Goodreads: www.goodreads.com/CaraPutman